FACES

Also by Shirley Lord

Small Beer at Claridge's
The Easy Way to Good Looks
You Are Beautiful (And How to Prove It)
Golden Hill
One of My Very Best Friends

FACES

Shirley Lord

CROWN PUBLISHERS, INC., NEW YORK

PUBLISHER'S NOTE: *This is a work of fiction. The characters, incidents, and dialogues are products of the author's imagination and are not to be construed as real. Where the names of actual persons, living or dead, are used, the situations, incidents, and dialogues concerning those persons are entirely fictional and are not intended to depict any actual events or change the entirely fictional nature of the work.*

Published by Crown Publishers, Inc., 225 Park Avenue South, New York, New York 10003

CROWN is a trademark of Crown Publishers, Inc.

Manufactured in the United States of America

Library of Congress Cataloging-in-Publication Data

Lord, Shirley.
Faces / by Shirley Lord.
p. cm.
I. Title.
PR6062.0724T4 1989 88-21445
823'.914—dc19 CIP
ISBN 0-517-57158-7
10 9 8 7 6 5 4 3 2 1
First Edition

To Abe

Acknowledgments

Thanks to my husband, A. M. Rosenthal, for his encouragement and valuable advice; to the distinguished surgeons John Q. Owsley, Jr., M.D., F.A.C.S, and Thomas D. Rees, M.D., F.A.C.S, for their guidance on the portions of this book relating to plastic surgery; to Polly Mellen, the brilliant Creative Fashion Director of *Vogue* magazine, for her inspiration; to Eugene Kennedy, Ph.D., Professor of Psychology, Loyola University of Chicago, author of *A Time for Being Human* (Image Books/Doubleday), for allowing me to quote some of his words of wisdom; to Rick Adams and Louise McCorkle, authors of *The California Highway 1 Book* (Ballantine Books), an intriguing guide to the California coastline.

My thanks also to Owen Laster, Betty A. Prashker, Nora Betty, and my son Mark Hussey, for their unfailing support and unerring suggestions, and to Colleen Sullivan for her help in delivering this manuscript.

CHAPTER ONE

Her thirty-five-day-a-year shooting contract stipulates that she be photographed by Richard Avedon, a proviso she's had since she signed with the company in 1974. Both a spokeswoman in print and on TV, Lauren Hutton is highly visible and, according to a Revlon executive, very effective. "As she gets older she continues to project a vitality, a reality," he says. "When we picked her we were looking for someone a woman could identify with, someone accessible and Lauren certainly is that . . ." As of last year Lauren Hutton was earning about $250,000 per annum to advertise products for Revlon . . .

WITH A SHAKY HAND SHE UNDERLINED THE LAST PARAGRAPH of the *Women's Wear Daily* article in red. She couldn't wait for Alf to read it. Should she read it to him over the phone? No, she would swing by after everything else was over—just when he'd begun to wonder where on earth she'd disappeared to. She would drape herself over his drawing board and put it right under his nose. Would he be surprised when he finally took the trouble to look up and look at *her*. Would he be surprised! Would he . . . would he? She took a Quaalude out of her purse and swallowed it down with a convulsive gulp as the taxi stopped at 2146 Ventura Park Boulevard.

At 10:15 A.M. on the thirtieth of May when even third-generation Valley dwellers were seeking the shade and moaning about the third week of ferocious ninety-degree temperatures, Teresa Millicent Shapwell, otherwise known as Teri Shephard or just Teri on her contact sheet, turned down Ventura Park Boulevard for the sixth time. She had been pacing up and down since the taxi dropped her there, but it wasn't only perspiration from the heat that matted her ash-blond hair and caused her mascara to smudge, emphasizing shadows beneath her eyes. Coming from the airport, even though the taxi was air-conditioned, she'd been sweating. She always sweated when she was nervous, even when coming to a decision, let alone carrying it out. Now it was indecision that caused her to continue to walk on stiletto heels that hadn't been designed for walking. The heels made her legs look good, very good, but the thin soles meant the pavement burned her feet with every step she took. She hadn't expected to walk much. She hadn't expected that out of nowhere would come terror about what she was about to do.

Anyone watching Teri Shephard that morning might have wondered what such a pretty woman was doing on Ventura Park Boulevard at all, let alone walking up and down it. It wasn't a place for window shopping. There were no shops and hardly any windows in the rows of low-level white office buildings, interspersed as many suburban Valley streets were with houses that had long ago been given up by families, stripped of personality, and taken over by small businesses. Now the searing heat emphasized the monotony, anonymity.

As Teri reached an intersection, she slipped off her shoe to rest her bare foot on her small suitcase. She had never felt more helpless. She looked to the left and right. If a taxi materialized she would take it to give herself more time to think. It would mean losing the deposit, if she changed her mind . . . but she was suddenly so scared.

She would wait five, ten minutes, then if one didn't turn up . . . she blinked back tears. Why the hell wasn't the lude working to bring on the resolve she'd felt the day before? Like switching on a tape she ran her husband's words through her mind. "Honey, it's time I traded you in for a younger model. Oh, sorry about that pun, baby. I couldn't help myself . . ."

The sun was making her giddy. There were no taxis. She winced as she put her shoe back on and began to limp toward 2146 once again. She wasn't a quitter. There was no turning back. Thank God, the lude was beginning to work. What on earth was she getting into such a state about? Hadn't she seen for herself what they had done for Magda, who had confided she was thirty-five, yet looked as if she had at least ten more good years ahead of her before the camera? Perhaps even Lauren Hutton had had something done? It was nothing to be ashamed of these days . . . even Marilyn Monroe had been a nobody until she'd had her chin fixed.

She was in charge of herself again and an excitement she hadn't felt in a long time surged as she read the brass plaque on the iron gate of the house set back at the end of the boulevard. THE FOUNTAIN REJUVENATION CLINIC. BY APPOINTMENT ONLY.

Her appointment had been made. The requested deposit sent. She was ready. She pressed the bell. Her new life was about to begin.

Two hours later the thirty-four-year old actress turned model (who only admitted to twenty-eight on her contact sheet) slowly opened the drawer by her bed and smiled to find her purse safely inside. She took out a mirror as carefully as if it were an egg and lay back to study her reflection. It was the last time she would look at the fine lines that had disgusted her for the past year, the last time she would even have to see the one little pit left over from a luckily short bout with acne in her adolescence, a pit that had traumatized her until Alf had taught her camouflage.

Teri floated on a Valium and Demoral cloud of confidence and looked at the familiar reflection as if it belonged to somebody else. In a way it already did. It was a face of failure—failed actress, despite all the promises, also-ran model, deceived wife and—for some reason Teri couldn't fathom she giggled as she thought of the last description—disinterested mother. Disinterested? Heck, no, that wasn't the right word. What was it? She loved her babes, didn't she? She both loved and feared them for what they were so innocently beginning to do to her career just by growing up.

Her thoughts were interrupted by the door opening and,

drowsy though she was, she recognized the head of the clinic approaching. Magda had showed her a photograph. Mysterious, marvelous, almost motherly Magda, who she really hardly knew, had kept her promise to put in a word for her. So she really was going to get the works from the top enchilada. She was going to look twenty-two again. The doctor's soothing voice added to her euphoria. "Are you feeling better? More relaxed?"

"Yes, Doctor," Teri whispered like a little girl. "Now I know I'm going to be in your hands . . . I'm happy . . . I'm so happy to meet you . . ."

"Good. I'm going to explain to you why I developed my special formula for young women like yourself with glamorous careers. You told us during the interview this morning that you had decided to have a facelift for the sake of your career, but after seeing what we had achieved for your friend Magda Dupaul, you were persuaded to seek us out. In fact, you are far too young to contemplate a facelift . . ."

Teri almost purred with pleasure.

"You could say a facelift takes care of face sag. It tightens up the skin like pulling a bedsheet tight, but it doesn't remove fine wrinkles—the frown lines between the eyes, those between nostrils and upper lip." The doctor gently traced the lines on her face with a finely pointed marker pen, but even this strange assault on her features did nothing to diminish Teri's happiness. She smiled into the doctor's eyes like a dutiful pupil, nodding assent with every word spoken.

"To use the same simile, although the bedsheet has, in effect, been tidied up, it is not fresh. It is marked. It has been lived in. This is where my miraculous face peel goes to work. My face peel cleanses the sheet, takes all the marks away to produce baby-fresh skin . . . a totally fresh sheet . . . you will soon see for yourself."

Oh, how she longed to see her skin baby fresh. She must have dozed off, dreaming of her babes' pink-and-white smoothness, the scent of talcum powder, tiny soft booties, and the joy of realizing that after both pregnancies, one so horribly fast after the other, she had no stretch marks on her abdomen and hadn't gained more than half a pound in those two tumultuous years. She was faintly aware of a white-coated nurse taking her blood pressure, as now without affecting her equilibrium Ben's words went through her mind again: ". . . time I traded you in for a younger model . . ."

A year ago it had been Ben's poor pun, a joke. But it wasn't a joke now. There had been too many unexplained absences and then too much explanation over nothing. She floated serenely, high above a truth she had had to acknowledge. For a second time in their seventeen-year-old marriage, their relationship had turned into—how had Jo, her brainy daughter described it?—Teri foggily searched for the phrase—"a cold war," that was what Jo had said.

But it hadn't been Ben who had made her take action. The danger signal had come from a much more serious source—from Alfred Victor—Alf, the maestro photographer who had got her the biggest modeling job of her life with the haircolor company, which had put real money in her bank account, the money she was spending now. It was Alf, who with his idea of humor, had told her his camera could no longer hide her wrinkles with a piece of chiffon over the lens. He'd told her that the day after she had discovered Ben was once again seeing another woman—a young girl.

She was moving, floating was a better word, out of the room, down the corridor, aware that whoever was pushing the wheelchair was wearing one of her favorite scents, only she couldn't remember the name. She'd opened a new bottle only the day before—or had it been the week before? The week she'd been waiting for, when Ben once again had mentioned an upcoming trip to the East Coast. "Something hot has come up," he'd said, not looking at her. "A chance to get in on a big development deal, baby . . ."

Of course, she had already found out what he was planning. Something hot was waiting for him all right—a baby-faced liberal-arts student from UCLA, who'd gone back East for the summer vacation, a rich babyface, who probably sat on his lap, as she herself had once done with soaking wet cunt, teasing, coaxing, playing baby to handsome Daddy Ben.

Teri had been proud of her performance. She had been so convincing she'd even seen the relief in his eyes as she'd boasted about the big location job that had finally come up for her—in Mexico, which meant she would be away on a big deal, too. "Not as big as yours, Daddy, but big enough."

The Mexican location had been Magda's idea to explain her

one or two weeks' absence from home, but she had in any case planned the time better than she'd ever planned anything. The kids were going to be away—Jo at a summer writing school, Alexa off with Barbara, her rich pal in Santa Barbara—and Ben away; hopefully getting indigestion with too much of a good thing. When he returned, as he had returned before, guilty and overanxious to be loving, there she would be, as good as new to fall in love with all over again.

She knew she was on an operating table, but there wasn't an ounce of fear in her, even though she had been told on arrival that she wouldn't be completely knocked out, which she'd begged for. All she could think of at that moment was the fountain, the lovely, cool fountain she'd seen in the entrance hall that morning. Everything Ann, the nurse with the sexy breasts, had told her would happen was happening and Ann had been right. There was nothing to be afraid of. The anesthetist injected her arm with something and quickly she felt even sleepier, yet she could still take in what was going on around her. She even recognized the masked nurse passing things to the doctor. It was Ann—she recognized her from her breasts.

Now her face was being cleaned with ether in preparation for the big peel. They wouldn't tell her what the peel was made of—it was a secret Eastern formula, but Magda had told her chemicals would be involved—that was why it was called "face peel with chemosurgery." The doctor had warned her to expect a burning sensation as each section of her face was painted with the peel formula—but that it wouldn't last a minute. Yes, it was beginning now.

As the doctor finished painting one section of her face, again as Teri had been told to expect, another nurse, not Ann, swiftly covered it with adhesive tape.

From far away Teri could hear them talking, laughing. For the first time she realized the doctor had a faint foreign accent like Magda's—it was fascinating. "Bax says they'll pay anything not to go under the knife. That's the great plus about acid. You can call it what you want to call it, but you have to call a knife a knife . . ." Teri wanted to laugh with them, but she couldn't move her lips anymore. "Bax wants four more locations—one up north. Did that order for more phenol come in, Ann? I'm going to try something out with alabaster particles."

The conversation flowed over Teri's head as she drifted happily in and out of sleep. There was no more burning. Instead of the trapped, claustrophobic feeling she'd dreaded experiencing from the adhesive-tape mask slowly covering her face right up to the hairline, it was almost comforting, like being a baby again, wrapped in swaddling clothes for the cold weather so only her eyes could peep out. Her eyes wanted to close, but she fought to keep them open, enjoying the feeling of eavesdropping on the "inside" conversation continuing above her head.

"This one certainly didn't need much to calm her down. Not like that boozing, society type we had last week. God, she was almost impossible to knock out—the more they drink, the more they cost us in anesthetic. Good, we're nearly through. I've got to head off that nosy reporter before I leave here tonight. Let's hope this one turns out to be our star."

Star. Teri whimpered inside. In a couple of days when the tape came off she would know whether she still had time to be a star. Suddenly she was asleep.

Did she love her mother?

"My Mother—a Perspective" was the theme they'd been given that morning. Juicy. Provocative. Dangerous! Jo rolled onto her stomach, feeling her sweat wet the sheet. It was a dangerous subject for the unwary. She'd hated herself for blushing so obviously that the other kids had laughed at her. Why had she blushed?

She started to write, "Why did I go red when I heard so many of the kids almost brag about hating their mothers? What was behind that involuntary blush?"

After a moment's thought she crossed out the word, *involuntary*. Superfluous. Blushing was always involuntary. She ought to know. She did too much of it.

It was a fairly good opening for the creative writing assignment. She liked it for its matter-of-fact, casual style—something about her writing that Mr. Peiffer had already commented on favorably. Sweat from her nose dripped onto the page, reminding her how incredibly moist she was all over. There were summer sounds outside the window. Bike bells, tennis volleys, splashing from the pool, screams of laughter, which somehow sounded different in summer than in winter. She didn't feel at all sorry for herself that on this hot afternoon she was inside thinking, writing, when she should have been outside "with the gang," playing her indifferent game of tennis or water polo, which was just an excuse to get close to some of the boys.

She was savoring the thought that for the first time in her life she could think of herself as "one of the gang." It wasn't such a super swinging gang. Alexa would certainly look down her perfect nose at all of them, but for Jo, feeling part of a group, any group, *belonging*, was like being elected Miss America.

Oh, boy, but it *was* hot. Jo jumped up, knocking Bobo's birth-control pills onto the floor. It had been a shock to discover, sharing a room with three girls more or less her age, that she was the only virgin among them. Not that she'd admitted it. She would rather have died. Instead, her reticence on the subject for some miraculous reason had just seemed mysterious to the others and she'd enjoyed cultivating an evasive, enigmatic personality, day by day slipping as easily into it as she slipped into her Lily Pulitzer print skirt.

There were a bunch of well-thumbed letters on Rita's pillow—all from Tom, the boy she was going to marry when she reached eighteen, even though he was only a garage mechanic and her parents said he wasn't good enough for her. Rita had already read out loud some of Tom's most passionate statements. Jo felt it was a kind of betrayal, even though they were really banal, but she'd oohed and ahhed just like the others, except when she'd felt keeping silent was more intriguing.

She opened the door to look down the corridor. No one in sight. She would be safe running to the decrepit old shower room in her bra and pants. She had to cool down before she wrote another word.

It was like giving her body a delicious long drink and she let the water rush down on her long and hard, staying under for much longer than the requested, "Five minute showers only please!" The thought of going back to the overcrowded, airless room was impossible. She lifted up her freckled face to the jet of water, imagining herself on a tropical island, naked under a waterfall, while watching from the crest of a hill was a . . . was a . . . There was an urgent knocking on the door. "How long are you going to be in there, darlin'?" It was Brad Parker from Texas, the heartthrob of the summer camp.

"I'm coming right out, Brad, right out."

She rushed so fast, she banged her toe painfully on the sink; but she didn't care. She was blushing again as she tried to make a skimpy towel into a sarong. "Here I come," she sang out, her heart beating fast. She opened the door to try to scoot past him. He stood there, all six feet four of him blocking her way.

"You're cute, Jo."

She couldn't believe he'd said it. "Cute?"

"Yes, you are, little baby face . . . but not babyish, here." Brad put his hands, his big brown hands, right over her breasts. What she would have done next, she would never know, because somebody started running up the stairs. Brad elegantly swung into the bathroom with a "see you . . ." leaving her gasping for breath as he shut the door behind him.

Had she imagined it?

The room was as hot as ever, but now she didn't care. Brad Parker's hands on her breasts! It was the most erotic experience of her life. What a summer! What a summer camp!

Was she beginning to show some sign of Alexa's beauty? Not a chance, yet why were things happening to her this summer that had never happened before? She'd learned the hard way not to expect anything from summer camps, certainly never the idyllic time promised in the ads, where skies were always cloudless by day, star filled at night.

There had been two or three disturbing days when she'd eavesdropped on her parents discussing the possibility of sending her to a sixteenth-century castle in Haute Provence, France, for ". . . the learning experience of a lifetime."

Discussing was hardly the right word. Arguing, if not downright fighting, was more accurate. It was the same every summer with Mom trying to introduce her to "all the things I never had" and Dad at first ridiculing and then downright despising everything Mom said.

"If you want to improve her mind, let her do it with somebody else's hard-earned cash," Dad had said. "Send her to that lost-and-found place in the desert, which guarantees she'll lose ten pounds and gain that new self-image you're always going on about." His tone had grown more and more sarcastic. "Get with it, Teri, for God's sake. Get her in shape, so some other guy will buy her that fancy education one day." On and on, and round and round the discussion had gone in familiar circles until, as usual, she had been the one to solve everything, Jo, the Peacemaker, trying to sound excited about the ad she had found in the San Diego paper.

"At Blue-Bird—for teenage coeds—you can milk a cow . . . blow hot glass . . . weave shawls and blankets . . . hit a home run . . . publish your poetry and prose . . . grow zucchini . . . swim in a water hole . . . achieve a Black Belt . . . fence with foils . . . bake a pie like mother used to make . . ." That was a joke. Jo couldn't remember her mother baking a pie in her life, but she'd circled "publish your poetry and prose." She had never seen that offered in a camp ad before and no matter what else her folks thought—endlessly comparing her to Alexa—they had to admit she'd always been dedicated to following a writing career. She'd been writing since she could use a pencil. Both of them wanted her out of the way during the long summer vacation. She knew that, and they didn't even try to pretend otherwise.

Mom had some big modeling assignment coming up in Mexico and Dad, well, Dad always had some reason for a heavy-duty business trip somewhere. They never worried about what to do with Alexa, although she was ten months younger. Alexa always had plans, big plans, with friends like Barbara Witten, the kind of friend Jo knew her parents wished they had themselves, who would send a car and driver at a moment's notice—even a plane ticket one Christmas—to whisk Alexa away to another world.

No wonder people fell over themselves for a place on Alexa's schedule, one of her sister's favorite new words. Alexa, her absolutely gorgeous sister, was worth every cent squandered on her. Jo didn't begrudge Alexa a thing. She just wished her folks didn't make her feel so "underfoot" no matter how hard she tried to prove she could be independent, too. For some reason, she made her folks uneasy. She didn't know why. It was Jo who had to go somewhere, who had to do something with her summer. Jo who had to be farmed out as if she couldn't be trusted to open a can of beans.

It was crazy, topsy-turvy, because it was Alexa who was always scraping the car as it made the tricky turn into the garage. Alexa, who had left the fudge cooking on the stove one weekend and nearly burned the house down. Alexa, who once ran through the glass door into the yard and who had had to have five stitches in her beautiful head. She had been looking after Alexa ever since she could remember. Perhaps that was why her parents never seemed to worry about Alexa.

"Look at this ad, Mom. I'd really love to go there—it sounds neat. I'd much sooner go to a camp where I could get something I've written printed than learn French . . . and anyway I don't want to go so far away from home. I might still get a call from Mike Tanner for that summer desk job on the *Union Tribune*." She didn't really expect that manna from heaven. She'd been typing Mike's free-lance short stories for a few months now, trying to make a little cash on the side, but Mike Tanner wasn't enough of a big shot in the newsroom to pull any strings, and as Jo knew from Alexa, you had to pull the right strings to get where you wanted to get in life. Nevertheless, she'd persevered. "Blue-Bird isn't that far away. Mom, I'd really love to go there this summer."

Of course, Dad had gone on making snide remarks about weight-loss camps, but there hadn't been any real intent on his part. He knew her weight yo-yo'd up and down, that she was chubby, but could never be called fat—although there was no way she would ever have a figure as great as Mom's or Alexa's. It had something to do with being an ectomorph or an endomorph—and whichever was the fatter morph of the two was her fate.

It was funny, the more she pretended to be excited about Blue-Bird, just to calm the atmosphere at home, the more genuinely excited she had started to become. She had forgotten about the disappointments of other years, of not getting along with the other kids, of always turning out to be the "loner" . . . "different" . . . going off with a book alone when even the plainest, dullest girls seemed to get hooked up with someone quickly, so that complete strangers twenty-four hours before they were exchanging petting experiences and whispering fascinating secrets to one another.

This summer *she* was doing all that—and more. Brad. Jo looked at herself in the mirror. She did have big breasts and they were firm, high, and her waist was a good feature, too, so much so Bobo said she should always wear three-inch belts to emphasize its smallness.

The sun was going down behind the mountain. It was her favorite time of day, when the last rays hit the red-flowering gum trees, so the blossoms blazed like exotic fireworks and a warm wind from the Mojave Desert far inland stroked the tall, feathery leaves of the plum palms.

In the distance, walking slowly down the mountain path, Jo saw Bobo and Rita, their arms intertwined, talking intensely together. Once a sight like that would have produced an intolerable outsider sense of loneliness and longing. Now, she smiled lovingly in their direction. The gang was reassembling. She would be able to tell them a little bit—just a little bit about her rendezvous with Brad—but most of it she would keep a secret. She was growing up at last.

Her face was made of glass. Very fine glass, the kind they made in Venice. She'd never been to Venice but Alf and she had drunk Champagne out of two Venetian "flutes"—that's what he'd called them—so incredibly thin she had been scared she'd be eating glass with each sip.

Alf was so sophisticated. He knew the right word, the right drink, the right everything for every occasion. He was also cruel, but sophisticated people always were. However hard she'd tried over the years, producers, directors, coaches, all the sophisticated pros had somehow always guessed she came from a small hick town and had had to learn how to be sophisticated from the movies—like a deaf child lip reading.

She moved her face very, very slowly from side to side. It was funny, but she knew she might break something if she moved faster.

Through tiny slits in the tape, Teri saw the room was darkening again. She brought her wrist up to her eyes to check her watch. Ten to nine. It had to be evening, but she had lost track of time. The most wonderful thing was, so far, her face didn't hurt.

Acid peel—*acid*—the word had frightened her for days after that first discussion with Magda. She'd imagined herself as Joan of Arc going up in flames, but instead of heat, just as Ann the nurse had predicted, her face felt cold, very cold and smooth under the tape.

What a sight she must look. Teri smothered a nervous giggle, not sure if anyone was in the room with her. Jo would say she looked like the phantom of the opera, just to prove how well read she was, the little monster. Alexa would more likely say something sarcastic like, ". . . And who did you kill on the highway today, Mom?" As for Ben—Teri felt tears in her eyes. Damn and blast Ben. Damn and blast all men. She fiercely concentrated on pushing the tears back. God knows what tears could do to an acid peel, particularly bitter tears over an unfaithful husband.

Oh, was she going to show him when she got out of there . . . was she going to prove what a great dame she still was! Alexa thought it was all Ben's fault that she wasn't a top model. Alexa, with her clever little asides that Ben never seemed to mind. If Jo ever said the things Alexa said—wow, a hurricane would turn the house over. Darling Jo. How different things might have been if she'd turned out to be the boy she'd foolishly promised Ben, who still, from time to time, said she'd tricked him into marrying her. Tricked! That was a joke. Married in pale blue, seven months pregnant, with a funny little bulge in her stomach, which someone had said looked as if she'd swallowed an olive. "That's Joe, my son," she could still remember Ben saying proudly, his arm around her thickening waist, affectionate, loving, adorable in fact. She was so young, so innocent, so trusting. Then, Lady Luck had always shone down on her, so it had never crossed her mind she would have a girl. Girls didn't run in her family or Ben's. But then she hadn't expected Ben to mind so much either. He'd insisted on calling the little scrap Joe with an *e*, not Josephine, but "Joe," writing it on the birth registration form as clearly as anything, although the clerk had raised her eyebrows. She'd never let him inflict the *e* on their little girl, though. She'd done her own share of insisting; writing "Jo;" thinking "Jo." The tears almost came back as she remembered one day Jo had told her with such pride that one of the girl characters in *Little Women* was called Jo, too.

Teri fidgeted restlessly in the bed, her thoughts far away in the El Cajon trailer park, remembering the flies, the heat, the baby crying—and then the horror of discovering they hadn't taken enough precautions—another baby on the way. There were the tears threatening again. She whimpered. She suddenly wanted to get out . . . to be already wrinkle-free, pink and glowing like she'd been back in the big time, in the sixties.

"Teri . . ." the doctor was beside her bed. "Teri, are you comfortable? Please be good and take some more liquid."

She nodded dutifully as a straw was inserted between her lips.

"Are you in pain? Sore? It is important you tell me if you are. As I told you this morning, press the buzzer twice for pain."

Again Teri shook her head, trying to convey both its fragility and the absence of pain. The doctor started to talk to her as if she was a really important person, explaining what to expect, what not to expect, and warning her, too. "I can see you look after your skin, except in one very important regard—the sun. Such a sad, sad situation in California, where the sun is always shining so beautifully. You must never go into the sun again. Never, never sunbathe, do you realize that, Teri? It is the sun that gave you the lines that caused you so much distress. Do you understand that, Teri? All my work, my research, is useless if you do not hide from the sun from now on. Are you going to promise me that—so that soon I will see your photographs everywhere I look?"

This was better than Champagne out of Venetian flutes, better than a couple of Quaaludes. This was the kind of talk that always made her feel high, like the few occasions Alf had predicted great things—like the day the creative guy at Clairol had winked and told her she'd got the job. She reached out and squeezed the doctor's hand, creaking through the tape, "Oh, I promise. Thank you, Doctor, thank you."

The doctor put a finger across her mouth. "Do not move your mouth now. Tomorrow, yes, but not tonight. Tomorrow afternoon we will remove the tape and soothe your skin with a special antibiotic powder I have created. The next day a wonderful new ointment will be used to help soften the crust before it is removed—and then . . ." the doctor paused. It was like a play, Teri thought, a play she knew and loved so much she knew the next words. Yes, here they came. ". . . you will see your lovely new skin, pink, shining with health, lustrous with youth."

Teri no longer felt restless. The voice was hypnotic. Although she'd slept more than she'd slept in years, her eyes were closing again.

There was a line a mile long around the movie house. Alexa guessed from the self-satisfied set to Barb's mouth that she didn't care. As usual she had a plan. That was what she liked most about Barb. Sure, it helped to have her kind of money, but she always had a neat plan for how to spend it. Barb brought the open Chevy to a screeching halt just where the line turned off State Street. She turned to Bugsy and Dave in the back and with a nonchalant wave at the man-sized posters of John Travolta on the walls, ordered, "Okay, boys, get in line. Lex and I'll be back around nine to take over from you. Then you can take the car, park it on Chapala, and pick us up when *Fever* is over. Okay? Over and out."

What dummies, Alexa thought, as the two lanky boys hopped out with sick smiles in her direction. That was another thing she liked about her best friend. Barb treated guys like gofers and the incredible thing was they fell for it—especially, as Barb had pointed out sardonically, whenever she was around. "They're hoping for a screw, you'd better believe it. With that bod, you lucky beast, what else do you expect?"

They had been swinging in the hammocks by the pool earlier that day, talking about sex—or rather Barb had been talking about it, her favorite subject after food and diet. It bored Alexa to sobs, but she put up with it because she loved staying with Barb. Who wouldn't? Her father, Paul Witten, was the top honcho of American Oil or Gas or Air or something equally essential to American life and it was a top honcho's home all right—from the long meandering drive lined with huge palms all the way to the big white stone house with the inner courtyard, modeled, so Barb had told her with a bored yawn, after one her last stepmother had seen in Andalusia, wherever that was. Alexa often thought if it had been Jo who was Barb's friend, she would have had the entire history of the place in twenty-four hours, probably right back to the time Santa Barbara was part of the Spanish empire. Alexa didn't care about the past. She luxuriated in the present . . . in the incredible deep plushness of her bed, in the deep brown towels in the guest bathroom, so thick when she draped one around her it was like wearing Mom's beaver coat.

Only that afternoon Alexa had thought Barb must be crazy to agree to see Bugsy and Dave again—two guys they'd met the day before roller skating at Palm Park. Now, they'd been turned into linemen, shuffling along for nearly two boring hours to make sure Barb and she had seats for the last performance of

Saturday Night Fever, waiting in line while Barb and she cruised the town.

"Where'd you get that bod from, anyway?" Barb had asked that afternoon, starting to sound petulant as she always did when she'd seen enough of Alexa in her bikini.

"My father, I guess . . ." she'd spoken without thinking, hiding her anger as she could hide every emotion, when Barb started to shake with laughter.

It was only in recent months she'd begun to realize being five-foot-ten wasn't the suicide jump of all time. As Barb prattled on about cocks and grass and gofers and grads, Alexa had daydreamed. Her height and her sea-colored eyes and probably her mouth, too, wide and kind of sensual like Carly Simon's, came from her father—but her skin, pale gold, matching her long pale gold hair, was definitely inherited from her mother.

Now, with her hair in a long pony tail, flaring out like a meteor as Barb stepped on the gas, Alexa wondered briefly where her mother was and who she was working for in Mexico. Certainly not for anything or anyone worthwhile. Certainly not for *Vogue* or *View* or *Bazaar*. As a model her mother was on the way out, Alexa knew that. At thirty-four or -five or whatever age Teri really was, she'd lost the look that Alexa had never been able to put into words, but a look that once upon a time had made her jealous of her mother. Now the situation was reversed.

She didn't need to be told by her father that her mother wished she'd never been born. It was too late to pretend to be her sister. As Dad had said more than once, "Get lost, kid. You're too visible today. Mom is getting a blue spell over her lost youth."

He didn't help. It was too bad pretty men just got better looking when they wrinkled up—even when they had a touch of gray around the temples. While Dad's looks improved and he lapped up all the attention from Mom's friends and now her friends, too, Mom just put on more blusher and pulled her hair tighter and tighter away from her face in that silly facelift band. It was too bad. Alexa sighed, shutting her eyes as Barb negotiated the turn off the highway onto Montacito. The only time she could think was when Barb was behind the wheel. Barb didn't like to talk when she was driving, thank God, and right now she liked driving her new red Chevy a lot.

It was crazy the hysterical way Mom had carried on when Alf Victor suggested she sit for some shots. She was too young. Alf had no right suggesting such a thing and on and on Mom had ranted. Alexa liked Alf Victor. He always treated her like a grownup. She remembered with gratitude the day Alf had let her stay around while he shot a detergent ad. Mom had never known about it—and never would. Why should she give Mom the satisfaction of knowing how turned off she'd been that dreary morning, watching another aging model endlessly grimace at the camera. Modeling was for the birds. Alexa didn't believe any of the crap published about the big-time money models were supposed to make. Sure, from time to time Mom landed a job that meant new clothes, even a new car once. It was the time *between* jobs that made nonsense of that kind of life. Perhaps it would have been different if the "master of the house" had ever delivered his "promises, promises." Alexa wrinkled her nose as if she had a bad smell under it as she thought of her father.

There was more *between* time waiting for *his* lackluster contribution to the family budget than there ever was with Mom.

Nope. She might be lucky and have a great bod, as Barb from time to time jealously admitted, but without brains it didn't get you anywhere. She was going to San Diego State in the fall to do a business management course and then she would head to New York, away from beach bums, the Bugsys and Daves and Bens of the world. With brains and a great bod she would land a head honcho of gas or oil or air and never have to live on credit again.

They were pulling into the country club because Barb had the hots for one of the boys who did valet parking. It was a boring place, but Alexa quite enjoyed seeing the covert looks from the old guys sitting with their wives, as wrinkled as prunes, all of them trying hard to look as if they were enjoying their martinis. It was a prison without bars.

She'd read in a book once that the king of England had had to give up his throne to marry the woman he loved, because she'd been divorced. From pictures Alexa thought she looked like a flat-chested frump. After a few years, the book reported, they'd apparently run out of anything to say to each other, so when in public they'd taken turns reciting the alphabet, smiling while they did it to make sure they looked as radiantly happy as ever. Marriage, hmph! Why so many of her friends were dying to get into it was beyond her.

The wrong valet was on duty. Barb glared at the red-faced boy who opened the car door as if he'd insulted her. "Do we want to go in?" The question, Alexa knew, didn't need an answer, but she shook her head anyway. Barb pulled the car door shut and, giving the startled boy one more glare, put her foot hard on the gas and shot forward.

How boring Barb could be. Now, Alexa knew, they would head for the drugstore, where Barb would eat too much ice cream and moan about "living in a sanitarium." As a framed old advertisement in the Witten pool house stated, Santa Barbara had once been called "The sanitarium of the Pacific, where visitors can luxuriate near the quiet restfulness of the waves' crests and ocean breezes, where the vital elements renew health . . ."

Not with the amount of grass being smoked in Santa Barbara today, Alexa thought. Barb was nuts. As a university town where the graduates never seemed to want to leave, there was plenty of action around. Even before the car pulled up, Alexa could hear the disco beat that was reverberating through the town, *Saturday Night Fever*. Now, John Travolta was someone she would like to meet. For him she would really show off her bod. For him she might let down her guard—well, at least for an hour or so. Alexa followed Barb into the drugstore, moving her body in time to the rhythm pouring out from the jukebox, immediately aware she was being watched, getting used to the idea and liking it more and more.

She was ill, very ill, she knew it. It had happened in the night, the feeling she couldn't breathe, tidal waves of sweat breaking through her body. There were low voices around her bed; faces loomed near, then far away, like looking at them through the wrong end of binoculars.

It was so unfair, but she felt so weak she couldn't scream out her outrage, that just when her face was going to be like new, her body, her stupid body, was letting her down.

The tape had come off the day before and she hadn't complained once, hadn't even moaned although the sound of tearing skin had been about the worst sound she'd ever heard in her whole life. She'd put up with it, murmuring her gratitude as Ann had cleaned her up and applied the special powder every two or three hours to the place where she knew her face had to be. It didn't feel like glass anymore.

She'd wanted desperately to brush her teeth but hadn't been able to open her stupid mouth. Where was her mouth? Teri touched it as tremulously as touching the mouth of a stranger. It was a mouth all right, an isolated soft space, surrounded by hard crusts, scabs that didn't allow it to open wider than a whisper.

She'd been told there would be no mirrors, no reflections until the next day, when the crust would peel off so naturally, it would be like taking a perfectly baked cake out of a cake tin. Words, words, words . . . and now it was nearly time and she felt so ill she almost didn't care how she looked. A thermometer had become more important than lipstick. Her blood pressure had become her most vital statistic.

Her body shivered and then blazed, while the place where her face had once been, suddenly, intolerably, added to the injustice of it all and started to throb as if her whole head was a bad tooth.

Was she dreaming? Was Magda really standing beside her bed, looking down with the kind of suffering, deeply sympathetic look on her face that only foreigners ever seemed to have—the look Ingrid Bergman had had in *Casablanca*.

Despite her misery, Teri could still admire Magda's high Slavic cheekbones that photographed so well, cheekbones that now were highlighted as if they were wet with tears or shining with some new kind of gloss—but why was Magda there? She wasn't supposed to be. They had a date, a special Fourth of July/Christmas Eve kind of date when she, Teri Shephard, would turn heads in the Polo Lounge of the Beverly Hills Hotel the way she'd once always turned heads in Jerry's drugstore. "Is that you, Magda?" Nobody answered. Teri didn't know anything anymore. She felt confused, her mind spinning with a mixture of inside and outside elements, hot and cold pain.

There had been snatches of conversation all day. She'd heard Ann, the nurse, speak in a bitter, sarcastic tone that Teri recognized because she'd so often sounded that way herself. ". . . bloody treacherous stuff . . . I told you all along phenol can penetrate the bloodstream. I told you she'd only taken a correspondence course. Russian diploma, my ass. I tell you, if a blood clot develops . . ."

If they had been talking about her, Teri didn't even have

the energy to be alarmed. She'd stayed still, concentrating on breathing, on not shivering, although she'd felt colder and colder, except for her face, which with every hour passing, every powdering, burned beneath its baking crust.

"Take the crust off!" she screamed. She knew she screamed, but her voice was so puny she could hardly hear herself. Then, as the drip went on dripping into her arm, she began to feel better, in fact astonishingly better, almost euphoric as if she'd climbed a volcano and been able to put out the flame.

It was 4:25 P.M. when the doctor came into the room with Ann and another woman in a white coat. Teri was still sweating but she knew she was going to be fine. The doctor told her so, but in any case Teri knew it already, although for some reason she was clenching and unclenching her hands like a prize-fighter before a fight. She was wheeled to the window, which didn't reflect anything. In any case she didn't want to look at herself while "they" were there. She wanted to savor the look of her new face alone, so she could revel in it without embarrassment.

Now it was like waiting in the wings before going on stage to become a star. They were removing the crust with ease with the special cream, all part of the magic formula, the doctor said. It took a while to realize she couldn't move her neck either now. It was locked in something. Teri could see beads of perspiration on the doctor's face above her. She shut her eyes tightly, only to open them again when she heard Ann gasp, "Oh, my God . . ." and saw a look of horror on the young nurse's face.

Terror soaked her body with sweat. There were tears in the doctor's eyes—tears? There was a long in-drawn breath before the doctor spoke in the same reassuring voice. "Another day of waiting, I'm afraid, Teri. We need to make some adjustments. Perhaps it will mean a visit to our convalescence clinic in Mexico. We will make all the arrangements. There is the presence of eschar, dead skin, which we have to correct."

"Eschar . . . what does that mean . . . eschar . . . Mexico . . . I don't have the time . . ." Teri's voice was squeaky, sounds squeezed out from between lips that had forgotten how to move, how to smile, scowl, open wide enough, for God's sake even, to let a toothbrush inside.

"You must rest now." The doctor wasn't looking at her, but stared at Ann as if she were an enemy, while Ann still had the look of horror on her face, looking away at the floor, at the wall, anywhere but at her. What was going on? They injected her again before she could lash out and stop it and in seconds a fog descended, blocking out all sights and sounds.

They had left the light on. Teri came to abruptly and scanned the room. It seemed empty. With great difficulty she sat up, her neck still like a padlock between shoulder and head, forcing her to move her whole body if she wanted to turn to the left or right. Now only one thing consumed her. She had to see herself, had to know now, this instant, what it was that needed adjustment, what needed a trip to a Mexican clinic? She slid off the bed, horribly weak, as if her body had been stripped of all its energy along with the skin off her face.

There was a silence about the place that was unnerving, but nothing and no one was going to deter her. Her purse was no longer in the drawer by the bed and she knew there was no mirror in the lavatory next to her room, but she had seen on arrival a bathroom somewhere at the end of the corridor. If she could make it to there, she could see for herself what else had to be done.

Teri half stumbled, half crawled along the wall, her nightdress marking it with sweat as she moved. The tidal waves were returning, but she kept on, gritting her teeth to get to her objective.

At first she thought the bathroom door was locked, but in her nervousness she turned the knob the wrong way. She clicked on the light and in her eagerness to get to the mirror over the sink left the door open behind her.

She shut her eyes as she stood before the mirror, then, taking a deep breath, slowly, opened them to see a monster staring back . . . a mottled monster of blood-red and stark-white ridges and nodules of skin where features—a nose, a chin, the high curve of cheekbones had once been, one side of the face puckered up from mouth to ear like shriveled meat. Only her eyes, her deep dark-brown eyes, told her the monster was related to her, to Teresa Millicent Shapwell, also known as Teri Shephard—dark brown eyes that stared from eyelids that seemed to be turned inside out.

The monster, who only a few days ago had been Teri

Shephard, wife, mother, and professional model, heard someone behind her.

"Can I help you?" somebody asked.

Teri turned to face a nurse, a strange nurse, who clutched her throat and backed away in anguished disbelief as Teri moved toward her, before crashing unconscious to the floor.

CHAPTER TWO

Jo didn't have a summer that year. She remembered it beginning too fiercely, too soon in May. She remembered the way the sun rose every morning like a huge orange bubble over the tennis courts at the summer camp, guaranteeing another scorching day, another day of daring to leave off her bra like the other girls did and anything else that had a strap that could burn into flesh. She remembered the glorious, giddy promise of two months of happiness ahead, rushing with the gang to the ocean to cool their feet in the tidepools with the hermit crabs and green-brown sea anemones. She remembered petting for the first time, petting with Brad from Texas in the back of an old Thunderbird to and from Bobby McGhee's in Newport Beach, where Brad actually knew people, even though he was from a state over a thousand miles away.

She remembered how easy it had been to put on her "mysterious look," because everything had been mystifying, wild, crazy, wonderful. Brad had known a guy who worked at the 7-Eleven, which in Newport Beach didn't just sell groceries, coffee, and doughnuts twenty-four hours a day, but rented out cars, not just Fords and any old Joes, but "Rolls-Royces, Mercs and Porsches." She could remember the way Brad rolled those names off his ever-seeking tongue. No 7-Eleven would ever seem the same again and she would always remember the eight-foot-high statue of John Wayne, which told everyone he'd lived nearby.

She remembered summer beginning, but it had ended abruptly the day she'd been told to report to the camp adviser's office and had seen her father sitting with his head in his hands, sobbing so hard the tears made odd little splashing sounds on the wooden arms of the chair.

Even now she felt ashamed that her first thought had been one of embarrassment that her father could make such a fool of himself, that even as handsome a man as her father could look so silly. Perhaps the brain played tricks and made you think terrible, superficial, disgusting thoughts when you were in shock. Perhaps it was the brain's way of giving you time to live for another second before you tried to drop dead before anything could be said to hurt you further.

But then it actually hadn't been any words that had made her knees buckle and her whole body start trembling. It had been the sight of tears in the codfish eyes of the owner of the camp—"the jailbird," as the gang always called him. When her father hadn't moved, Jailbird had come over in that odd stealthy way of his to lead her to a chair and clumsily stroke her shoulder.

"Bad news. I'm so sorry, Jo. Bad news . . . your father . . ." The owner had glared at her father, as if he'd suddenly realized it wasn't his problem, his responsibility. "Mr. Shapwell, your daughter Jo is here—your daughter . . ."

Even now, five months later, with summer long over, Jo could still hardly accept it. Her mother gone—gone.

She would never know how long she'd stayed in that office, with her father gulping, sobbing, stopping, starting to sob all over again as he'd told her that Mom had been killed in a car crash in the mountains in Mexico.

"My Teri, my little Teri," he'd said over and over, his voice breaking every time he'd tried to go into detail.

Two nights before he'd been called by the Mexican police in Tijuana, asking him to come to identify the . . . the . . . her father had never been able to say the word, because it wasn't *body*. There had been no body to identify. There had only been "remains." It had taken days and days for Jo to learn the whole story, that her mother had been totally incinerated in a car that had hurtled down a mountainside and exploded at a point in the Sierra Madres where rainfall had washed away part of the road.

At first she hadn't wanted to hear, had put her hands over her ears, shutting her eyes, screaming she didn't want to know, crazily trying to think where she'd been two nights before.

A Hawaiian High had been blowing. Her hair had caught in Bobo's fraternity pin and Brad had come to the rescue. They'd had a milkshake in town. They'd walked for hours and jeered at the luxury homes they'd passed . . . and all the time that she had been laughing and flirting and having the very best time she'd ever had, her mother, her sweet, trusting, adorable mother, had been driving to her death.

She'd had hysterics. She wasn't proud of it, but at least it had made her father act like a man again. In the morning, like a prisoner going into solitary, she'd packed her things, not aware of what anyone said, not even Brad, who'd put his Texas address in her purse without her even realizing it.

On the long drive north to tell Alexa and bring her home, she had hardly exchanged a word with her father. They'd both cried, drying their faces as they stopped for coffee or a hamburger or to go to the bathroom. She had never questioned her father that they should not warn Alexa first. It couldn't be told on the phone. It couldn't be told to another person to tell Alexa. "The family has to be together," her father had said. The words had sounded foreign coming from him.

"Afoot and lighthearted I take to the open road." It was one of her favorite Walt Whitman sayings and it had mocked her every mile they drove from Long Beach's oil wells to Malibu's gold-plated houses on stilts and on and on until they'd crossed the Santa Barbara county line.

Her father had been scared. She knew the signs only too well. "I've gotta have a quick one," he'd said.

"It's not a good idea." She'd sounded like her mother and that had brought on the tears again. She would never again hear her mother say the phrases that had been as predictable as the weatherman's jokes on their local TV station. She would

never again be able to watch starry eyed as her mother sat before her dressing table and took years away with eye pencil and concealer stick. She would never again be able to cut out an ad or an editorial picture of her mother in a magazine to add to her bulging scrapbook.

Just as her father had never taken any notice of her mother, so he'd taken no notice of her and one scotch had followed another, but at least she'd been able to take over the driving.

Looking back, Jo realized how much they'd taken for granted, driving straight up the coast to break the news to Alexa and to bring her home. For what? A funeral of remains? The two of them, father and daughter, had been in a fog, not talking, because they'd never talked much and what had brought them together had been too agonizing to think about, let alone discuss.

They had taken for granted that Alexa would be sitting in the palatial Santa Barbara house just waiting for them to drop in and, of course, she hadn't even been there.

When they'd finally located the Wittens' hidden entrance, having stopped for directions three times, and had driven up and up and round and round the magnificent drive, Ben had been incoherent with despair and drink. As usual, Jo had had to muster up his courage and almost push him up the steps under the towering colonnade to a front door with no doorbell in sight. Perhaps their shadows had caused suspicion because after knocking feebly on the wood and looking everywhere for something to announce their arrival, the door had been opened by a distinguished-looking man who'd turned out to be the butler.

What a mess it had all been, the kind of disorganized, miserable mess Ben had always managed to surround them with every time he put his mind to it.

"Miss Alexa? You have just missed her. She left with Miss Barbara to visit Mr. Witten in San Francisco. I believe they will be there until the weekend."

There must have been something in their faces that neither her father nor she had been able to say. Jo would always be grateful to the Witten butler that, with her father silent and white beside her, she didn't have to go into much. "Our mother . . ." the butler had put out a steadying hand. Jo had choked on the next words, but a little bit of it had escaped.

"Oh, my, oh dear, how terrible. Come in miss . . . Miss Shapwell. Come in, Mr. Shapwell. Come in while I try to reach Mr. Witten's office."

And so the family hadn't been all together when Alexa received the news.

The message light was flashing, but it wasn't the office line. Paul Witten shrugged. It could wait. Or rather she could wait. He wasn't in the mood for any reheated, warmed-over chick. Was it a sign of getting old that the sight of Alexa Shapwell had made the thought of the talented, ambidextrous lady waiting so impatiently for news of his arrival suddenly so uninteresting? Was he turning into a lecherous old sugar daddy?

Hell, no, but God, what a difference six months could make to an adolescent—*some* adolescents. It sure hadn't happened to his own spoiled little heiress. He bounced into his large elaborate bathroom-cum-exercise-room as if he were going on court to face his toughest opponent. In a way, getting ready to receive Miss Alexa Shapwell was like taking on an unknown challenger, his favorite sort of game.

Was the vision who'd stepped off the company plane really one and the same Alexa, the gawky, awkward screwball of last winter, who instead of sitting on the sofa had managed to sit half on a sidetable, effectively smashing one of Eldora's favorite hideous Spanish figurines? It had gained her a modicum of his affection then. As he jumped on the trampoline, he felt a return of the euphoria he'd experienced a month ago, on being released from his last marriage and never having to watch a flamenco again. The thought of Alexa's long legs, which looked as if they started under her armpits, stirred his penis even as he jumped higher and higher. What a pity he hadn't known about the metamorphosis that had taken place. He would have made a point of visiting Santa Barbara as soon as she arrived. The thought of that lovely body swimming in his pool, swinging in his hammock was simply delicious—like sampling a perfect martini or having Ashkenazi play his Steinway in the drawing room.

How old was she? Seventeen? Eighteen? No more. She was a changeling, half angel, half devil with those curious gray-green eyes and that wide mocking mouth that seemed about to say "fuck you, you old fogey." He laughed aloud as he went into the shower.

It was going to be a helluva lot of fun showing Miss Shapwell around tonight. Thank God, his own Barbie doll had to pay her usual duty call on her mother. If he hadn't decided to stay one more day before leaving for Europe, he would have missed Miss Shapwell's visit altogether.

Was she like most of the young nowadays, well-equipped with knowledge of popped-in protection? It had shocked him to learn from Daisy, the girl he had been crazy enough to marry after leaving Barbie's mother, that his own daughter was probably on birth-control pills. Now, two marriages later—both to women he should have kept as mistresses—he was grateful that his daughter had enough sense not to get into trouble and end up with a jerk who would spend her money as fast as he earned it.

Well, he wasn't a fool. He would enjoy a close, very close evening of flirtation and if Alexa showed signs of knowing what to do with his mammoth erection, he wouldn't discourage it. Otherwise, he'd send her back to Santa Barbara none the wiser and see what another semester might teach her.

Dark gray suit, gray-and-white silk tie, Bulgari cuff links, Harvey and Hudson crisp white shirt—it all looked good and so did the face and body that went with it. Paul Witten combed his thick dark-brown hair, only slightly graying at the temples, spooned some caviar on toast for himself, and tasted the Montrachet as the doorbell rang.

The warm smile of welcome turned sour as he opened the door to see his daughter Barbara, standing like a guard beside the changeling beauty, both with grim expressions. For one of the few times in his life his composure left him.

"What in God's name are you doing here, Barbara?" came out before he realized what a giveaway question it was, coupled with his aggravated tone.

"Alexa's mother has been killed—in a car crash. Her sister and father are waiting for us back home. We've got to go back now . . ." it was only later that Paul Witten remembered it was his daughter, Barbie, not Alexa, who then burst into tears.

* * *

Someone—Jo would never know who—had chosen St. Paul's letter to the Corinthians about love for the funeral. "Love is patient and kind; love is not jealous, or conceited or proud; love does not keep a record of wrongs . . . love never gives up . . . there are faith, hope and love; but the greatest of these is love." The priest had spoken so sweetly and innocently, drawing conclusions about a woman he'd never known, trying to give some comfort in his sermon to the distraught man sobbing noisily in the front pew.

Jo had sobbed, too, almost suffocating as she'd tried not to make a sound. It was Alexa who'd pointed out that St. Paul's letter had been an ironic, almost chilling choice, adding to the melancholy, the sense of what-might-should-have-been.

"Love is the greatest of all." Had her mother, Teresa Millicent, ever had reason to believe it? Experience it? Perhaps once upon a time.

Jo could remember almost word for word the way her mother had sometimes reminisced about the "good old days" . . . about her "whirlwind romance with your dad, who swept me off my feet—straight to El Cajon trailer park." It was funny that the "good old days" had been when she and Dad had been almost broke, but Teresa Millicent had never sounded bitter. Self-mocking perhaps, and wistful. Yes, more and more wistful but never bitter, even though for the last few years love had been in pretty short supply at 804 East Mission Highway. The white stucco house with its rumpus room and big yard with garden furniture, table and chairs with gaily striped seats, was several rungs up the real-estate ladder from El Cajon, yet that early love had somehow been snuffed out on the way.

There was no point in dwelling on it. The past was the past. There was nothing to be gained, as she kept telling Alexa, from reminding Dad that he hadn't made Mom happy. "Can't you see he's living with that?" She could see it. There was a scared, half-pleading look in his eyes. Even the way he sat hunched over, looking into space, was full of guilt.

If Alexa could see it, she obviously didn't care. Her voice was always sharp when she spoke to him, which was as little as possible.

Aunt Clare, Dad's cousin, had written to say the service had been lovely. The service had been the worst.

Alexa said she'd heard Dad boast to someone on the phone that the church had been packed, "as if Mom was making a special appearance." Jo hated it when Alexa was that sarcastic, even though she knew Alexa was suffering, that her remarks and coldness to their father were her way of trying to cover it up.

Anyway, it was a lie. No matter what Dad said or didn't say, Alexa was going to twist it—but the church had been half empty, or half full. Alexa would put it one way, she the other, but it didn't matter. People didn't matter. Nothing mattered.

Jo would wake up in the middle of the night, shaking, seeing again the coffin, the wrong-sized coffin, too big, much too big. However hard she tried, macabre thoughts would cram her mind. What could have been inside? A burnt-out skeleton? The "remains"? The coffin had been a terrible shock, followed so soon after by another one from Alf Victor.

Jo had tried over and over again to get Dad to explain, but he always shut her up, at first gently, then losing his temper, bawling at her not to drive him crazy with what Alf Victor had or had not said. "It isn't going to bring your mom back, is it?"he'd yell, his face white and taut.

So she tried to forget what Alf had told Dad at the lunch following the funeral—that he didn't know what on earth Teri had been up to in Mexico. "She couldn't have been on her way to any location. She didn't have any job in Mexico. I would have known about it if she had!" Jo could still hear Alf Victor's dogged voice. She knew he had been telling the truth. If it had been a modeling assignment, Alf would have known, that was sure. Her mother hadn't moved a step without him professionally for as long as she could remember. Alf had told her mother what to wear, when to cut her hair. Alexa always said Mom wouldn't even go to the bathroom without Alf's permission.

"I don't know what she was up to, but it was nothing to do with work." So where *had* she been going? What *had* she been up to? The questions gnawed at her, depleting her energy, her interest in getting on with life.

Alexa was no help. She wouldn't even let Jo finish, but cut into her stumbling sentences with the only thing she seemed to have on her mind nowadays. "Mom should have left Dad years ago when she found out he was messing around. Mom had enough going for her to really go places. The only way to win with guys is to treat 'em like they treat women. Love 'em and leave 'em. Alexa's vehemence had left Jo breathless. Alexa was like a volcano, erupting when everyone around had forgotten there was a volcano in their midst, erupting and scorching everything, everyone in sight, then just as suddenly retreating into herself, cool, remote, contained again.

Alexa had looked right through her father, not showing any emotion or saying a word when he'd entreated them to go through their mother's things. "I can't face it, kids. Take what you want and put the rest in the trunk in the garage. I'll send it to the mission one day, but right now get everything out of my sight."

Jo hadn't been able to face it either—not then, maybe not ever. "Take whatever you want, Lex . . ." Her voice had choked up. "Maybe later, in a month or so, I'll take a look. Put everything you don't want, like Dad says, in the trunk . . ." And Alexa had gone into Mom's little dressing room and Jo had swallowed hard later when she had seen Alexa packing away some of Mom's purses, scarves, and accessories in the big drawer under her bed and hanging up some of Mom's silk pajamas, a couple of her good suits, and Mom's precious silver fox boa and beaver coat in her wardrobe.

She hadn't known how Alexa could do it, but she'd known it had hurt like hell. For the first and only time since the news, Jo had seen tears coursing down Alexa's cheeks.

Slowly, it seemed to Jo, her father and Alexa slipped back—or was it moved forward—to pick up the pieces and resume their usual way of life.

From time to time she saw a haunted look in her father's eyes. Was he remembering, reliving the horror of the moment he'd told her about when the Mexican police had found Mom's favorite red-and-white Yves Saint Laurent scarf fiercely flapping in the wind from the branch of a tree, somehow swept out of the car as it fell down, down, down? The scarf—the only thing left totally unscorched?

Was he seeing again the twisted ugly mess of metal smoldering in the brush, all that remained of the dark red Plymouth, rented from Hertz in San Diego so trustingly only the day before by Teresa Millicent Shapwell?

As the weeks went by he didn't pale and jump or cry out "Jesus" anymore when the phone rang at night—on the nights he was home. And like "before"—either on Saturday or Sunday—he started to barbecue lunch for them, hot dogs and steak his special way, known as "Ben's burnt blessings" or the "3B," charred black outside, deliciously pink inside. In Dad's opinion, as he often said, barbecuing lunch expressed "what family life in California is all about."

At first, when Mom had installed the fancy brick charcoal oven outside, it had been a new toy to show off and most weekends he'd encouraged neighbors, pals, and some of Mom's friends from her old model agency to "drop by for a bloody and a 3B around eleven." His expansiveness hadn't lasted long, especially when Mom had started to rebel over the butcher's bill. Well, why shouldn't she have rebelled? Usually she'd been the one paying for it!

It had been at one of the early weekend barbecues that Dad first set eyes on Libby Nelson from New York City, taking liberal arts at UCLA. She'd arrived, uninvited, with her aunt and uncle, all on their way for an athletic few days at the Rancho La Puerta health spa across the border. From Mom's flustered behavior, Jo had gathered "Uncle Les" was a Mr. Big Shot casting director from a Los Angeles advertising agency. Of course, Alexa had to crack, "I bet Mom wishes that little group hadn't stopped by. Boy, have you ever in your life seen such a juvenile delinquent?" It was an apt description for Libby Nelson.

In abbreviated white shorts and pale pink halter top, which only just contained her lavish breasts, Libby had flaunted her body like a candidate for a *Playboy* centerfold. She'd flirted in the most obvious way with their own father, who to Jo's embarrassment had lapped it up, as if Libby had arrived gift-wrapped just for him and not even C.O.D.

For months, Alexa had hinted their father was "messing around with Libby—who isn't just liberal in the arts department!"

Jo had refused to listen, yet deep down had known something more than usual was wrong because Mom had been so nervous, so unsure of herself, even when checking in with Alf Victor to see if any work was on the horizon.

Then, suddenly, a couple of weeks or so before Alexa left for Santa Barbara and she went to summer camp, Mom had brightened up, implying she was in the running for a big commercial that was going to be shot in Mexico. Even when Jo had overheard Dad tell Mom that while she was away, he would probably be away, too, "looking into a big deal on the East Coast," Mom hadn't sounded too fazed. That was what made the mystery so much worse. However much she searched her mind, Jo could not remember any details about the Mexican job. She was fooling herself. She realized now—too late—that Mom hadn't volunteered any, which was also very unusual.

Jo had never told Alexa that Dad had been planning a trip to the East Coast while Mom was away, because she knew her sister would pounce on the news as positive proof Dad was having an affair with young Libby, back in New York for the summer break. And, of course, Dad had never made the trip. The news of the accident had come from the Mexican police before his departure . . . and now he was as free as air to have as many affairs as his conscience would allow.

"Hello?"

"It's me, Barb . . . Hello? Bar-ba-ra, get it?"

"Okay, okay. I know it isn't Barbra Streisand."

"Hey, what's *that* meant to mean? What's eating you?"

Alexa bit her lip. It wasn't like her to allow moods to disrupt the cool image she endeavored to show to the outside world. Quite the contrary—and she didn't want to get on the wrong side of Barb, especially now.

"Sorry, Barb." Alexa paused and decided there was nothing to be gained from being "loyal." She never revealed much about her family's shortcomings, but Barb knew, if anyone did, that she wasn't wild about her father.

Alexa tightened her grip on the phone as if she had resolved something. "I am sick of being here, Barb. It's so damned depressing. Business management is for the birds—at least it certainly isn't going to be my life's work. I've gotta get out of here—do something different." When Barb didn't respond, Alexa went on talking, which was also not like her.

"I moved in with a bunch of kids taking the same courses, but first one, then another dropped out and I just couldn't afford the rent, so decided to move back home and commute, but . . ." she gulped, then rushed on, ". . . I told you once my old man was messing around with someone not much older than me. Well, I think he's at it again, and this time it's worse. He's trying to make us all *friends*—all one big happy family. It's sick."

"That sure didn't take long." There was no surprise in Barb's voice. In fact, she sounded bored.

Alexa got the message. "Okay, I'm sorry to go on so much about me. What's up? What's happening in your life?"

"Oh, nothing much. Dad's got a bunch of movie people in and out of here for the next week or so. They're on their way up north to make an epic about an axman in the Redwoods. There's a broad with no beam and no tits who's swinging from the trees trying to make Dad notice her. Some hope. She's not his type." The bored tone didn't leave Barb's voice. "The phone never stops and it's never for me. Rob's left the club to join an oil rig or something equally disgusting. There's not one decent cock . . ." Barb yawned in midsentence, ". . . in town. Not one. It's been so-oo dreary and Dad's been nagging me so much, I've half agreed to go to interpreters' school in Geneva, but I still can't make up my mind what I really want to do—except find a good lay."

Alexa hardly heard her prattle on. Movie people. Staying with Barb in the Santa Barbara house. What an opportunity. She took a deep breath. It would never do to let Barb know how eager she was for an invitation. She changed the subject. "How's your weight?"

Barb sighed so heavily through the phone it was like the first sign of a Santa Ana wind approaching. "Lousy." Her tone sharpened. "I suppose you're your usual gorgeous size six soaking wet."

"I've got a great new diet and . . ." Alexa had a brainstorm. ". . . a terrific new guy. Met him in class. Greg Fletcher. He's mad for me, keeps talking about us sailing to Santa Catalina and if I don't get seasick, taking me with him when he tries a run down to Hawaii—Polynesia—you know, like the Kon Tiki raft trip. I'm sure in the mood to get away from it all . . ."

"Has he got a friend?" Alexa knew Barb would ask that question.

"Yep—but he's up somewhere near you, finding his soul before the great expedition." It was going better than she'd dreamed.

Barb caught the bait. "You mean in Santa Barbara?" Barb paused. She wasn't totally caught yet. She answered her own question. "He can't be. There's no one new here, except deadbeats and dropouts . . ."

"I think Greg said he was in Mendocino or Mendocito? I always get them mixed up. Greg's going up to visit him soon. I might go with him." Alexa couldn't believe how easily half fiction was turning into realistic-sounding fact. There was a Greg. He was okay, but too "into himself" to be really interested in anyone else. He *was* going on a Kon Tiki–type expedition with a friend called Ignatius—Iggie for short—who was somewhere up north, but neither had suggested she be part of the crew—yet.

"Boy, your life's always so much fun . . ." Barb was coming to life. "Can you come up here for a while—cut out of class—and let's maybe go find the soul searcher before I have to depart for the boring civilized Swiss?"

Alexa took another deep breath again to stop sounding too enthusiastic. She hated being a dropout in one way, yet in another—with daily evidence of her father's involvement with Libby, that oversexed piece of trash—she knew she would never be able to finish the semester without a major and probably irreparable row. She was too much in debt to take on another apartment, yet couldn't live at home for much longer, putting up with her father's deceits, innuendos, the false air of gaiety, then just as sudden ice-cold silences, the way her poor mother had. Jo might be able to bear it, but she couldn't. And she was just getting into her prime. Moviemakers—she had to meet the moviemakers, who might be able to see in her what Alf Victor had told her just the other day was there—star quality.

She'd bumped into him on the corner of Pine and Hilltop and he'd held her at arm's length saying softly, "Well, well, well . . ." in that low-key, but so flattering way of his. He'd invited her back to his studio for a cup of coffee. She'd intended to ask him where he thought Mom had really been going the day of her accident, but although Jo thought she was heartless, Alexa knew she still couldn't talk about it without losing her cool.

Looking her over more and more appreciatively, Alf had started to talk to her about cameras of all things, explaining how a lens could kind of "develop" any lurking beauty to print for posterity on film. He'd told her, for instance, how ordinary Mia Farrow looked in real life, a face without much character, he'd explained, yet the camera captured something the eye couldn't see—captured it to turn her into a beauty in print and on film. Apparently, it was the same with many models. She hadn't stayed long, but it had been long enough to know that if Alf hadn't been serious before about taking some test shots, he certainly was now. She still had no intention of just becoming a model, but it was encouraging that he felt with the right camerawork she could really be someone—someone people who were really in the movie business might spot right away, so she might end up being an actress.

Her silence had gone on long enough. "That sounds like a great idea, Barb. I'd love it."

When Alexa put the phone down she had a headache. She knew it was because she was going to have to break the news to Jo that she wasn't going to finish the semester. Well, Jo would just have to lump it. They would never understand each other.

Alexa's features softened as she thought about her sister, who in some funny way the more she acted like a little mother, seemed younger although she was ten months older. Jo had certainly been devastated by Mom's death, but the job at the *Union Tribune* seemed to have helped. Now, instead of acting as Mom's slave, running the house, looking after her while Mom concentrated on her career, Jo was Mike Tanner's girl Friday—which was a hell of a lot healthier.

She knew Jo would go to college one day, when she'd saved up enough, because she was serious about writing a masterpiece and always said you had to have a good background in other people's masterpieces before you could write one of your own.

By the time Jo came in from work about eight or nine that night, Alexa had decided not to tell her what she planned to do. Why give her another blow just when she was getting back on her feet? Neither of them could expect any support from their muscle-bound father. She hadn't told Barb half the story—that the beast had even dropped hints that he might be thinking of marrying again and moving East . . . that they couldn't expect to live "rent free forever."

As if his money had been used for the house at 804 East Mission. She knew very well, and so did Jo, that Mom had made the down payment and probably many of the monthly mortgage payments, too. It wasn't as if he seemed short of cash at the moment either. One of his crazy deals must have come in, because he'd bought a new car and when she stopped to think about it, he seemed to have new clothes—no doubt to impress the juvenile delinquent.

Sometimes Alexa felt like murdering him. Mom must often have felt the same way and it was just that kind of anger building up that ruined lives—as it had ruined Mom's—using up energy for a useless purpose, energy that had to be used for growing, learning, succeeding.

The phone call from Barb was a turning point, a signal that she had to move out fast before she wasted her life. It was worth taking the risk of coping with a pass or two from Barb's father.

Luckily on her last trip to the Witten palace, he'd been on the East Coast, but from one or two of Barb's caustic remarks, Alexa knew she hadn't missed the interested look in her own papa's eyes. Oh, how Alexa hated men. She couldn't afford to lose Barb's friendship over that . . .

Alexa wryly smiled at the thought of becoming her best friend's stepmother. Oh, God, was she letting her imagination run away with her! She had no intention of marrying anyone—ever—even if she had the chance of becoming the next Mrs. Oil, Gas, or Air.

Although she felt like kicking herself right into the deep blue Pacific, when she went in next day, Alexa found she couldn't bring herself to just drop out of class. If she could only earn the credits she needed to be accepted back for the new term . . . if she worked day and night perhaps she could just scrape by. It would mean missing some good sorority parties, but although she'd been flattered at first to be invited to join so many during Preference Night, it all seemed like kid stuff now. So she was on the way to being a big shot in Kappa Delta. That wasn't going to impress anyone at Twentieth-Century Fox. She would have been better off in rush week staying as she'd meant to stay. GDI, Gamma Delta Iota—or God Damn Independent!

All the same, when it came right down to it, there was something in her nature that couldn't let everything slide.

To Jo's amazement, Alexa turned into a workaholic, up at dawn studying feverishly, not missing one class, working until midnight or later every night, refusing to answer the phone, no matter who was on the other end.

A week later Jo understood why such an amazing transformation had taken place. She came back to find an oversized postcard of Marilyn Monroe's famous calendar picture stuck to her dressing-table mirror. She felt faint to see it. It was the way she had received so many messages from her mother. This was the first time Alexa had done it. Jo hoped it would be the last.

> Darling Jo, I don't know whether I am going back to State next semester or not. I don't think I am the business management type, but don't be mad at me. I've sweated all week, as you know, to get everything in shape in case I do want to sign on for more slog. Right now, I am A-OK for acceptance if I want it, so I'm off to meet some movie hotshots staying with Barb in Santa Barbara—that's where I'll be if you need me. I've decided I'd like to get "discovered" sooner than later. Take care of yourself . . .

Jo shook her head as she read Alexa's scrawled P.S. "If Dad bothers to ask you where I've gone, tell him to the sane town where cradle snatchers get arrested."

It wasn't very funny but it was typical of Alexa. Jo stretched out on her bed and reread the postcard. At least she knew Alexa would be well looked after in Santa Barbara, and she was too tired to worry about whether Alexa would drop out of college or not. Too tired and too busy working to worry about a little sister, who was obviously more and more capable of deciding things for herself.

Alexa had borrowed a body stocking from Amy, one of the girls who taught aerobics for extra cash whenever an empty classroom was available. It was scarlet, streaking across her torso in a way it could never streak across Amy's, emphasizing every curve, turning every movement Alexa made into a seductive invitation.

She knew without looking at anybody that people were staring at her as she crossed the huge drawing room to curl up on an ottoman beside Barb. She knew, because she had been practicing her entrance upstairs in her usual guest bedroom. First, she'd worn a tight-fitting jersey skirt over the stocking. Then, she'd had a better idea. She tried on the bottom half of a new beach outfit she'd received for her birthday—very low-cut cotton matador pants, which few people would be able to wear. They balanced—precariously even on her—on the hip line, before dipping in a V-shape back and front, clinging tightly to rump and thighs before flaring out at the knees. As Alexa walked, she knew the trousers were cut low enough to show the way the skin-tight body stocking curved into the soft spaces between her legs and the crease of her behind. It looked as if her body was painted in a shimmering, fiery glow from the neck, down over perfectly shaped breasts, flat belly, and long back, the dark V of the trousers pointing like arrows to what lay beneath.

She had pirouetted before the long cheval glass for a good fifteen minutes, stretched, sat, and practiced a variety of movements before she was satisfied that there wasn't an outfit in the world that could be at once so concealing, yet so seductive.

Barb scowled at her as she had never scowled before. "Who are you trying to impress?" she muttered, but Alexa smiled serenely into space as if she knew everyone had been waiting for her arrival. A heavyset, deeply tanned man loped over to stand looking down at her. "And who are you, you beautiful creature? Are you a surprise package from William Morris?"

Paul Witten put a casual arm around Mr. Heavyset's shoulders. "What makes you think William Morris would be so generous? Let me introduce you to my daughter's close friend, Alexa Shapwell, who I don't think has ever been on a film set in her life, have you, Lex?"

As she shook her head, Alexa smiled the cool, contained smile she'd also been practicing upstairs but it wasn't easy keeping her cool. The interest she'd generated in the room was obvious. Everyone was looking at her as she'd hoped, but it wasn't easy to receive so much attention, particularly the kind she was getting from a lanky redhead leaning against the marble fireplace.

Alexa guessed it had to be the one Barb had described on the phone—"no tits, no beam"—for her figure was like that of a boy, but Barb hadn't mentioned how pretty she was with huge blue eyes that were now blazing with fury.

"Paul, can I have some more Champagne, honey?" The voice carried a soft, fascinating burr. The perfect host, Paul went over to refill Blue Eyes' glass, then came back to Alexa. "Let me introduce you, my dear, to my talented guests."

There had to be fifteen, twenty people in the room, but it was so large Alexa hadn't realized it until Paul Witten tucked her arm in his and guided her around. Blue Eyes turned out to be Kathleen O'Hagan, a young actress from Ireland ". . . with a brilliant future." She did not seem mollified by Paul's flattering introduction. Alexa could feel her gaze on her back like a laser ray. Producers, writers, bankers . . . Nelson . . . Boy . . . Georgina . . . Peg . . . Allen . . . she didn't know what they were all doing there, but in less than ten mintues she knew she had been right to put together such a provocative, memorable outfit.

Most of the people, she'd already learned to her chagrin from Barb, were moving on in the morning. They'd already spent too long on financial details and even as she was being introduced she could hear someone say, "Time's running out on us. We've got to come in on time and on budget on this one."

Quickly, the attention she'd received in the elegant room dissipated. These movie people were real movie people. Her arrival had caused a small sensation, but they were used to sensations. Now it was over and back to business for everyone—except, Alexa knew, for Paul Witten and the heavy-set guy, who'd apparently mistaken her for a new face, a new talent he'd heard about, who he'd been trying to entice into working for him.

Alexa knew she had a lot of work to do patching things up with Barb, who stormed out of the room when she realized Alexa had agreed to stay for dinner. Barb had earlier pulled her to one side during the interminable cocktail hour and hissed, "We are not staying for dinner. Do you understand that, Lex? Don't let my fucked-up father persuade you . . . it's Dullsville . . . I've been going bananas listening to all this shit about percentages. We are cutting out, I told Dad so."

But Alexa had no intention of "cutting out," for instead of the time she'd thought she had, now she knew she had only one night to impress *someone*, only one night to be "discovered." In any case, Paul Witten was not about to be overruled by his own daughter as to where this particular houseguest was having dinner.

But Barb had been right. The dinner *was* Dullsville, long and tedious, especially as there was no more apparent interest in her from Mr. Heavyset. He turned out to be another Paul, Paul Gruen, the producer of *Tall Man's Shadow*, the movie Paul Witten was partly financing, about to start on location in and around Mendocino, a couple of hundred miles north of San Francisco.

Alexa was dismayed to find she wasn't seated next to either—but she didn't let it show.

The two men on either side of her, Boy and Allen, talked over her, rude bastards, about budgets and schedules during three of the four courses. When they finally turned to acknowledge her existence and asked her perfunctory questions about herself, she soon wished they'd get back to the dollars and cents that so obviously obsessed them, for what could she add to the conversation? What could she say about herself that had even a dime's worth of value? She hadn't done anything, been anywhere. She was a nobody. She spent the remainder of the dinner returning Paul Witten's suggestive smiles and nods, resolving that everything was going to change. With whom and through whom Alexa didn't know, but she determined something was going to happen—and soon—to make her into a "somebody."

The dinner ended about nine-thirty and a group went to the screening room to see *Grease*, a new movie, not yet released, with John Travolta and Olivia Newton-John. A month, a week, even the day before, Alexa would have been in ecstasy to sit in a private screening room with movie professionals to see a movie before it was released to the rest of the world.

Now, she was guarding every minute of her time as carefully as if it were her life's savings.

"Can you play backgammon?" Paul Witten seemed absentminded as he brushed a piece of hair away from her cheek. It made her nervous. Did he realize how revolted she was, even by the thought of his touch or of having to touch him? What a sickening innocent she was. She had to fight herself. Act a part, even if it meant doing something she loathed. She shook her head but gave him a wide smile.

"I'll teach you. I'm a good teacher—about a lot of things, you'll see." She could certainly see that other women might be excited by that remark. Paul Witten was so smooth, there was nothing overdone or objectionable in his tone. His very matter-of-factness would make him attractive to most women—of that

Alexa was sure. It was a kind of sophistication she'd never experienced. He didn't excite her in any way, but other than when he touched her, he didn't offend her either.

Paul Witten was a good backgammon teacher. After an hour or so, Alexa relaxed sufficiently to begin to enjoy the game, although it seemed much too easy, kid stuff, which it obviously couldn't be.

"I was leaving tomorrow to spend a day or so on location with Paul, but that can be a bore. When Barbara told me you were coming up to spend a few days, I postponed my trip." Paul Witten winked at her across the pink-and-gold terrazzo marble backgammon table. "It's time I got to know the one friend who can influence my daughter. I believe you ride?"

"Not very well."

"Barbara's never really cared for it. We'll take some easy trails late tomorrow afternoon. As I'm now here for a couple of days, I've got a few things to deal with in the morning, but . . ." Paul Witten covered her hand for a second. ". . . I'll be back at the house around three-thirty. It will be fun."

"What will be fun?" Blue Eyes was back from the screening room, running her hand down Paul Witten's back. He didn't like it. Alexa could see that, but either Blue Eyes didn't see it or chose to ignore it when he moved away slightly.

"Riding." His tone was clipped, all business. "Alexa's a good horsewoman. I am going to introduce her to some of our special trails on the property."

"When?" The soft burr was frayed.

"Oh, sometime tomorrow when you're on your way to becoming a star—when you go off to work. What time are you leaving?"

"But I thought you were coming with us?" The Irish actress made a quick recovery. "We're leaving early—I can't think why, as the plane's chartered, but Mr. Producer said something about saying good-bye about nine . . ."

"I hate good-byes." Paul Witten spoke so sweetly, he could have been swearing eternal love.

Blue Eyes was obviously used to it. "So do I," she replied lightly, ". . . but not goodnights." With one last fierce look in Alexa's direction, she bent to kiss Paul's cheek and murmured, "You're right. It's time I went back to work. All play and no work isn't good for a star's future, that's for sure—but at least come and say goodnight later, darling." She didn't wait for an answer, but walked quickly out of the room, closing the door firmly behind her.

"The girl's crazy," Paul Witten said coolly.

Alexa looked anxiously toward the door. Would it be opened soon by the producer, the other Paul, the Paul who really mattered in the movie world? Blue Eyes was right. Anyone could play anytime. It was *work* that made stars, not play. Paul Gruen had seemed interested in her before dinner. She had to see him again. She wasn't going to be left behind to ride horses and end up in the hay with her best friend's father.

She began to feel panicky. "I think perhaps it's time I went to bed. I am kind of tired. Would you mind?"

"Not at all." Paul was once again the perfect host, helping her out of her chair, taking her to the door. "Have you everything you need? Is your room cool enough? Not too cool?" He laughed lightly, as if to show how amusing it was for him to be acting like a nursemaid to his daughter's best friend. The way he pinched her rump, however, before she went upstairs, was a reminder that his intentions were not those of a nursemaid at all.

Alexa locked her bedroom door and stared at the reflection that had given her so much satisfaction hours before. All she had accomplished was to antagonize Barb so much she would probably never invite her to Santa Barbara again. Worse, she'd increased Paul Witten's attraction to her, so that she would be fending off his passes, if she was able to, for the next few days, which would be a nightmare.

What a mess . . . yet she had been sure that Paul Gruen had taken more than a cursory interest in her—personally or professionally she didn't know or care.

Alexa stared gloomily out of the window, across sweeping lawns, where magnificent trees and pieces of sculpture were so cleverly lit that the scene was like a lavish theater set. She had been right to come, but she had come too late. She should have squashed her conscientiousness and arrived earlier. What could she do now to make sure Paul Gruen didn't forget her?

Before she switched out the light she had made plans, A and B. She had heard Boy and Allen complain during dinner about the difficulty and cost of chartering a plane in Northern California, apparently much more of a problem than chartering in the south. "Let's face it, the Pacific Northwest is still savage. Any pilot worth his wings doesn't want to land on those strips hacked out of the redwoods overnight up there. I'd say we were lucky to make that deal with AirLink . . ."

She would get up very early and try to "hitch" a ride on the AirLink plane by asking Paul Gruen straight out.

If that didn't work, she would do everything in her power to make things up with Barb . . . tell her she knew where Greg was meeting Iggie up in the Redwoods . . . then, try to persuade her to cut out and drive up north in search of adventure. That, Alexa decided before she fell asleep, wouldn't be that difficult.

As it was, she didn't need to use either plan. Paul Gruen found her before she went to look for him.

As she got out of the shower about seven the following morning, there was a firm tap on her door. It was probably Barb, although Alexa had never known her to get up so early—but then, perhaps, she had been out all night and had never gone to bed. It wouldn't be the first time. Alexa also knew if Barb had something on her mind there was nothing she liked more than a fierce, no-words-barred fight, the sooner the better.

She didn't bother to look in the mirror before she went to the door, wrapped in a towel, water dripping down her back from her wet hair.

"Oh, Mr. Gruen . . ." Alexa automatically tightened the towel around her. He came into the room as if he belonged there, but he didn't attempt to touch her.

"You're a beauteous creature. If you've never been on a movie set, d'you want to get a taste of it now? D'you want to come along on location for a couple of days? I'd like to get some test shots of you . . ."

"Oh yes, oh yes . . ." There was nothing cool, contained, or "acted" about Alexa's joyful response now.

CHAPTER THREE

In less than an hour, about-to-be-a-movie-star Alexa Shapwell was sitting beside top-shot Hollywood producer Paul Gruen in a dark Mercedes on the way to Santa Barbara's county airport.

Before Alexa left, she had the presence of mind to write a note to Barb—as insurance.

> I know you must be mad at me, but I had a call last night from Greg. Seems Iggie and he are near where your father's film is going to be made. I had the chance of a lift up there with the film crew. I'll call you when I know what's going on, so we can all meet up.

Whether Barb believed her or not was unimportant. It would kill two birds with one message. Barb would know she was still thinking of her, and, Paul Witten would be totally turned off—at least Alexa hoped so.

When Blue Eyes got on the Gulf Stream and saw Alexa sitting there, her mouth dropped open, but then, just as the evening before, she made an instant recovery to give her an enormous smile. "Got thrown off your horse?"

Whatever the actress was thinking, she could think with pleasure. Alexa didn't care. Probably she thought she'd been a failure in Paul Witten's bed. Let her think it, if it improved her temper.

Alexa smiled her perfectly cool smile. "Let's just say I need more practice . . ."

Except for Kathleen O'Hagan everyone else on the plane ignored her, even Paul Gruen, but Alexa felt relaxed, free, not tied down by a nagging sense of losing opportunities, or meeting responsibilities to anyone, except herself.

When the pilot announced they were making a descent into San Francisco, Kathleen O'Hagan and somebody whose name Alexa had forgotten said simultaneously, "What are we stopping here for?"

Paul Gruen didn't bother to look up from *Variety* as he answered, "Alexa and I are getting off here. I'll join you later in Mendocino—probably tomorrow."

"*I'll* join you . . ." not "*We'll* join you." Alexa's spirits dropped as the plane dropped. Hell, Gruen obviously thought she was a good-time girl and nothing else. She would soon show him how wrong he was. She knew just where to kick to finish his good times forever, but how could she stay out of his bed and still retain his interest in her to get the promised film test?

Inexplicably, the loss of her mother stabbed Alexa almost as if she was hearing the news for the first time. It was strange—as the months had passed since her mother's death, her memories of her had dwelled more and more on her laughter, on her jokes against herself, than on the sourness that since her teens had developed between them.

Would Mom have known what to do? Probably. Her blind love for her husband would have protected her, shown her what to do naturally—but she, Alexa, didn't love anybody and never would.

Act cool, she told herself fiercely in the limousine on the way to the Fairmont Hotel, where Paul Gruen casually told her he kept a permanent suite.

In the lobby Alexa knew she wasn't going to be able to fake it. Gruen was too assured, too powerful. He didn't look left or right, or acknowledge any of the servile smiles of recognition. People moved out of his way, as they would on seeing an express train bearing down on them. Fear attacked her. She could see goose bumps on her arms, and, predictably, as always happened when she had the jitters—although she'd never had them like this before—she began to feel hungry, ravenous.

It was a curious thing that no one had ever been able to explain. Most people lost their appetites before an exam or a swim race or having to make a speech and a fool of themselves before their peers. She always, but *always*, felt a gnawing hunger that made her stomach growl.

"I'm starving," she said as he opened the door to the suite. It was a little-girl voice that she loathed, but he didn't look at her as he strode ahead into a room as dark as if it was night instead of just past eleven o'clock in the morning. "The kitchen's off to the right. There should be some crackers and cheese. I've got to make some phone calls."

He didn't attempt to pull the drapes, but switched on a lamp beside a low divan. "Beat it," he said as she hovered uncertainly in the hallway.

Her hands trembled with anger as she opened one cupboard after another in the kitchen and found nothing but a half-empty box of cereal. There was a sad-looking orange in the refrigerator and a pack of cream cheese.

Alexa fumed. What the hell was she wasting her time for in the kitchen? She was in one of the most famous hotels in the world, wasn't she? There was a directory of services in a kitchen drawer and without pausing she called room service. "This is . . . just a minute . . ." There was no number on the telephone. "This is Mr. Gruen's apartment—on the twentieth floor . . ."

"Mr. Gruen's?" The voice at the other end sounded surprised.

"I'd like a club sandwich, no, make it two clubs with extra bacon. Some yogurt. Do you have banana . . . ?" The voice still sounded surprised. "Oh, strawberry will do okay. Iced coffee with chocolate ice cream and, oh yes . . ." She swung open the refrigerator door again. Nothing to drink there either. "Send up a couple of diet cokes and a jug of milk, please, and can you hurry?"

With the thought of food arriving, her fear of what might happen in the next few hours—momentarily blotted out by her flash of anger—returned. She could hear Gruen's voice droning on in the next room. It was a brilliantly bright day outside, yet his apartment was as dark as an opium den in Chinatown.

Through a kitchen swing door, Alexa walked into an impressive dining room. Fourteen high-backed chairs, like pews she'd seen in church, surrounded an ebony table, so shiny she could see her face, ghostly pale, looking down into it. There was something strange about the seating arrangement. Little stools were placed behind every chair, upholstered in the same velvet as the regal chair seats. Odd. Were the stools for the wraps of women guests . . . or their purses? Purse! Where had she left her purse? And her duffel bag? For a moment Alexa felt so nervous, she couldn't remember carrying either into the hotel. She ran back into the kitchen and out into the hallway on the other side. Thank God, there were her purse and dear old duffel where she had left them by the entrance door.

She had an enormous urge to grab her things and scoot for freedom—but why? Gruen hadn't laid a finger on her—yet. He hadn't even given her a glance, yet the whole apartment was full of something—sinister . . . yes, that was it . . . sinister. He was still talking on the phone, so she slunk down the hallway on the left to find out if there were any more exits.

Sunlight blinded her as she opened the door at the end of the hall. Here, white shoji blinds emphasized the light pouring into an exquisite Japanese bedroom, with tatami mats on either side of the widest bed she had ever seen—the lowest, too, as it stood only about three feet from the floor.

Her stomach growled loudly as she went into a black mirrored bathroom to find the loo. Facing her as she sat on the toilet was a sculpture set into a recess. It took her a minute or two to realize the sculpture was of a naked woman crouching at a man's feet as she sucked his mammoth penis. Alexa shivered. Now, she knew she had to get out fast, but as she stealthily went back to the entrance, the doorbell rang.

She stood frozen as Paul Gruen ambled over to open the door.

"What the hell is that?" He sounded as angry as if he had just stepped into dogshit. Alexa could hear glasses and cutlery tinkling, as the waiter prepared to move a table inside. Not a chance. "Take it away," Paul Gruen bellowed. "You know I never order room service. You think I'm going to pay two hundred percent for some fucking pieces of bread? Take it away and make sure you don't send a bill to my office or you'll wish you'd never been born." The waiter made the mistake of trying to argue with the red-faced man, who shot out his huge paw and pushed him back to shut the door in his face.

"Alexa, where are you?" Gruen roared.

"I'm here." It was no little-girl voice now. Alexa blazed with anger as she thought of her club sandwiches being sent away. "You mean, tight-fisted, two-bit . . ." she stormed down the hall to pick up her things. The next minute Gruen threw her across his shoulder like some bag of burlap. "So you're that hungry, are you, you pushy little broad! Well, I'm going to take your mind off your stomach and move it elsewhere."

She couldn't scream. Her breath came in gasps. She could only bleat, "Put me down, put me down" as he moved toward the low divan, picking something up from a table as he went.

She soon discovered what it was—and there was no way she could resist. In one easy maneuver Gruen forced her face down across his knees, pulled her skirt up to her waist, and ripped her bikini brief in two, to expose her bare behind. "Here's something to take your mind off food, young lady," he whispered.

However much she writhed and tried to twist out of his grasp, he had her pinioned. To her shame and terror, Alexa saw their reflections in a mirrored wall across the room. She, helpless, half naked, slung over his lap, as his huge hand descended, holding a silver-handled whip. She clenched her teeth to stop crying as he started to whip her with slow, unhurried strokes. It wasn't how much it hurt. The whip stung enough to make her flinch. It was the terrible indignity that made her want to scream. Now she really knew how it felt to want to kill someone—and as he whipped, he hummed under his breath and she knew, although she couldn't move her head to see his face, that he was smiling, having a wonderful time.

Beneath her T-shirt, his penis was swelling, his body heaving, as he whipped her steadily with his right hand. His left hand holding her head, the lower part of his body began to move agitatedly up and down, up and down, until suddenly her T-shirt was soaked through and he screamed out, "You cunt," released his hold, and let her fall to the floor.

Alexa bit her lip so hard she tasted blood. She wouldn't

give him the satisfaction of seeing her cry—or scream—or anything! She looked up at him with hatred, and realized with another shudder of disgust that whatever she chose to do or not do, wouldn't affect him. He'd received what he wanted. He was slumped back, his eyes half closed, almost asleep.

"You rat." Her voice was unsteady, but there was no mistaking her desperation. "You mean, low, filthy rat." As she looked around the room to find something to strike him with, Gruen slowly sat up, as if to remind her of his powerful physique.

"Here . . ." He put his hand in his pocket and before she knew what she was doing, she caught the package of peanuts—airline peanuts—he threw down at her. "Eat up—and if you're a good girl I'll take you to McDonald's for dinner . . ."

"You're crazy. You should be locked up." With or without her briefs she was leaving. Alexa rushed toward the big entrance door, bending down to pick up her stuff. When she tried to open the door, she realized why he hadn't moved to stop her.

"Unlock this door or I'll call the police."

"And what are you going to say, Miss High and Mighty? That you got a taste of the whip? That obedience isn't your strong suit? What charges are you going to bring, you little trollop." He threw his head back and started to laugh.

She had never felt more demoralized, more helpless. What a fool she'd been. She'd walked straight into a prison with a raving lunatic, who wouldn't even buy her a sandwich. Self-pity was building up. Before it could break out in front of him, she ran down the corridor to the Japanese bedroom, throwing herself on the low bed to let the tears flow.

All afternoon she lay there, waiting for his footsteps. There was no key to this room, no way to bolt the door. The only weapon she could find to defend herself with was a long bath brush, which he could snap in two with his little finger. But no footsteps came.

As time passed, her hunger and anger came back. She started to feel stronger. She took a shower, bathed her sore behind in a bidet in the black mirrored bathroom. She could see a slight redness, but nothing to indicate what she had really been through.

She changed into jeans and another T-shirt, seeing the

crimson body stocking crumpled up at the bottom of the duffel bag. Just seeing it there made her want to throw up. Now, all she longed to do was hide her looks and slink away in anonymity to merge with the crowd.

Surely, he couldn't keep her in the suite as a prisoner? What would Paul Witten do if he ever found out his famous producer friend had a kinky liking for the whip? How could she get the message to him—to Barb—to *anyone*, to escape from this nightmare?

She had just started to doze when Paul Gruen came marching into the room. He looked freshly showered, glistening with health and strength in a black kimono. "Come with me, Alexa. I'm going to feed you—if you are a good girl."

She stood up, her face full of loathing, but there was no alternative but to follow him.

Escape was uppermost in her mind now. How to escape!

He led the way to the dining room, now lit by torchères and slender silver candelabras. She stiffened with resentment when she saw the table was set only for one. He put his huge hand around the back of her neck and moved her toward the low stool beside his chair. "Kneel here and wash my feet."

"I won't." She arched back as he forced her down to her knees. "Wash my feet and you'll be fed. Disobey and you'll go hungry." Beside the stool was a silver bowl, filled with small rolled-up white towels. She could smell lilacs. The towels were scented with lilac fragrance. Her stomach churned. "I'd sooner starve . . ."

"Come now, don't be difficult. Here, take this."

He held out a tantalizing piece of pâté on toast. Alexa shut her eyes. She would rather be tortured, whipped, strapped, caned, but all the same saliva filled her mouth, when, thank God, the phone rang.

"Fuck." The huge man reached down the back of the chair seat and to Alexa's horror pulled out a long, thin chain and clipped it around her neck. She couldn't move nearer the table. She couldn't move back without toppling the tall chair.

He was gone for about twenty minutes. She kept thinking she was about to faint, but then her anger welled up to save her. Her hair was stuck to her nape. Perspiration ran down her nose. Her humiliation was soaking her body in sweat.

When he returned he had changed. He was in sports

clothes, a tan jacket and slacks. He nonchalantly unclipped the chain and said in a matter-of-fact voice, as if nothing unusual had happened, "There's a problem. We can't go to Mendocino tomorrow. I've got to return to L.A. It's a pity, but let's just say you are very much unfinished business—the business of your discipline. Paul Witten called. His daughter is apparently worried about your whereabouts. I told him you're a screen-struck young kid, who could easily get people in trouble—but I also told him I'm going to give you a test when you learn some manners."

Alexa snarled. "I wouldn't work for you if you were the last man on earth. You should be locked up. You're a madman. Mr. Witten won't believe what I have to tell him about his great producer friend. You're crazy."

Paul Gruen ran his hand casually over her breast as if she hadn't spoken. "You can come back with me now to Los Angeles and I'll get a part written into the picture for you . . . or you can go back to kindergarten—and I'll see you when you've grown up." He put out his hand as if to ask her to shake on a deal.

She didn't think twice. She lunged forward to sink her teeth in the fleshy part of his palm. To her fury and frustration, he shook her off like an ant.

"Go back to where you came from, kid," he drawled, obviously bored. "In a year or two maybe you will have calmed down or thawed out. Right now, you ice the hots out of any man."

He was gone. Alexa couldn't believe it. She waited five, ten minutes before gobbling down the pâté, then creeping out of the dining room, expecting him to be standing there, whip in hand. She spent another twenty or thirty minutes going from room to room, her heart beating wildly before testing the front door and finding it open.

Oh God, now the fear was back. What could she do? What could she say to Barb?

It seemed as if days had passed, yet it wasn't even ten o'clock. Paul Gruen was right about one thing. She did need to calm down. Alexa took a long, cool shower, did some yoga exercises, then dialed the familiar Santa Barbara number.

After talking to Barb she complimented herself. She wasn't a bad actress after all. She had sounded like the old Alexa, the one who was cool, man, and never fazed about anything. She had said all the right things to entice Barb, who was going to pick her up at the hotel in the morning, when they would head north.

It was the land of opportunity. Even the country road signs were intriguing. " 'Son,' for the rich sons of Sonoma, Barb." Alexa laughed as they drove through the green-and-gold wine country and on to the land of the pink, lush pear farms. As usual, Barb wasn't saying much as she concentrated on driving, negotiating the twisting turns on the way up to the Pacific Northwest.

Alexa knew that Barb knew they might not really be searching for Greg and Iggie; that it was more likely Alexa wanted to find the *Tall Man's Shadow* crew working somewhere up near Elk.

But even if Greg and Iggie weren't the prey, Barb had stumbled on another reason to visit Mendocino, and beyond. "D'you know the Maserati of marijuana is grown up in Mendocino?" she asked Alexa, after the ice was broken, when they met on Thursday morning. "It's incredible. It's California's largest crop . . . a guy told me you can start smelling it from the county line. Boy, what a place, nobody cares, not even the Feds, because grass saved the whole economy up there after timber collapsed . . ."

Barb's font of irrelevant information was another reason she fascinated Alexa. Right now, she felt she almost loved her, because of the huge tide of relief that had washed through her when Barb appeared to accept so quickly the story she had left behind in her note.

Alexa had finally sat up all night in a chair she'd pulled up close to the front door. She hadn't dared to sleep in case the monster returned, but after changing her mind over and over again, she'd decided not to mention the Fairmont incident to Barb. Paul Gruen would never talk about it—well, certainly not to Barb. Maybe to her father, but *he* would never tell his darling daughter either.

" 'Men' for Mendocino," Barb screamed out, as they crossed the Gualala River and started to see the small county sign, MEN, along the roadside. "Men . . . men . . . men . . ." they sang in unison as they spotted each signpost, the road dipping and curving around tiny one-time timber camps, each sitting snugly in rivermouth clearings between dark forest and deep blue ocean. The explosion of surf against dark rocks, the staunch pines and salt-smelling cypress among wind-sculptured rocks, the whole dramatic coastline appealed to something deep in Alexa.

The previous twenty-four hours receded as if they had never happened. Her spirits rose. She felt liberated, happy—happier than she could remember feeling for a long, long time.

They stopped for ham and eggs at a motel outside Sea Ranch, and Barb's discontented look disappeared when she saw—smelled—two young bearded men enjoying a joint in a corner booth. Winking at Alexa, she sidled over to them and from her coy look, Alexa guessed she was asking if they had any grass to spare. If it kept Barb happy, it was okay with her.

Alexa decided she never wanted to leave this place of redwood trees, wild ocean, big sky. Somewhere, farther up, was the "lost coast" she'd heard the film people talk about, sixty thousand acres of coastal wilderness. She didn't know what she wanted anymore. A film test? Not if it meant holing up with a crazy producer; not if it meant holing up with any man. Something would turn up. Despite Barb's liking for marijuana, Alexa knew no amount of smoking pot could ever bring her the exhilarating sense of freedom she was experiencing now.

Barb had told her, with a smug look of satisfaction, that her father was mad she'd hitched a lift with the film crew; that he'd dismissed her contemptuously as "just another cheap free-loader," but Barb had also let out that he was still intending to check in with the unit in a day or so.

As Alexa sat at the counter watching Barb flirt with the two guys, who looked as if they'd been crying "timber" all their lives, the last bit of tension drained out of her. If they found the *Tall Man's Shadow* unit and Paul Witten was there, maybe she could still land a part in the film, perhaps as an extra. With Paul Witten, she would be safe from the whip man. It was weird to think of Witten as a protector, weird to find herself sitting miles from anywhere, hypnotized by the rolling ocean, not sure about anything, yet not worried either. A strange, sneaking feeling was building up in her that life was about to change for the better—that MEN, short for Mendocino, was a sign that was somehow going to bring her good luck.

* * *

Alexa's collect call made Jo worry about her all the more. Alexa hadn't sounded like herself, screaming through the phone what a great time she was having, that she'd met a famous Hollywood producer who was trying to sweep her off her feet. It hadn't sounded like her cool, couldn't-care-less sister one bit.

Jo stared moodily into the darkening garden. Why she hadn't asked Alexa exactly where she was or whether she was coming back for the new semester at State she would never know.

Jo sighed. She would have to call Barbara Witten. She didn't want to act like Alexa's nursemaid, but there was nothing else for it. If she didn't care about Alexa, who would? Certainly not her father, who before driving off two nights before—for what he'd called a "two-day golfing business trip"—had told her as if he meant it that he'd washed his hands of his good-for-nothing daughter.

Jo knew her father was going to La Costa. How he could afford it she didn't know, but she'd heard him make the reservation over the phone. He wasn't very smart about hiding anything. Perhaps he didn't care anymore about showing any signs of bereavement. Why should he? She was the only one left at home to deal with his moods. She heard herself sighing like some old maid and irritably reached for the phone. Whether Alexa liked it or not, she had to track her down and talk some sense into her to make her realize she was drifting in the same irresponsible way she had always accused their father of drifting.

Barbara Witten answered the phone herself and in two seconds made it horribly clear she didn't know and didn't want to know where Alexa was. Red-faced, Jo pressed on, "Where did you see her last?"

Barb snapped back, "Trying to make it with my father in a Mendocino motel!"

Jo stared at the receiver in disbelief. Barb had hung up on her. Alexa and she must have had some monumental falling out. She was trembling. She didn't know why. Perhaps because Barbara Witten had obviously meant to be insulting, perhaps because Jo suddenly had the feeling Alexa was in Big trouble.

She pushed open the door to Alexa's tiny bedroom. Who

else could she call who might know where Alexa was? Who else might Alexa have called collect with more news about "being discovered"? Jo's mind was blank. She knelt down to pull open the big drawer beneath Alexa's bed. It was the place she kept all kinds of things—notes, old exam papers, old diaries, address books, lists. The first thing Jo saw, which brought tears to her eyes, was one of her mother's favorite purses—large, dark-blue crocodile—if a crocodile could ever have been dark blue. Beneath it was a jumble of her mother's belts and scarves.

Jo opened the purse, expecting to find it empty, but it was crammed with papers, postcards, a "things-to-do-today" pad. With a stab of pain she saw it was covered in her mother's neat handwriting with lists of names to call, names her mother had always been calling, hoping to be considered for a job.

A letter, in huge, oversized writing on pale mauve paper with just one word, MAGDA, printed in dark mauve on top, caught her attention. There was no phone number, no address, just MAGDA.

> Darling, wear a large hat and dark glasses. Twelve noon, Polo Lounge, Beverly Hills Hotel, fourth of June.

The fourth of June! It was a date her mother could never have kept. By then she was dead, burned to death in the car wreck over the border. Jo breathed deeply, as if she were in a race, as she reread the short scrawled note.

Who was Magda? And why had she instructed her mother to turn up virtually in disguise: ". . . a large hat and dark glasses"? Beneath the letter was a bank statement with a bunch of returned checks clipped to it—May checks—"Teri Shephard" checks, a sign her mother had always said proudly, of her own earning ability. They were the last checks her mother had ever written.

Tears ran down Jo's cheeks as she leafed through them, each one bringing back a memory, a reminder of how much her mother had contributed to the family, often supporting them entirely.

Sixty-four dollars to Wilkinson's, the grocer . . . one hundred and two dollars to Jed the butcher . . . five hundred dollars to the Blue-Bird Summer Camp . . . to Saks for a new dress . . . to The Fountain. Jo stopped, put a still-trembling hand to her throat, staring at a check made out to The Fountain, a certified check for a fortune . . . for eighteen hundred dollars dated May 30, only four days before her mother's death.

What did it mean? Where and what was The Fountain? All thought of finding Alexa disappeared. What could her mother have possibly bought for so much money?

Jo stared into the garden as if to summon up a waterfall or some garden fixture that eighteen hundred dollars might represent. Of course, there was nothing there. She turned the check over. On the back was an almost indecipherable signature. The first word looked like *Svetlana,* but it was impossible to decipher the second part of the signature. It was stamped, FOR DEPOSIT ONLY, THE BANK OF CALIFORNIA. Jo turned the check over and over. She knew her mother. Eighteen hundred dollars would have been a major investment for her. Teresa Millicent had never squandered money. Jo clearly could remember her saying with her light laugh, "You don't forget so easily what a dollar means, when you've had to count every nickel and dime every day . . ." Her mother had always spent the major part of her modeling income on the needs of her family, so where did The Fountain fit in?

Jo called Alf Victor next day, but he was busy shooting in the studio. She left her name, but he didn't call back. She wasn't surprised. She wasn't important. He had often been too busy to call her mother back, so why should it be any different for her.

When her father called about five o'clock to say he was on his way home, Jo could hardly wait for his return. Dad would know about The Fountain. Dad would explain.

Jo reasoned to herself if she only knew what her mother had been doing in Mexico . . . if she only knew where Teri had been going and why, then she wouldn't still feel so unsettled about her mother's death and worried about a check made out to a mystery place and a date with a mysterious woman called Magda.

Nobody had been able to answer those important questions. Nobody, not even Alexa, had seemed to care. Perhaps the check and the letter could provide simple answers to the questions that Jo now realized had been nagging her since she'd heard Alf Victor state adamantly at the funeral that her mother had not been on her way to any location.

"Hi, Jo . . ." her father returned in a good mood, burned

from the sun, swaggering from some success. On the golf course or in the bedroom? Jo didn't care. She just wanted him to put her mind at rest once and for all. If her father knew where her mother had been going in Mexico and didn't care to tell her—that was one thing. If he didn't know and didn't care, she cared and she was going to find out.

Ben was in his most fatherly mood, legs up on the coffee table, throwing her some popcorn, boasting about the deal he was about to sign, a deal that was, he said, "a sure thing."

He yawned and poured himself a scotch. Jo swallowed hard and took The Fountain check and the letter from Magda out of her purse. "Dad . . ."

"Yep, baby, what's on your mind? Have you heard from that crazy sister of yours?" Jo shook her head. She held out the check and the letter.

"Dad, I found these in Mom's blue purse among lots of other papers of hers. I thought you ought to take a look at them . . . you probably just stuffed the checks away without looking at them."

Her father stared at the two pieces of paper as if she had handed him a time bomb.

Everything came out—her unhappiness, her anxiety, her confusion. "Dad, if you know where Mom was going, *please* tell me. I can't stand not knowing why she was in Mexico. It's all such a mystery. Do you know why she spent so much money at this shop, this place, The Fountain? What d'you think it all means?"

Her father stood up, shaking with agitation. Jo cowered against the chair, almost expecting him to strike her, although he never had, but he went over to the window, clutching his head as if he was in pain. As she started to speak, he yelled, "Shut up, shut up!" He began to pace up and down the room, muttering, speaking to himself. "I don't know. I don't know. Is it any business of ours what she did with her money? God knows she spent too much of it on you and your good-for-nothing sister." Despite what he was saying, Jo went to him, to try to calm him down. His eyes were wet, red. She put another scotch in his hand and he drank it down in one gulp, sinking back on the sofa. He looked at the check and letter again, before stuffing them into his pocket. "Where did you find these?" He was making an effort to control himself, but his mouth was twitching.

"In Alexa's room . . . Don't you remember, you asked us to take away Mom's things . . . to get everything out of your sight? You must have put Mom's bank statement and all the old checks in Mom's purse yourself, just so they weren't hanging around . . ."

Her father got up, rushed into Alexa's bedroom, and started yanking out the drawers of her dressing table, one after the other, spilling the contents on the floor. Bikini briefs, lipsticks, T-shirts, a jumble of femininity . . . empty fragrance bottles, jars of cream, potpourri . . . but no papers, no diaries, no checkbooks or checks. Had he forgotten about Alexa's other drawer? Apparently he had.

He started to shake Jo by the shoulders. "Don't you understand, baby? I can't face thinking about it. It drives me crazy. No, I don't know where Teri was going. I don't know anything . . . but it's too late to do anything about it now. Why torture me? Why torture yourself? You're obsessed. Where is that purse of your mother's?"

He followed Jo into her room where, unable to speak anymore, she took the blue purse out of her closet and handed it to him. He opened it, shut it, opened it again, then looked at Jo helplessly. "Honey, I don't know what the hell your mother was really up to. I'll try to find out . . . honest I will . . . but . . . why? Okay, okay . . ." She hadn't spoken, but he was answering some inner voice. "I'll try. I promise you I'll try to find out what all this means." His voice broke. Again he said, "Why are we torturing ourselves? It won't change anything . . . She's not coming back . . ."

Clutching the purse, he slowly walked out of the small bedroom, down the hall, and out the front door. Moments later Jo heard the car start up and watched from the window as her father drove fast out the gate, down the street. As soon as the car turned the bend in the road, she went back to Alexa's room. She still trembled, now with a mixture of fear and anger, but she'd made a resolution. She was going to go through everything in Alexa's secret drawer . . . every bank statement—everything that could have anything to do with her mother. She might be obsessed, but there were enough reasons for it. She didn't believe for one moment that her father was going to do anything to find out what the check to The Fountain represented, what the letter from Magda was all about. If he was tortured being reminded of her mother's death, *she* was tortured because she didn't *need* to be reminded. It was never far from her thoughts. There was something wrong. She could smell it. She was going to find out what it all meant.

Her father didn't come back that night, but Jo didn't care. She felt she would never care again whether he came back. She would never make the mistake of confiding her fears to him again either . . . and she had found something to bolster her belief that something was wrong. Another check for three hundred dollars made out by her mother to The Fountain with the same scrawled signature on the back. This time the name "Svetlana" was unmistakable, but the last name was more indecipherable than ever. Her mother had written this check the month before, in April.

Jo stared at the check for ages. The three hundred dollars had to have been a deposit for something. The eighteen hundred dollars had to have been payment in full—but for what?

Jo remembered the trunk in the garage, the trunk packed with all her mother's things that Alexa had not taken, the trunk that had lain there, forgotten by all the family for months. It was two o'clock in the morning and all her energy was drained. After work the next day Jo promised herself she would go through everything in the trunk, however much time it took. Perhaps she would ask Mike Tanner if he could help her solve the mystery of The Fountain. He wasn't only her boss. He'd become her friend. She should have confided her fears, her confusion to him weeks, months ago. He had a trained journalist's mind, an instinct for tracking down facts fast.

Relief sent her to bed and she slept deeply, resisting her alarm clock at 7 A.M. to open her eyes. The events of the previous evening suddenly jolted her wide awake. Now she viewed her father as a hindrance, someone who was so weak he wanted to turn his back on the truth, who hadn't the courage to find out, once and for all, exactly what had led up to the tragedy.

Mike Tanner was out of the office, but in a way, despite her thoughts of the night before, Jo was relieved. She had plenty of work to do. As she typed, she reflected again that once she'd satisfied herself she had examined everything her mother had left behind, most of it in the trunk, she would have more clues to work with. Then she would sit down with Mike and ask for his help.

Her father's car was in the driveway when she got home. Knowing him, Jo didn't think he would want to stay home with her that evening. He didn't speak to her as she came in, and she didn't speak to him as they passed each other in the kitchen.

About seven-thirty, she heard him call Libby and tell her he would meet her in an hour "at the usual place." With set expression, Jo confronted him as he tied his tie in the bedroom. "Dad, can I have the check and the Magda letter back? I'd like to see what I can find out . . ."

He looked at her through the reflection in the mirror. He sounded calm, cold even, as he answered her. "Leave it with me. I've already started to make inquiries. I'll tell you everything I find out—if I find out anything—as soon as I do, I promise." He didn't say another word until he slammed out about thirty minutes later. Again Jo watched, waiting for the car to turn the bend in the road.

She'd already changed into jeans and an old shirt to prepare for a long stay in the dusty garage. She needn't have bothered.

Before she switched on the garage light she knew what she would find. The trunk was gone.

CHAPTER FOUR

NOW HE KNEW WHO SHE REMINDED HIM OF. . . . SHE WAS A MIX OF two old movie stars. There was the wide, sensual mouth and slinkiness of Lauren Bacall in *To Have and Have Not* and the golden glow of Rita Hayworth in *Gilda*. Watching these two movie greats over and over again on the late, late TV shows, battling with his usual insomnia, Cal Robinson had often mused that knowing them and having an opportunity to work with both of them in their heyday might well have been worth being born a few years earlier. Female stars today just didn't have their allure, their glorious earthy sexuality.

It was strange he hadn't noticed the girl when he'd given her his order—always the same in this part of the world—baked Dungeness crab, a plate of fried squid, and a carafe of his favorite Sonoma wine, but then he was always distracted when he came back to Mendocino. Too many memories pulled at him. There was too much "nature"—flora, fauna, and much too much ocean.

How often had he vowed never to return? Hundreds of times, yet there was always something that pulled him back, something masochistic in his nature, he guessed, that sent him to the one place he had spent nearly twenty years trying to forget.

He never did his best work here and things were particularly sour on this shoot. He wasn't getting the feel of it and the editor *Town and Country* had sent along wasn't helping either. Too gushing one moment, too assertive the next, with so far not one original thought in her overstyled head. Not that he was a barrel of fun to be with. Why they wanted to cover the annual Whale Festival was beyond him anyway.

Cal made a mental note to call Pony, his agent, to quit booking him with jobs that meant days and days away from the studio—however much they paid. He also had to impress on Pony never to consider any location jobs in or around Mendocino again.

As he ate, he carefully watched the girl with the incredible body as she moved around the restaurant taking and delivering orders. She was quick, efficient, but she was having trouble getting away from some of the tables. He could understand why. Much to the irritation of their female companions, some guys were trying to chat her up to keep her at their table longer. He was going to do the same.

Every so often, he noticed, she stopped by the large scenic window to take a deep, indrawn breath as she stared out at the endless Pacific.

Through the window he could see thick clusters of dark-blue-and-white lupine bushes waving in the wind all the way to the cliff's edge, where, a hundred feet below, dark-blue Pacific rollers crashed on boulders, sending silver spray high into the air.

"Never turn your back on the Pacific Ocean. Those sneakers, forty feet high some of 'em, can be deadly up along Mendocino's western edge." He could hear his father's voice even after all these years. It was a warning that hadn't been remembered until it was too late, on a honeymoon that a vast "sneaker" wave had ended in tragedy.

Cal drank the rest of his wine as the beautiful creature approached his table.

"There are some great desserts—blackberry and raspberry crumble . . . it's made here . . . redwood forest cake, that's with rum . . ."

"Any with pot?"

She wasn't fazed. She must have heard it a dozen times. She might have been yawning as she replied serenely, "No pot served here. Do you want dessert?"

He shook his head and ordered another carafe of wine in order to keep the table. He wanted to study her more as the light changed with Northern California suddenness from blue day to dark blue night. She was worth some film. Unlike many photographers, Cal didn't often make that decision about anyone not ravenously hungry to be a model. If someone he respected brought someone along, that was one thing, but he'd never gone around like some typecast Hollywood talent scout looking for that certain "face" . . . that special "body" in the most unlikely places.

When she went into the kitchen about nine-thirty, she didn't come back. To his irritation a mousy-looking waitress asked him pointedly if he wanted anything else and left his check on the table before he asked for it. "Where's the girl who waited on me?" he asked the cashier as he paid the bill. "I want to leave her a special tip—she was good."

Cal smothered his annoyance as the beady-eyed young man taking his money smirked. "She's off early tonight. You can leave something in this tray. She'll get it . . ."

Feeling frustrated, Cal walked out into the forecourt, the ocean breeze ruffling his hair, flipping his jacket. As he went to his car he heard a woman shout, "Get away from me, you louse . . ."

As his eyes adjusted to the light he saw the girl trying to extricate herself from one of the guys who had been ogling her back in the restaurant.

It wasn't like him—he hated getting involved in anybody else's troubles or business—but there was something about this girl that demanded his attention. Cal ambled over as nonchalantly as he could and said in a cold, drop-dead voice, "Take your hands off my girl or you'll end up as a whale's breakfast and you'd better believe it." The guy was taller, heavier than Cal but there was something in Cal's manner and voice that got through.

"You're a lucky fella," the man slurred tipsily. "Thought this was meant to be a friendly country . . ." He hiccupped. "Thought gals like this got shared up here. She's one sweet ass . . ." Cal didn't let him finish. It was easy to spin him around and send him sprawling into the lupine bushes lining the drive.

He put his hand possessively under the girl's arm and guided her toward his car.

"Thanks," she said without a note of appreciation in her voice. "I can deal with drunks, but you made it a whole lot quicker."

"Think nothing of it. I am a lucky fella. I wanted to talk to you anyway, but you vanished before I could get to first base. Do you feel like a drink in town?"

Was it the ocean getting noisy or was she whispering so he had to lean his head toward her to catch her, "Don't waste your time."

So she was one of those independent stuck-up little broads, was she? Well, he would soon change that attitude. He felt his stomach muscles tighten as he looked at the girl's face suddenly illuminated by a ring of light as someone opened the restaurant door.

She looked tense as Cal turned to see the drunk stagger to his feet and make a move toward them. He opened the car door and, as he expected, she got in. As he drove on to the main road he said, "It's not what you think. I've got an interesting business proposal for you. I'll tell you about it in town."

He could tell the way she sat upright like a telephone pole she didn't believe a word he said. Well, why should she? She must be propositioned twenty times a day, he thought, as the twinkling lights of Mendocino, like a make-believe city perched daintily on the headland, came into view. He pulled up outside his favorite little bar near the Fire Station. "D'you want to hear more over a club soda?" There was no trace of a smile, but she nodded and followed him inside.

She stayed tense and taut for a good thirty minutes while Cal talked. He could hardly believe that he, Cal Robinson, nationally known, award-winning photographer, was actually trying to prove himself to some unknown, probably spaced-out female.

She had smirked, almost as irritatingly as the cashier had smirked, when he'd told her he was a photographer from San Francisco on assignment for *Town and Country*. The smirk had changed into a look of downright cynicism when he told her she might have "something."

"I suppose you've heard it all before?"

She didn't bother to look at him. "Yep."

"But not from a professional, someone who's willing to pay you for some shots?"

She laughed derisively. "I've been paid all right, but never enough."

"Do you want some grass?"

"Never touch the stuff." She fiddled with her purse as if about to leave.

Cal inwardly groaned as across the bar he saw the *Town and Country* editor move toward him. "Hi, Cal. I wondered where you were. I left a message for you at the hotel." She looked pointedly at the girl and stuck her hand out. "I'm Tonia Brace from *Town and Country* . . ."

"Alexa Shapwell." The girl took the hand without enthusiasm.

Cal decided Tonia wasn't so bad after all when she gushed, "Oh, Cal, no wonder they say you're the best in the country. However did you find Alexa? She's perfect for the red bikini . . ."

Cal shook his head. "Not so fast. We just bumped into each other. I'm not sure Alexa is interested . . ."

The editor cocked her head to one side in a way Cal supposed she thought was wise and reflective. "Let me call the boss in New York and tell him about your lucky find. He knows you're not too happy with the current model situation." Neither of them encouraged her to stay and when, after a few more minutes of small talk, she left, Alexa leaned forward with the first sign of interest she'd shown. "So you really are working for *Town and Country*? I didn't believe you . . ."

She must have wanted someone to talk to after all. Cal reckoned, because from being cold and withdrawn, she let the floodgates down and the words rushed out. "I've been out here about six weeks . . . working with a film crew in the forests, west of Elk . . . but . . . my . . . my part was pretty small . . ." She kneaded her fingers together nervously. "Let's just say I was promised a lot, but nothing came of it . . ."

The more she talked, the more vulnerable she seemed—and the more captivated Cal became by her bone structure. "Are you tired?"

Alexa shook her head vigorously. "No, I'm not a bit tired. Why?"

"I've a sudden urge to take some shots of you. Some Polaroids. There's a little room off to the right. No one is ever there. I'll go get my camera and meet you there in ten minutes. Comb your hair and you'll be ready."

Was she crazy? After all her promises to herself, was she about to believe so soon yet another man who told her she had "potential" . . . "something other girls don't have"? Why should this Cal Robinson be any different from Paul Witten?

She had escaped the whip man and Paul Witten to be alone, to earn a little money by day in order to walk under the stars at night, to listen to the ocean, to pick the lupines and poppies and put them in a Coke bottle by her tiny bed and not have to do anything mentally strenuous except remember lunch and dinner orders.

And yet . . . and yet . . . Alexa giggled as she combed her hair in the tiny rest room and smeared on some lip gloss . . . ever since she'd driven up Highway 1 with Barb bitching beside her, she'd had the unmistakable feeling that she was on her way to a date with good fortune. It had been there all the time—even on the last, worst day.

The irony was after Barb met up with Chuck and Lonnie, the two guys in the motel outside Sea Ranch, who not only looked the part, but turned out to be real life "timbermen," she hadn't had to think of a way to interest Barb in finding the film crew.

On the contrary, Chuck and Lonnie had played right into her hands. Out of work for weeks, they'd been heading north, because through the "timbervine" they'd heard a movie was about to be made ". . . about Long Walker, ma'am, the fastest axman ever to hit the coast."

The word had been around that plenty of work was available and plenty of dollars, too ". . . for guys like us who know how to use the old poleax and the California double bitted, too—not as actors," they'd guffawed through their marijuana haze, "but for when the film guys need some real live logging going on. You can't mess around with chopping. A lotta folks can get hurt. They need guys like us."

Alexa hadn't needed to look at Barb to know how quickly she would take advantage of the situation—if she liked them. And she had liked them, particularly Chuck. Alexa had had to bury her face in her huge coffee cup to keep Barb from seeing her grin, when she'd heard her say laconically, "Well, boys, it's your lucky day. That's just where we're headed. My dad's the one making the film. Well, he's put up most of the money. If you want to strike it hot, now's the time . . ."

They were grisly and tough looking, but it hadn't taken more than twenty-four hours to turn them into gofers, as docile and daffy as Bugsy and Dave had ever been. At least, that's what Alexa had thought at first and they'd been wonderfully useful, knowing how to get to where they'd been told the film crew was setting up, deep in the redwoods, near the logging camps between Gualala and Mendocino, where Long Walker had established his legendary reputation.

Whether it was because it was so wild and Chuck and Lonnie were completely at home in that environment, or whether it was Barb's connection to the moneybags, they'd been given the greatest reception. Even Kathleen O'Hagan had emerged from her trailer to give them both her idea of a welcoming hug.

Everything had been swell for forty-eight hours—although Barb had begun to show signs of restlessness at the tortoise-slow pace of moviemaking.

Alexa had been amazed at how long even the smallest scene seemed to take, but she had also been much too fascinated to be bored, at once understanding all the talk in Santa Barbara about dollars, high costs, low costs, budgets. It had been translated into what she saw set up in the forest—an enclave of trailers for the stars, the wardrobes, the kitchens that never seemed to run out of food for endlessly hungry cameramen, first, second and third assistants, continuity girls, and extras, dozens and dozens of extras, all of them taller than any men she had ever seen, just as the trees, the fantastic redwood trees were taller than any trees she had ever seen.

There was an old woodsman, hired by the movie company to check on "authenticity," who enthralled her with stories of the first loggers, who arrived in Mendocino County at the time of the Gold Rush and "who created an instant town, Gualala, beside the fast-running river that flowed through the trees to the sea. One by one the giant trees were cut, hauled over wet timber skids by fifteen-hundred-pound bulls to the river's edge, where they waited for a freshet, that's a sudden surge of the river, to take the logs downstream to the mill . . ." Alexa wanted to hear more and more, reliving the robust past as the actors and actresses put on their costumes and sets sprang up to roll back the years to the turn of the century.

She'd lied to Cal Robinson because she never did get a part in the movie.

Just when she'd stopped looking over her shoulder and started to relax, Paul Witten and Paul Gruen had arrived. She had already planned what to do when this inevitably happened. She was going to play "Siamese twin" and stay so close to Barb's side that neither Paul could give her any problems—but Barb wasn't very cooperative.

By then she had developed a crush on Chuck of monumental proportions, but the more attached she'd become, the more standoffish Chuck had become—typical male reaction, thought Alexa.

In any case Alexa hadn't had to worry about Paul Gruen, who from the day he arrived to the day he left a week later, never acknowledged her existence. Paul Witten was another matter.

He had greeted her coolly and at first hadn't paid much attention. Now, as Alexa combed her hair for the fifth time and unbuttoned the top two buttons of her twill shirt, she grimaced. She had had a good feeling all right, enjoying being a movie "hanger-on," still hoping a miracle might happen, just as it did in the movies—that someone would get sick—that she, watching and knowing every scene, would be plucked out of obscurity to "save the day/save the movie." But it hadn't happened and now probably never would—certainly if either Paul could do anything to prevent it.

Because of Chuck, Barb hadn't wanted to leave the location site, preferring to stay in one of the tents the film crew had rigged up for the extras in the forest. They were like no tents Alexa had ever seen; roomy enough for people of normal height to stand up in, with a shower tent attached, an "outdoor" carpet on the floor, and the plushest sleeping bags, more comfortable than her bed at home.

As soon as Barb's father arrived, however, things had had to change. That first evening there had been a big scene, when he'd learned his Barbie doll hadn't been driving back to the Heritage House or the Fools Rush Inn, where most of the top echelon were staying, but had been shacking up in the forest. When he'd discovered Chuck was the reason, he'd solved it the way he probably solved most things. He'd "bought" him—driving them all, Lonnie, too, back to a hotel in town, where he'd told Barb in a voice that brooked no contradiction she was to stay—and only for another two weeks at most.

Barb had cried all over Alexa that night, telling her that for once her father had put his foot down. After two weeks, there was to be no more fooling around. She was being shipped off to Geneva to the interpreter school, whether she liked it or not. If she showed any resistance, he had made it clear there would be no more allowance, and not even any more "automatic use" of the Santa Barbara house. She had no other option, she'd sobbed, because, as Alexa knew, she'd never gotten along with her mother.

The next day Barb had told Alexa she was going to sneak back to Santa Barbara to get her jewelry and then sell it ". . . to go away with Chuck. I'm crazy about him. Once Dad realizes I'm serious, he won't treat me like a kid anymore."

Alexa had tried to talk Barb out of it. That was probably why Barb blamed her for what happened next. Even now Alexa couldn't understand how Barb could ever have believed she would blab to her father. It must have been the grass, finally getting to her after getting high every night.

It seemed more like three years ago than three weeks ago when everything had blown up. It was funny. Paul Gruen had come into her room in Santa Barbara when she had just washed her hair. This time Paul Witten had walked into her Mendocino hotel room unannounced just before seven, as she had emerged dripping from the shower.

The odd thing was at first he had thrown her a towel, telling her he wanted to talk to her about Barb, but just as she'd wrapped it around her, he'd made a grab for her.

The towel had fallen to the floor and she had been so startled that he'd run his well-trained fingers all over her, before she'd had a chance to fight him off. The door had opened and Barb had been standing there, white and shaking, screaming every kind of curse at both of them, before making a dive at her father's throat, crying hysterically he'd ruined her life, that she would kill him and then kill herself. Somehow Paul Witten had managed to extricate himself and push Barb out into the corridor and that, thank God, was the last she had seen of either of them.

Peg, one of the production secretaries, had later told her that Barb's father had given Chuck and Lonnie one-way tickets to Alaska with guaranteed forty-thousand-dollar-a-year jobs in the oil business, providing neither of them ever contacted Barb again. She had tried to call Barb several times, but Barb had refused to talk to her ever again.

Cal Robinson drew in his breath. He was experienced enough to know that the Polaroid he was looking at didn't lie. Alexa Shapwell was a great-looking girl, with a body that turned heads and evoked wild figments of imagination, but that often fizzled out on film. Not with this one. Not with Alexa. He had been right. There was something world class here. Of course, he would have to take proper shots, some in Mendocino, but more important, some in his studio. He would have to get her to San Francisco to his studio.

Cal casually passed six or seven Polaroids to her.

"What d'you think?" she asked, hardly looking at them.

"I don't think. I know. You can be a top model. I want you to come to San Francisco with me when I finish this job . . ."

"How much will you pay?" Alexa asked suspiciously. "My mother was a model. I want the going rate." She looked so intense, Cal tried to control his smile.

"And what's that?" He could see she was trying to look composed, sophisticated.

"Well, my mother was a pro. She got . . ." Alexa tried frantically to remember, but she couldn't. Oh, well, she'd try anyway. "She got a hundred dollars an hour," she blustered.

Cal met her look straight on and was impressed to see he didn't faze her one bit. "How old are you, Alexa?"

"Eighteen, nearly nineteen . . ." she lied, adding a year to her age. "Well, is one hundred okay with you?"

"Yes, I think so." He gave her one of his lopsided, most attractive smiles. "I think, in fact, you're going to be paid a great deal more than that by your nineteenth birthday . . ." He paused, winked, and added, ". . . whether it's this year or next."

Alexa ignored his crack. "When do we leave?"

"When I'm through here. In a few more days."

"Can I do the red bikini shot the *Town and Country* editor mentioned?"

Boy, she didn't miss a trick. "No," Cal said softly. "I'm saving you for something much more special. I think you may be *Vogue*'s next cover girl."

He didn't attempt to touch me, Alexa thought, as an hour later she turned out the light in the bed sit that went with her waitress job. She lay still so she could hear, far away, the waves breaking around the headland. Was she making a mistake to jump so soon in another direction . . . to turn her back on the peace and quiet she loved so much? It was a dead-end life of drifting, she knew that, but it was without pain . . . but probably without much pleasure in the long run, too. There was something about Cal Robinson she liked. He didn't make her nerve endings tingle the way Paul Witten always had even before he put a finger on her. Cal seemed to take what she had to say seriously.

She didn't have to make a decision right away. He was going to be working in Mendocino for the next week and by the end of that, she would know through her own in-built antennae whether he was interested in her professionally or privately. It certainly wasn't going to be a mixture of both as far as she was concerned.

If she still felt he meant what he said, she would go with him to San Francisco to work on what he called her "portfolio." She had no intention of staying a model. Her views on that as a career had not changed, but after the events of the past few weeks she was clearer headed, tougher—at least she hoped so.

A modeling career, Cal Robinson had intimated, could bring in real money, not the on and off, never certain checks her mother had had to live with.

Alexa shut her eyes, vowing she would model only for as long as it took to amass enough money to retire on. Then she would return to Mendocino and buy an art gallery or a gift shop. If she couldn't make that much, part of a storefront for the spring-and-summer season, like, she had discovered, so many people did—people who, somewhere along their lives, had lost sight of where they were going, who hadn't given up, but who had dropped out of the rat race.

Before she slept, Alexa thought again of her mother, her brave little mother as she now regarded her. "I'll make it,

Mom," she whispered in the dark. "I'll make it just for you."

"Will you stop apologizing, kid? Calm down and speak slowly. You're not bothering me. I want to listen. I want to help, okay? Let's take it from the beginning."

Jo tried to stop the tears that the kindness in Mike Tanner's voice evoked, but she couldn't. They'd been pent up for too long.

"I'm sorry . . ." she said again. The skinny, wiry man, who looked more like a pale egghead university professor than a born-and-bred Californian, hot-shot newspaper reporter, held out a handkerchief with a huge ink stain on it.

"That's better," he said, when Jo laughed as she dabbed her tears away. "Now, shoot." Mike pushed his glasses on top of his head as he always did when he wanted to concentrate, and he put a brotherly hand momentarily over hers.

"Alf Victor wouldn't give me the time of day, but I managed to remember the model agency representing Mom before she met him—about five or six years ago. I called and they vaguely remembered a model called Magda DePaul or Duval or something like that . . . but they hadn't represented her for quite a while. They thought she'd had to go back to Europe, something about her papers not being in order."

"What was the name, DePaul or Duval?"

"I called about three times and every time I spoke to somebody new. No one could exactly remember because except for the owner, who I never got through to, nobody there now had actually been at the agency five or six years ago."

"You're sure Magda's letter was giving your mom instructions to wear a large hat and dark glasses?" Mike Tanner felt a wave of empathy for his young assistant as he saw her gulp and her fingers grip the edge of the table.

"Yes, yes, Mike . . . that was what struck me as so odd. Oh God, I wish I could show you the letter. My father keeps saying he's looking into it—but he just makes excuses when I ask to see the letter again. For all I know he could have lost it—but I'll never forget what it said. Why would my mother be frightened of being recognized? If the letter had been from a man . . . but then no man would write like that . . ." Jo drummed her fingers on the table. "Was she trying to avoid someone? It doesn't make sense."

"No, kid, it doesn't." Mike looked at the check Jo had handed him earlier that evening. "The first thing we have to do is find out what this Fountain is all about and where it's located. That shouldn't be difficult. I think you're right. The second check that your father took was obviously a final payment for something—this check was a first deposit. If it wasn't for a purchase, it was obviously for services rendered—perhaps The Fountain's a spa or someplace like that . . ."

"But why wouldn't Mom have told us she was going there?"

"That's what I don't understand, especially as you say your Mom liked to talk to you about her work, about the things she bought, her diet, all those kind of female things."

Mike looked kindly at the freckle-faced girl staring at him with such desperation. There was probably a simple solution as to what Teri Shephard had been up to. It probably involved another man, but from what Jo had told him, that answer wouldn't break her heart. Her father sounded as if he'd always been a bum husband and father, too. He wanted to help. He hoped he could get the answers fast.

He deliberated now whether or not to tell Jo that he was considering an offer from the local TV station, one he was probably going to accept. He wouldn't be able to take her with him, at least not at first, maybe never. He decided, seeing how upset the conversation had made her, not to break the news now. He would get some facts together first—some solid facts about The Fountain and perhaps about this mysterious Magda, too. By then, he would know whether the station would meet his price and promise of future prospects.

As Jo walked into the house, the phone was ringing. When she heard Alexa's voice she felt for the second time that day the clouds about to lift. How many times had she rehearsed what she would say to her errant sister when she finally heard from her, but as soon as she heard Alexa's voice, her anger evaporated as it always did—her anger, but not her concern.

Alexa read her mind. "I know you must be as mad as hell, Sis, but I didn't want to call you till everything was great. Just like I told you, it's all happening. I guess you could say I've been 'discovered' just like I hoped I would be. I met this incredible photographer, Cal Robinson. Have you ever heard of him?" Before Jo could answer, Alexa rushed on. "He's based in

San Francisco, but he's known everywhere—not just in the U.S., but in Paris, London, Rome. He thinks I can be really big time. He knows *everyone*, *Vogue* editors, *View*, *Cosmo*, *Town and Country*, fashion designers, all the best contacts on the Coast and in New York."

Jo finally got a word in. "What happened to Mr. Hollywood Producer Moneybags—the one you told me about last time you called . . . last month, or was it last year?" She tried to add some ice to her voice.

Alexa dismissed him as Jo was used to her dismissing everyone. "Oh, him! He was only after one thing—like most guys. He didn't want to pay for it either. He was a real mean shit. I told him to get lost, but Jo, this one is different. I swear it. He's really a pro. He knows dozens of gorgeous girls, but he's not interested in any of them—only for work. His wife drowned up here years ago and he's never been able to get over it. He's the first man I've ever met who sees me only as a piece of saleable meat."

"I don't like the sound of that . . ."

Alexa laughed, but not hysterically like she'd laughed the last time. This sounded more like her old happy-go-lucky sister. "Don't worry, Jo. I mean saleable on film . . . in pictures, photographs."

Before Alexa could put the phone down Jo interrupted. "Where are you? Give me a number where I can at least contact you. I had a terrible time trying to find out where you were. I had to call Barb . . ."

Alexa was silent for a minute, then said, "Don't tell me about that. I don't want to have a nightmare tonight. I'll explain everything when I see you. I don't have a number to give you now. I'm on my way to San Francisco with Cal tomorrow. I promise when I'm settled I'll call, but in any case you can always leave a message for me at his studio. He's bound to be listed. Jo, he's for real. He's big time!"

"Yes, I love it. Yes." *Click.* "Okay. Hands on your tushy, Lex. No, for chrissakes, not there. On your rump. Touch it. Love it. Stroke it. Yes, that's better." *Click.* "Separate those impossibly long legs of yours. Let me see them wider . . . wider . . . Think about your body as if it were an incredibly precious jewel." *Click.*

Alexa was used to Cal by now, understood his staccato, often irritable instructions, often knew what he was going to say before he said it. He was usually right.

There had been weeks and weeks of teaching her to "think about her body" . . . showing her how to use it "minimally for maximo results," a favorite directive of his. Today, Alexa felt sluggish, as if she'd slept for twenty-four hours, when she'd hardly slept at all. Three furtive cups of coffee hadn't helped. Cal didn't like her to drink coffee. He said it yellowed the skin.

If he was going to be irritable today, then so was she. She was fed up that it was an ad retake for an important West Coast sportswear manufacturer. How much longer was he going to keep her under wraps? When was she going to be ready for the long-promised editorial exposure? When was her portfolio going to be good enough in his opinion? He'd kept his word about paying her a hundred dollars an hour, which meant she already had more money than she knew what to do with. She never had time to spend it. It was work, work, and then more work, and everything she had ever thought about modeling as a career was true. It was a deadly profession. Only Cal's expert training on how to present herself made it worthwhile. Nothing could buy that training, Alexa knew that. It was years of experience, of dealing with great-looking girls. Everything he taught her, Alexa knew, would be twice as useful in movies, where even the slightest extra movement could look exaggerated, unreal. She had always strived to look, feel, be cool. Now, she was sure she could control herself sufficiently to present whatever image was called for.

The buzzer went off downstairs, announcing that someone had been let into the inner sanctuary, the room leading to the studio elevator, usually off limits whenever Cal was working. Whoever or whatever it was Cal had to be expecting, allowing the interruption—at least Alexa hoped so.

Away from the studio Cal acted like a big brother, caring for her in a way no one else had, except Jo. Best of all, it was "caring" for professional reasons. He checked on her weight, her diet, making sure she walked a mile or so a day. He checked on her sleep, making sure her bedtime gave her at least seven or eight hours of sleep a night.

In the studio, however, all vestiges of big brother vanished. Alexa had already decided his personality was as variable as the San Francisco weather, which as she had now been told at least a dozen times—and had discovered for herself—could literally change from neighborhood to neighborhood, from block to block—from gloomy, chilly gray on Sunset, to brilliant, glowing sun in Golden Gate Park, to blanketing fog enshrouding the studio just off Telegraph Hill.

Cal had installed her in a small apartment nearby that he sometimes referred to as "little Sis's place," other times as "cousin Paddy's place," still others as "my pal Paddy's pad." Sister, cousin, mistress, pal—whoever Paddy was, Alexa couldn't have cared less. Paddy was away for a year in Europe and that was all that counted, because although the apartment was small, it was "chic"—that was the only word for it—with dark-red burnished walls, gold lamps, and a huge picture window in the streamlined, eat-in kitchen that showed off a postcard view of the Golden Gate Bridge and the hills and slopes of the city she had already grown to love.

Cal seemed occasionally amused, occasionally put out by her obvious indifference to the fact he wasn't attracted to her.

Alexa was overjoyed. Her instincts had been right for once. Cal Robinson was interested in her professionally and that was it, nothing more. He had never attempted to touch her out of the studio. In the studio, nobody could ever have misinterpreted his positioning of her as "touching." It was more like "manhandling." He literally pulled her shoulders back when he didn't think she was responding fast enough to his commands; he "shouted" her into the position he wanted, if she didn't get it right after the first two or three times. No, touching was far too intimate a word to describe how he moved her around.

In fact, in the studio Cal was a tireless tyrant, insisting they work on and on and on until he was sure he was "getting the shot," while she felt she was about to fall on her knees with exhaustion.

Today, he seemed more tense than usual, more tyrannical, barking at Twinny, his Chinese assistant, to move faster, when Twinny was already greased lightening, bitingly sarcastic about the way Sonia Stafford had styled her hair, running his hands through it, so all the carefully inserted pins fell to the floor, rubbing off some of her eyeshadow himself.

Something was up, but until the buzzer went off Alexa had felt too soporific to care.

"Twinny, let's go. Up that strobe. Lift that board. Alexa,

where are your legs? Part them—think body, think stride, jut . . ."

For the first few seconds Alexa's reactions were mechanical, dull, until she saw a woman, a strange-looking woman, standing behind Cal and—Alexa could hardly believe it—following every instruction he was giving her. She, too, was opening her legs, touching her rump, moving as if to stride, jutting her body forward. When Cal bellowed, "bat those lashes, Alex, let me have them . . ." the woman, whoever she was, batted her eyelashes, too!

At first, there was something nerve-racking about her being there, yet slowly something mesmerizing, too. Alexa found herself not only listening to Cal, but copying the stranger's interpretations of Cal's commands, coming now faster and faster.

When Cal stopped to change film, he didn't introduce her and didn't tell her to take a break either. Sonia Stafford nervously squirted water onto her hair to lick it back from her face and added some bronzer to her forehead to give the "touch of sunglow" Cal had acerbicly snapped he wanted. He was about to start shooting again when the stranger shouted, actually shouted, "No, wait!" All sluggishness left Alexa. This was going to be interesting. She didn't have a clue who this five-foot-nothing with sleek blond hair and deep dark tan was, but now surely she would find out. There were bound to be fireworks. Nobody told Cal Robinson to wait or to stop or to do anything in his studio, his kingdom. To Alexa's amazement, apparently this feisty little nugget could and did.

"Something's been bothering me, Cal. She can't wear underpants with that skirt when she stands that way. I like the look, but it doesn't work with underpants. Take 'em off."

Alexa looked peevishly at Cal. Surely he would tell this stranger to go screw herself. He didn't. He nodded his agreement abruptly instead and Alexa turned to go into the dressing room. "Don't lose the mood, the momentum, Cal . . ." the interfering so-and-so was giving orders again, and, goddamn it, again, Cal agreed with her, saying quickly, "Don't waste time, Alexa. Take the pants off now. Throw 'em to Sonia."

The weirdo was right. Goddamn it, she was right. Time off the set could break the mood and it could take ages to recover it. The weirdo was right about the underpants, too. It was ridiculous, Alexa realized now, to wear them with a snakeskin wrapped skirt, which because of the material had felt one size too small ever since she'd put it on.

There were no more interruptions, but Alexa was aware of the woman's presence the entire time—of her eyes, which looked black, menacing, hypnotic, and her bushy brows, which communicated approval or disdain during the grueling day-long session.

About seven Cal called it a day and after Alexa showered and dressed, she went as she usually did to curl up on the shaggy old sofa in Cal's office. She couldn't wait to find out who bushy brows was. She had to be "someone," that was sure. Even the dark-gray track suit she had been wearing, which made her look like a cross between an alpine yodeler and child gymnast, Alexa sensed had to have been made by a leading designer.

Cal had put on a clean T-shirt when he ambled into the office. Alexa brightened up. This usually meant dinner out somewhere. "Sorry, Lex. Not tonight. Go home and fix yourself a sandwich. You saw Penelope Waverly here today. She and I have to smoke a pipe of peace together and talk some business."

"What's that supposed to mean? I could hardly work with her there. Who is Penelope Waverly?" Alexa sounded like a shrew and that was just the way she wanted to sound. She was now so fed up, she wanted to scream at him.

Cal propped his feet up on the desk. "Probably the person who is going to influence your career the most, young lady. Penelope Waverly is the powerhouse fashion editor of *View*, known for her people-spotting, talent-scouting ability. She left the *New York Times* because she was given a piece of the pie at *View*."

"What do you mean 'a piece of the pie'?" Alexa interrupted.

"Equity, my little dumb friend, a piece of the action, profits, and with that frosty-faced Blair Benson, at the helm, they're making plenty of profit all right. I heard Penelope was in town. I knew eventually she'd come to see my latest sulky little discovery sitting here. Pen and I have had our differences in the past. She accused me of letting someone slip through her pincers to sign up with *Vogue*. It had nothing to do with me, but obviously *Vogue* is *View*'s only competition." Cal leaned back and closed his eyes. "Whew, she's a bloody marvel. She saw things in you I hadn't even thought of. We're going to sign a peace treaty tonight and tomorrow, my love, you're going to sit for *View* with the great Waverly in charge of the sitting. It's that audition for the star part you've been bitching about."

Alexa didn't answer, waited until Cal opened his eyes to look at her coolly, reflectively. Then, and only then, did she give him a dazzling smile, arching back so that her black halter top opened to show the curve of her breasts. "I'll do my best for you, Cal," she said demurely.

"You sure will, baby. Get a lot of beauty sleep. I'll pick you up just before eight."

"New York, New York, it's a wonderful town . . ." Alexa couldn't get rid of the song as she headed for the dressing room the next morning.

There was a black man lying on the sofa, so thin and hungry-looking she started to back out, colliding with Penelope Waverly on her way in. "This is going to be fun," Waverly said right out, making no attempt to introduce herself. "Have you met Mims? He is the best there is, flew up from L.A. when I told him there wasn't anyone around here who knew how to handle lip gloss, let alone eyelash curlers. Gee whiz, you are a good-looking gal, aren't you . . ." Penelope Waverly hardly stopped talking for the next forty minutes. Even when she darted out of the dressing room to confer with Cal in the studio or rummage in the huge clothes closet, Alexa could hear her comments, all running together like a one-woman monologue.

Alexa had decided over breakfast she would be cooperative but withdrawn. She didn't have a chance to be anything else.

While Penelope talked, Mims, the black makeup artist, studied her, pulled her hair in different directions, up, back, away from, over her face, and with long skinny fingers acting like calipers measured her bone structure, the space between her eyes, the distance from temple to chin. Alexa felt it was all very affected.

What was she going to wear for this long, longed-for audition? After an hour of what she considered more wasted time than usual, Alexa found out. Penelope came in with a long low "whoopee . . ." holding out an enormous sand-colored towel as if it was the latest creation from Paris. "See this color, Mims. Fix it in your eye, in your soul. I want her to be . . ." Penelope lowered her voice dramatically. ". . . I want people to think she's this color all over."

Alexa stared impassively in the glass, hoping the tiny little nerve she felt twitching beneath her eye wasn't showing. To her relief Mims left when Penelope asked, no, ordered her, "to strip off . . ."

Although Alexa was now used to undressing in front of other models, hairdressers, makeup artists, there was something acutely embarrassing about taking off her jeans and shirt with Penelope Waverly's eyes fixed on her every movement. "Take your bra off, your pants. I want to see what kind of skin you have all over. Some gals, gee whiz, have this rub-ber-y kind of flabbo on their backsides." Penelope gave a monumental shudder as if she were talking about a rare disease. Alexa began to hate her, but she still did as she was told, clasping her arms around her breasts as Penelope walked around her as if inspecting a statue.

"Very, very nice. Cal always was a good picker." The editor started to wind the towel around her from neck to ankle, all the time muttering to herself, "I was right. I was right."

She spent a good twenty, thirty minutes tying the towel, untying it, leaving her breasts exposed, covering her completely like a mummy, until she murmured she had "the shape—the shape of sun, sand, sex." Penelope clapped her hands together like a little girl and screamed for Mims, who came in with a huge artist's board covered with dollops and dabs of different shades of brown, all the way from cream to mahogany.

"You've got it, you've got it," Penelope cried with delight as Mims dipped a spatula swiftly into three or four shades, blended them together in his palm with a long lean finger and started to apply the color from her neck up to her forehead. Her skin started to match the color of the towel exactly. The makeup session lasted ninety minutes. Alexa thought she'd go crazy, but when Mims finally stepped back and she looked at herself she realized he deserved his reputation.

She hardly recognized herself. She looked as if she were growing out of the sand towel like some brilliant, exotic flower.

Her lips and eyes were gold; her skin was sand-colored like the palest, finest yellow-gold sand.

"Are you testing me for a remake of *Goldfinger*?" Alexa asked coldly, the only sentence she'd uttered since stepping into the dressing room at 8:30 A.M. Penelope ignored her cold tone.

"No, gal, far more interesting than that. You'll see. Aren't you enjoying all this?"

Alexa stared woodenly ahead. The thought of now going through a lengthy hairdressing session made her feel ill, but suddenly, with a shout from Cal, "How's it going in there?" everything speeded up. There was to be no elaborate hairstyle. Mims plaited her long gold hair into one thick braid, sprayed it with a gold film so that it clung to her head, emphasizing its shape and making it look more like something emerging from the sand than ever.

Another towel was produced, a fresh one, a replica of the first. By now Alexa no longer cared that Mims stayed in the room staring at her, while Penelope whipped the first towel away and as dextrously as before, wound the fresh towel around her, this time pinning it fiercely into place at the back, draping it so that one shoulder was exposed and one leg all the way up to the crotch.

She waved Mims out of the room as Cal called out one more time, "What's going on? How long? Let's get going before she has another birthday!"

Penelope put her face alarmingly close to Alexa's and turned her to face the mirror. "Look at yourself, gal," she whispered hoarsely. "Remember you cost two dollars . . . two dollars . . ." When Alexa looked nonplussed, Penelope whirled her around, before twisting her to face the mirror again. "Buy me . . . buy . . . think 'buy me,' " she whispered in her ear, now so close her hot breath tickled. "This is for a cover, Alexa. Think, 'buy me . . . buy me . . . only two dollars' . . ."

As Penelope led her triumphantly onto the studio floor, Alexa thought of Paul Gruen. She felt as if she were about to be auctioned. How he would have loved to see her trussed up like this. How he would have enjoyed seeing her obey all the instructions that were now going to be given. In a second, though, all those kinds of rebellious thoughts left her as Penelope carefully explained how she wanted her to lie back on the white linen divan in the center of the studio floor.

Three hours later Alexa had stopped hating Penelope. Mims had made her look like an exotic flower. Penelope made her feel like one, so precious she had to be isolated, surrounded as she now was, by big white boards and standing lights. There had been many sessions with minimal sets like this, but no one, not even Cal, had made her feel so special, out there alone on the set.

"Hold your beautiful chin down, gal. Look out from under those silky dreamy lashes. You're waking up from a languorous nap. Lids go down, pause, slowly open . . ."

Mims was a dream, too, Alexa decided. Always there before anyone had to say a word about more gold foam for her hair, a touch of coral blended onto her shoulder to bring back the glow. Cal and Penelope worked together like an orchestra leader with a choreographer and she was the dancer, following the movements as if she had been rehearsing them all her life. For the first time, Alexa discovered it was actually possible to enjoy being photographed.

It was over. She was spent, but in a different way than usual, when physical tiredness linked with mental exhaustion made her angry, frustrated. Now, although she felt she couldn't move another muscle, mentally she was exhilarated, knowing without anyone saying a word that the sitting had been a success. She sat in the dressing room, staring at her reflection as Mims deftly removed every vestige of sand color from her skin. She looked wan without it, but when he sponged her face with an ice-cold tonic and the natural pink began to come back, so did some of her vitality.

"How did I do, Mims?" She smiled broadly to show she only wanted confirmation, not reassurance. The black man, who hadn't smiled once, now briefly showed large white teeth.

"You'll do." He leaned on the back of the chair, staring somberly at her reflection. "Do you want to make some real money? The kind that will blow your mind?"

Alexa was startled but didn't show it. "Sure, who doesn't? What do I have to do? Rob a bank?"

The whiter-than-white teeth flashed. "Nothing so easy." He winked. "I know someone . . . someone who would appreciate your style." Alexa fidgeted in the chair, uncomfortable as Mims slowly looked her over in the mirror.

"He is a very hard man to please, because he is an expert collector—a collector of beautiful things, of beautiful women . . ." He pronounced it "boo-ti-ful" as if talking to a child. "He relies on Mims. He knows Mims recognizes the best. What's your phone number?"

Alexa was about to get up and tell him to get lost, when to her relief Penelope came back. "Mims, outside . . ." Penelope stood in the doorway, looking at Alexa with pride as if she was now her own creation. "I want to say some important things to this gal."

Penelope kicked the door shut as Mims left and leaned against it reflectively. "Alexa, I've just spoken to Blair Benson, the owner and executive editor of *View*. She wants to see for herself what I've discovered. I want you to leave with me in the morning for New York. You're raw, untrained, but Cal Robinson isn't often wrong. You're almost certainly cover material, even though today was a disaster."

For all Alexa's pride in her self-control, she lost it. She repeated the word, almost screeching, "*Disaster*?"

"Yes, gal. Cal Robinson isn't the photographer for you. He sees the talent, knows it, strokes it, but he doesn't know how to unleash this sleeping tiger. Turbulence, gal. I know just the photographer to release your turbulence. Don't worry. Cal will be rewarded for finding you—he's wonderful with Farrah and Margaux, even Renny . . . but not you."

Penelope was speaking more to herself than to her. Alexa didn't care. She was wrestling with her own thoughts. What should she do? It wasn't a hard decision to make.

New York was where the big money was, Cal always said that himself. If this weirdo, who made her feel so good on the set, felt Cal wasn't the right photographer for her, perhaps he never would be . . . perhaps that was the reason it had taken so long to get her portfolio just right, the reason she was still modeling for sportswear ads and soap commercials, stuck just like Mom had been stuck with second-rate stuff, when she had been told so often she had "star quality."

Cal had been good to her, there was no question about that. She would never forget it, but much as she loved living in Frisco, it was where the opportunities were that counted. It was again time to move on.

Penelope didn't seem to need her answer in any case. She had taken it for granted. "Be ready with your bags packed tomorrow morning. I'll pick you up at eight. We'll catch the ten A.M. TWA." Penelope placed her hands firmly on Alexa's shoulders. "Don't tell Cal now. I don't want any teary farewell scenes, any upset that will mean you don't sleep. I don't want anything upsetting to show on that lovely face of yours, gal."

She clutched Alexa's shoulders and stared directly into her eyes. "Cal told me you are not having an affair—but underneath that ice layer of yours, you're not in love with him, pining, lusting after him, are you?"

Alexa's derisive laugh was all Penelope needed. She released her hold on her, but still looked directly in her eyes. "You really are a self-contained little number, aren't you? Cool, steady, and so gorgeous . . . that's a star-studded combination, gal . . . and I am going to make damn sure that it's going to make millions for *View* and for you."

To Alexa's surprise, Penelope suddenly sat down and looked like a tired old lady. "Do as I say and you'll go far, Alexa. I promise you. Now, gal, promise no upsetting goodbyes tonight."

Alexa nodded dutifully. The last thing she wanted was an upsetting scene with Cal. When she was well established in New York, he would understand. When she was a big star, she would insist he take some pictures sometimes . . . it would only be a matter of time before she could repay him for his faith in her.

"Act as you usually do," Penelope whispered her last instruction, scribbling down her address before she left the studio. "Don't let him suspect I'm spiriting you away. All's fair in love and work, right, gal?"

Alexa let loose her most radiant smile, although she was annoyed to find her hand trembling. "Right, Penelope. I'll be ready for you at eight."

Nevertheless, it took all of her acting ability to respond to Cal when, later in his office, over a carafe of his favorite Sonoma wine, he thought he was telling her big news. "You've passed the test, kid. Penelope is going to recommend you to Blair Benson, the owner of *View*, and that's as good as being a *View* star already. Blair is a 'hands-on' boss all the way."

Alexa sipped the wine cautiously, afraid something would slip out if she drank too much.

"Pen's a feisty devil, but she sure knows what she wants

and gets it." Cal leaned forward to tap her knee. "Don't daydream now, Lex. This is important stuff. Penelope is a very powerful lady who can help you more than you'll ever know, but I am not going to let her take you over. We've got to handle this very, very carefully. I told her last night we were going to move at my pace, not hers."

Alexa heard him, but no alarm bells went off. She didn't want to handle things "carefully" or "move at his pace" anymore. The minutes were ticking away. She was more than ready to move. A revealing thought came to her. Cal was always telling her the really big money was on the East Coast, so what was he doing on the West Coast? Okay, so he did sittings for *Town and Country* and other magazines and he'd explained why he'd had a falling out with *View*, but in the three months she had been working with him, there hadn't been a peep from *Vogue*, the biggest of them all. No, Cal Robinson was in a backwater, perhaps of his own choosing, perhaps not. In either case, Alexa didn't want to stay there with him a minute longer than was necessary.

Cal whistled. "Well, you're sure a cool customer. Here I am telling you all this good news and you look as if I'm sending you to sleep."

Alexa pushed her glass away and smiled sweetly. "I am excited, really I am, but . . ." She stifled a yawn. "It's been a long, long day. I'm dead."

He was immediately, unusually conciliatory.

"You're right. Guess what, we won't work tomorrow, how's that?" As he spoke, he flipped through his desk diary. He frowned. "Well, I guess you won't work, but I see now I've got to. I was going to take you down to Carmel, but Pony's filled up my only free day for a week. We'll do it next week. D'you want to celebrate in Chinatown tonight? You can sleep late tomorrow."

For a second Alexa hesitated, attracted despite everything by Cal's sweet, lopsided grin. The tiny nerve ending was back flicking below her eye. Was she being a fool leaving the guardianship of this great guy, who promised to steer her to the top—even if it was at "his pace"? There must have been something in her face that worried Cal.

"What's wrong Alexa? What's bothering you?"

The moment passed. She got to her feet and laughed.

"Nothing, Cal. Nothing. Give me a Chinese raincheck. I've just got to get some sleep."

Penelope Waverly placed her traveling rolling pin beneath her aching feet as she waited for Blair Benson to come on the line. She refused to think about being tired, but she wasn't about to have swollen ankles either, particularly not before another coastal plane hop. The rolling-pin idea worked wonders. As she rolled her feet back and forth over the hotel carpet, she decided she was beginning to feel soothed, and, in any case, she had such good news to impart.

Blair came straight to the point as usual. "Did you get her out from under?"

"With no trouble, dear boss. As I told you last night, I was pretty sure Cal Robinson was telling the truth—that there is absolutely nothing going on between them. When I told the little monster the incredible lie that Cal Robinson wasn't the photographer for her, she was ours, hook, line, and whatever else you want to call it. Cal will be mad for a couple of months, but he'll get over it. I tell you Blair, this gal's got it. She is going to sell thousands and thousands of copies. She'll leap out at 'em on the newsstands and leave every other book gasping for help. We couldn't have Cal Robinson breathing down our necks, interfering, telling us who could shoot her and who not . . . what she should wear and what not. I told him last night that the only way I would work with a totally untrained girl was on my terms. He told me he'd think about it, but I knew you weren't interested in waiting . . . that we need a new face now!"

As Penelope paused for breath in her nonstop diatribe, Blair quickly interrupted. "Well done, Pen. When are you lassoing her and bringing her in?"

"Why, dear boss, tomorrow of course. We will be in New York in time for tea . . ."

CHAPTER FIVE

NEWSPAPER NETWORKING—THE OLD BOYS' NETWORK—THERE WAS nothing like it for producing results. Whether it existed to such a degree in other professions, Mike didn't know, but he doubted it.

In combat zones, in the trenches, yes, but otherwise nothing could come close to the camaraderie and exchange of valuable leads that existed in the world of ink-stained comrades. Today and for the rest of his week's vacation he was going to tap it, good and hard, cash in on some outstanding favors, and all for the sake of a freckle-faced kid, whose beautiful boobs belied her otherwise innocent exterior—but she was growing up fast.

It was the week before he started his new career in television and he felt just great. As he moved his glasses down from the top of his head to study his decrepit address book, Mike chuckled. "You're going to be a four-eyed Mike Wallace," the producer had said. Well, he was sure going to give it a whirl. He already knew TV networking existed. He'd been beaten out on a few stories because of it.

He had already done some legwork for Jo. There was no "Fountain" listed in San Diego, Orange, San Marin, or Los Angeles counties but that didn't mean much. He had been through the newspaper morgue and hadn't been able to find any reference to The Fountain there either.

The Living Page editor had been adamant that it wasn't a spa or she would have known it. She'd been a doll. When he had insisted that it was really important that she know for sure, she'd called a pal, who knew the West Coast editor of *Vogue*, who'd reported back, equally certain there was no spa of that name in the whole of California. So what and where was The Fountain? He was pretty sure, whatever it was, it was in or near Los Angeles. According to Jo, her mother had made a date to meet a mystery woman called Magda in the bar of the Beverly Hills Hotel a few days after she'd written the big check, the one that had gotten Jo so worked up.

Mike had had a hunch that perhaps The Fountain, despite the ambiguity of its name, might be somewhere for alcoholics to dry out, but a few well-chosen questions to Jo had scuttled that theory. Teri had apparently even watered down her spritzers. "Mom said alcohol increased your appetite and ruined your figure," Jo had told him. "She always said she was lucky she didn't even like the stuff."

Mike tried to open his book at the *B* section but as usual had difficulty. The *B* had long been worn away with use. More people's names began with *B* than any other; then there was the column he hardly ever looked at for "birds," followed by the section "business contacts." He'd been to college with Burt Stokler, who'd been a reporter for the business section of *The Los Angeles Times* for five or six years. They had often exchanged leads in their respective cities.

"So, you're losing your byline, eh, Mike? Looking to become a famous face instead?"

Mike put up with Burt's cracks for a few minutes, then came to the point.

"I need your help, pal. I am trying to locate a place called The Fountain—in business about two years ago—some kind of service business, don't know what. A check for eighteen hundred dollars, signed by Teri Shephard on May 30, 1977, was put into their 'deposit only' account in the Bank of California. For various reasons, my hunch is The Fountain is somewhere in or around L.A., so the branch of the bank is probably there, too. There was another check made out to The Fountain by Teri dated April 29, also deposited in a 'deposit only' Bank of California account, both authorized on the back with a signature like 'Svetlana' something or other . . ."

"Doesn't sound like much of a story. Do I really have to waste my time on this?"

Mike knew Burt well enough not to be put off by his lukewarm response.

"Believe me, there's a story, and when I know it, you will hear it—on the six o'clock news . . ."

"Fuck you."

They arranged to meet for a drink the next night at a favorite hangout for *Los Angeles Timer*s.

Next, Mike made a call to the Loretta Pearson Modeling Agency, where Teri Shephard had been a star attraction, until the late sixties, when bookings had dropped off. Then she'd met Alf Victor, who, Jo had told him innocently, "Remodeled Mom to give her a more modern look."

The West Coast *Vogue* editor was supposed to have called on his behalf and she hadn't let him down.

"Mike Tanner of Station KCST . . ." It was ridiculous, but he felt like adding "an affiliate of NBC" for extra effect, but of course he didn't, and it wasn't necessary. There was no mistaking the expectation in the secretary's voice.

"Oh yes, Mr. Tanner, Ms. Pearson is expecting you," she cooed. "Twelve noon . . ." They were obviously expecting TV coverage, so let them think it. If television opened doors more easily than print, that was great and maybe a story on a modeling agency wasn't such a bad idea anyway. People were always interested in dream factories.

Mike looked at his watch. If he left now he would be exactly on time for his appointment with Alf Victor. He was always on time, but there was something about this pompous ass of a fancy photographer that already made him grit his teeth and made him want to be late on purpose.

In his long apprentice years at *The Union Tribune* over and over again Mike had found those really at the top, those really going places, always returned calls and behaved with a certain amount of courtesy. It was always the jumped-up guys who swallowed their own PR, who were so impressed with themselves, they were "too busy" to call back, who broke dates and never knew how to say "sorry, pal."

Mike was convinced Alf Victor fell into the latter category, although Alf had been quick enough to return his call. Mike hadn't liked his tone, shaded with condescension, although his curiosity had obviously been triggered as to what Mike Tanner, formerly of *The Union Tribune* and now with the hottest TV station in Southern California, could possibly want to discuss with him. Mike had told him it couldn't be discussed over the phone.

As Mike drove downtown, he noted the increasing number of construction cranes pointing into the sky. The skyline of his city was changing daily.

"San Diego City and County have moved into the civic fastlane. Few Californians still have the outdated picture of the city and its ambiance of a sleepy navy town. It's boom time downtown and in the suburban hills, the snarl of earth-moving equipment has replaced birdsong, peace, and tranquility . . ." He was doing it again, composing newspaper copy in his head, when he now had to train his mind to think of words that stayed in the mind when *heard*, not read. He stepped on the gas and decided, as usual, to be exactly on time.

Alf Victor was already waiting for him in a booth in the bar on Z Street, a bottle of Perrier Jouët on ice beside him. He didn't miss Mike's amused smirk, although it was off his face in a second.

"I always drink Champagne before the opera. Have you seen Levine's *Bohème*? I am told he does a tolerably good job." Alf Victor didn't wait for an answer. He continued, "Would you like to join me in a glass or do you want . . . eh . . . something else?"

"Champagne would be fine."

Mike hadn't expected the photographer to look so macho. There was a lot of strength in the shoulders beneath the well-cut black linen blazer, a lot of sexuality in the dark intense face. He looked more like a Spanish matador than a shutterbug. No wonder pretty women listened to him, probably fell in love with him, although Jo hadn't given him that impression about her mother.

For about ten minutes Mike allowed Alf to give him a short treatise as to what was wrong with and what could be put right about the San Diego Opera Company. Alf's acid remarks probably went over big with those who moved in the opera and so-called San Diego social circuit. Alf dropped names inconspicuously, but Mike was too much of an observer not to get the message that Alf was passing along: "I know people who count. I am a sophisticated, knowledgeable intellectual. Don't underestimate me, sonny. I move in the fast lane and you'd better believe it."

Halfway through his second glass of Champagne, Alf Victor did surprise him. He put a monocle in his right eye and leaned forward to put his face only a few inches away. Mike decided Alf had to be gay after all. The monocle took away Alf's masculinity as quickly as if he'd put a flower in his hair.

"So, fire away. Is it about me or my models? The has-beens or the will-bes?"

Feeling a second's disloyalty to Jo, Mike spoke carefully. "I suppose you'd call her a has-been. She's dead. I want to ask you about Teresa Shapwell or Teri Shephard, as she called herself, someone whose career I believe you rebuilt when it crumbled in the late sixties, early seventies?"

Alf Victor pouted like a child who'd been told he couldn't go out to play. "Teri Shephard? Why on earth are you interested in her? She wasn't interesting alive, let alone dead."

Mike fingered his full glass of Champagne. It would have been wonderful to have tipped it over the photographer's glossy head, but he restrained himself. "There are some unexplained questions about her death. Where she was going? Why she was in Mexico? You apparently told her family she wasn't on a location trip."

The photographer exaggerated a yawn. "The press never fails to amaze me. What are you dreaming up about that poor little creature? Is it just a slow week? No axmen around carving up bodies? No corrupt city fathers involved in deals over the planned new convention center?"

Mike laughed easily, although he longed to stuff Alf's monocle in his mouth. "It's forty minutes to curtain up. Time enough to answer my Teri Shephard questions and move on to your current discoveries. . . . What about telling me where you think Teri was going in Mexico? Could she have been double-crossing you, working for someone else when you were supposed to be her exclusive agent?"

Alf Victor sneered. "No way, no way. I'd already had to warn her that bookings were getting difficult. She'd taken too much sun over the years. Her skin was going. Chiffon over the lens and all that sort of thing wasn't helping, and retouching can't give back spirit, youth, freshness. I was having trouble getting the pictures—and if I was having trouble, how could I use her, recommend her? I am a photographer, not a philanthropist."

"Who's Magda?"

"Magda?" Alf screwed up his nose as if Mike had mentioned a vile smell. "Magda who?"

"Teri made a date to meet someone called Magda on June fourth. By then she'd been killed, but in any case Teri was going in the wrong direction. The meeting with Magda was to have been in the Polo Lounge of the Beverly Hills Hotel."

Alf shrugged. "So what? Magda . . . Magda . . . It's vaguely familiar, but models often call themselves Magda or Wanda or Carola or Teri . . ." he smiled thinly. "Teri was a mistake. I told her it was a cheap name, but she convinced me she'd been using it for so long, it had good recognition. You know, for catalogue, mail-order work." He sipped his Champagne carefully. "Teri was a pretty woman. Yes, once a very pretty woman with a great body, but she was too emotional. She was married to this bum, a pretty beach bum who only had to snap his fingers and she'd have a breakout or she'd lose a couple of pounds just before a bra shoot . . ." Alf sighed heavily as if remembering a broken world treaty. "Overnight she started to age. He'd told her so, too . . . Bill . . . Bob . . . whatever her husband's name was—and in the end I also had to tell her."

"Tell her what?"

"That she was getting too old . . . that she should think of retiring and let her daughter take over. Now, there's potential. That's who you should be interested in. Alexa's the future, not the past." Alf Victor paused to see if he had Mike's full attention. "Perhaps that's really why you wanted to see me. One never knows what reporters are really after." He held up his glass and stared at the pale gold liquid bubbles. "Teri's daughter has a skin this color with hair to match. I wonder where she's hiding? I ran into her one day last year . . . told her I'd be willing to take some shots . . . help her with her clothes, her style . . . the same thing I did for her mother, but with much . . ." he paused to stress the word, "*much* more enthusiasm."

The temptation to pour the remainder of the Champagne into Alf Victor's lap was growing again, but Mike pressed on. "Magda wrote to tell Teri to wear a large hat and dark glasses, as if she didn't want anyone to know they were meeting."

"Wait a minute, Magda . . ." Now Alf was irritable as if prodded awake out of a deep, satisfying sleep. "Oh, yes, now I remember. There was this Estonian Amazon on a shoot one day. Teri seemed to know her from somewhere. The client had sent her along for me to consider for a group shot. Magda. Yes, I remember, wonderful bones, but terrible teeth. She couldn't smile—I forbade her to smile." Alf paused as he tapped his monocle on the rim of the Champagne glass. "Magda Dupaul, that was her name. I used her once, but once was enough, and I haven't seen her in at least a couple of years. . . ."

"Magda Dupaul? Yes, we used to represent her. A beautiful girl but undisciplined, unreliable, very unreliable." The founder and owner of the Loretta Pearson Modeling Agency needed to go to Weight Watchers badly. She was a story, Mike decided, as he watched her amble across her spacious office to shut out the sun rays that were about to blind him.

"Is that better, Mr. Tanner? The sun really gets to you in that spot, I know. It's called the hot spot for more reasons than one." She giggled girlishly. "It's kinda useful, a sort of natural searchlight when I'm trying to get the truth out of some of my girls."

In Mike's estimation, there were at least two hundred pounds of Loretta Pearson and he couldn't see why she would need any help getting the truth out of anyone.

"I'm trying to locate her, Mrs. Pearson . . ."

"Ms. Pearson," she corrected him amiably.

"Sorry, Ms. Pearson. I believe you also represented a Teri Shephard some years ago? About 'sixty-eight or 'sixty-nine? Did you represent Magda Dupaul at that time, too?"

"Believe we did, believe we did. Teri Shephard? Was killed, wasn't she?"

Mike nodded.

"Read about it somewhere. Poor, silly girl. Always guessed she'd end up in trouble."

"She was killed in a car crash, Ms. Pearson, driving in the Sierra Madres in Mexico. There was a heavy rainstorm—part of the road was washed away. It was a tragedy. As you probably know Teri had two daughters. The eldest one, Jo, worked for me—she's a friend and I'm trying to check into one or two things on her behalf."

For such an enormous woman Loretta Pearson moved with speed. As Mike was talking, she bounced in and out of what looked like a huge filing cupboard to return with a blue bound file in her hand. "Is this who you're trying to find?"

Mike opened the file without answering. A composite of black-and-white photographs showed a haunting face in profile and full face, while a striking full-length picture showed the same girl in a black leather bikini. "Magda Dupaul, 5 feet 11½ inches, 38 inches, 24 inches, 35 inches, size 9 shoes, raven-black hair, dark brown eyes, pale complexion" read the captions. Mike looked again at the face, at the sharply angled cheekbones that so obviously came from a Slavic country, and eyes so large they looked almost out of proportion to the rest of the face.

"Why don't you represent her now? Why do you say she was so unreliable?"

Ms. Pearson threw up her arms, dozens of bracelets jangling together like tambourines. "She never turned up. We would book her and she wouldn't turn up. Once she didn't turn up for a year, said she'd had an emergency back home, wherever home really was. First she says she comes from Hungary . . ." Ms. Pearson flashed Mike a smile that sent shivers down his back. " 'That's where I come from. Why I have such gorgeous skin.' Then she forgets and tells me her folks are back home in Sofia, as if I don't know where Sofia is, then it's Estonia . . ."

Mike interrupted softly. "Where is she now?"

Loretta shrugged her huge shoulders. "Haven't seen her in over two years. We got her this great job—print and TV ads for a new hotel in Vegas. We paid to get her teeth fixed, took it out of the advance. She wasn't a kid either; it's never that easy getting good jobs for girls over twenty-five . . . maybe she was twenty-seven . . . I don't know, but she had a great-looking body, firm all over . . ." Loretta Pearson ran a fat hand down her own arm, then seemed to shake with anger. "About a week before the job, her sister called up, said something about Magda's papers weren't in order, that she had to leave the country for thirty-six hours to get a new visa—that she'd be back in time to go to work. Never heard from her again. I never want to hear from her again either!" As she finished her sentence Mike caught a glimpse of another, not so amiable Ms. Pearson, who made her models sit in the full glare of the sun to get the truth, the whole truth, and nothing but the truth.

"Do you know where I can reach her sister?"

"Nope. Until she called, I didn't even know Magda had a sister and with the number of lies she told me, who knows if she ever did?" The phone rang as it had been ringing since Mike's arrival. This time, however, the buzzer on Ms. Pearson's desk buzzed and she indicated the appointment was at an end.

"I'd like to come back sometime, Ms. Pearson. Perhaps to do a story about your new hopefuls . . ."

Ms. Pearson's chin wobbled as she nodded cheerfully, "Anytime, Mike, anytime—and if I ever hear anything from Magda, I'll give you a call, but she'll never get any more work from me. She's too old now anyway."

It was the second time in twenty-four hours Mike realized he'd been taught how short was the lifespan of a model. Too old at twenty-nine!

He was about to leave when he had another thought. "Can you remember more or less the date of Magda's Vegas job?"

"I sure can. I'd booked to go to Vegas with her. I like to gamble, you know, blackjack, not much serious stuff. I was so mad, I went anyway and lost a couple of thousand bucks."

"When?"

"June—let's see—yep, it was June tenth two years ago. That was the date she was supposed to start work in Vegas on location. Her so-called sister said she'd be away a week. That was over two years ago . . ."

He hadn't accomplished much, but he'd learned a model was considered "over the hill" at twenty-nine and already on the skids after twenty-five. Poor Teri Shephard had obviously been told she hadn't long to go, both by the husband she adored and the photographer in charge of her career.

At 7 P.M., as Mike waited in the mock-Tudor pub in downtown Los Angeles for his old college roommate, he reflected on how bleak the future must have looked to Teri Shephard two years ago. She had paid out over two thousand dollars to a place called The Fountain—two thousand dollars she could apparently ill afford. She had been searching for something that she obviously thought worth that kind of investment. What could it have been that she felt The Fountain could supply? The Fountain . . . The Fountain . . . Something clicked. Of course, that was it. It had to be. The Fountain of Youth—that was what Teri Shephard had been searching for—youth. As Mike scribbled down some notes, somebody whacked him across the back. Burt Stokler had arrived.

"This place looks like shit, but it has the best draft beer in the country. Let's move to the back of the bar where we can get merrily pissed, dear friend."

It was their usual rite on meeting that no business be discussed until two or three drinks had been downed, but tonight Mike was too restless to play the game. He had to know if his theory was right and if so, how The Fountain delivered its promise of "youth." With drugs? By injection? It all seemed crazy to him, yet he was sure he was on the right track. What a story it might make after all—a Fountain offering "youth" had endless television possibilities. Mike Wallace, watch out, here I come.

"Okay, Mike, what's eating you? You're like a guy who wants to fart in the boardroom. Relax, for chrissake. What's up? No, don't tell me. I'll put your bloody mind at rest right now. Whatever your Teri was up to, it had to be for your sake, buddy. She went to The Fountain for rejuvenation, kiddo. The Fountain's full title was The Fountain Rejuvenation Clinic."

"Goddamn it, I was right. I was right." In his excitement Mike knocked the tumbler of beer into his lap. "Oh, shit!" He ineffectually tried to dry off his pants, then forgot about it. Burt was laughing hysterically. Soon so was he. As Burt ordered more beer, Mike forced himself to calm down. There was only one way. He told Burt as much as he knew about Teri's death.

"So, it's not the mother, it's the daughter you're after, an orphan in the storm. You never change, comrade. Okay, for the orphan's sake, here are some facts. The Fountain Rejuvenation Clinic seemed to be a pretty prosperous outfit, specializing in face treatments, not lifts, but some kind of peel treatment that smoothed out the old bags, if you'll forgive the expression. My friends at the bank in the Valley were pretty pissed off when they shut down operations about a year, or a year and a half ago—maybe about six or seven months after your Teri wrote her last check to them. Seems they were on the verge of a big expansion and the bank was all for it. They were liquid, too damn liquid, never borrowing enough, and they were talking about a big loan to open more Fountains in other states."

"Who are 'they'?"

"The owner of record was a hotshot young real-estate lawyer here called Denny Upton. Who was really behind the setup I didn't have time to find out. In any case, I figured it's your problem, not mine. Seems there was something fishy about The Fountain, despite their lily-white, debt-free position. When I inquired as to why The Fountain shut off its faucet of youth, when it was spurting so much cash, my bank pal didn't know that much, but remembered the postal authorities had come along and charged them with false advertising by mail. Upton put in an appearance and there were a couple of patsies who were supposed to answer specific accusations—a director of the company called Magda something or other who could never be found . . ."

"Magda!" Mike just saved another tumbler from going over. "I can't believe it."

Burt threw his large head back and laughed again. "Neither can I. I've never seen you so thrown. It's turning into a whodunit. Where does Magda fit in your scenario?"

"I don't know. I thought she was just a pal, a model Teri knew. I agree with you it's fishy, very fishy. Jo found a note among her mom's things—a note from a Magda confirming a date with Teri in the Polo Lounge on June fourth, telling her to turn up in dark glasses and a large hat. She never made it, of course. She was killed June third, but why Magda asked her to come in disguise . . ."

Burt interrupted. "It wasn't a disguise."

Mike looked blankly at his friend. "I don't get it. Why the dark glasses, the large hat?"

"Simply one old bag telling another old bag how to appear in public after a face peel. I gather it's not a very pretty sight until it calms down, when 'youth' is miraculously restored. I should say *if* it calms down . . ."

"How do you know so much?" Mike was furious that Burt's explanation of the note made so much sense. Why hadn't he thought of that himself?

"I don't, sonny boy. I just add two and two together and come up with a so-called rejuvenation business that was turning over several hundred thousand dollars a year in nice tidy profits, until clever old Uncle Sam caught up with their 'promises, promises,' which presumably they weren't always able to deliver."

Mike's palms dampened. Had The Fountain been able to deliver its promise to Teri before her tragic death? He had to go on for Jo's sake, but for a second he wished he had never started to track down Teri Shephard's last days.

"How long was The Fountain in business?"

"About three years. Why don't you sit down with Upton? He'll be able to tell you." Burt was beginning to look bored. "Look, I don't know much more, nor do I care to. They were fined but allowed to continue to operate as a beauty clinic, providing they stopped putting out their crazy ads. Somebody who actually worked at the place, who occasionally signed checks, took most of the blast in court." Burt plunged a large hand into the sagging pocket of his denim jacket and came out with a crumpled note. "I could remember seductive Magda's name. The other patsy, who did most of the testifying, and was apparently let off with a warning, was . . ." Burt scrutinized the scrap of paper. "Let's see—Ann Pershing of Culver City. Seems she was in charge of nurse admin, but pretty well ran the place, because this Magda was rarely there."

"That figures. Magda was also a model." Mike had the feeling he had lost Burt. He was now talking to himself. "Okay, but how about some action? Is The Daisy still swinging?" Burt's attention span righted itself.

"Let's go, boy."

The next morning the inside of Mike's mouth felt like a subway john. God, he'd tied one on all right with Burt the night before. It was always a mistake, but this week it was a serious mistake.

He saw his clothes strewn from the front door to the side of his bed. A terrible-looking mess. He felt sorry for himself. He needed a woman to look after him. He needed his little girl Friday, Jo. It was ten-thirty. Room service stopped at ten and he had no energy to crawl downstairs for his greet-the-day first cup of coffee.

As he stared morosely at the ceiling, the facts he'd amassed about Teri Shephard filed neatly across his brain. He was getting somewhere, but did he want to get there? He was filled with a sense of something ominous, something he didn't want to find out because he didn't want Jo to find out. Well, there was nothing for it. She had to know eventually. Perhaps it was better if they came to the conclusion together. He knew his Jo. She wouldn't forgive him if he didn't ask her to join him as he neared the end of the trail.

It was Wednesday. This was a transition week for Jo anyway. She would be tidying up what he'd left behind, getting ready for the new guru, her new boss who wasn't moving to the paper for another few days.

Mike realized now he needed Jo with him. He didn't want to face receiving any more bad news alone. It would be better for Jo to discover the truth at the same time he did.

Several phone calls later, fortified by an hour in a Turkish bath and several cups of coffee in a nearby coffee shop, Mike called Jo at the paper in San Diego.

Quickly he told her all he had learned. There were no squeals of shock, no gasps or sighs. Jo was, as she always was at her desk, cool and calm.

"Denny Upton is away for a week on the East Coast, but I left all my numbers with his secretary, who seems pretty efficient. The luckiest break came from the state's register of nurses. I found out where Ann Pershing lives. She doesn't seem to be working right now. I'm going to pay her a short visit tomorrow. Would you like to come with me?"

He heard Jo sigh. It was a sigh, Mike knew, of gratitude and relief.

"I'll be at your hotel in the morning, boss. Please don't change your mind about my coming."

She was well read on the subject of aging, particularly female aging. She could and did quote De Beauvoir and Sontag. Did she believe one word of what she read and said? No.

Ann Pershing tweezed out a gray hair and stared morosely into the mirror, which still bore an ugly crack from the jar of Fountain Replenishing Cream she'd thrown at it several months before. It was early, only ten to eleven, but she needed a drink. These days she often needed an early drink to face the day and several late night drinks to find fast oblivion in sleep. She was getting compulsive about it, compulsive . . . impulsive . . . two character defects she had been warned about since high school.

Today it was imperative to keep both defects under firm control. Even though she was as clean as a sterilized mask and had nothing to be ashamed of, dealing with the media, off the record for humanitarian purposes, just as much as on, was tricky. She was going to need all her cylinders working.

Ann bit her lip to keep from groaning out loud. Being in love and being rejected, humiliated, was as painful as pleurisy. Every so often, like every ten minutes, she would think of something else he'd said, some oddball compliment like the one about her high-class cylinders that could outspeed anyone's, a compliment she would never hear again because he'd moved on and up and out of her life completely, reaching a plateau where, he'd told her clearly and cruelly, she didn't and could never belong.

Compulsive . . . impulsive . . . that had been one of his regular criticisms, too. Well, now he would pay. She would talk and talk. She poured one measure of vodka into a small glass. Just one little drink to steady her nerves, so she could decide exactly how much she would tell this smartass TV journalist and how much she would keep to herself.

As she sipped the drink slowly—as if it were red hot—she decided she had to be careful. Much as she longed to tear the bitch's reputation into rags and send her like some rotten cargo back to the foreign ghetto she came from, did she want to bring him tumbling down, too?

She knew she didn't. Hell, she still loved him desperately, but it wasn't only that. She looked around her small but well-furnished apartment. She was still on the payroll and if she played her cards right, she not only would continue to be, but she could insist on a good fat raise.

Also she realized she still nurtured some hope that he might change his mind and decide she could be of some use after all, could play a part in the new business, which from the beginning had zoomed in the most fantastic way.

As she drained the last drop of vodka, she looked tearfully

at the lily on her sideboard, bent over with its own weight almost down to the glass top, but still blooming. Her hope was as fragile as the lily. Without support soon she would snap, just as the lily was going to snap.

With her second glass of vodka, Ann began to feel more optimistic. She knew too much to be thrown onto the dust heap. If she hadn't just read an article about the company, in, of all things, a Palm Springs glossy magazine, she would never have agreed to see this Mike Tanner.

His call had come minutes after she'd ripped the magazine in two and had been pacing around the apartment like a crazed creature at the injustice of life.

His call had thrown her off guard. She'd been arguing with herself ever since as to whether she should disappear for a couple of days, but what was the use?

The news ferrets always found you in the end and, as she'd been emphasizing to herself over and over again, she was in the clear.

She had spoken up like a nice, well-trained, well-educated nurse at the hearing and helped The Fountain get out of what could have been a hell of a mess. It was Bax's decision that they close down a few months later. They hadn't been told to close. They could still have operated as a beauty clinic, providing they didn't use those crazy medical ads anymore, but obviously Bax had already made other plans, big plans, far bigger than the chain of Fountain clinics on the drawing board.

It was incredible that she should have sprayed some lily-of-the-valley room freshener around when her doorbell rang from downstairs. Incredible because for a moment the scent made her think of the pretty model Teri Shephard who'd told her how much she loved the smell of lily-of-the-valley. Minutes later Mike Tanner came up with his girl Friday who turned out to be, of all people, Teri's daughter Jo.

She was furious. Tanner hadn't breathed a word about bringing anyone with him. He hadn't mentioned Teri Shephard. He'd just said on the phone he wanted to ask her a few questions about The Fountain and other places like it—and all the time he'd only wanted to know about Teri.

She'd meant to be gracious, but she was so angry she was anything but. Careful, careful, Ann, she told herself, even as she was blurting out, "I think this is an imposition. You didn't say you were bringing anyone with you. What's this all about anyway? You said you wanted to ask me about The Fountain and other beauty clinics. You're here under false pretenses. I think it's . . . it's outrageous."

He had to be a soothing sort of guy, because before long, she had calmed down enough to ask them to sit down, but she could feel a nerve in her temple beating away.

She took a deep breath and looked longingly at the cupboard where the vodka was stored.

"Ms. Pershing, I'm sorry, really I am, but I think you'll forgive us when I explain."

Ann Pershing felt a lump in her throat when she saw the young girl, a cute little thing, blush all the way from the neck up.

Her mind whirled with conflicting thoughts as Jo stumbled. ". . . You see, Mom told me lots about her life, but that summer—I was going to summer camp and my sister to stay with friends—she just said she was going on a modeling assignment in Mexico. The next we knew . . ." A tear zigzagged down Jo's cheek. ". . . Dad came to collect us to tell us she'd been killed in a crash . . . and then . . ." Mike patted Jo's back to encourage her to go on, ". . . it came out that nobody knew what Mom was doing in Mexico. She hadn't been on a modeling job at all. Then I found out she'd been to The Fountain. Oh, Nurse Pershing, really all I want to know is where Mom was going. Can't you understand that? Everyone knows she had an accident, but everything surrounding it is so mysterious. Was . . . was my mom at The Fountain for that . . . that youth treatment?"

This was terrible. It was worse than she'd ever imagined, sitting face to face with this nice, freckle-faced kid with the huge eyes, an innocent, not there with her media boss to trap her, but just to find out what her mom had been up to . . . of that Ann was sure.

She couldn't look at her anymore. She looked instead at the lily, which now was hanging just by a thread of its stem before it broke right off.

"Ms. Pershing, we don't want you to tell us anything that invades patient-doctor confidentiality, but as you can tell, the mystery surrounding Jo's mother's death has distressed her to the point it's affecting her work, her future. She just wants to know what happened at The Fountain and where her mother was heading." Mike paused, then said casually, looking straight at her, "We know she had a date with Magda, one of your co-directors at The Fountain on June fourth, the day after she was killed, but she was heading in the opposite direction and nobody seems to know why."

Ann slumped back in the armchair, eyes closed, trying to blot out the memory of Teri's face that terrible day the tape came off. Perhaps it was the memory, perhaps it was the sight of Teri's daughter's sweet trusting face searching hers, but suddenly Ann felt she had to tell the truth.

She leaned forward, a feeling surging through her that she hadn't felt in ages—a feeling she'd once always had, of wanting to be the best kind of nurse, caring for those who put their trust in her so completely, working hard to give the best she had in her. Was there still something decent left to give? Oh God, she hoped so.

Ann took Jo's hands in hers. "Your mother was beautiful, but, well, like so many in her profession, the going was getting tough. She wanted to look younger . . ."

Jo didn't answer, just held onto the nurse's hands as if she wouldn't let them go until she knew everything. Ann heard her own voice as if it were somebody else talking, a flat monotone, stating facts without emotion.

"The Fountain started out all right. There were face treatments, programs to help skin, stop smoking . . ." She hesitated.

Mike prompted her. "There were special face-peeling treatments, weren't there? I read about the false-advertising-by-mail case. We don't need to go into that. Did Teri come to The Fountain for the youth face peel?"

Ann nodded, her throat muscles tightening. She desperately wanted another drink. "Yes, she came . . ." She pulled her hands away from the young girl.

"Did Magda carry out the peel?"

"God, no. That phony . . ." Impulsive . . . compulsive . . . the words rang in her brain. She put her hand over her mouth as if to stop herself talking. Her hand was trembling. Why was she talking to these people? What was she getting into.

The lily fell with a plop onto the sideboard. It was an

omen. Ann tried to force down a sudden attack of fear, as Jo pleaded "Please, please, Nurse Pershing, just tell me what happened to my mother."

"It didn't work." The words were wrenched out. She wasn't going to tell them why . . . she wasn't going to break their hearts as hers had been broken with the greed of it all, the laxity, the experiments with that deadly phenol that could skin a three-thousand-year-old sun-baked rock.

"What do you mean?" Jo cried. "What do you mean?"

The phone rang twice, then stopped as Ann went to pick it up. She had to get rid of them, had to end what could only be a destroying conversation for her, for them. As calmly as she could she tried to let the daughter down lightly.

"The peel was not an entire success. Your mother . . ." she gulped, remembering again, against her will, the horrifying sight of Teri's face. She stiffened. Why should she let the phony Slav off the hook? "I didn't know at the time the doctor was not qualified to carry out the treatment . . . the chemosurgery . . . the acid peel was applied too strongly . . . your mother's skin was damaged."

"No!" Jo screamed. "No . . ." she screamed again. "Was she disfigured?"

The nurse in her came to life. She put her arm around the kid's shoulders. "It could have been put right. There was a certain amount of disfigurement, but it could have been put right. There had been other cases."

She was lying. It had never happened like that before. They'd all said, all the scheming lot of them, that something could be done, but she had never believed them. She felt Mike Tanner's eyes accusing her. She rushed on. "I was off for a couple of days after your mother's peel. When I came back to the clinic she'd left. Then somebody told me it was in the papers—her car had gone over the cliff. It was terrible. A terrible way to die . . ."

"Suicide . . ." The kid was crying. "Mom must have committed suicide. Oh, I can't believe this. It's so much worse . . . oh, oh . . ." She was crying as if she would never stop. Even the young media guy didn't seem to know what to do.

He stood up and almost barked at her, "Where is this Magda?"

She had just decided to tell him and rat on the whole crummy bunch when the phone rang again. This time it didn't stop. She went into the bedroom, somehow knowing it was him. It had to be him and it was.

"Ann . . ." There was that old electric note in his voice, one she hadn't heard for a long time. She could feel her pants getting moist as he spoke swiftly, urgently. "There's a young TV guy around asking questions about The Fountain . . ."

"He's here."

"What!"

She was triumphant, hearing for the first time the shock in his voice, shock from a man who was always so totally in control, but it was gone in a second.

"Ann, I need to see you, but I can't leave right now. I've got a better idea. You come to me. There's a lot going on that can concern you. I know I can trust you. Don't jeopardize us. Don't jeopardize your future." He paused, then added softly, " . . . with me. Tell him nothing. Get rid of him. I'll call you back in an hour with all the arrangements, and when we meet . . ." He paused again and lowered his voice still more, "I'll give you what you like so much. Come dressed for the occasion, Kajira."

He had said it again, the one word he'd whispered in her hair, in her ear, when he'd introduced her to the kind of love-making she hadn't known could exist anywhere outside a harem.

She was a different person when she went back into the sitting room and they were different, too.

Jo was composed, wiping away her tears. Mike was tense, alert.

Before she could speak, he was at her like a damned district attorney. "What was Magda's role in all this . . . and Svetlana, who is she?"

But she was on cloud nine, eyes shining, body already throbbing with anticipation. Nobody could worry her now. Like a young girl she bubbled the words out. ". . . I haven't any more time to talk to you. I'm sorry I had to tell you such terrible things, but . . . but . . ." She normally would never have said such a thing, but she was in a hurry to get rid of them and she didn't think. "Perhaps it was all for the best. Your mom could never have worked again. I'm sorry, I can't tell you any more . . ." Once more she repeated lamely, "Perhaps it was all for the best."

"Can I come back?"

Teri's daughter looked so pathetic, Ann lied once more. "Of course you can. Call me about six tonight. I'll try to answer anything you want to ask me then, but there's not much more I can tell you."

At six, at six-thirty, and then every half hour after that, until midnight, Jo called Ann Pershing's number, but there was no reply. At seven the next morning she caught a cab with Mike to go back to the nurse's apartment. There was no response to the doorbell and when they rang the superintendent's bell—as by now they expected—he told them irritably she'd gone away for a couple of weeks and if she thought he was going to act as her answering service, she'd made a big mistake.

"Do you know where she's gone?" Mike knew the question was futile even as the super answered, "Who knows, who cares?"

Mike looked at Jo, defeated, pale, shrinking back into the corner of the cab returning to the hotel. She was supposed to catch the 9:30 A.M. commuter back to San Diego, but Mike knew he wasn't going to let her go.

He pulled her roughly into his arms, smothered her face with kisses.

"Mike . . ." There was bewilderment, then the sweetest look he'd ever seen on a girl's face. It said it all. "Is this really happening to me? Can I really be this lucky?"

It was terrifying the way this surge of longing, of loving, of wanting to protect every inch of her, swept over him. He had heard about it happening, but he'd never believed it could happen to him. He didn't know what it meant. He had no intention of being serious with anyone, least of all Jo, little, freckle-faced Jo—but he didn't want to return to being her big, brotherly friend either.

"Mike . . ."

"Don't say anything." He ran his fingers over her lips, traced the curve of her soft cheeks, her ears, felt the soft tendrils at the nape of her neck. She was returning his kisses, her mouth hungry for his. He could feel his body, her body getting hot. He touched her breasts, her big, beautiful, firm breasts. The nipples stiffened.

Neither of them said a word as he paid the taxi off and led her to his room, the untidy, rumpled room he had left only an hour before, the blinds still drawn, his clothes all over the floor.

The funny thing was now he felt shy, not awkward, but shy. They stood facing each other in the darkened room. She started to remove his glasses, but he stopped her. "Not yet, not now. I want to study you . . . savor you . . ." He laid her down gently on the bed. She looked up at him questioningly. He wondered why he'd never realized what delicate, long lashes she had.

"Oh, Mike, you're not just sorry for me, are you?" she whispered.

"Hush, hush, you silly baby." He wanted to be gentle with her, but it was difficult. His longing was growing. He started to unbutton her shirt, a button flying to the floor. Her breathing was getting fast, faster, like his. They were both racing to the same point. It was her warm blush that blacked out his caution, his resolve. He didn't wait to unhook her bra, fiercely pulling it down to her waist, crazy to suck her full, delicious breasts.

It was incredible, she was holding them up for him, her body moving to show she was yielding, she was ready. His hand slipped inside her skirt beneath her panties, his fingers on her belly moving down to find her hot, moist place.

"Wait . . . wait . . ." Jo cried excitedly. In seconds she had slipped out of her skirt and pulled her panties off, to reveal a tangled mound of black hair. She was wet; he knew it; could smell her wetness, her longing.

He sat astride her, opening the small mouth beneath the hair, looking at the pink folds of skin that came together like the most perfect virgin shell.

His tongue probed it open as Jo writhed, moaned, clutched him, trying to pull him up and into her. He was intoxicated by her, but he tried to retain control.

He rolled her over onto her belly, lying on her so his penis was hard against the soft crease of her behind.

"Am I the first, Jo?" He had to know.

Her reply was muffled in the pillow, but she half turned and cried fiercely, "Yes, yes, yes, you're the first, but don't worry. I've been on birth control . . ." He rammed his mouth on hers. There would be no more talk. His fingers caressed the soft flesh between her legs until he could stand it no longer. He turned her over. She was smiling up at him, her arms pulling him closer. As Mike slid into her, at first slowly, then more and more insistently, aggressively, she wrapped her legs tightly around his back, her whole being wide open for him. He couldn't believe her wild abandon as he thrust deeper, deeper, deeper. They were coming together, wildly, passionately. It was just unbelievable . . . little Jo . . .

It was unbelievable all right. All the way back to San Diego, all day at the office, all night unable to sleep, Jo went over again and again what had happened in Mike's hotel room.

She had never expected it would happen like that. She had always taken for granted that when she lost her virginity, she would be madly in love with a man in love with her; that "love" would have been uppermost in their minds, "love" leading to a relationship, to a togetherness, that she had supposed would end in marriage . . . yet "love" had never been mentioned.

Was she sorry? Ashamed? She didn't know how she felt. It had all happened so quickly. It had all been so unexpected. She was only sure about one thing. She longed for it all to happen again and again and again. She tried to remember minute by minute every touch of his hands, his lips.

At first, Mike said he would come back to San Diego with her, then he changed his mind. She could remember clearly the way his face had changed, tender, gentle one minute, angry, tense the next, his face so close, as they'd lain exhausted in the bed, that when he'd spoken his breath had been hot on her cheek. "I've got a few days left, baby. I want to find out more about those bastards. I want to try to find that bloody woman Magda and get through to the lawyer, Upton. I think it would make more sense if I stayed around here. Obviously Pershing was warned not to talk to us. Remember how different she was when she came back from that phone call? Perhaps it was Upton calling her—or someone who'd heard about my calls to Upton. Whoever it was, I'm pretty sure the call was warning her to keep her mouth shut. I've got to find out where she went."

Jo had felt so grateful for his anger, his determination to keep going after them, the terrible people who had ruined her mother's life. She'd felt so protected, too, lying in his arms, drifting in and out of the kind of sleep she'd never had before, a wonderful sleep that could surely only follow lovemaking, a sleep where you were always conscious of another's closeness, of your lover's breath all over you.

There was another part of it, too. She'd felt so overwhelmingly relieved, so sure that now the future was going to be all right, that Mike was going to take care of everything—and take care of her, too.

Forty-eight hours later she didn't feel like that anymore. He hadn't phoned, not once in forty-eight long hours. Even after twenty-four Jo had begun to wonder if she had been a disappointment in bed—whether she should have given herself to him so easily, so eagerly? Now, she wished he had come back with her, then hated herself for even thinking that. He was working for her, wasn't he? Trying to get to the bottom of the whole tragic mess.

She was so miserable by Friday she could hardly concentrate on anything. If she wasn't worrying about Mike, she was weeping inside for her mother. Had she committed suicide? The fact she had been killed in a car crash across the border was no longer so mysterious. Probably she hadn't cared where she was going . . . she'd just picked up a car in San Diego and driven through the night. Perhaps she hadn't intended to kill herself—but she hadn't cared about living either. But how had she traveled from The Fountain back to San Diego? Had she been so badly disfigured she was unrecognizable?

Mom had been so sensitive about even the slightest little zit, perhaps what Nurse Pershing had tried to tell her had been the truth—that the damage could have been rectified, but Mom wouldn't believe it?

Questions, questions—there were so many racing through her brain. They were questions that perhaps Nurse Pershing could have answered—questions that perhaps Mike could answer now—if only he would phone.

As she let herself into the house about six o'clock on Friday evening, the phone was ringing. It was Alexa. She had been longing to hear how Alexa was getting on in New York, but the disappointment that it wasn't Mike was so great she had trouble saying hello.

It didn't matter. Once again this was an Alexa so excited that there was no way she could be expected to hear anyone else's, not even Jo's, despondency.

"It's all happening, Sis. Everything I dreamed of. The people at *View* love me. I'm their newest star. Everyone wants to meet me. New York is heaven. There are places here open all night . . . the City literally never sleeps. It's just great. It's too great . . . that's why I'm calling you . . ."

As Alexa was talking, Jo was speaking to herself. Calm down. Don't be upset it's not Mike. Tell Alexa what you've just found out.

"Alexa." Her voice was so despairing. Alexa paused in her outpouring.

"Alexa, I've just found out the most terrible thing about Mom . . ."

"Mom?" Alexa sounded as if she had never heard the word before.

"Yes, Mom. Goddamn it . . . our mother . . . She probably killed herself intentionally—do you understand what I'm trying to tell you? I—Mike Tanner—we—he called me to come to Los Angeles. He found out Mom went to a place called The Fountain. Remember, I told you about the checks, about the letter from someone called Magda?"

"Yes, yes . . ." Alexa was obviously impatient. "I haven't got much time, Sis. They're waiting for me. What about The Fountain?"

Jo wanted to reach out across three thousand miles and strangle her self-centered sister. "This is what about The Fountain! Mom went there trying to get her looks back, trying to get rid of her wrinkles. I don't know exactly what happened, but they did a lousy job. Mike and I found a nurse who'd run the place with this Magda . . . she told us . . ." Jo was sobbing now, not altogether sure it was because of what she was saying. There was a lot of missing Mike in the sobs, too. "Mom had a face peel—a lousy, terrible face peel, there. It went wrong. It sounds like she was disfigured . . ."

"Jo, you don't *know* this. Just because a nurse told you. How do you know that for sure? Why are you upsetting yourself like this? Why are you turning up all this stuff? What good is it?"

Alexa's apparent indifference blew the sobs right out of her. "How can you be so callous? You sound just like Dad. Don't you care that some lousy people took Mom's money and scarred her for life? Don't you care she thought she was ruined?

That she took a car and drove herself over a cliff . . . ?" She was screaming.

There was a click. Jo stared at the receiver in disbelief. Her own sister had hung up on her. Then the phone rang again.

"Jo, darling, Jo please . . ." It was Alexa. "I had to do that to make you calm down. Please don't say anything more till we meet. Listen to me, I do care, but you could be wrong, too. Listen to what I have to say. I want you to come to New York—to live with me, help me, chaperone me, be my big sister like you've always been. I need you—love you—my life's so crazy, I need a manager. Honest I do . . ."

"Oh, Alexa, I need you, too, but don't you see, I've got to find out—got to get revenge . . . Oh, I don't know what I want . . . anyway, you don't really mean it, do you?"

"Of course, I do. I can pay you. I'm earning big money. I've got an agent—all the top models have to have an agent to look after money, all that kind of thing—but I need more than that. I need someone I can trust. Anyway . . ." Alexa stopped talking. Jo could hear her take a big breath across the miles. When she didn't say anything for another few seconds, Jo felt nervous.

"What, what is it? What now?"

There was another big breath. "I have to go now, Jo darling, but I really mean it. You must come to New York. I can't tell you much now except there's someone I want you to meet. Bye." Alexa had hung up again. This time Jo knew she would not call back.

"There's someone I want you to meet." There had been a different sound in Alexa's voice. It wasn't her usual '"famous movie producer/photographer/big-time money/big-time people" routine. There had been a note in Alexa's voice she had never heard before—or was it because before Mike she wouldn't have been able to recognize it? Was Alexa in love? Or was she able to hear a different note because now she was in love? Or was she?

Jo walked aimlessly around the house that she had once thought of as home. It wasn't anymore. It hadn't been for a long time.

"It's a place to hang my hat," she'd heard her father say recently over the phone, probably to Libby, although she wasn't even sure of that anymore.

Since the night, weeks before, when he'd returned from

his golfing trip to La Costa and taken away The Fountain check and the letter from Magda, she'd deliberately distanced herself from him. It hadn't been difficult. He hadn't made any overtures to mend fences, but then there hadn't been many opportunities.

He was always in a rush to be somewhere, go somewhere. He hadn't been home when she'd returned from L.A. Looking back, she couldn't remember the last two or three consecutive nights he'd spent in the house. They were both using it as a place to hang their hats.

She had no affection for the place anyway. There were too many reminders of Mom and now she knew what had happened to her in her last days, Jo knew, it would be impossible for her to stay there much longer. It would drive her crazy.

Should she go to New York? There wouldn't have been any decision to make, but for Mike. She would have gone on the next available plane, if only to see what Alexa was up to, to meet whoever it was she wanted her to meet.

Jo sighed. Most of all she longed to get into Alexa's head what had happened to Mom and try to instill in her the same burning anger to get even, to track down the perpetrators, to make sure they never had the chance to ruin anyone else's life. If possible to get them behind bars.

Jo couldn't sleep. She got up at 2 A.M., then 3 A.M. to pace around the house, tormented by her thoughts. She finally collapsed on the sofa around five-thirty, dreaming she was on an operating table surrounded by masked figures. Far away in the distance she could hear a bell ringing, an emergency bell sounding an alarm, alerting someone—was it Mike?—that she was in terrible trouble.

Groggily she came out of sleep to realize it was the phone ringing again and again and again. Thinking she was in her bed, she groped her way to where her bedroom door should be, crashed into the coffee table, and knocked over a chair. The collision opened her eyes. "Hello?"

"Jo, baby. Thank God, you're there. Are you alone?"

"Oh, Mike . . ." She was in love all right. The sound of his voice went through her system like an adrenaline injection. "Oh, Mike, yes, yes, yes . . ."

"Can I come over? There's something I want to tell you that just came over the wire. I know it's early, but . . ."

She was now as awake as if she'd had an ice-cold shower.

"Oh, come quickly. I've been so worried about you. When did you get back?" She stopped short. No recriminations. No questions. There had to be no recriminations or questions *ever*. That was the way her parents' fights had always started.

"I got home last night. I'm on my way, baby."

It was eight-fifteen. The house was a mess and so was she, but her lover was on his way. Thank God it was Saturday and she didn't have to go to work. On the way to the shower she caught sight of her face. It was flushed, her eyes dilated as if she were on something. She was throbbing just at the thought of Mike, at the thought that the reality of him was only minutes away.

There was a robe Alexa had left behind that Jo had always liked. On her it took on an entirely different personality. It was baggy and short on Alexa. It was slinky and ankle-length on Jo, rounding out her rump, not quite closing over her breasts.

It was a corny phrase, but it was in her mind as the doorbell rang. "Time stood still." There couldn't have been any time at all between opening the door and going straight into his arms. There was a faint smell of spice about him, an aftershave she'd never noticed before and she knew she smelled of roses, from the shower gel and toilet water she'd sprayed all over. She wanted him, oh, she wanted him so much, to feel his probing, his penetration.

It was so natural to touch him, to reassure herself that he was growing for her, hard, harder, big, bigger.

Even as she felt him, she knew he was trying to resist, trying to back away, but she wouldn't let it happen, wouldn't allow it.

They were on the floor, on the carpet in the hallway, the robe open all the way, to show him her body had been waiting for him.

"No, Jo, no . . ." he was saying. She took no notice, pushing away fears, ignoring the fact he obviously hadn't been driven by the same unrelenting passion to see her that she'd had to see him, the passion that had driven her mad for the past few days.

He kept saying "no,"even as she kissed his neck, opening his trousers to find it, guide it. She had to make him find her as irresistible as he was to her. Yes, yes, it was so. Now, he was ramming her legs wide apart, sucking her breasts, heaving himself into her so roughly the edge of the hall rug cut through the cotton of the robe like a knife against her thighs. She didn't feel the pain. Her body was crying out, singing with his as he took her there in the hallway.

Afterward, there was a difference. The first time in the Los Angeles hotel had been followed by such tenderness, such caring, it had been easy to delude herself into believing there could be a "happy ever after."

It was different this time. There was tenderness, but there was guilt, too. She'd been around too much guilt with her father and mother not to recognize it immediately. Had Mike been making love to another woman in the last three days? Could it really be possible? She would never know, because she would never ask him.

They sat awkwardly in the sitting room, she pulling the robe around her as if she were sitting with a stranger. He tried to be relaxed, but she could see it was an effort. She was numb, brain and body, as if the last frenzied minutes had been the kind of operation she'd been dreaming she was about to have.

"Jo, I'm sorry . . ." Mike looked down at his hands.

"Don't be." She didn't know for sure what he was sorry about, but she could guess. There was nothing she could do about it except pretend she didn't care. "What did you want to tell me so urgently?"

It was the best question, the only question. At once he became like the old Mike, the one she'd known and trusted before she'd made the mistake of falling in love.

"Burt Stokler, he's my old roommate—I think I told you he helped me open up the leads to the lawyer Denny Upton and then to Ann Pershing."

Jo leaned back against the sofa for support. The nightmare was back and this time it was worse. Mike didn't love her. He was her friend, but it wasn't enough anymore.

"There was a message from Burt on my answering service when I got back last night. I wrote it down . . ." Mike took a notepad out of his jacket. "Burt dictated a report to me—of a story that's in today's L.A. *Times* from one of the wire services." Mike hunched forward, with an expression she knew well from watching him at work in the newsroom—it was so intent he looked angry. "A body was found stabbed today in the twenty-first stairwell of the luxurious East River Hotel in

New York City. The victim, 38-year-old Ann Pershing, a registered nurse, resident of Culver City, California, was staying in the hotel . . ."

The numbness went. "Oh, my God." Jo leaned forward, forgetting to clutch the robe, as intent and as angry looking as Mike.

He read on, "She was found less than three hours after she checked in. She died of a single puncture wound on the right side of her neck, which cut the jugular and vertebral artery, causing a severe hemorrhage. The killer's motive is obscure. The slaying, the first in memory at the celebrated hotel overlooking the East River, has stunned the management . . ."

Mike was speaking, but Jo wasn't listening. New York. Ann Pershing had gone to New York and she had been murdered there.

She looked at Mike. Her voice quavered. "Murdered—she was murdered because she knew too much, isn't that so, Mike? It has to be."

"Yes." He was grim. "You were right from the beginning, Jo. Now I've really got to get down to business."

She went over to the window and looked outside at the familiar garden furniture her mother had bought. "They're in New York, the people who caused my mother's death are in New York."

There was no answer from Mike, but she wouldn't have heard one anyway, because she was too consumed with her thoughts.

Alexa's phone call had come at the right time. In a few hours she would be on her way to join her.

CHAPTER SIX

Ralph Lauren has a Hawker Siddeley jet. Estimated cost, six and a half million dollars. Add another two fifty thousand for a redesigned "loftier" interior ordered by Ralph (as you know, five-foot-six in his high-heeled boots), who found the cabin cramped his style. Perry Ellis owns a Cessna seaplane to get to his pad on Fire Island. Calvin Klein is into chartering Lear jets the way most folk grab an Avis. There is enough stuff here for a piece on American designers flying high. Their income is staggering. Can we meet to talk about it for June or July?

BLAIR BENSON CHECKED THE MEMO FROM THE FEATURES DEPARTment with a red marker pen and tossed it on top of a couple of manuscripts in the tray marked APPROVED.

She had been right to hire Arthur Reddish away from the competition. His memo hardly conveyed the tough investigative reporting that would go into the story. If there were any clouds on the rich designers' horizons, clouds that could bring them back to earth with a bump, "Radish," as Reddish was invariably called, would certainly find them. He was a one-man fact-finding missionary and as creator of the magazine's tremendously successful "I Reveal" pieces, it was worth putting up with his irascible temper. With a name like Reddish, Blair reflected, a permanently red complexion, and his unexpected, hot flashes of temper, he must have been saddled with his "radish" nickname since childhood.

Snowflakes drifted past the windows of her eighteenth-floor corner office. Blair frowned. If they increased, she would have to close the office early to allow the commuters some way to get home by nightfall. She sighed. It was a vicious circle. She wasn't about to pay above the going glossy-magazine rate for junior editors and assistants, which meant fewer and fewer of the toilers could afford to live in Manhattan.

It wasn't like the good old days when Diana Vreeland had been known to turn down requests for raises with the stock answer, "Why don't you ask Daddy to increase your allowance?" Few ink-stained wretches had private incomes these days, with "Daddies" more and more pressured to pay their own bills, . . . unless they were successful fashion designers, she thought wryly.

The pale-gray private phone behind her rang simultaneously with her intercom beep. Without putting the receiver to her ear, she said "One moment" into the mouthpiece. Her hand shook slightly as she pressed down the hold button, then clicked on the intercom switch.

"The run-through's ready to roll, boss." As usual, Penelope Waverly was punctual to the second.

Blair didn't mean to sound bad tempered, but she couldn't help herself. "Did you Polaroid Shapwell's ankles? I'm not sending thick ankles to Hawaii, however much you're in love with the rest of her. Something about her ankles bothers me."

"Remember, we changed her name to Wells, not Shapwell. Alexa is showing more and more 'attitude' these days, but her ankles are di-vine." Nothing seemed to faze Penelope. "Can we start, Blair? I don't want the gals to start muttering about getting caught in a snowdrift . . ."

"Give me ten minutes." Blair looked at the dark-red ormolu clock that exactly matched her dark-red lacquered desk. "Bring in the bodies at two-ten."

She leaned back to pick up the gray phone. She told herself it wasn't her mind that was answering the call, it was her body.

Her primitive, eager body, he called it, that was "all animal instinct, which needs constant taming." As if he had ordered her to feel them, she could feel the slight welts beneath her beautifully cut gray flannel pants that Valentino had told her she had to have. She was alive to the soreness of sucked and pulled nipples beneath the matching gray velour sweater. It was as if she were again in his bedroom, naked, with the dildo he had shafted into her behind, the dildo he had forced her to live with for an hour on Saturday afternoon, and, worse, again later, when dressed, she had acted as "hostess" to a group of his Middle Eastern business colleagues. She had been a hostess who could never sit down, who never spoke. She had smoked with them and served them drinks and canapés, moving slowly, oh so slowly around the two-story Fifth Avenue sitting room in the white grosgrain dress with the balloon skirt he had bought her for "good behavior"—the dress that had been the bridal finale of a recent new collection.

As usual, he spoke to her like a stranger, a courteous but all-business stranger, telling her when their next meeting would take place, as if he were giving her the doctor's appointment she had been waiting for. In a way he was. For almost a year now, she had known her health depended on him, mental and physical. Looking back—when she dared to look back—she couldn't understand how it had happened, but she accepted, helplessly, hopelessly, the fact he had taken over her life.

In less than three or four minutes, their conversation was over. It ended as it always did with an abrupt command, one that was totally out of keeping with her professional position, one to remind her who she really was. Also as usual his voice flooded her with energy, the energy she was famous for, that even got written about in *Women's Wear Daily*. She was addicted to him. Even his voice was enough of a shot to send her racing ahead with her huge workload of responsibilities—after she had followed his curt command.

She dipped the bronze letter opener he had given her into the flask of iced water she always kept on her desk. She stood up, unzipped her pants, and slid the ice-cold blade carefully beneath her flannel long johns, shivering as the metal passed over her flat belly and pubic hair. She opened her legs to allow the blade to slip between the folds of her vagina, the icy shock contracting the folds of hot wet skin, stirring her, making her giddy with desire for him, for the dildo, for anything thick and forceful, the way he had taught her, no, commanded her to be stirred. She could feel her sex oozing out as her vagina tried to suck against the metal.

"Stay wet," had been his last words. She moaned softly as her body throbbed for more masturbation, but obedient to everything he had said, she wiped the letter opener with a tissue and returned it to its leather case, zipped up her pants, and sat down to buzz Penelope's office.

"Okay, Pen, what's holding you up?" she asked coldly. "Let the show hit the road."

Was it any wonder that Alexa had changed so much? The alarm clock was chirping away like some psychotic bird, but Jo had already been awake for hours, tossing, turning, trying to pinpoint what it was that made her now feel so awkward, so inhibited whenever she was alone with Alexa. Not that they were together that much, with or without people. Since her arrival in New York three months before, Jo had continually been trying to keep up with Alexa and not often making it.

If she had ever thought Alexa was irresponsible, there was a worse word for it now. Alexa had become totally unreliable. She wasn't just late. Sometimes she didn't turn up at all. If she told Jo she would be in one studio, often she would be in another. She didn't only break dates, she disappeared for twenty-four/forty-eight hours, without apologies, usually with a casual, indifferent excuse: ". . . shooting . . . filming . . . photographers are impossible animals. Pen Waverly sent me somewhere else . . . Blair took me to meet some people."

Alexa was in a unique position. Jo realized that now. *View* had made her a star overnight. Penelope Waverly had made it her personal responsibility to "produce her"—changing her name to Alexa Wells—"Shapwell will *never* do"—making sure she wore only clothes that emphasized everything "positive" about her looks . . . teaching her to make up in a certain way . . . to wear her hair in one of three ways . . . to go to all the right "people-watching places" at "exactly the right time . . . never before 9:30 P.M. at Elaine's and on Sunday nights—just after Woody Allen gets to his regular back table" and ". . . to Mortimer's any night of the week and lunch on the weekend" and ". . . to Le Cirque for lunch but not for dinner . . ." Alexa had laughed as she told Jo, "Pen's banned me from model hangouts, Oren and Aretsky, McMullen's—at least for now."

Alexa had also told Jo the first day she arrived that the one word this extraordinary talent spotter disliked was "potential."

"She pretends to watch for it, develop it, but when Pen puts her seal of approval on a 'gal,' she already has to be so good, her 'potential' has been reached!" After forty-eight hours in New York, Jo had begun to loathe the sound of Penelope's name.

Even before Alexa's first cover appeared, Jo learned, model agencies had been frantically wooing her with bait of extraordinary personal services—chauffeured limousines, valets, and —something Alexa told Jo she'd soon learned was a really big attraction—"delicious gourmet dinners, delivered at any time, day or night. Believe me, after two or three days in the studio, when your knees are buckling from exhaustion so you can't even boil water, that's a big plus."

Alexa had confided early on, "When I called you, I wasn't thinking straight. I thought we could handle everything between us—with a good accountant that *View* said they would provide, so I could invest in the right T bills, CDs and everything like that . . ." Jo had been amazed at how effortlessly, casually Alexa already regarded the huge amounts of money she was earning. She hadn't given her an exact figure, but working it out herself, Jo knew it couldn't be less than two hundred thousand dollars a year—and Mom had thought she was making big time money with one hundred dollars an hour!

Jo had quickly caught on that by surrounding Alexa with their own chosen people, *View* was ensuring there was no risk of losing her to the competition. Alexa hadn't needed her to tell her so either. She was already champing at the bit.

For the last two months, Jo had been taking bookkeeping courses between trying to keep track of Alexa's appointments, plus interviewing the biggest model agencies in the country. She had tried to resurrect Alexa's wry sense of humor, pointing out how ironic it was that she, Jo Shapwell, was interviewing the biggest and the best on her sister's behalf, instead of the other way around. "D'you know how tough it is for a girl to get signed up with Ford or Elite or any of the big agencies? And here they are, fighting with each other to get a piece of you. Isn't it a blast!"

There hadn't even been the suggestion of a smile from

Alexa. "Just remember, Jo, any agency we choose is there to run my business, not my life. Other models have told me their agencies practically tell them when to go to the bathroom. Cal Robinson tried that on me in San Francisco . . . telling me what to eat, what not to drink. I don't need it. I don't want it. I won't have it. I'm not going to be influenced by *View* on this either. I want your gut reaction, not theirs. One of these days, Cal Robinson, or someone like him, will find them another cover girl, then where will I be? I don't want to work so hard either. I want to be able to book myself out for a day, a week, a month if I want to."She had spoken in a tough, sharp way but then, out of the blue, she'd winked. Her tone had softened. "That is, when I have my first million bucks in the bank . . ."

As Jo stretched out, trying to will her body to make the move out of bed, she wondered if Alexa had returned the night before. She'd waited up for her until, at one o'clock, she couldn't keep her eyes open a second longer. It was as if Alexa had totally forgotten all the things she'd said over the phone about need and love, calling for her help, the call that had motivated her fast move to the East Coast.

Jo gritted her teeth. If Alexa had forgotten, she certainly hadn't—and wasn't about to either.

All right, so she had had an ulterior motive in moving to New York—two ulterior motives. She had wanted to be in New York when the police found out who murdered the nurse Ann Pershing. So far they didn't seem to have a clue. Much more important, she had to admit to herself, she'd wanted to move as far away from Mike as possible, so she would never again be in danger of believing he really cared about her, so she would never again have to risk the chance she might throw herself at him—literally. Every time she thought about the early morning scene at home in San Diego, she blushed with shame and humiliation.

She was still pining, but whenever her thoughts drifted back to the skinny young hotshot reporter, who had only called three or four times since her arrival, she deliberately clamped down on herself and tried to concentrate on Alexa. She told herself every day how relieved she was that she had come; she just hoped she was in time to keep Alexa from losing all sense of values.

Time was her enemy. Whenever she checked on the time,

she would find herself subtracting three hours. If it was six-forty-five in New York, it was only three-forty-five on the West Coast and Mike, she hoped, was fast asleep, alone in his bed. Oh, Mike, if only you felt as I do. Would she ever get over him? *Clamp*. There she went again. Alexa, she told herself fiercely, keep your mind on Alexa.

What was behind the ultracareful way Alexa now chose her words? What was it that made her speak, move like a robot? She was hiding something.

Alexa had always liked to be phlegmatic, cultivating a cool, unemotional exterior, but she, Jo, her big sister, had always been able to plumb the enigmatic depths that Alexa liked to swim in. Now, Jo found she couldn't—something was different.

She pressed the switch beside her bed that operated heavy peach-colored drapes. They moved soundlessly apart to show that not only had the snow stopped, but it appeared to be a brilliant sunny day. If she didn't know she was in New York, crazy city that it was with such seesawing weather, she might have thought it was as warm outside as in Southern California.

In the hermetically sealed eleventh-floor apartment that was Alexa's temporary home—"a gift from *View*"—on the corner of East 57th and Sutton Place South, the only way to know what to put on in the morning was to dial "weather" and that meant calling information, because New York City didn't believe in easily memorized numbers for imparting such simple facts of life.

Jo squinted in the sunlight flooding the corner desk as she turned the pages of the appointment book. "Acting class 11:30 A.M. . . . voice lesson . . . 2 P.M.—Hiro Studio . . . 6:30 P.M. B.F." There was that reference to B.F. again.

When Jo had asked Alexa what it stood for, Alexa had played dumb in the worst way. "Bloody Fool, that's what it means, Sis. I'm a bloody fool. This is a crazy city to live in. Why don't you go back to sunny California?" She had said it affectionately, sweetly, but it had reinforced the awkwardness between them.

The worst thing was Alexa's apparent indifference to what had happened to their mother. It stuck in Jo's throat like a lump, building in size every time she attempted to talk about it, when Alexa either looked over her shoulder with a bored look or changed the subject, even when she was in midsentence. Okay, so Alexa was tired. Jo knew most days Alexa worked the kind of grueling hours shop assistants worked—on her feet for hours and hours and worse, like a store dummy, going through endless hair, makeup, and clothes changes.

As she headed for the kitchen, she heard Alexa's shower gushing. So she had come home last night. There were many nights when she didn't, and there was nothing Jo could do about it, although she always tried.

As she put on the coffeepot, she saw a bundle of mail on the kitchen table with a FROM VIEW BY MESSENGER label on it. Fan mail—it had to be fan mail, which, along with the flowers, the boxes of free makeup and perfume that arrived in a steady flow every week was the only thing that put back the old smile on Alexa's beautiful face.

As she turned on the waffle machine and heated up syrup, Alexa appeared in the doorway staring at her.

"What's that look for?"

Alexa slumped down moodily at the table, flicking the elastic band that surrounded the letters. "I've got a big decision to make, Jo."

Jo flipped the waffles over and drowned them in syrup the way Alexa liked them. For once she didn't jump in, overeager for Alexa to finish her sentence. Let her understand what it was like to live with long silences, unfinished sentences, and unanswered questions. Either Alexa didn't get the message or, more likely, didn't care, for she didn't speak again, but sipped her mug of coffee and didn't start on the waffles as she usually did.

Only when Jo switched on the "Today" show did she come to life. "A big cosmetics company has approached me about being their . . . spokesperson . . . their superstar . . ." Alexa sighed as if she had just announced her death sentence.

Jo wasn't going to let her get away with it. "Is that so bad? Don't people like Farrah Fawcett and Margaux Hemingway and what's that Lauder model's name, Karen something or other, get hundreds and hundreds of thousands of dollars advertising products?"

"Graham, Karen Graham," Alexa responded in a monotone. She sighed again, this time so heavily Jo lost her temper.

"I'm really getting fed up with you, Lex. You called me after months of nothing to ask me to come to New York . . ." She tried to mimic Alexa's voice, ". . . chaperone me, be my big sister like you've always been . . . I need you, love you. I need a manager, honest I do."

"Jo . . ." Alexa flushed, trying to interrupt, but Jo was too furious to be deterred.

"Sister, you don't need a manager! You need a keeper! But what happens when I get here? I have to act like a private eye to find you. You say you'll be one place and you're in another. You've been acting like a zombie ever since I arrived. You say there's someone you want me to meet, then you say, 'not yet' . . . You don't want me to meet this 'someone' yet—whoever it is, probably the 'bloody fool' in your appointment book every other week for the last few weeks!" She could hear herself almost screaming.

Alexa tried to put her arm around her, but Jo pushed her away. "You won't get rid of me easily, Alexa, and I'm disgusted with your callousness over Mom. You won't listen because you're too wrapped up in your selfish self as usual—too busy counting your millions, and now you sit here as if you've got cancer because you have a chance to earn more millions. Why don't you spend some of it helping me find the people who sent Mom to her death? I told you about Ann Pershing. She was murdered, murdered, don't you understand what I'm trying to tell you! Murdered!" As she shouted out the last word the phone rang and they both jumped.

"I'll take it in my room." Alexa was up and running. Jo stared at the phone. She wanted to pick it up and listen in, something she would never have dreamed of doing once. Instead, she nibbled on one of the waffles, watching a dirty-looking tugboat edge down the river toward the ocean.

When Alexa came back, Jo had cooled down. Whatever was bothering, changing Alexa, she knew her sister well enough to know that she would not find out by yelling at her. Alexa didn't refer to Jo's outburst, but she was no longer in a sighing, mournful mood either. She yanked the elastic band off the mail and smiled to herself as she read the top few letters. "Jo, you know I've got a secret admirer in Oregon." Alexa sounded strangely shy.

Jo would not allow herself to be mollified. "I'm sure you've got them all over the place," she replied coldly.

Alexa laughed. "No, you don't understand. This is really strange. I've been getting mail, letters, well, notes really, from someone who must have seen me, known me when I was up in the Pacific Northwest—perhaps on location in the forest or when I was in Mendocino. It's kinda sweet, but shivery, too. It's from someone who seems to know the real me . . ."

"Who is the real you, Lex?"

Alexa ignored the asperity in Jo's voice. She started to read aloud. " 'Loved the pictures in December *View*. I bet you were the kind of little girl who liked to try to mend the broken wings of tiny birds, who tried to keep secret pets in your room, who cried when your folks couldn't afford to buy you a pony one Christmas. I bet now you're rich and successful you ride like a pro.' "

Alexa looked at Jo excitedly. "Isn't that incredible, Jo. Don't you remember how I tried to keep a rabbit in my room? How I yelled at Dad when he took it away?"

Jo nodded without really thinking as Alexa handed her the letter.

The first thing she noticed was that it was signed only with the letter *M*. *M* for Magda? Jo brushed the crazy thought away. She was obsessed, but then there were plenty of reasons to be obsessed. As she quickly skimmed the typewritten contents, she nodded again. Yes, there was a sense of "understanding the real Alexa"—if there was such a person. On the envelope, stapled to the letter, was the address: P.O. Box 825, Portland, Oregon.

"I've been receiving them ever since my first *View* cover appeared. Sometimes he asks me for an autographed picture. I must have sent at least three. I know he must be a redwoods man," Alexa continued dreamily. "It's the place where I really belong, Jo. It's the place where men are really men—where people can find themselves."

Now, it was Jo's turn to sigh heavily. "Somewhere along the way, we've both got lost, Sis."

There were tears in Alexa's eyes, but a note of purpose in her voice as she suddenly grabbed Jo's hand. "Sis, this contract—this deal with the cosmetics group, it could help us solve a lot of things, believe me. Not just because of the big bucks . . ."

"What do you mean?"

It was the old Alexa, the fierce volcano about to erupt but not quite yet. There was a sense of smoldering, of fire—yet somehow just kept under control. It was comforting to see her come so completely alive, yet unnerving to realize her little sis had changed so much her zombie role might be an act that could even fool her.

Alexa looked her in the eyes, a challenging look of bravado. Jo wondered if Alexa could feel what she could see—a tiny nerve flickering just below her left eye. It was, for her, a comforting sign—that Alexa was acting like a tough guy, but that, just as in her own case, there was a lot of up-front courage, but a lot of inside insecurity. They were both still so young.

"I haven't been wasting time, Jo. Just be patient. Things are going to work out."

She was tired of being patient. "You're talking in riddles. I'm not going to let you upset me again today. One thing's certain, though, if you're going to sign anything with a cosmetics company, you can't use the *View* legal team. They won't be very happy about you signing up with a commercial enterprise. I've at least learned that much since my short indoctrination into this crazy world. We're going to have to decide this week on the agency you want to work with long term. You can't keep postponing it."

"You decide."

"All right, I will."

Alexa frowned and looked at her watch. "God, look at the time—and you're supposed to be my manager. Okay, you decide. But just make sure you decide on the best—with the lowest commission. I hate the thought of parting with a cent."

Time—it was all a question of time before he got a hot lead that would tie up the messy, unfinished business of Teri Shephard's death and provide both the beginning and the end of the special he had in the back of his mind.

Mike Tanner read quickly through the notes in his project file.

> The advertising of cosmetic surgery on local television stations, in newspapers and magazines, has grown exponentially since the Federal Trade Commission ruled that

> physicians should be allowed to advertise four years ago. Cosmetic surgery ads are now especially common in the states of New York, California, Florida, and Texas, and are the targets of increasing criticism from reputable plastic surgeons, who emphasize that there is a very fine line between publicizing a doctor's practice and promoting the surgery he or she performs. Another big concern is that more and more ads are being placed by plastic surgeons who have their own office surgical facilities where, notes Robert Goldwyn, M.D., Chairman of the Department of Plastic Surgery at Harvard Medical School, "Operations are performed in total privacy, unlike in a hospital, where other surgeons can informally observe plastic surgery patients and evaluate whether or not a woman actually needs the procedure being performed."

Mike glanced at his watch. It was good stuff. Should he tell little Jo some of it, make her realize he was by no means finished with his investigations on her behalf, just because she had hopped it to the East Coast?

It was 10:30 A.M.; 1:30 P.M. in New York, which meant Jo would probably be at some fancy lunch, wheeling and dealing on behalf of her superstar sister. Well, Alf Victor had certainly been one hundred percent right about her. Alexa was superstar material all right, and obviously her modeling career would soon lead to the big or little screen. Would Jo continue to be a camp follower? Had she given up her writing? Would she lose her own special identity being guardian, shadow to Miss Alexa? Mike hoped not.

Giving in to an impulse, he dialed the New York apartment, but crashed the receiver down as soon as he heard a recording machine announce, "Nobody is here at this time, but if you will leave your name, etc., etc. . . ."

It was probably just as well. He had difficulty talking to Jo right now. The last call had been stilted, phony. She obviously thought he had acted like a shit, and perhaps he had, perhaps he hadn't. He'd tried to resist her advances. So, she had been a virgin on the pill and he had fallen into the trap of thinking she was as liberated as all the other young virgins, who boasted they wanted freedom, too.

As he thought about Jo, the sweetness of her skin, the

curls at the nape of her neck, his penis stirred. He did care about her, but he didn't care about being tied down, not one little bit. Nope, it was just as well her high-and-mighty sister had an answering machine and not a live-in receiver of calls. That way Jo would never know how many times he had picked up the phone on impulse just to say hi and keep in touch.

When he had proof, real proof, that The Fountain had once upon a time operated elsewhere, under a different name with the same management, and that a particularly nasty rap was involved with the closing of that one, then he would certainly pass on the news fast. Then only a few more steps would be needed to find out where the perpetrators were operating now. It seemed highly likely they would be practicing and prospering in New York City.

Mike went back to his notebook:

> Thomas Rees, M.D., of New York University, told me a recent survey revealed an extraordinarily large number of cosmetic surgery patients choose a surgeon from the Yellow Pages. Dr. Rees is also concerned over the fact that younger surgeons, faced with the reality of huge malpractice insurance costs and escalating expenses, don't have the luxury of turning down patients for cosmetic surgery and that these surgeons are placing ads that promote dissatisfaction with a woman's or man's looks, holding out a false promise of surgical perfection.

Wow! It was a snake pit, and one that could make a devastating hour-long TV special. As Mike put the project file away, Ann Pershing's words came back to him. "Your mother was beautiful, but like so many in her profession, the going was getting tough . . . she wanted to look younger. The doctor was not qualified to carry out that treatment. Your mother's skin was damaged—yes, there was a certain amount of disfigurement . . . then I heard her car had gone over the cliff . . . a terrible way to die."

"Suicide. She committed suicide." The memory of Jo's cry still sent a chill through him. Mike crashed his hand down on the desk so noisily even his owl-faced, sleepy secretary turned around to see what was up. "A problem?" she inquired without a trace of concern.

"Yep, a problem," he snapped. "A problem I'm trying to solve."

"That she devil, that little vixen, that double-crossing, fat-ankled, no-good deceiver . . ."

"Calm down, Pen." Blair Benson didn't turn around to acknowledge Penelope's arrival in the planning room. Instead, she crossed her immaculate Geoffrey Beene–clad feet and leaned over the light box to inspect the latest batch of pictures from Paris.

"Don't you care, boss? After all I've—you've . . ."

"Care about what?"

Penelope was about to froth at the mouth. "I know you know because Rab told me that Eileen called . . ."

Blair still studied the Kodachromes with fierce concentration. "That was indiscreet of him."

"Oh, shit . . ." Penelope kicked the door and stormed out.

Blair wanted to kick the door, too. She wanted to kick it down, kick the wall, the light box, but most of all she wanted to land the pointed toe of her impeccable boot right in the center of Alexa Shapwell Wells's oval-shaped face. She wanted to yank her out of *View* and start a grapevine rumor of instability and insanity and alcoholism and degenerate fucking of dogs, ponies, you-name-it, she'll-do-it sort of thing, but she couldn't.

Her hands, her tongue were tied. She couldn't say or do a thing about the biggest defection in the history of cover girls.

She still couldn't believe it, couldn't believe he would steal what was such a trifle to him, but such a valuable asset to her. And he told her he hadn't even said more than a few words to her—just enough words to know that she had had to have acting classes and voice lessons in order to take the next step in her career.

Blair held on to the light box feeling faint. She had never felt faint before in her life. What was he doing to her? She needed something to get through the day. She had never needed anything before. Well, so now she did . . . Something that would enable her to smile, to say congratulations to the bitch, who would never, never, never appear in *View* again.

As she thought it to herself, she knew she was beaten before she even uttered the edict.

Of course, Alexa would still be there. He would want it. She would produce. As Blair went down the long corridor to her office, she could see, straight ahead, Penelope holding her head in her hands. It was very effective. All the little girls were huddling in groups, wondering what to do to soothe the savage, brilliant genius.

As she approached, they popped back into their pigeonholes. On the whole, despite her misery, Blair decided it was healthy the way the staff reacted to news that appeared to diminish in some way the prospects of the magazine. It was called loyalty, which Alexa Wells, or whatever name she now used, seemed to know nothing about.

Rab Robson, her homosexual secretary, was loping about in her office, which she didn't like. She gave him her iciest look, but as she expected he didn't freeze or show any reaction. "Alexa Wells is here." Rab allowed himself what Blair supposed was a wince of nausea. "She wonders if you have a few minutes—she wants to tell you her news herself . . ."

"If she wants to see me, she will have to wait thirty minutes. Send her in at three-thirty."

Rab waddled out with his strange ducklike walk, and thirty minutes to the second waddled back with *View*'s most successful cover girl ever.

Blair stood up, aware and enjoying Alexa's unusual discomfiture. They stood eye to eye, shaking hands. Blair even pecked her cheek.

As Rab closed the double doors behind him, Blair gestured to the sofas by the window. There was to be no help from her in prompting any conversation. She was a leader in the field of building insecurity. Oh, but Alexa was beautiful. This girl, unlike so many top models, was just as extraordinary away from the camera. Blair could feel bile in her throat as she took in with a professional eye the slanting curve of cheekbones that today were makeup free.

Despite Penelope's curse about her ankles, they were, as Pen had once described them, "di-vine"—even though, like so many models today, Alexa was wearing sneakers. Her independence was already showing. The sneakers weren't pristine. In fact, they were grubby.

Despite Blair's obvious restrained reception, Alexa soon exhibited her usual, nothing-can-intimidate-me manner. As

Blair leaned back and observed her through large black-rimmed glasses, so Alexa also leaned back and purposefully crossed her long, long legs. "I wanted to tell you myself that I've decided to accept an offer from the Devi Cosmetics Company." She appeared even more nonchalant as she continued, "I will always be eternally grateful to you—and Pen—but . . ." her voice wavered for a second, "this is the kind of contract nobody could turn down."

"What do they want you to do?"

Alexa laughed, tossing back her glorious hair. "Well, you know more about this kind of thing than I do. Devi is famous, isn't it, for its antiaging cream? I gather it's been created from some kind of ancient Indian formula." She chuckled like an overgrown schoolgirl. "It's a riot, they're going to call me The Face, Now and Forever—sort of suggesting that with their cream, no one need ever change . . . age. It's a five-year deal with a renewal review clause every year. I guess if I remember what Pen has been lecturing me about for months, I won't change that much in five years and by then it won't matter." She turned her strange, sea-green eyes directly on Blair like searchlights. "I'll be independently wealthy by then."

The meeting did not get easier. After Alexa started to chat companionably about Devi meaning Indian goddess, Blair decided she had had enough.

She stood up abruptly and returned to her desk, indicating she now had important work to do, more important people to see. Alexa didn't seem bothered at all.

She leaned cheerfully over the desk and said, "I hope you're not too mad at me. I hope I'll still be seen in *View*—on the editorial pages, I mean, not just in the ads. Wish me luck."

She held out her hand gracefully.

It was impossible not to shake it. Blair wished she had pincers to snap off each finger one by one, but there was nothing she could do, not now, not yet, perhaps never.

Was she still cooking up that disgusting mess of crunched-up tacos with overboiled onions, mashed potatoes . . . and worse, eating the atrocity with a spoon?

Did she still turn her watch back when she was running more than thirty minutes late, before giving an amazingly convincing performance as one of the few unfortunate creatures on God's earth who could blame Rolex for unpunctuality?

Was she already losing her unique look of innocence trying to be evil—or was it vice versa? Had New York hardened her eyes, spoiled her sweet natural posture, changed her as it had changed so many he'd known?

Cal Robinson poured himself some Sonoma and collapsed in his favorite armchair to reread the story in the *San Francisco Chronicle*. It was illustrated with two pictures of Alexa, one taken by him soon after she'd come back with him from Mendocino, the other a PR shot from this crazy-sounding company, Devi, as The Face, Now and Forever.

The *Chronicle* had, for once, written a nice blurb about him, too. "*View* cover girl Alexa Wells was first discovered by the internationally known San Francisco–based photographer, Caldicot Robinson." Who the hell in the business would recognize him from that, but then who cared? He had much more business than he could handle.

Long ago he'd lost his anger over Alexa's defection. In fact, Cal couldn't remember feeling angry at all. In some ways he'd realized later, he'd never expected Alexa to stay, to be patient, to do things his way—and she'd probably been right. Good timing had never been his thing.

Cal drank a couple of glasses of wine before giving in to the impulse that had been building all day to call her to congratulate her.

Even as he dialed the number he'd been given months back from a model who'd worked with Alexa at *View*, he felt foolish. Even thinking about Alexa brought out the big brother in Cal. He guessed it always would. No matter how high she climbed—and he had a hunch it would be all the way to the top, to the megabuck marriage, the movie career, whatever she wanted—for him there would always be this pocket of vulnerability about her, vulnerability that would make him feel she needed protection.

"Lex?" He couldn't believe his luck when a breathless young voice answered on the first ring.

"No, sorry. It's Jo . . . Jo Shapwell, Alexa's sister. Who's this?"

"Cal Robinson, I'm . . . I'm . . ."

"I know who you are." There was a smile in her voice that

made Cal feel good. What she said next made him feel even better. "Alexa's talked so much about you . . . about how wonderful you were to her. She'll be sick, *sick* she missed you. She's just crazed right now. You know she's signed with this big cosmetics company."

"That's why I'm calling. To give her my best—to congratulate her." Cal laughed. "I guess between Pen Waverly and me, she's just had to lose all her bad habits, right? And now Pen and *View* are going to lose her. Pen must be as sore as hell. Lex has really hit the jackpot with this, right?"

The warmth in Alexa's sister's voice came over the wire. Jo sounded a very different customer from the cool, contained Ms. Wells.

"Cal, I know your call will mean the world to Alexa . . ." Jo paused, then said shyly, "She should have called you herself long ago . . . well, I think she was scared you wouldn't talk to her. She's always said the first chance she got she wanted to work with you again. Perhaps it will happen with the Devi campaign . . ."

Cal laughed again. It was ridiculous, but the fact that Alexa had cared, had felt sorry, had talked about him made him feel ten feet tall. All the same, the last thing in the world he wanted was to get mixed up with any Indian cosmetics company. "I'll try to reach her again—perhaps tomorrow. I'm pretty busy myself. Tell her not to worry. All is forgiven . . ."

Jo cut in. "We won't be here tomorrow. We're moving to a Devi apartment. I think it's on the park somewhere. As soon as we're in, I know Alexa will call you."

"Sure thing . . . sure thing. Well, it was nice talking to you." Cal was glad he'd called, even though he'd missed Alexa. At least the ice was broken.

There were commercials on television luring couples to Essex House on Central Park South for a honeymoon or a second honeymoon weekend—"at a price you won't be able to resist . . . with a Sunday morning Champagne breakfast in bed and the whole park stretched out before you like your own private garden."

For Alexa, it looked as if Central Park were going to be her garden for the next year and for four more years after that—if Devi took up the option on her contract and if she was still happy being their "Face, Now and Forever."

The Devi apartment on Central Park South, part of the deal for the year, was the kind of place Jo had thought only existed in the make-believe world of movies.

Central Park South, she'd discovered, was really West 59th Street, sloping gently up to Columbus Circle from the Plaza Hotel on Fifth Avenue. The Devi apartment was at the top of the hill on the thirty-second floor, commanding a view that was so breathtaking, it was like two glasses of Champagne down in a gulp.

As usual, Alexa was taking it all in her stride, including the fact that in one hour she would be meeting the American press for the first time as the Devi Face, about to be made into even more of a celebrity.

As sister of the star, Jo had been persuaded to have her first facial from a pair of practiced Devi hands, followed by a makeup from one of America's leading makeup artists, who turned out to be a jolly girl from the north of England named Linda Mason. Linda's visit had been more relaxing than the tranquilizer Jo had taken the day before, when, unlike the days in the other apartment on East 57th Street, the phone hadn't stopped ringing and neither had the doorbell.

Alexa was still in hot rollers and her favorite kimono, which bore traces of the chocolate bars she had promised Penelope to give up. Not that Penelope probably cared anymore whether she was a chocoholic or not. She probably hoped Alexa was covered in zits, but she wasn't, and Jo knew that she probably never would be. "Lex, the limo will be here in thirty minutes. You know the traffic is awful . . ."

Alexa sat staring out over the green panorama. "It'll only take ten minutes to get to Le Cirque . . ." As she spoke, she uncurled herself and came over to Jo to give her an unaccustomed kiss. "I don't want to look eager."

"Believe me, you don't." Jo didn't want to snap, but despite Linda turning her into a reasonable facsimile of a good-looking girl, she felt like the ugly sister looking at Alexa's beautiful, only lightly made-up face.

When Alexa whirled back into the room twenty minutes later, Jo gasped. Whatever natural beauty Alexa had, Penelope had obviously taught her how to use every molecule of it. Devi had sent her to Scaasi because, Lex had explained, "he is the master of entrance and exit dresses . . ."

"I've never heard of him . . ."

Alexa had looked at her in the new, faintly amused way she had started to adopt, which made Jo feel like hitting her. "Perhaps you know him as Isaacs? He turned his name around as soon as he started to hit the jackpot. Believe me, he's a master of design."

Now, Jo could see for herself Devi and Lex were right. Scaasi, or whatever his name was, had achieved the impossible. The delicate gold organza dress made you think of an Indian princess and an all-American girl at the same time. The color of the fabric matched Alexa's hair and skin. The shape of the dress made you aware all over again of the length and slenderness of her legs, her torso, as well as the roundness of her breasts, her rump. She was, at once, unapproachable and desirable. "Wow," was all Jo was able to say, then again softly, "wow . . ."

Alexa laughed. "You're pretty wow yourself." The intercom from downstairs buzzed. "That will be good old Barry."

"Who's he? Is he Devi's owner? The mystery man you're always hinting about that I'm going to meet one of these days?"

To Jo's surprise, Alexa flushed. "Nope. I doubt he will be there. He's really behind the scenes. Barry Hunter is the East Coast legal eagle of Devi, a real hotshot Wall Street lawyer financier . . ."

"I wish you'd told me he was picking us up. I'm nervous enough without dealing with any legal genius. What am I supposed to talk about?"

Again, Alexa was unusually affectionate as she gave Jo a quick hug. "You'll like him. That's why he's such a hotshot. He seems like your average boy next door, sweet, unassuming, until you see him dealing with another lawyer, when a bit of his piranha instinct shows through."

Jo moaned inside. Your average boy next door . . . Average boy reporter turned into TV rapier-thrust commentator. Oh, Mike. Oh, Mike . . . She pushed the thought of him away as the doorbell rang and she went to answer it.

Alexa was right. From the moment Jo looked into Barry's deep blue eyes, she liked him, trusted him. He had unruly sandy hair that he obviously tried to slick down, but a tiny bit still stuck out at the side. It had emphasized the boyishness of his looks, despite the serious dark-blue suit and impeccably starched pin-striped shirt.

To Jo's astonishment and growing sense of relief and happiness, Barry hardly left her side at the party, which grew in size from the moment they stepped through an arch of topiary trees into L'Orangerie, the private room of one of New York's most successful restaurants, Le Cirque. There was an intoxicating scent in the room, which came from tiny candles and baskets of potpourri, held in bowers of branches and ferns.

Alexa moved through the room on the arm of Beni Huvaut, the president of the company, a tall majestic Sikh, wearing a deep crimson turban with his dark suit.

"She's like a moonbeam," Barry murmured approvingly as he saw the reaction of reporters, TV cameramen. "You can see even they recognize she's different."

No expense had been spared at the party to feed and entertain the media. There were oysters served on gold plates, Beluga caviar in tall silver containers, surrounded by oceans of ice; bowls and bowls of colorful curried hor d'oeuvres and a huge side of lamb, cooked, Barry explained, "the way they cook it on the Northwest Frontier . . ." It was carved in slices so thin it looked like pink smoked salmon on the pale pink plates.

Would the *View* crowd turn up, members of the top echelon, some of whom Jo had gotten to know during her attempts to "manage" Alexa before the model agency had taken over? She hoped some of them would. Not Blair Benson, who made her skin creep, although she had never understood why. Especially not Penelope, despite the fact she had to take most of the credit for Alexa's zoom to stardom. Penelope had always ignored her, so Jo didn't care if she came or not—except for Alexa's sake. Jo knew that Alexa really cared for Pen, as she always called her, cared and had had a couple of guilt attacks during the past month, knowing how much time and effort Penelope had put into "producing the product" as Alexa often deprecatingly described herself.

If Blair and Penelope came to the launch party, would it mean they had forgiven her, or, more likely, would it mean they were there for obvious "business" reasons? According to Alexa, Devi was about to become a big *View* advertiser, so they could hardly not put in an appearance.

By seven o'clock the room was so crowded that Jo kept getting separated from Barry, but he always found her again.

As she smiled her gratitude, she saw Brown Schneider, *View*'s beauty features editor, sidle in. She always seemed to sidle into space, but it was impossible to miss her. Over six feet tall with huge owlish spectacles, Brown's appearance indicated her academic background. Someone had told Jo she had a Ph.D. that she never used. What she was doing covering the beauty scene, Jo had never been able to figure out.

Even now she looked out of place and she certainly looked and talked as if she didn't belong in the world of cosmetics and perfumes, spas and salons—but she wrote as if she understood its immense appeal to women of all types and ages.

Her candid, occasionally even scathing, pieces on the beauty and pharmaceutical industries were followed as avidly by the beauty manufacturers as by the savvy *View* readers. An accolade from her meant a sure winner at the beauty counter, whereas if she criticized something, she did it so cleverly that there had been few advertising withdrawals, only a threat or two.

She had always been nice to Jo, and Jo appreciated it. How would Brown write about the Devi antiage/forever-young concept? Only the day before, Jo had read Brown's comments about the introduction of a new reducing cream in Europe . . . "Promised for the U.S. in a year or two. We should have been issued seat belts," Brown had written, "to ensure we stayed until airborne on the hot air pouring out from well-intentioned research-and-development vice presidents, who called themselves scientists. Instead, alas, even before a king-sized model of the magic tube was produced, people were bailing out from the launch party, which cost about ninety thousand dollars. I hope this sum will not be retrieved from sales of the cream, which is the perfect epitome for 'hopelessness in a jar.' Oversized Europeans would be better off investing in a treadmill. Next year, remember I told you so . . ."

It was impossible for Jo to get through the crush to Brown and, in any case, there was a sudden clash of cymbals announcing that something was about to happen. As Jo turned toward the back of the room, where there was a rostrum and microphone, she saw Blair Benson surrounded by a circle of reporters with Radish, or Arthur Reddish, another "*View* voyeur" as Alexa called him, at her side. So Blair had come to give her support after all.

In Jo's opinion, despite the heaps of expensive caviar,

endless Champagne, the many varieties of delicious Indian breads and other subtle touches of the East, Beni Huvaut's singsong welcoming speech introduced the first amateur note to the proceedings. Barry Hunter's face gave nothing away. Jo tried to look through the sipping, murmuring crowds to where Blair Benson was holding court, but there were just too many in the way to see her reaction.

"Our own goddess, Alexa Wells, The Face, Now and Forever," Huvaut rhapsodized, closing his eyes as if about to meditate.

With such a fast paced, know-it-all New York crowd, Jo was surprised no one laughed, or least snickered a little. Perhaps the party was really going too well or perhaps her sister, her own little sister, did have the ability to mesmerize—for everyone was smiling, not in a sarcastic, cynical way but as if they really believed in the possibility of a face staying the same, "Now and Forever."

Jo realized she was smiling, too, really smiling, not just a top coat to hide pain inside, but a genuinely happy smile because an attractive, apparently sweet man was being so attentive. Whether it was out of politeness Jo didn't know, but it felt good, warming.

She was in such a haze of Champagne and well-being because of Barry, it wasn't until the room had almost emptied that she realized Alexa had gone. With whom? Where? There was no anxiety in her questions, but the fact that she asked them was enough for Barry to chide her laughingly, "Don't worry. I believe your sister is quite able to look after herself." Jo took him at his word and happily went with him to have a nightcap at Doubles, which turned out to be a private club in a deep red velvet, subterranean pocket beneath Fifth Avenue.

It was the first time in months she had felt like a person in her own right; the first time she had felt attractive and not like some orphan who a man had taken pity on and given what he thought she needed most.

Her body didn't respond to Barry the way she had responded so immediately to Mike, not even when they danced so closely that she could feel his hardness against her thin skirt. Barry took the pain away. Next time . . . if there was a next time . . . Jo knew she might begin to respond—if she dared risk trusting a man again.

The next day began the whirl of TV, radio, and store appearances for Alexa—and Jo was right there, the girl Friday, behind her. If Tuesday was New York, Wednesday was Boston, Thursday Washington, D.C., and Friday, Saturday, and Sunday, the nationwide Devi tour began to go south.

As she sat soaking her feet with Alexa in a Miami hotel suite whirlpool bath, the phone rang. It was Barry, asking her to dinner the first night she was back in New York, which he knew very well was in two weeks' time.

"Do you like him?" Alexa was frowning, looking down at the foaming pale-turquoise-colored water.

Jo knew she was blushing. She couldn't help it. She had never told Alexa about Mike, but Alexa knew something had happened to change her. Alexa knew something, someone had hurt her enough to put her even more on her guard and sometimes cause her to turn away because there were tears in her eyes.

"Yes, I guess I do. You were right. He does seem like the boy next door . . . but I don't know him and it's . . . it's going to take me a long time to trust anyone again."

"Don't!" Alexa's command was fierce.

Jo looked at her, startled. "What do you mean?"

"Don't trust him. Don't trust any man."

Jo took her feet slowly out of the soothing water and began to dry them. She didn't answer Alexa, because there was nothing to say. Alexa would never trust any man—she knew that. Perhaps it was because of Mom and Dad, but more likely it was because of her great beauty, which meant that she was prey to every man, no matter how committed he might be to somebody else.

As she went toward the bedroom, Jo said sadly, "It's different for you, Lex. You're so special. I can understand how you feel about men, but I am—ordinary—like most girls . . . women. I need to trust. I've got to trust in order to function."

As Jo switched out the light around midnight, it was the first time in months she didn't subtract three hours from the time. Instead, she lay awake in the dark, thinking of what she would wear in two weeks' time.

* * *

"Don't dress up," he'd said. Jo wished she'd believed him, understood him, understood New York dressing. For her, "informal" was much more of a nightmare than the "black-tie" invitations she'd come to understand meant long dress or at least "best dress."

They were at Mortimer's, which she knew was one of the most "in" places in New York. She had never been there and she had been dreaming about her date with Barry for fourteen days and nights in sterile hotel suites in Atlanta, Dallas, Houston, Los Angeles, San Francisco, Portland, and on the way back East in Chicago, Detroit, and Philadelphia.

She could have worn jeans and a T-shirt. She looked good in both but she was in an Oscar De La Renta suit that was a little too tight, because she'd gained a couple of pounds on Alexa's whiz-around tour.

If the suit made her feel uncomfortable, the dashing blond who had just joined their table uninvited made her feel doubly so.

Barry had just finished telling her what an "insiders' club" Mortimer's really was, when the woman appeared, gave Barry a big hello kiss, and pulled up a chair from the next table. There was no way Jo could tell if Barry cared or not. As soon as he told the uninvited one that she was Alexa Wells's sister, the blond launched into a monologue that told Jo she had to be a photographer or a one-time model or something to do with that celluloid world.

"She's incredible," the blond cooed. "Most of the 'go-see girls' look completely different at night than during the day. You know, Barry, what I'm talking about, now that you're in my world." She slipped a hand into her pocket and pulled out a bunch of Polaroid shots. "Here is a new girl, A.M. and P.M. See how different her face looks at night after all the muscle tension has accumulated?"

Jo tried to look interested, but inside she was seething, her skirt feeling tighter and tighter as every second passed. Soon, however, Blondie was on her way, never noticing, Jo was sure, how charmingly and adroitly Barry got rid of her. Before Jo could speak, he summoned a waiter. "Take this chair away and make sure there's no chair near my table. I don't want to be interrupted again."

"Who was that?"

Barry tweaked her under the chin. "A very important movie agent from the West Coast, the kind always looking for talent and finding it. Who knows, perhaps one of these days, we'll allow her to discover Alexa—but not yet."

"What does 'go see' mean?" Jo frowned. It sounded so cheap.

Barry put his hand on her knee and deliberately brought his face close to hers, encouraging her to laugh as he said, "It means a girl 'goes to see' somebody important, a *View* editor, an advertising talent scout, a major cosmetics company. In your case, it means you 'go see' an able, oversexed young lawyer . . ."

It was a wonderful evening, until Barry started on a long paean of praise about the Devi company and the brilliant, beautiful woman who was responsible for the product behind its startling success. "It's difficult for people like us to understand someone like Madame Devi," he mused, holding his wineglass up to the candlelight. "She shuns public life. She's dedicated to research." He seemed to forget Jo was sitting beside him as he went on. "I've never met anyone quite like her. She's, well, unforgettable—it's easy to fall in love with her."

Jo's appetite went as quickly as it had come. She recognized the stomach twinges. She felt jealous, irrationally jealous of a woman she knew nothing about, somebody she'd never met, who obviously meant the world to a man she hardly knew.

She didn't know how to handle it, so she said nothing. It didn't matter in any case, because Barry went on and on through the main course extolling Madame Devi's research, which "will really benefit women everywhere."

She tried not to feel skeptical, tried to relate what he was saying to the meandering, meaningless phrases in Beni Huvaut's "now and forever" speech. As if Barry read her mind, he touched her knee again. "Beni's just a front man. I think, personally, it's a mistake. He's charming, but he hardly adds anything to the company's identity. We don't need him now that we have your beautiful sister doing such a good job. Do you realize since the announcement and her tour, sales have gone sky high?"

Jo shook her head. She didn't care. It was terrible, but she realized she didn't care at all whether the Devi product was selling or not. She wanted Barry's full attention on her, not on her sister, not on Madame Devi, but still Barry went on.

"American women don't realize how lucky they are. Madame Devi spent her young years in India. She fell in love with the country, studied with a famous herbalist up in the Himalayas, and somehow stumbled on the origins of this extraordinary formula. It really is unique. I thought it was rubbish, but it isn't. Have you tried it?"

Jo shook her head again, only hearing one word out of three, wondering just how exquisite Madame Devi really was. Was she dark, fair? Like Alexa or completely different?

Barry continued. "Of course, this 'Young Forever' concept is a gold mine . . ."

Jo shivered. Against her will, the discoveries of recent months crowded in. Mike crowded in. She could feel tears about to form. She couldn't believe the evening was turning into such a disaster, but Barry didn't seem to notice her increasing despondency and her descent into gloom. He leaned forward, smiling at her. "Coffee? Brandy?"

She murmured no, but he didn't pay any attention. "Two cognacs," he ordered, before turning to face her again. "Yes, we are very happy with your sister."

Jo tried to smile and regain the optimistic feeling she had had waiting for him to pick her up. At that precise moment, she spotted Alexa standing in the crowded doorway, hand in hand with a dark, intense-looking man she did not recognize. There were no tables that Jo could see. People had been waiting by the bar to be seated for ages. The man that Barry had pointed out earlier as the owner was going over to greet them. Jo watched as the stranger shook the owner's hand and they both looked at their watches.

"Barry . . ." Jo drew his attention to the entrance. "My sister has just arrived with someone who I don't think has a reservation."

As he looked at them Barry jumped to his feet. "How wonderful. They must join us. What a wonderful coincidence! Don't you know . . ." She didn't hear the end of his sentence, as he made his way between the tables to the doorway where Alexa and the man were still standing.

Jo could see Alexa wasn't very pleased. The feeling was mutual. She had left the house early that morning when Jo hadn't known where she was to meet Barry.

Was the man she was with the one she had once wanted Jo to meet so much? Certainly Barry wanted her to meet him. He was as excited as a schoolboy. "Jo, this is Dr. Marcus Lanning, Madame Devi's son. Won't you join us, Marc, Alexa?" They both shook their heads together.

"No, no. Glenn's found us a table in the next room. We want to be quiet, to catch up. I want to hear about the party, the tour . . ." the dark-haired doctor said.

Jo knew she had to be grinning, too. Madame Devi's son? Marcus Lanning had to be at least thirty, if not older, so Madame Devi obviously had to be in her late forties, early fifties—at least fifteen years or so older than Barry Hunter. Why on earth had she felt so stupidly jealous, so irritable, listening to Barry sing the old girl's praises? She probably was a genius, probably did have a world-beating formula.

Suddenly, the candlelight was brighter, the restaurant no longer just noisy but full of gaiety and laughter. Jo smiled up at Alexa, who gave her one of her most ludicrous winks—just like the old days when she had teased Mom. There was a twinge of pain as Jo thought about Mom and how proud she would have been of Alexa—or would she? Jo dismissed the thought as her sister walked into the next room, followed by Madame Devi's son. Barry watched her, too, seeing the heads turn as she passed by.

He looked at Jo reflectively. "Your sister is a devastatingly beautiful woman, but she is also a very lucky one." No matter what he said now, Jo felt she would agree with him constantly.

"Yes," she agreed dutifully. "Yes."

She hung on every word as he grew more expansive, sipping his cognac. "You see, Madame Devi has a loving godfather behind her, a man with an international empire. For Madame Devi, this product is the result of a lifetime's work. For him?" Barry covered her hand briefly with his, "For him, it's just one investment in a huge consortium of investments all over the world . . . but . . ." He obviously wanted Jo to give him her full attention because he paused until he felt he had it. "For a man who is all business, he has an unusually well-developed eye for a beautiful woman—of a certain type and temperament."

Jo began to feel uncomfortable again, yet didn't know why. "Who is he?"

"He prefers to remain anonymous—for the time being. One of these days when he sees where the company is going, he will probably announce his participation, but he doesn't have to now."

"Why are you telling me about him?"

"Because he is the genius who chose Alexa as the company

spokesperson, the company image, if you like. He saw her on one of his visits here—on a *View* cover—and he knew immediately she was the perfect Devi woman—so you see what I mean when I say your sister is a lucky girl."

Barry drew his chair closer. "And you're a beautiful, lucky girl, too. One of these days, you will meet him . . ." He put his fingertips just under her skirt. The tablecloth hid the fact. She could feel herself growing moist. She was responding and she wasn't sure she wanted to. She hadn't liked the suggestive note in his voice when he'd talked about Alexa and the mysterious money man. There had been something strange about it. Jo tried to turn the subject away from Alexa and herself and thought the best way to do it would be to get back to Madame Devi.

"You said Madame Devi spent her early years in India? She wasn't born there then? Is she American, or is she Indian?"

Barry wasn't paying much attention to her questions. He was playing with her knee, moving his fingers toward her thigh. His voice when he spoke was thicker. "No, no. She's not Indian—but her thinking is Indian. She doesn't like it to be generally known, but in fact she was born in Russia." As he spoke he didn't look at her and his hand moved higher and higher. Because he wasn't looking at her, he didn't see her pale and close her eyes as he murmured absentmindedly, "Her real name is Svetlana . . . a beautiful name, don't you think. I like it almost more than Devi. Svetlana Sorgiokov—that's the name she was born with . . ."

She was going to be sick. She stood up so quickly she stepped on his toe. "I'm sorry, I have to go to the ladies' room. I'm sorry."

She wasn't sorry. She was terrified. Svetlana, Svetlana. She had to get home. Her head was reeling with the alcohol, with emotion. It couldn't be the same—it couldn't be related . . . Outside the ladies' room was a pay phone. Mike. She had to reach Mike.

As Jo dialed the operator to call collect, she realized she couldn't remember Mike's number.

She felt someone watching her. She put the phone down. There was Barry, leaning against the wall, smiling, looking at her with his deep-blue eyes—warm, trustworthy Barry, just like the boy next door—who could also act like a piranha.

CHAPTER SEVEN

LAUGHING COUPLES SAUNTERED INTO THE PARK, EATING ICE cream, holding hands. The sun was out. It was Saturday afternoon. All was right with the world thirty-two stories below. Alexa turned her back on Central Park, envy gnawing, frustration building. It was becoming a familiar, disturbing pattern. She looked around the perfect sitting room, full of beautiful, expensive objects, furniture. It was empty of everything and anything she cared about.

As if to remind her that these days she was rarely alone, Kiko, her black-belt Thai houseman, soundlessly approached, bearing a bowl of freshly roasted sesame seeds and a silver salver she knew would contain an iced tea unlike any other iced tea in the world. It tasted like rose petals would taste if made into iced tea . . . rose petals with a surprising, delicious tang of orange. Kiko had arrived unexpectedly, unannounced, and installed himself in the studio apartment next door, which had miraculously become vacant in a no-vacant-apartment city. Kiko, Barry had explained later, was a "bonus," one way to say an extra "thank you" as Devi sales climbed toward the thirty-million-dollar mark.

He could cook like a dream, press even her most delicate lingerie and gossamer-thread dresses so that every time they looked like new. He had a sweet, quick smile, was unfailingly polite, pleasant. She guessed she liked him—if you could like anyone you didn't really trust.

She had been properly appreciative to Barry, who she had also never totally trusted. She hadn't been able to resist teasing him, however, adding that Kiko was "no substitute for a Siamese cat . . ."

As Alexa munched on the sesame seeds, she analyzed the three Alexas she had become. There was the Alexa who was public property; a body to be touched, pulled, raided—a ribbon from her hair, if not a hair from her head, a snatch of fabric from a dress that, for public appearances, the Devi designers had made too accessible to grasping hands.

As *View*'s number-one cover girl, it had taken her no time to become used to people turning to stare, to whisper or even shout, "Aren't you . . . isn't she . . ." as she passed by. For nearly two years, she had enjoyed it, the head turning, the focus, the ever present curiosity from strangers, who hoped she, too, had to cope with zits, with hair that fell out of shape, with problems of how much to eat or not eat in order to stay such a perfect size four or was it six?

As Devi's Face, Now and Forever, it had also taken no time for her to loathe it. It was fame of a very different kind, huge, fierce, unrelenting, as her face appeared on billboards taller and wider than a two-story house, on prime-time TV commercials, and in dozens of double-spread color ads in national magazines and Sunday newspaper sections. No wonder people felt they owned her. She was a regular "visitor" to their homes, when they were at their most relaxed, shoes off, doing whatever they felt like doing indoors, safe in their own nest, letting it all hang out . . . She "watched" them from their TV sets as they watched her.

Then there was the professional Alexa, owned and operated by Devi, Inc., fed by them, dressed by them, housed by them, even entertained by their chosen consort, and, above all, trained and trained by them on how to prove and corroborate the unprovable and uncorroborated, the ability of a cream to allow human skin to withstand the ravages of time—now and forever. She was very, very good at the job, but where was the girl she used to be? Had she turned into a Devi puppet? She knew, thank God, she had not, although sadly she realized that even Jo didn't understand that the least visible and less and less known Alexa was still alive and well. "That Alexa" mostly surfaced when the rest of the world was asleep, when, lying awake, she would resolve to resurrect her long-ago ambition—to become rich enough to retire to Mendocino or points north, even to Oregon where her most faithful fan still apparently lived. He was still writing, not as much as before, unless the Devi people were checking and confiscating her mail. She wouldn't put it past young Barry . . . Oh, God, she was getting paranoid!

She had been on the cover of *Time, Newsweek,* twice on *People.* The full heat of stardom burned so fiercely, every so often she felt her inner self burning to death, while everyone around her seemed singed by it, spoiled, changed.

She walked restlessly into her bedroom. There was a photograph of Princess Diana and Prince Charles on honeymoon on the front page of the *New York Times.* From what she had read and seen on television, Princess Di seemed like a simple girl, child really. How long would it take to change her? Did she have any idea what it was like to live under a nonstop searchlight, now and forever? Of course not, but at least she had a husband who was used to it, who would be able to encourage her to kick her shoes off when they were behind closed doors, to kick them off and laugh and laugh at the idiocy of it all. She had no one to laugh with. Every so often she thought of calling Cal Robinson. She'd been thrilled to learn from Jo that he'd been big enough to call with "no hard feelings," congratulations and all that jazz. . . . But she really had nothing to say to him . . . and certainly not over the phone, which stilted up so much conversation that should have been real.

There was a picture of Jo beside her bed, darling little Jo, who had changed so much since her arrival in New York. She had become withdrawn, acting less and less like a big sister. She even talked to her as if she were a stranger. Alexa bit her nail. She knew she had begun to reply like one.

It was all for the best that Jo had gone back to San Diego for a couple of weeks to do something for her old boss, Mike

Tanner. At least that's what she'd said when she'd left in such a hurry the week before. She missed her dreadfully, but in one way she hoped Jo would stay in California. New York wasn't for her. She'd given in to a weak impulse, calling Jo to urge, beg her to come to live with her, regretting it almost as soon as she had put the phone down. Already it had been too late.

Why had she done it? Perhaps because of her father's crazy letter, warning her to be careful in New York City, that it was full of snakes and snake charmers who would ruin her . . . that a modeling career, especially in New York City, could easily lead to an early death.

He hadn't mentioned her mother, but it was obvious that, although he had written the letter in some drunken stupor, he'd been thinking of Mom. It had been crazy, yet there was something frightening about it, too. As if he knew something she didn't, would never know . . . Then when she'd called Jo on impulse, really to cheer herself up and tell Jo how wonderful everything was, Jo had responded with the terrible news she had just found out about Mom, disfigured in an unauthorized beauty clinic, hiring a car to drive herself over a Mexican cliff.

Alexa had been terrified to think of Jo coping with it all alone. She had sent for her in a hurry, wanting to share the good things, forget the bad, but it had started so badly with the inexplicable murder of her mother's nurse, Ann Pershing, only days after she'd talked to Jo and Mike, only hours after her arrival at a New York hotel. It had made the veiled warnings in her father's letter all the more real. She had never told Jo about the letter. Knowing Jo, she would almost certainly have called their father and asked him what he was referring to . . . or perhaps asked Mike Tanner to confront him with it—and who knew where that would have led?

So, from the beginning, there had been too many undercurrents, too many things unexplained, still unexplained. She'd decided to try to sort everything out herself first, but Jo had been so obstinate, wanting to stick her nose in, getting in deeper and deeper when neither of them really knew what they were getting into. She needed help of a special kind. She wanted to talk about her father's letter with someone, that damned letter she had never answered . . . about the innuendos that had triggered her already suspicious nature. But who could she talk to? No one.

It was ironic that the most unapproachable, impossible

man to know—according to Barry—the mysterious, magnetic Mr. Forga, was the one who, so far, had helped her the most.

He had asked her to call him Bax, but she hadn't been able to. It was strange. He attracted her, yet frightened her, too. No one else had such an effect on her.

Alexa opened the drawer by her bed to read, as she often read, the opening paragraph of the little book Mr. Forga had written on loneliness when, a long time ago, he'd told her, he had been a practicing psychiatrist.

> There is an everyday loneliness that has never been identified—the loneliness that fills the hours when we can do nothing but wait, the loneliness of lovers who are separated by jobs, miles, circumstances they cannot control. Isolation characterizes the life of the loner who scorns friends in the name of loftier values. The loners practice a crippled religion. They are the most miserable of all. But they dare not let themselves feel the pain of their loneliness, because they cannot, or will not, admit it. Those who wait to be saved from loneliness will experience even more anguish and injury than the individual who makes himself vulnerable by moving toward people.

Loners . . . crippled loners. Alexa knew that Mr. Forga thought she was one—suspicious, unable to let the real girl show through, even to his experienced questions, few though they were. Tears pricked the back of her eyes. Mr. Forga, brilliant, mysterious Mr. Forga, once a psychiatrist, now a multimillionaire, was, Barry implied, the real money behind Devi, and the man who had chosen her from a *View* cover, as the face women would be able to believe in most of all. It was eerie. He seemed to understand her more than anyone she had ever met, yet she still held back. He was trying to make her trust him, trust people, that was all—yet he scared her. She had to admit it, although he rarely moved from behind his giant marble desk as she sat facing him, listening much more than talking.

Alexa turned the page.

> Love is friendship that has caught fire. It is found in the sweet and sour of reality, rather than in the "always out of

> reach" stars in the heavens. Love is the force that connects the broken parts of life, filling in the hollows and bridging the gaps. . . . Love has a great deal to do with one's upbringing. People who were deprived of love early in life have a hard time giving it. A child cannot be loved too much, but he can be overindulged. . . . The chaos in a family that provides no models makes it difficult for children to achieve the growth necessary to sustain a love relationship.

Alexa put the book down as she thought again of her nonparent, her nonfather, Ben. He had always created the chaos. He had made it impossible for the Shapwells to become a family. He had been and probably always would be a callow, selfish nonperson. She was glad she had never answered his letter or his couple of phone calls. Even his voice on her answering machine had given her heartburn. "Hey, baby, how you doing?" She had heard him say that a hundred times to Teri, her long-suffering, hard-working, idealistic little mother, who perhaps with the right love and encouragement could have become a good model, perhaps a top model—as if that were one of life's great achievements! It was all really so tawdry and Mom had paid for it the worst possible way, trying to buy back a youth she probably had never really had . . . and then being disfigured. Alexa shut off her train of thought. Jo wanted revenge, and went about getting it one way. Well, she wanted revenge, too, but her way was more subtle—perhaps devious was a better word. Jo was too public about her investigations. She knew that wasn't the way to achieve results. One day—perhaps sooner than later—she would be able to confide in Jo, who would be amazed by how much she knew . . . but . . . Alexa sighed . . . she, too, knew far too little.

There was a postcard from Santa Fe on her side table. From Marc. She reread it, a little of the dark cloud lifting. She liked him—in fact, she liked him a lot. He made her laugh. Surprisingly, now that he had been away a week, she missed him, too—and was actively looking forward to his return the next day.

Did he have the ability, the strength to help her move permanently out of the morass of despair she nowadays often fell into?

He had been "detailed," she knew, to act as her escort when he could fit it into his own busy schedule. In the beginning, she had thought sardonically, it was to ensure she stuck by the Devi rules—laid down, she was sure, by Baxter Forga. Early to bed, early to rise, no alcohol, good nutrition, less rather than more to eat (a rule she found particularly difficult to follow), at least an hour's exercise a day and a healthy amount of sex—if Marc and she found the idea mutually attractive. So far, although there was an attraction there all right—Marc was, after all, tall, dark, and saturninely handsome—they hadn't slept together, but the last good-bye kiss and caress of her breasts had, for once, not been a turn-off, but a turn-on. Was the psychiatrist in Mr. Forga helping her find herself—at least as far as sex was concerned? How astonished Mr. Forga and Marc would be to know that he, Marc, was the first man whose touch had aroused in her something other than revulsion?

She had wanted to laugh out loud when Barry first told her he was going to introduce her to Madame Devi's son. Barry was so enthralled by Madame Devi, the same note of devotion and respect had been in his voice when he'd mentioned "Madame's son." Alexa had been sure, despite the virility of his looks, that Marcus Lanning would be a mother's-boy wimp, or a homosexual, but Marc hadn't turned out to be either—far from it. He was self-contained about himself and his family—just like she was—but also, just like she was, opinionated about everything else with a quick, often self-deprecating wit. He was occasionally even scathing about the Devi "young forever" concept. He obviously didn't like to talk about his mother or her Devi "tunnel-vision" as he put it. He liked to talk about the world, which he'd seen a lot of, as a young naval doctor, before deciding to quit the navy and come home to work.

"I'm sure your mother must have welcomed that." She'd made the obvious comment without thinking, but his answer had given her plenty to think about.

"I'm not sure she ever noticed . . ."

Why else had Marc been asked to squire around "the most desirable property since Marilyn Monroe?" That was how Barry had told her he'd put it to Marc, proving once again what a hayseed he really was beneath his Paul Stuart immaculate suit.

Alexa was sure it was to preclude any "outside entanglements" that might get in the way of living and breathing for Devi twenty-four hours a day.

How little most people realized what being a top model or a living image for a product meant. It was just like being a top athlete, part of the training—or "maintaining"—precluded any relationships that might get in the way of presenting a perfectly fit body and mind to the world. What had Mr. Forga told her the week before without a trace of a smile? "The definition of love is a sleepless night with a sick child . . . or a sleepless night with a healthy adult. You luckily do not have to suffer the first, and you cannot afford the second. That kind of love is infatuation, instant desire. It is one set of glands calling to another. I repeat, love is friendship that has caught fire. It takes root and grows one day at a time . . . never causing an emotional upheaval. Never forget, grief is one of the fastest ways to age the skin."

It was one of the few times he had moved from behind his awe-inspiring desk. It was the first and only time he had stood up as she had said good-bye, moved to her to touch her forehead with two lean fingers. Her eyes had become fixed on his dark, almost black eyes, deep, hypnotic. She had felt as if she were going to fall asleep on her feet. It had been over in a second—at least she thought so—but it had been a disturbing, strange sensation.

One of the few questions he'd asked her had come that day. About Marc. "Do you like his company?" It was an old-fashioned way of putting it. She had hesitated, and she had seen he was pleased by her hesitation. Now, she wondered, if Kiko had read the postcard and tried to interpret the initials beneath Marc's signature to pass the information on.

F.O.T.M.D.P.S.M.M. "Fan of the most desirable property since Marilyn Monroe . . ." It was a sweet joke, but if you were a "desirable property" under constant surveillance, it might not be regarded as a joke. Perhaps it could be regarded as an indication that it was a relationship that had to be watched.

Alexa yawned. It was all too early to know. She didn't really know Marc, and Marc didn't appear to want to delve down to find out if there was a real person beneath The Face, Now and Forever.

The sun blazed into the bedroom with sudden intensity. From her luxurious white silk-covered bed, Alexa saw people stretched out on the meadow. On impulse, she decided to join them. She put on running shorts, dark glasses, and clipped her Walkman over her ears to head out for a long run. So Kiko would probably run soundlessly behind her. She had no doubt he could do everything she could do and better, but at least she would feel anonymous, "normal," just part of the crowd.

As perspiration poured out, Alexa felt her inner self come to life. She forced herself to go faster, faster, until after about an hour she collapsed on a shady piece of grass. She just missed a busy row of ants, which came out of nowhere at her toe tip to stretch in an organized line to an anthill a few feet away. She studied them as she waited to regain her breath. They all looked exactly alike, but were they? Was one ant more beautiful than another in the ant world? More industrious? More ambitious? For the first time that she could remember, she told herself she wanted to be like everyone else, even as another voice urged her to accept the fact she wasn't. She was different, not necessarily better (except in the looks department) but different. "Exceptional," was Mr. Forga's way of describing her. She shivered despite her sweat as she thought again of the power and presence of the man, who was the real money behind Devi. He never wanted anyone to know when she went to see him. He never telephoned her directly. He summoned her to call him, through Barry, or more recently, through Kiko. Although the desk was always the same, gigantic and made of marble, the location was not. Alexa shivered again. Who was he really? Where was he from? He was a total mystery . . . and obviously wanted to remain so.

She was as wary as ever, she told herself, as the ant line swerved in a new direction. Her built-in defense system could be switched into play instantaneously and yet—she had to admit—although she fought hard to maintain the essential space between her outer and inner self, there was something about Mr. Forga that was beginning to act on her psyche like a drug. Had she been hypnotized the week before when their eyes had somehow locked together for those few seconds? As she was lost in thought, the ants disappeared.

It wasn't until she was nearing the apartment, when she slowed down to tie her shoelace, that Kiko materialized, kneeling down, looking as cool as if he had just stepped out of a shower, to tie her shoelace for her. He ran silently beside her for the rest of the way.

Thank God, she'd come, Jo kept telling herself, convincing herself she had been right to rush off impulsively after waking

Mike up in the middle of the California night. In her terror, she'd forgotten the time difference, clinging to the phone as if it were a buoy, her body wet through with sweat as if she had been drowning.

Mike had a trained journalist's mind, all right. It hadn't taken a second for him to sound alert, ready to take action, although she'd realized later it had been just before 3 A.M. in San Diego.

All the love she'd ever dreamed he might feel for her had been in his voice, as if he'd been dreaming about her, too.

All she'd had to do was whisper in a funny half cry, half plea, "I'm scared, Mike. I'm scared . . ." It had been an understatement that terrible night, tossing and turning, again and again remembering "Svetlana" written on the back of her mother's check, with the indecipherable word beside it. Could the second part of the signature have been "Sorgiokov"? The insane thought had taken root as every minute passed until the urge to call Mike had grown overpowering.

He hadn't been able to come to her. He'd insisted she get on a plane the first thing the next morning. Like receiving the most beautiful gift in the world, Jo had realized there was absolutely nothing to stop her.

"I'm going home for a couple of weeks," she'd told Alexa at 8 A.M., her bag packed, a taxi at the door. She'd meant it. "Home"—it wasn't East Mission Drive. It was Mike Tanner. Since that morning in the Los Angeles hotel, home had been and probably always would be Mike Tanner, whether "home" meant Jo Shapwell to him or not.

During the long flight west, Jo had rehearsed meeting him, concentrating on holding in check the longing to throw herself into his arms, as she had seen so many women meet their men at airports, train stations—not in real life so much, but at the movies, on TV.

If his arms were out waiting, she'd go straight into them, but if they weren't, she'd simply hold out her hand and say, fervently, sincerely, "Thank you, Mike, for being here when I need you." The rehearsal had been unnecessary. Mike hadn't been at the airport, couldn't be there, said the message handed to her by an American Airlines staffer immediately after the plane doors opened. It had been like a corny sitcom joke. Mike had had to cover a fire. She was to go home and he would call and then come over as soon as he could—if possible before his nightly six o'clock broadcast.

As always, she had followed his instructions, getting a cab to 804 East Mission, only then aware that she would be seeing her father for the first time in eight, almost nine months—or would she?

She hadn't called to say she was coming home. Home? East Mission wasn't her home anymore, and now she couldn't assume Mike was "home" either. He was a big-shot TV newsman in this city, fond of her, that was sure, but not crazy about her as she was about him. Jo had felt homeless, bereft.

As the taxi had drawn up outside the familiar white stucco house, her hand had been trembling. She hadn't even been sure her key would still fit the lock or if Libby, or a Libby look-alike, would be inside. But the key had fit and there had been nobody there.

Why would there have been? She had stifled a scream when she'd stepped into the hallway and seen the living room stacked with packing cases, the kitchen the same, Alexa's and her tiny bedroom empty of everything.

Only her parents' bedroom—Ben's room—hadn't been totally packed up. The double bed had been slept in, one side table gone, the other still in use with the phone on top, beside an answering machine, blinking that it had a message to deliver.

Jo had gone into the yard to sit on a packing case that probably contained the barbecue grill, her heart thumping, more scared than ever, until the phone had cut through her hurtling thoughts. It had been Mike, apologizing for not being at the airport to meet her. When she'd told him the state of 804 East Mission, he'd taken charge. "Don't unpack there. Go to my place. I'll call the super and tell him to let you in. There's a back room with a camp bed. You can stay with me for a few days, then we'll see what to do . . ."

Before she'd left the house that she knew she would never return to again, she'd had the sense to listen to the message. It was a voice she didn't recognize, certainly not Libby's drawl, but still high-school pert, giggly, reporting, "Big Daddy Ben, don't be mad. The movers couldn't finish this week, but you'll be all through by Monday and I'll be waiting in the hot tub, all juicy and ready for my big boy. Don't forget to call the video guy. The wall's all set for the new installation."

So Big Daddy Ben was moving to a new juicy girl, a hot tub, a new video installation with all the old furniture. Would he send a change-of-address card? A sense of failure, of bitterness, yet resignation, had stayed with her all day. She couldn't blame her father for not calling or writing to tell her. She'd hardly been in touch with him since her move east. Nevertheless, it seemed like the final betrayal.

The shock of the packing cases, her father's imminent move, had calmed her down and made it easier for her to wait for Mike like the good friend he probably wanted her to be, not the sex-crazed, hungry-for-love creature he'd last encountered.

All the same, on his arrival it had been impossible not to respond to his kiss, straight on the mouth, his hands gripping the back of her head. She'd had to fight back tears, determined not to arouse his pity, which, she'd decided long ago, had been the trigger to his desire in Los Angeles.

His phone had put the brake on any emotional outbreaks. It rang every five, ten minutes after he'd walked in the door. It seemed Mike was now always on call, and at certain times of the day he could never switch the damn thing off. Finally, after he'd spent an hour dictating a story he would deliver later that day, they had gone out to a small Italian restaurant. There, over capuccino, she'd told him the whole story of the conversation with Barry Hunter, the hotshot Devi lawyer, who had revealed to her the identity of Madame Devi . . . "Not an Indian alchemist or an Indian anything, but Russian . . . a Russian Svetlana. It's a common Russian name, but it's all too much of a coincidence, isn't it?" she'd pleaded.

"Damn right, little Jo. Damn right." Mike had stroked her cheek and told her how insanely busy he'd been, working on a number of investigative pieces about the enormous development projects going on in the city. "I've always intended to get back to the beauty clinic story," he'd said earnestly. "Not just for you and your mom's sake. Come back with me to the studio and you can read my files on the whole sorry phony-plastic-surgery, face-peel, lotion-and-potion mess. Tomorrow we'll start trying to decipher that signature."

It was funny. She'd slipped right back into her girl Friday role, nobody questioning her existence as she'd sat at a table in Mike's cramped back office, sometimes answering the phone and getting coffee when he asked for it. The rest of the time she had started to read the huge amount of material Mike had amassed, files marked "follow-up" first, those that he'd apologetically told her he just hadn't been able to follow up at all, because other stories had taken precedence. The file was packed with clippings about lawsuits, women suing facial wizards, youth practitioners, private clinics, salons for loss of looks, disfigurement, stopping just short of death, but no mistaking the living deaths.

She'd watched Mike on his nightly TV spot and fallen more in love than ever, more in love, yet feeling further away from him. There was a reserve she'd seen and felt on and off camera. That first night he'd sent her back to his place with a number she could call for a wonderful home-delivery pizza. "Order it about nine," he'd said. "I'll be through with my meeting by then and when it's fresh, it's best . . ."

But he hadn't come home by nine, ten, or eleven, and after all the disappointments, one piling up on top of another, Jo had fallen into an exhausted sleep on the camp bed in the back room, the pizza uneaten.

If day one had been painful, days two and three had more than made up for it.

"I'd forgotten it's the weekend," he'd said ruefully, wandering into the back room around six-thirty the next morning, rumpled, sleepy. "The damned check's in my safety deposit box: we can't get to it until Monday . . . but guess what, we're going to forget all our cares. I'm taking some time off. We're going to head to the beach—or go up to Julian and drink some of that cider of theirs . . ."

But they hadn't done either. She'd sat on the end of the camp bed and it had collapsed to the floor. She hadn't had to do a thing. Mike had flung himself on top of her, sucking, pulling, licking until they'd rolled together in a corner, hands, feet, tongues, bodies interlocking. He had made all the moves, as hungry, if not hungrier than she could remember herself ever being the last time they had made love. They hadn't moved out of the apartment all day, just going to his room, to his futon to make love again and again, between sleeping, whispering, eating—he as loving as she'd ever dreamed a man could be.

Was it a commitment? Did he love her after all?

She'd held on to each minute of the forty-eight hours, daring to hope it might never end, saying to herself on the way to reality and the safety deposit box on Monday morning that twice he'd said over the weekend, "I won't let you down, little Jo. I'll never let you down again . . ."

And now it was Friday, and she was following up on his brilliant Monday brainwave when after scrutinizing the slanted second name from every angle, they'd given up trying to decipher it, trying to make it fit "Sorgiokov" or anything else using the Western alphabet.

"I know what I'll do," he'd grinned like a little boy. "I'll talk to Astra, the astrologer. She often works for the San Diego police. If she's not into graphology, too, I bet she'll know someone who is . . ." and Astra had known someone and now Jo, after making a dozen or more phone calls to track him down, had managed to make an appointment to show the check to Edward Vale III, who, Astra had told Mike, was used to deciphering hieroglyphics on five-thousand-year-old Egyptian mummies, let alone scrawls on twentieth-century checks. The cab passed East Mission Drive on the way to what Mr. Vale called his "Graphology Center." Jo averted her eyes.

"You'll be all through by Monday," the hot-tub girl had said on the answering machine to Big Daddy Ben. Now, it was Friday, so presumably the house was totally empty. Anything Alexa and she had left behind had been packed up, perhaps in storage, more likely sent, like Mom's big trunk, to the Salvation Army or the Mission. Again, there was more resignation and sadness than anger—and surprisingly, when Jo had called Alexa with the news their father was moving out, so far address unknown, Alexa hadn't been her usual biting self. On the contrary. She had been full of concern over how Jo felt.

"It's for the best, Jo," she'd said. "That house has nothing to do with us anymore. It was never much of a home, even when Mom was alive. Let's look forward, not back." Alexa had abruptly changed the subject as she so often did. "What's up with Mike? Are you going to work for him again—write for TV?" Alexa's enthusiasm for Jo to stay in San Diego had been impossible to miss, but Jo didn't bite.

"There isn't a job for me here, Lex. I thought I was working for you. I'll be back in New York next week."

It was true. Mike hadn't suggested she stay. There was nothing short term or long term about their relationship. This was the way it had to be these days—not just one-, two-, or three-night stands, but a long, loving friendship that included sex as a matter of course, along with cappuccinos, pizzas, and—in Mike's case—some investigative reporting on her behalf, which might also be useful to him professionally.

Jo shut her eyes to block out the tears that her thoughts produced. What was wrong with her? Her relationship with Mike wasn't over. It was just beginning. It might or might not lead to . . . what? Now and forever? Happy ever after? That was all a mirage. Nothing like that happened anymore.

The cabdriver woke her up. "We're here, miss."

The Graphology Center was a white stucco house not unlike the one on East Mission, except it was surrounded with trees heavy with oranges. Jo pressed the bell beneath the sign E.V.III. A querulous voice barked, "Announce yourself. Speak up. Speak up." She spoke into the security mike. A buzzer buzzed and she pushed the front door open to step into a dark, furniture-filled hall. "In here, in here."

She went in the direction of the voice and, when her eyes grew accustomed to the gloom, saw sitting behind a desk stacked high with books a Noël Coward look-alike in dark-blue dressing gown. "Sit down, sit down." Edward Vale waved a vague hand in the direction of a chair. Finding one empty enough to sit on was difficult. There were books, magazines, pamphlets everywhere, pages fluttering as an old-fashioned fan wheezed overhead.

Jo's optimism wavered. This eccentric wasn't going to be able to decipher anything.

"Thank you for seeing me. I've been told how busy . . ."

Edward Vale interrupted her. "Yes, you are a very fortunate young lady. I only have this half hour free until this time next week." Jo opened her purse to hand him her mother's check. He peremptorily put up a hand. "Two hundred dollars, please—cash."

Mike had warned her she would have to pay on the spot, but she hadn't expected this. She gave him the money. He counted it slowly, infuriatingly slowly. She could feel her anger building, but finally he gestured for the check.

"Svetlana . . ." He repeated the name phonetically several times. Jo could hardly contain her irritation.

"Yes, yes, Svetlana . . . but Svetlana what?"

Only the soft flutter of pages moving, as the fan turned in

the overfurnished, cluttered room, broke the silence as Edward Vale brought the check up close to his eyes as if they could devour it. "Henn . . ." He sounded as if he was speaking to himself. "No, no, not Henn . . . certainly not Henn . . ."

Jo clutched the edge of the chair seat, tension making her sick to her stomach. Another minute passed. "Could it be . . ." she started to say.

He shushed her violently. "Ssshh . . ." Then he handed the check back. "It's a foreign hand, Austro-Hungarian school, and yet it's a simple English name. Strange."

Edward Vale pursed his lips as if it was a personal affront. "It's Lann, or possibly even Lane, an unusual juxtaposition of the letter 'n' and the last letter . . . definitely written by someone unused to the Western alphabet."

Lann . . . Lane . . . Lanning? Despite Edward Vale's determined tone that forbade any other question, Jo pressed on. "Could it possibly be Lanning?"

"Extremely unlikely. No, I would say definitely no. If you are asking me again about this last word, I must say again no. If you would like to leave the check with me, I will discuss it with my students. A Xerox will not do." He answered her before she even thought of the possibility. "But the answer will still be no."

Jo wouldn't give up. Perhaps because her eyes welled with tears and perhaps because somewhere there was a small crack where compassion existed in Edward Vale's formidable exterior, unexpectedly his expression softened. He pushed some of the books aside to lean across the desk in a more approachable, confiding way. "I cannot find what is not there—but perhaps you do not know that when someone is using a name that is not his own . . . or a name he has invented for some purpose, he unconsciously can incorporate in the new signature some part of his usual name. Lanning is not written here. Whoever was perhaps trying to write Lane—a simple, easily forgotten, and so often adopted name . . ." He paused and resumed his stentorian stance and tone ". . . I say, perhaps, please remember that, perhaps whoever it was, began to write 'Lann' by mistake. I do not like conjectures, but it is an unusual combination of letters."

On the way back to Mike's apartment Jo wanted to scream, her anxiety and confusion was so great. Marcus Lanning, that was the name of Madame Devi's son. How proud and excited Barry Hunter had been to introduce her to Marcus Lanning. Jo shut her eyes, remembering all too well . . . "her real name is Svetlana . . . Svetlana Sorgiokov—that's the name she was born with . . ."

But Svetlana had married a man called Lanning, and given birth to a son—to Marcus Lanning, who Alexa was going out with, a man who, for once in her self-absorbed life, seemed to have the ability to occupy her thoughts and arouse her emotions.

"There's someone I want you to meet," Alexa had said months and months ago, when she had first urged her to come to New York. Was Marcus Lanning that someone? Jo had never been able to find out. Alexa had always enjoyed being mysterious, covering her tracks. How long had she been seeing Marcus? Had he been the one to bring Alexa to his mother's attention? Jo didn't know, just as she didn't know so much about Alexa's new life in the fast lane.

Lane. She was back to that frustrating name again, so near, yet not near enough to fit together all the parts of the terrible jigsaw.

She sat hunched forward, trying to deep breathe herself into calm, the way she'd read women about to give birth reduced their pain, but that was physical pain. This was mental. Even though there was nothing to prove it, Jo was certain Alexa was surrounded by some kind of danger. If Madame Devi, Svetlana Lanning, née Sorgiokov, was one and the same Svetlana Lane of The Fountain disfiguring clinic, was it possible she didn't know that Alexa Shapwell, the Devi Face, Now and Forever, was the daughter of Teri Shephard, the woman The Fountain had disfigured—the woman Svetlana Lane had caused to commit suicide?

And what about the mystery man behind the Devi enterprise? The man that Alexa had once told her with eyes shining could buy and sell the whole world . . . who had decided after being shown only one *View* cover that she was the face women everywhere would believe in—did he know everything about Madame Devi? Did he know about her past? If Madame Devi and Svetlana Lane were one and the same person, was it possible that he didn't know he was dealing with someone who, years before, had been convicted of false advertising by mail, promising youth and beauty, delivering ugliness and despair?

Jo felt a swift surge of anger at Alexa. It was ridiculous. She didn't even know Mr. Moneybags's name. If she knew it, she could find out more. How could Alexa be so secretive? If only she knew more . . . if . . . if . . . if . . . Her mind was reeling. She felt sick.

When she arrived back at Mike's apartment, she was so exhausted she lay down on the camp bed and immediately fell asleep, nightmare following nightmare.

Later that night, curled up on Mike's lap, she went over the facts with him, trying to make sense of everything. "Looking back, I can understand it, Mike. Mom was pretty, really pretty, but I guess as she was getting older, jobs were getting harder and harder to get . . ." One sentence tumbled after another. "Then, well, as I've told you their marriage—Mom's and Dad's, wasn't good. He was easily flattered. There was this young hotshot, juvenile delinquent, Alexa always called her. I'm pretty sure now Alexa was right, that Dad and this kid, really a kid, were having an affair. Perhaps it went on after Mom's death, too. She—Mom, she was always fascinated by anything foreign. She probably saw an ad for this face peel—advertised as Eastern magic or from India or something like that. Mom had a childish belief in anything like that. She was always trying to persuade Dad to send me overseas—to get culture—to France—to castles in the sky . . . you know, that sort of thing . . ."

Mike crushed her closer to him. We're going to solve this together. You'll see. I'm here." Yes, Jo thought to herself, you're here now, but what will you say when I tell you I've got to go back to New York to warn Alexa—that I can't do it over the phone. I've got to get her away from Devi. Are you going to be able to come back with me?

"Where does Magda fit into all of this?"

Jo slumped against Mike's shoulder. "I don't know. Perhaps it was Magda who told Mom about the peel. Svetlana and Magda were obviously in the business together, but I just don't know." She gulped. The moment had come. She looked up at Mike, hoping her eyes would convey how she felt about him. "I've got to go back to New York, Mike. I've got to tell Alexa everything face to face and try to make her understand what this means—or may mean. I've got to try to get her away from

Devi and back to modeling. Right now she's the hottest thing around. I want her out of that crowd—whatever the truth is. It's all too much of a terrible coincidence." She'd meant to stay calm, but it was impossible. She knew she sounded, looked agitated.

Mike looked grim, the way she remembered he always looked when a story was going badly. "Jo, I understand all that, but I don't want you to go back alone, and I can't leave San Diego now. Any minute this development scam is going to break. Can't you wait a couple of weeks, maybe ten days, until I can come back with you? I don't want you going back alone . . ."

"A couple of weeks!"

"Well, maybe not, but at least a week. It doesn't have to be wasted time. You can research some of those cases in the files—there's one—I can't remember where—that seemed to link it in one or two ways to The Fountain, but I can't remember exactly how or why."

Mike pulled her closer to him. "Jo, it's different now. I feel differently about us." He did. She could tell he did. He was unhooking her bra, releasing her breasts for his mouth, his face flushed, anxious. She turned to straddle him, slipping out of her panties, feeling his fingers opening her wide, wider, soaking three, four fingers deep into her wetness. She was writhing, on the edge of coming, knowing that he now wanted her as much as she wanted him. Of course, she couldn't leave him. "Oh, Mike . . ." He was in her, deep, huge, a thick pulsating force twisting her body and mind into a whirlwind of sensations. It went on and on . . .

When Alexa called at 7:45 A.M., Mike had already left for a breakfast date. "Jo, darling . . ." Alexa's voice sounded sleepy, as if Jo wakened her instead of the other way around. "Jo, are you having a good time with your boss? I miss you."

There was Mike's smell in the bed. Her vagina was sore, her arms faintly bruised from his grip, his passion. Happiness soared for a second; then guilt overtook her.

"Yes, Lex. Is everything all right?"

Alexa's reply was more slurred. "Oh, yes, your little sister is really going to hit the big time. Guess what . . ." Alexa giggled inanely. "I'm going to be a face clinic . . ."

"What!" Jo swallowed hard. "Speak up, I can hardly hear you . . . what do you mean?"

"Barry told me last night. Mr. Forga's going to open Devi clinics all over the country—all over the world." Alexa stopped short, as if she realized she'd said too much. Jo realized why. Forger. Mr. Forger—that had to be Mr. Moneybags's name. Jo longed to ask Alexa how he spelled it, what his first name was, but she didn't dare, and in any case, Alexa was now rattling on so fast, she began to sound out of breath.

". . . I'm going to be the biggest star. I'm going to get part of the . . . what's the word? The . . . I forget the word . . ."

"Equity?"

"Yeah, that's it . . . equity . . . and I'm going to meet the old girl herself when she comes to town to announce it. I'm going to earn millions, zillions . . ."

"When is Madame Devi arriving?"

"Don't sound so harsh, Sis. What's wrong? Isn't Mike treating you well . . ." Again Alexa started to giggle. "Don't come back here, Jo. New York isn't for you . . ."

"I'm sorry, Lex, but you don't sound like yourself. You sound as if you're on something . . ."

"I am." There was a pause; then Alexa whispered conspiratorially, "My friend, Dr. Marcus Lanning, and I are on happiness pills."

Jo drew in her breath sharply. *Doctor* Marcus Lanning. She had forgotten that Barry had introduced him as a doctor. Doctor of what?

Alexa's next sentence brought a flush to her face. She could feel it.

"Marc's taking me to Morocco to celebrate . . ."

"When?" Again her question snapped out like a bullet from a gun.

"Sis . . . Sis," Alexa murmured reprovingly. "You sound so cross . . . next week before the announcement . . ." Alexa paused. ". . . That is, if Devi allows it."

By the time Jo put the phone down, she knew she couldn't wait a couple of weeks for Mike to come back with her. She couldn't wait a week—a day. She had to go back at once, to instill somehow in Alexa the full purport of what she now knew, and then get Alexa and her future out of Devi's hands.

Jo booked a seat on the three o'clock afternoon flight. She

couldn't risk staying one more night with Mike. Her willpower wasn't up to it and too much was at stake. Mike called before she could call him. He understood. He always understood that duty came before everything else. "I'll drive you to the airport." He did. They kissed deeply on the curbside as a porter took her bag away. Before she walked into the terminal building, he held her shoulders and said, "I won't let you down, Jo. As soon as I can, I'll come to New York. It's really different now. I don't know what's going to happen between us, but it feels very good to me . . ."

CHAPTER EIGHT

THERE WAS A TINY PEARL BUTTON ON THE BATHROOM FLOOR, THE faint smell of violets in the shower, and two cups, two saucers draining in the kitchen rack. Jo. They all stood for Jo. They added up to the sinking, sick feeling in the pit of his stomach. He felt unnerved, unable to concentrate, full of self-hatred. He'd let her go back; hadn't even attempted to persuade her that a few more days, all right, ten more days—perhaps fourteen—wouldn't make any difference; that Alexa was big enough to look after herself and, in any case, had resisted so far all attempts on Jo's part to be guided, protected, or even warned about anything.

Mike told himself he hadn't said a thing because he had known it was useless to say anything logical about Jo's relationship with her sister. Although Jo was one of the most level-headed females he had ever known, as far as "family" was concerned, she was a walking example of "blood is thicker than water." Sister Alexa was obviously the most self-centered bitch of all time—but whatever she did or didn't do, as far as Jo was concerned, she was still the little sister who needed her care.

Mike kicked the wastepaper basket across the room, even as he tried to push down a rising sense of panic. He'd allowed her to fly straight back into the firing line. All right, all right, hold on there, he told himself. Let's take a long cool look at this again. Now Jo was no longer in his apartment, playing havoc with his emotions just by looking at him in that sweet, shy way of hers, disrupting his usual orderly method of weighing situations and assessing facts, he decided he would sit down at the old pine desk his father had left him and attempt to evaluate everything as if he were new to the story.

On a large piece of paper he wrote, "Fact" on the left and "Theory" on the right.

"Fact One: fading model Teri Shephard, with unfaithful, youthful-looking husband, saved up enough bucks to go to a San Fernando Valley face factory called The Fountain for a 'youth peel,' either advertised or recommended to her by model pal, Magda Dupaul, as a guaranteed way to restore youth and beauty. Magda, as Teri may or may not have known, was associated with The Fountain." In the margin, Mike wrote, "Probably had been given a piece of the action." He paused, then wrote quickly, "The Fountain had operated very profitably without any complaints, problems, or bad publicity for at least two or three years."

He got up to pace around his living room as he went through points in his mind, absentmindedly tidying up books and papers before sitting again to write under "Theory": "According to head nurse and administrator Ann Pershing, spokeswoman for The Fountain, Teri Shephard was disfigured by the peel." He moved his pen to the left side of the paper to write, "A car rented by Teri Shephard on June 3 from Hertz in San Diego skidded over a cliff in the Sierra Madres, exploded, and Teri Shephard burned to death."

Mike looked at his watch. 8:30 P.M. 11:30 P.M. at JFK where Jo would probably just be landing. The sick empty feeling returned. He doodled, shook his head, and went on, still writing under "Fact."

"The owner of record, a lawyer . . ." He paused, uneasy, as if he were missing a clue . . . damn it, he couldn't remember the guy's name, but he didn't want to stop. He continued on a fresh line. "Nurse Pershing and Magda Dupaul were called to testify seven months after Teri's death, when The Fountain was accused by the postal authorities of false advertising by mail. Although a subpoena was issued ordering Magda Dupaul's appearance before the court, she never turned up." Mike thought of something, jumped up, went over to his filing cabinet to look for a notebook. Yes, there was the name in his notebook. "The owner of record, Denny Upton, defended The Fountain's activities. The Fountain was fined, but allowed to continue to operate as a beauty clinic, provided the misleading ads were dropped." Mike stared into space. He had been astonished to learn there was nothing in the Food and Drug Act to prevent The Fountain from still using the peel process, providing they made no claims as to its miraculous age-restoring properties. Had someone else been "peeled" beyond recognition? There was no proof of that, but nevertheless, The Fountain had closed without warning a few months after the postal authority's hearing. He had tried to ferret out why without success. There seemed to be no apparent reason, for, if anything, business had continued to boom.

Moving to the right-hand column, Mike scribbled, "Magda Dupaul has never surfaced again. She probably left the country. Her agent, Loretta Pearson, implied there was trouble with her immigration status."

He sucked the end of his pen before adding another sidebar: "Q: Why wasn't Svetlana Lane asked to testify? Why was her name on the back of Teri's checks and not Magda's or Ann Pershing's? What was her role at The Fountain? Was she, in fact, the 'peeler'?"

Mike returned to the "Fact" column with grim determination. "Ann Pershing was murdered the day of her arrival in New York City on November 10, three days after admitting to Teri Shephard's daughter Jo and myself that her mother had been disfigured by The Fountain's peel."

Mike stared out of the window. Why had Ann Pershing gone to New York so suddenly? Why had she been murdered? To be silenced? What could she have known that meant so much to someone that her life had to be taken?

According to Jo, the murder had occurred about five months before Devi made its formal offer to Alexa. Jo had been certain from the beginning that Ann Pershing's death was related to her mother's disfigurement and death. Now, no matter how much he'd tried to reason with her, Jo was equally convinced it was also related to Devi's roller-coaster success. He sighed. Was it possible it was all one bizarre "life is stranger than fiction" coincidence? Svetlana Lane and Svetlana Lanning—were they one and the same person? And if so, did that mean Svetlana Lanning—today's Madame Devi—had once been The Fountain's peeler, creator of the famous youth-restoring peel? If so, there was plenty of reason to get rid of the nurse.

Jo was convinced of it, yet there was no proof. It was an extraordinary, deeply disturbing similarity of name, but that was all. There was the question of Teri's own name. She had used her own bank account in her professional name, Teri Shephard, for those checks to The Fountain.

Again Mike went to his filing cabinet to look at the report he'd typed up following the meeting with Ann Pershing. What had she said about Teri's death? That she'd heard about it from someone who had seen an item in a San Diego paper. As methodical as ever, Mike had found and stapled the relevant clips to the report. It hadn't been much of a news story, but now he read the two short clips word for word: "Local model Teri Shephard loses her life in Sierra Madres car crash inferno . . ." was one headline. "Heartbroken husband Ben Shapwell confirmed his wife, who used Teri Shephard as her professional name, was on her way to a Mexican modeling assignment. The Mexican police say she never had a chance—that accidents often happen to drivers not familiar with the tortuous mountain roads, subject to landslides following heavy rain. Teri Shephard is survived by her husband and two teen-age daughters." Just one mention of the name Shapwell in a couple of local papers. It was unlikely the name Jo Shapwell rang any bells in New York, if indeed what had happened to Teri Shephard at The Fountain cast a shadow over Devi's immaculate reputation. As for Alexa, according to Jo, she had been called Alexa Wells from day one in New York.

Mike poured himself a vodka on the rocks and took it to the window to look south toward Mexico, not even twenty miles away.

He hadn't been able to get much out of the Hertz office. No one had remembered a "disfigured woman" coming in. The young clerk had even smirked when she'd asked him to repeat the word *disfigured*. Embarrassment, he guessed. The most he'd been able to get was a vague recollection of someone bundled up, in big glasses with a sombrero pulled down over her face. "Gee whiz," the girl had complained irritatingly, "we're so busy in here, filling in all these forms, we don't waste much time looking at people, you know . . ."

The phone broke his concentration. Jo. It had to be Jo calling on landing at JFK, but it wasn't. It was Crager, one of his key news sources on the real-estate wheeler dealing going on in the city, someone he'd been trying to get to for days. For a second it all seemed unimportant, but he forced himself to listen. "Just like you thought, Mike, high tech is going to the South Bay. All that down-and-out stuff you have to pass by on the way to Mexico, well, some smart son of a bitch is buying up those dilapidated shit shacks like they were diamonds selling as paste." It was a story, a good one, but Mike still had to force himself to ask questions, keep Crager interested in talking. They arranged to meet for lunch the next day in Old Town, San Diego, where nobody except bug-eyed tourists lunched. Crager's final sentence sent Mike right back to stare at his Fact and Theory sheet. "There's a joker in this South Bay deal, Mike. A megabucks joker who's got more money than any of the big guys you've been yelping about on the tube."

"A joker . . . a megabucks joker." Jo had used the term "megarich" about a mystery man who was apparently the real money and power behind Devi, an international financier, who used the Concorde the way most people used the subway. "He's someone who doesn't want to be known," Jo had said, someone so powerful and wealthy that even Devi's staggering success was just an interesting little diversification as far as he was concerned. What was his main business? Jo didn't know, just as she didn't know where Madame Devi lived, worked, or even where her creative think-tank laboratory was situated.

Jo had bolted, she'd told him, bolted too quickly, just as she'd begun to gain the Devi lawyer guy's confidence. She had been unusually diffident about Barry—what was his name? Hogan? No, that wasn't it. Hunter. Barry Hunter. He'd teased her about it in bed during the past glorious weekend. God knew, he couldn't blame her if she'd been attracted to another man, to Barry Hunter, to Barry anyone. It was a miracle she still cared as much as she did after the way he'd treated her.

He couldn't think straight anymore. The memory of Jo in

his bed the past weekend engulfed him. The thought of her exquisite breasts, her hard nipples, filled him with longing.

He drank a Coke, brushed his teeth, read his Fact and Theory columns over again. They only had Ann Pershing's word that Teri had been disfigured. Why had she told them? Was she trying to get revenge against The Fountain because she'd been the fall guy in court? Mike remembered Pershing's messy but well-furnished apartment. There was nothing run-down about it, but he'd found out that although she was still on the nurses' register, since The Fountain had closed three years before, Ann Pershing had hardly worked at all.

Mike closed his eyes, propped his feet on the desk. Everything considered, the way Teri had died, Ann Pershing's murder, the disfigurement probably had taken place.

Something was bugging him and he couldn't think what it was. Something that was in the follow-up file in his office at the studio. He felt so restless he decided to go there. By the time he arrived, he estimated, Jo would just about have reached the Central Park South apartment in New York.

The relief he felt when she answered the phone was like taking a tranquilizer. "God, I've been so worried about you, puss. Was your flight okay? Is your superstar sister there?"

"Everything's fine . . . Alexa's asleep," Jo whispered. "I just peeked in to make sure she hadn't given me the slip. I'm going to set my alarm so I can tackle her before her exercise class . . ."

Mike resisted the urge to keep her on the phone, to go over moment by moment the time they'd spent together, touching, feeling, longing. Who knew who might be listening in on the Devi-paid-for line? He tried to keep his voice free of fear for her, strong, confident, tried to convey without spelling it all out how fast theory could become fact with two imaginative minds at work. "We've got to keep cool about this, baby. We may be assuming much too much." There was a click on the line.

"Jo . . ."

"Yes, I'm still here . . ."

"Jo, I love you." He hadn't said it before. Why he hadn't said it when she was tight in his arms and he was deep, deep inside her, he didn't know, but it had been there all along. Now he knew it. Her joy came across three thousand miles of wire, untrammeled, pure, simple. There was another click before she replied. "I love you, Mike."

"Until tomorrow. Sleep well, my puss."

He couldn't move when he put the phone down. He was suffused with so many feelings, of ecstasy, love, pain, fear. He put his head in his arms, whispering her name. "Jo . . . Jo . . ." until he was calm again. So where was the follow-up file that he had so casually, carelessly given to Jo to go through? What was in it that he knew had some relevance? He hadn't looked at it in months. It was a crime, but there it was. He'd reneged. No more. Real-estate scams, development crooks, multi-megabucks-millionaires behind land takeovers that were going for peanuts in some areas—they would all have to take a back seat until he could prove without any doubt that Jo's suspicions were groundless.

He was suddenly as alert and clear headed as he was before he went on the air. He found the file, opened it, and set to work.

"Down on the Wrinkle Farm . . . Where the Harvest is Always Good . . ." was the first headline he read in a Miami newspaper. He skimmed through it, remembering that he had clipped it because despite its sardonic tone, it gave a clear picture of the enormous profits to be derived from what the paper described as "dubious, often secret face-saving, peeling formulas."

". . . from $1,000 to $4,000 a time, 100 patients a week."

"A 23-year-old Lexington, Kentucky, acne sufferer was scarred for life following chemosurgery with phenol, also called carbolic, a poison easily absorbed into the system through the skin. Doctors say her kidneys have been infected . . ."

"Wife of surgeon in Los Angeles sues 'miracle' doctor for half a million dollars; says 'youth peel' caused pneumonia and pericarditis . . ."

Case after case, name after name, complications Mike couldn't even comprehend. ". . . In addition to scarring, the chemosurgery produced ectropion, a condition in which the eyelids turn inside out, and keloids, growths of skin in thick white ridges and nodules . . ."

There was a long, serious piece on chemosurgery and face-peeling that he'd kept from the *New York Times*. Now he made some notes from it: ". . . a medical procedure, employed by surgeons to erase superficial wrinkles, acne pits . . . more and more being used by nonmedical practitioners in this country and abroad, who promote the technique as a 'miraculous discovery' that produces baby-fresh skin. A spokesman for the Food and Drug Administration said, 'the government is hamstrung in prosecuting face-peel quacks because they do not fall under any precise regulation. To come under our jurisdiction the chemicals have to be shipped across state lines.' " Mike let out his breath. He'd always known the subject could make a terrific TV special, yet probably because of his mixed-up feelings for Jo, he'd suppressed his natural journalistic instinct to go after it.

Not anymore. This was a national story. Okay, so he had to continue to do his job covering the local scene, but if he wanted to get ahead, this was a natural for him to gain national recognition.

He read on, adrenaline building. "The Secretary of the Committee on Cutaneous Health and Cosmetics of the American Medical Association estimated today there are at least one hundred nonprofessional clinics operating in the United States, but nobody knows for sure how many. They are principally in Florida and California. We've also found that many of the ads in newspapers are for clinics operating in Mexico, Canada, and the Caribbean. The lay practitioners, who often call themselves 'facial rejuvenators' are usually beauticians, whose education background often consists of only a high-school diploma and a hairdressing course . . ."

There was too much good stuff in the piece to continue to make notes. Mike found a red marker pen and underlined ". . . the emphasis on youth in the United States accounts for the rising popularity of beautifying techniques such as plastic surgery and the chemical peel. The setup is perfect for the unscrupulous person. He or she is dealing with a patient who wants something desperately—youth."

Beneath the *Times* piece was something he'd cut out from an American Medical Association journal. For a second he wondered why it was there. Then he remembered. He had seen the author, Dr. John Owsley, a respected national authority on plastic surgery, on TV and made a note to try to see him as Dr. Owsley lived and practiced in San Francisco. "When chemosurgery is performed by qualified physicians, the patient is usually hospitalized for a . . ." Dr. Owsley had written in the journal. "Some doctors give their patients a medicated moisturizer or hyperemollient to apply; others cover the skin with a waterproof tape that enhances the peel before providing the moisturizer. Twenty-four hours after the skin is exposed to the air, a scab forms, which falls off after about a week, revealing very pink, very sun-sensitive skin . . ."

Mike got up to stretch his legs and his thoughts. Jo had told him the date on the certified check Teri had written for eighteen hundred dollars had been May 30. Teri's accident had been on June 3. That meant she could only have stayed at The Fountain for a maximum of four days, if that. There had been no week of waiting for the scab to fall off naturally, so obviously no "qualified" physician had been in charge of the peel.

Botched noses, "silicone" bosoms that changed location overnight, ruined life after ruined life . . . it was incredible how trusting, how naïve women could be, handing over their faces, their bodies to strangers they would never invite across their doorstep if they rang the bell.

Suddenly he had it, the story that contained the line that, buried deep in his subconscious, had bugged him for so long. It was from a Las Vegas paper, a feature story called "The Pursuit of Youth," but it wasn't the feature that provided the clue he had been looking for. He had read the story from top to bottom, weeks, maybe months ago, and had caught sight of a name that had jogged his memory—but until tonight hadn't jogged it enough.

In a paragraph at the bottom of the page was a six-line news item. Its placing was either a cynical subeditor's joke or more likely an ironic coincidence, appearing as it did on the same page as the feature that extolled new rejuvenators, including the benefits of a vibrating mattress.

"Adele Petersohn, who sued the Spring Skin Clinic in Paradise Valley for two million dollars last year, alleging she was permanently disfigured following a 'youth' peel treatment, has settled out of court for an undisclosed sum, according to Upton and Fuller, lawyers acting for the defendants. Mr. Upton confirmed the Spring Skin Clinic is no longer in business."

Mr. Upton of Upton and Fuller . . . Denny Upton, the owner of record of The Fountain. He'd seen it, yet not seen it and if he'd mentioned Upton's name to Jo, after he'd learned it from Burt Stokler, he'd certainly never repeated it to her. What a careless idiot he'd been.

He didn't leave the studio until after 1 A.M., finishing the file of misery, then going through the phone books. It was easier to find the number than he'd thought. In fact, Adele Petersohn was listed in Las Vegas twice. He gulped as he read the listing: Adele Petersohn, Shop of Magic . . . Adele Petersohn, residence.

The story stayed in his mind on the drive home and when he went to bed. He dreamed he was driving through the desert into a tunnel, which turned into the tunnel of love he'd once visited at a fairground when he was sixteen years old . . . but this tunnel was inhabited by gargoyles and monstrous, misshapen devils. He woke at four, at five, each time falling back into a pit.

After a jug of black coffee and a fierce ice-cold shower, he was ready to face every gargoyle, every monster, and even Madame Devi with a pot of disfiguring peel lotion held menacingly in long white hands with scarlet nails.

It was 8:30 A.M. Should he call Ms. or Mrs. Petersohn at home? Las Vegas was a city that never slept, except for those that earned their living there, but shops, he remembered, never opened much before ten. By 8:45 he couldn't wait any longer. He dialed the number. No reply. He dialed every ten minutes after that until 9:30. Then he switched to the Magic Shop number. A high, light voice with an attractive lilt of Scandinavia answered: "Shop of Magic . . ."

"May I speak to Adele Petersohn?"

"This is she."

He didn't know what to say. He stumbled, stuttered, even getting his name out. "Mike . . . Mike Tanner. Mike Tanner of station KCST, San Diego."

"Yes?" The voice was cool, no sign of hostility to the press, but no welcome sign either.

He took a chance, decided to lay it out straight, but it still came out clumsily. "This is . . . um . . . Ms. Petersohn, I'm working on a story that I believe is important. Something that has to be done . . . about fraudulent clinics run by unethical, unscrupulous fly-by-nighters who profess to be skin doctors . . ." There was no response at the other end.

"I wondered if I could come to see you. I believe—this is, I am sure, painful for you, but I believe you . . ."

"I was a victim." The voice was lower now, but he thought more interested, encouraging him to go on.

"Yes, yes, Ms. Petersohn. I have been reading about your case and many others—oh, so many others . . ."

"I am sure. Why do you want to see me? I am not an exhibit." There was no anger in her voice. She spoke as if she were filing the details of a passport application.

He liked her. He couldn't see her, but the thought came quickly, perhaps too quickly—she's a willing witness. "Ms. . . . Mrs. . . . Petersohn, I don't want to intrude into your privacy. I'm not calling you for any sensational TV show. I want to ask you a few questions, then perhaps at your convenience we could meet."

"Go ahead."

"Who owned the Spring Skin Clinic in Paradise Valley?"

"I'm not sure."

Mike felt a tremor of anger, of disbelief. He subdued it and began to say, "But surely . . ." when she interrupted.

"I think it was opened and perhaps wholly owned in the beginning by the woman . . ." She paused. When next she spoke, her voice was full of hate. "The Russian woman, the witch. Magda. Magda Dupaul. You remember the witch in Snow White? Mirror, mirror on the wall, who is the fairest of us all? That was Magda Dupaul." Mike tried to remain calm. Venom came across the wire in waves.

"Yes, yes, Ms. Petersohn, Magda Dupaul—she was beautiful as you say, but evil?"

She was not listening. She went on. "If I knew where she was now, I would tie her down and drip acid, on her face drop by drop, slowly, slowly in her eyes, over her nose, her perfect cheekbones, drop by drop . . . I have looked for her, but I have always been a moment too late. Once, yes, literally a moment. She disappeared into the desert—into the Beverly Hills canyons with her profits of sin, thousands and thousands of dollars . . ."

"Did you follow her to The Fountain?"

"What Fountain? The Fountain of Trevi?" The voice, full of hate, let out a high, hyenalike laugh.

Mike persisted. "You say in the beginning the Spring Skin Clinic was wholly owned by Magda Dupaul when you were a . . ." he hesitated, "a patient . . ." The woman was obviously only just on the brink of sanity, but he had to go on. "When you were a patient, was there a partner there? Svetlana Lane? Lanning? Sorgiokov?"

"All those names . . . what do you mean . . . I think there was a partner, not more than one . . ."

"Does the name Svetlana mean anything to you?"

"No."

"Do the names Lanning . . ." He spoke very slowly now, enunciating every syllable carefully. "Sorgiokov . . ." and then, "Lane mean anything to you?"

There was silence, and a slight difference in her tone. "Dr. Lane, you mean Dr. Lane. Yes, she was there. She came to see me. She was . . . she was different from the rest of them . . ."

"Dr. Lane?"

"Dr. . . . Professor . . . Nobel prize winner . . . I don't know—that's what she called herself."

"You say she came to see you. Did she perform the . . . the peel?"

A shrill scream cut into his eardrum, a scream of a mind in pain, deranged. "Yes, no, yes, no. They were probably all in it. Do you know how many skin grafts I've had. Those Russian swine burned me so badly, they destroyed me. The doctors I've seen . . . every one . . . they all say the same thing—I can't grow any more skin."

"My God, my God." Mike was sweating. He meant it when he said, "I hope they had to pay plenty. Two million dollars, wasn't it?"

There was the hyenalike laugh again. "Not with that fancy hotshot lawyer they had. Still, all I had to do was look at the judge. I can still see the horror in his eyes. They tried plenty of tricks, but it cost them nearly a million . . ."

A million. Mike shut his eyes. So even then, Magda Dupaul and Svetlana Lane and whoever else was involved had been able to cough up a million and still move on a year or so later to open up shop in the San Fernando valley.

"I'd really like to come to talk to you some more, Ms. Petersohn, to track these people down, expose them, save others from your terrible experience . . ."

"What did you say your station is? ABC?"

"It's the San Diego affiliate of NBC. This could be a national story." He was expecting her to mention money, but it wasn't money she wanted.

He felt the hair stand up on the back of his neck as she began to talk closer into the phone. "Do you want to put me on

TV? It would make a good story, all right. You see, the reason I opened the Magic Shop—you can guess, can't you?" She didn't wait for an answer. "Let the camera zoom up the Strip. I can just see it now. Close in on the street. Film the shop from the outside. Get the storefront close up, see, so all the folks know just where the Magic Shop is. As the camera is working, you can be talking, telling people what I went through . . . how I used to wear a big hat, dark glasses, and still see how terrified people were to go near me . . . that's okay, I'm used to reading that about myself . . ."

Mike couldn't guess where it was leading, but it was somewhere he didn't care for, that much he knew. In any case, he didn't want to stop her. One day she was going to be useful, that willing witness he'd sensed in her voice from the beginning.

"See, then, when you've given me the big buildup, the shop door opens . . ." She started to whisper. Had she ever been an actress? She certainly knew how to add drama to every sentence. "And the reason I bought the Magic Shop with some of the damage money becomes clear . . ." She started to laugh. It was a horrible sound. "You see, it gives me the perfect excuse to wear masks . . . monkey faces, clowns . . . no one's seen my face in daylight around here ever since I had the shop. Masks . . . all kinds of masks . . . just like the phantom of the opera . . ."

It was macabre. The hysterical note just held in check. The thought of the disfigured woman behind the mask. The ironic thing was she was right. Adele Petersohn, peeled and disfigured by either Magda or Svetlana or both, did belong in the TV special on the subject and a lot of her production suggestions weren't that bad either. Mike shivered as he brought the conversation to a close. Either Ms. Petersohn had been driven crazy by her terrible experience or she had the most extraordinary business sense he had ever encountered.

He promised he would call her in a week to set up a date for a camera crew to film just what she had suggested, then, wet through with nervous sweat, he took another shower before he left for the studio.

"Barry's called three times, wondering where you were . . . when you'd get back."

Alexa had crumbs around her mouth from the freshly baked corn muffins that Kiko had just brought in; her hair didn't look as if it had seen a comb in a month. She looked adorable.

With sunlight adding luster to the copper pots and pans decorating the big kitchen cabinet, the smell of Brazilian coffee and bacon sizzling on the stove, Jo felt her tautness, the feeling of dread she'd had on entering the apartment the night before, slip away. Perhaps it was because Alexa looked so relaxed, drowsy like a child just awakened from a nap, but happy because she knew she was going to a picnic or a circus or something fun. Even the mention of Barry's name didn't disturb her. Did she feel more at ease with Alexa than she had in months because of Mike? Jo was so sure Mike had something—probably everything—to do with it. He'd said it; he'd actually said it on the phone the night before . . . "I love you," and she had said it, too. Reciprocated love was protection. It made everything in life easier to handle. She smiled at Alexa and said simply, "Did you tell Barry I'd gone to San Diego, gone home?"

"Sure. It wasn't a secret, was it?"

"Nope, but remember when you told me not to trust him?"

Alexa nodded carelessly.

"Well, I don't. I don't want him to know my business but . . ." Jo looked around the big kitchen to make sure Kiko wasn't lurking about. "I intend to find out more about his business first."

Alexa lost her drowsiness. "You mean his? Or do you mean mine—that is, Devi? What's it all about, Sis?"

Jo put her finger across her lips. "Are you going to your usual workout class today?"

Alexa yawned. "Probably, although I should really go to see Mr. Scaasi to get some exotic harem clothes."

Jo frowned. "Are you really going to Morocco with Marcus Lanning?"

"Of course. Why not? Do you realize I've never ever been out of this country. It's incredible. Here I am sitting on all this money and I've never been anywhere, seen anything . . ." Alexa looked defensive. "In any case, I like him."

"That's obvious."

"You needn't bite my head off. I thought you'd be pleased that at last I've found a man I can enjoy . . ."

Jo thought she saw Kiko outside in the hallway. She

winked at Alexa and said loudly, "I'll walk over with you to the gym. I might even give the Nautilus a try. I can't seem to shake off those pounds I put on from that last eating orgy called a Devi tour . . ."

As impassive as ever, Kiko was waiting by the front door as they were leaving. "Ms. Wells. I have a message for you. Please call the master before noon today. Here is the number."

"The master? Who's that?" Jo asked in the elevator, a sense of foreboding coming back. Alexa laughed.

"That's Kiko language. In our lingo, dear, it's boss, but in this case, big, big boss."

"What's his name? Forger? The one you mentioned on the phone? Is he the one you've wanted me to meet for so long?"

Alexa put on her big dark glasses before they left the building to head down Central Park South toward the Plaza on Fifth Avenue. "His name is Baxter Forga . . ." She paused, and then spelled it out. "F-O-R-G-A. I've also heard him called Boris." Jo's pulse quickened. At last Alexa was forthcoming.

"And is he the one?"

"Yes, he is the one I wanted you to meet, but not now and maybe never. He's a mystery man. I realize now he doesn't want to meet people—well, not many. He lives in a world you and I really don't know anything about."

Jo cut in abruptly. "That's funny coming from you. What's so different about his style and the life you've always led—or at least seemed to lead in Santa Barbara on all those visits. I never saw a mansion like that one. It was like a hotel."

"Oh, that's not what I mean." At the Sixth Avenue traffic lights they stopped, and Alexa took Jo's arm tightly. "Look, I'm not playing games or trying to be evasive anymore. I don't know enough about the mysterious Mr. Forga. Once, when I was first brought into the presence"—she was trying to sound sarcastic, but not succeeding very well—"I thought he was a kind of grand protector who would look after my big sis and me . . . that he was going to turn into some good old Uncle Sam." She laughed, "I mean, Jo, the kind of father figure we both need and have never had, but it wasn't to be." She changed the subject abruptly as usual. "Did you find out where Dad moved to? Where our things are?"

Jo shook her head. "Let's have a coffee at the Plaza. I can't concentrate talking in the street."

To her relief, Alexa agreed and for the next thirty or forty minutes, Jo told Alexa everything. "I know I acted on impulse, but when I turned around and saw Barry watching me in the doorway at Mortimer's as I tried to remember Mike's number, all I could think about was you telling me he could be a piranha."

"Oh, Jo . . ." Alexa looked mortified. "I think you overreacted." She leaned toward Jo looking her straight in the eyes. "Why did you come back? Do you realize what you're suggesting? That Madame Devi was Mom's peeler? Or at least involved in it . . . now I understand why you're so worried about Marc. You think he has to be involved, too?" Alexa laughed but Jo didn't think Alexa thought what she had just said was very funny. "I agree, it's a terrible coincidence, but you know there are millions of Svetlanas in Russia . . . Svetlana Lanning—Svetlana Lane—it's close—but then so is Karen Graham the model and Katherine Graham the publisher . . ." Alexa wrinkled her brow. "And Ginny Hutton and Lauren Hutton, two models, not one . . ."

Jo shrugged. "You're right. I told you I acted impulsively, rushing off like that. But there were too many similarities, too much atmosphere of mystery. I promised Mike . . ." To her annoyance, Jo felt a blush rise up from her collarbone to flood her face, but although Alexa must have noticed, she said nothing. "I've promised Mike not to jump to conclusions so quickly, to cool it, at least until he gets here."

"Is it serious, Sis?" She couldn't remember when Alexa had spoken so lovingly.

Jo blushed again. "I think so." She shook her head, reproving herself. "No, I know so. We're in love. It's just wonderful, marvelous."

"You shouldn't have come back. You should have stayed with Mike. Honest. I think you were on edge because things were so unresolved between you. Everything seemed suspicious, peculiar, because of all you've gone through. I agree, there are some mysteries about Devi. But that's the nature of the business—the way they like to market this Now and Forever stuff . . ." Despite the air conditioning, Jo saw perspiration above Alexa's lips. "You've got to promise me, Jo, you really will cool it. Mike's right. There's no proof. A lot of funny stuff, coincidences, but no proof to link what happened to Mom and what's happened to me with Devi. That's all good, isn't it? And, okay, so the nurse who squealed got murdered. The fact you saw her just a few days before probably had nothing to do with it." Alexa looked at her earnestly. "Promise me, Jo, you won't go jumping to conclusions again. Find out what you like from Barry . . . about Devi . . . or whatever else you want to find out about. But don't put two and two together and come up with tragedy. You never know where that might lead."

Nothing Alexa said changed her mind, but all the same Jo felt much calmer about things, more resolved to get to know Barry Hunter better and find out more about Madame Devi's identity. If she turned out to be the Svetlana she thought she was, then perhaps she might be doing the mysterious Mr. Forga a good turn—and Alexa, too. If she was wrong, and there was no connection at all between the two Svetlanas, no one would be more relieved and happy to discover it than she herself.

"She's modern . . ."

"He shouldn't have let her smile. Hedy Lamarr was never allowed to smile. . . . She had a stupid smile."

"What the hell has Hedy Lamarr to do with 1983?"

"The same as Valerie Demerest has to do with 1983. I just told you. Dennis shouldn't have let her smile."

"Oh, shit, excuse my French." Penelope Waverly, *View*'s fashion fairy godmother, laid her wand, her magnifying glass, down on the light box and whirled to face Toby Jenkins, the art director. "I can't believe Blair said she's modern. She's wearing that divine Calvin denim as if it was prewar Biarritz."

"Excuse me . . ." Brown Schneider's tone contradicted her polite expression. "This is ignorance-is-bliss time, but can you explain to me, Pen, dear, as only the shoulder straps of Calvin's divine blue denim are showing on the cover, how a prewar message is conveyed by Ms. Demerest?"

There was a tense silence in the planning room, but everyone there knew that Brown was the only one, apart from Blair Benson herself, who Penelope would condescend to answer, however ludicrous the question. Brown was *View*'s celebrated intellectual. Even Pen acknowledged that.

Even so, today, with such a strained atmosphere, it was obvious Pen found Brown's question almost too much to deal with. "My dear Brown, I don't think any of us at this time of crisis can spend precious minutes explaining how the selling aspect of a cover may even start with the shoes—which are never seen—but which can build momentum with every other piece of apparel a cover girl wears. I am sure, out there are people you know with Ph.D.s on the subject, but . . ." Pen let out a long, carefully developed moan, ". . . we are in trouble. I know you found this wondrous creature for us, otherwise we would not be stealing you from your ivory tower to waste time in the planning room with visuals, but Ms. Demerest is not going to make it. I told Blair that from the beginning, but she wouldn't listen to me." Pen pointed an empty cigarette holder at four or five mock *View* covers pegged to the wall. "Look at these cover tries. Kim . . . Christine . . . Fava . . . they're great, but they're not . . . not . . ."

"Alexa, The Face, Now and Forever," the art director said laconically.

"Where is Blair?" Pen ignored him and looked impatiently at her watch. "What's happening to her famous punctuality?" The intercom beeped as she turned back to the light box. Pen's assistant, hovering in the corridor, was given the nod to pick it up. "Blair wants you in her office for the run-through."

"What run-through?" Pen screamed at no one in particular. "She's got the days all mixed up. What the hell is going on?"

All the same, she rushed out, speeding through the long corridor, crying over her shoulder as she went, "Resolve the cover crisis. Let's retake Demerest in that Issey Miyake . . . that won't get a smile out of her. Hooray."

Young fashion editors were in the first of Blair's outer offices, arranging bathing suits and track suits into color groups. Two models, one black, one with very white skin, were sitting in bathrobes, watching them without speaking. Pen muttered to herself, looking at her watch, acting out perfectly the part of a frustrated, tortured producer. "This run-through was for tomorrow, Rab. There's too much amateur night around here. What's going on?"

Blair's secretary shrugged his eloquent shoulders. *"Je ne sais pas . . ."*

"Oh, yes, you do, you old queen," Pen muttered again under her breath. She pushed Blair's half-open door, then stopped in the doorway dramatically. Blair looked sick, really sick. "Blair, what's the matter? Shall I call the nurse? You look wretched . . . terrible!"

Blair tried to dismiss Penelope with one of her coldest looks but failed. "I just had a nosebleed, God knows why. It's over. I'm feeling better already. I just came in. That's why everything is late. I went to get a shot from the doctor."

"You look as if you could do with a shot of scotch or something . . ."

Pen stood on one foot and then the other. "You know somebody screwed up. Did you see the Demerest cover tries? They're just in."

"I don't need to ask. No good, eh?"

"Not good enough, although Toby will try to tell you otherwise . . . 'modern' . . ." Pen mimicked the art director's description. "I don't know why you listened to Brown. She's a wonderful, talented bluestocking, but she doesn't know a Watteau from a Wyatt, let alone what makes a good cover."

Rab knocked on the door and came in. "Do you want to start the run-through? You have an appointment with the doctor at four . . ." He couldn't look more sly if he tried, Pen decided. But what the hell was really up with Blair? She'd just told her she'd been to the doctor and now here was another appointment at four? Either Blair was suffering from something she didn't want anyone to know about, or she was up to something else.

Blair looked curtly at Rab. "I changed my appointment. I went at lunchtime. Yes, we'll begin." They were halfway through the run-through that proceeded amazingly smoothly, when the pale gray phone behind Blair's desk rang. Pen could remember that happening only once before. Then there had been a major think tank in progress, a comparative study, which went on every three or four months, comparing *Vogue* and *View* one page at a time. Even Ed and Eve Post had been there, making their sardonic remarks about food, as they sold their proposal for a new food, wine, and restaurant column under the pseudonym of Signposts. Even though Pen knew Blair had only just charmed them into joining the magazine, they, along with everyone else, had been unceremoniously shooed out of the room. That phone call had had the immediacy of a fire alarm, and it was the same again today.

The phone rang again and although one of the models was wearing only the bottom half of the Galanos swimsuit, Blair ordered them all "out . . . out . . . out." It was a very uncomfortable moment.

Penelope stalked back to her office to look at Polaroids from the afternoon showing so far. When Blair whistled for them to return, she decided she would take her time. Whether Blair was sick or not, there was no need for this unprofessional behavior. It was also so unlike her. She was rarely late without a damn good reason, and Pen couldn't ever remember her mixing up a run-through date, which with models' time, was an expensive item on the fashion budget. Was something ominous going on? Was Blair selling the magazine? Looking for new management? There had been murmurs about the aptitude and style of the ad manager for some time, but that couldn't be the reason. Business was good. No, it had to be something else . . .

As it was, Pen didn't receive any summons back. Blair came into her office about twenty minutes later, closed the door behind her, and slumped into Pen's wonderful old planter's chair. From her tight-lipped expression Pen knew Blair had something unpleasant to say and she also knew she wasn't about to explain it.

Even so, when Blair made her terse announcement, it startled Pen enough that she threw her arms into the air.

"Don't worry about reshooting Demerest," Blair began. "Please don't ask me any questions and I do mean *any* questions. We are going back to your dream girl . . ." She couldn't help revealing some of her bitterness. "We're going to shoot your recent bête noir . . . mine, too . . ."

"You don't mean . . ."

"Yes, I do mean Ms. Alexa Wells, Devi's Face, Now and Forever . . ."

"I can't believe it . . ." Pen wheezed. "That's like giving Devi a million-dollar ad for free . . ."

"You heard me, Pen. That is my decision and nothing is going to change my mind."

Alexa was late, and she told the taxi driver so imperiously, implying he was to blame for catching every red light from Central Park South to East End Avenue, as usual a different address from the one she had visited before.

The driver mumbled unintelligibly, but all the same started to negotiate the traffic. It was the first time Mr. Forga had not sent the car, the long gray stretch with the wonderful dark windows that gave the world outside such a soft, seductive glaze, at the same time ensuring whoever was inside could not be seen at all. It was a reprimand, of that Alexa was sure, an indication that the master of Devi, Mr. Baxter Forga, was not pleased about her planned five-day vacation, squeezed in between the day she moved on a step further from just being The Face, Now and Forever, to the day she became a big shareholder in the whole enormous Devi empire.

Instead, as she had expected to be fifteen, twenty minutes late, she arrived outside an imposing brownstone house only twelve minutes after the appointed time.

A familiar mixture of fear and anticipation churned her stomach. He would think she was being deliberately late—that every time they met she had changed, if only imperceptibly, that she was—inevitably—becoming spoiled by her spectacular success, showing a newfound independence that he had indicated once before he did not like and would not tolerate.

It would take time to lull his fears, subdue his suspicion, and above all overcome the opposition she expected to the upcoming vacation. She thought she knew how to do it. She was determined, but she was becoming careless. The driver confirmed it. Instead of having the fare ready, she spent another minute or so finding money. It gave him time to turn to look at her. As she handed him a five-dollar bill he said, "There's something about you that's familiar, miss. Aren't you . . . what's her name . . . you know, the most beautiful face or something like that?" She wasn't supposed to be "recognized" off duty—particularly when keeping an appointment with Mr. Forga. That had always been an edict.

"Keep the change." She jumped out of the cab, adjusting her dark glasses, pushing a few stray golden hairs back into place in her chignon, habits that like nervous tics always appeared on the occasions when Forga summoned her.

The door was ajar as it was whenever, wherever they met and also as usual, except for the soft glimmer of a dark-blue Rigaud candle, the hallway was unlit. Her self-confidence started to crumble as she heard his voice call from the landing above. "Alexa, please come up. I am looking forward to seeing you. It seems longer than two weeks."

The stairs were highly polished black lacquer and she climbed them timidly, not only because she felt she was on a black ice slope, but because for the first time Mr. Forga was not waiting for her in an office environment behind a massive marble desk. He was at the top of the stairs, his face illuminated by a spotlight, which also shone on a striking ebony sculpture of a kneeling woman behind him, her head thrown back so far an ebony sweep of hair touched the ground. As Alexa reached the top step, she heard the front door below click shut.

"This is an important occasion, my dear . . ."

Her hands were moist with nervousness but he didn't this time shake her hand. She followed him down a deeply carpeted hallway into, she supposed, a sitting room with gold brocade sofas, tapestries on the walls, and other ebony sculptures in beautifully lit alcoves.

She felt awkward, uncomfortable, like a little girl at her first grown-up party. Take hold of yourself, Alexa, take hold of yourself. Her nervousness grew as he patted a space beside him on one of the giant sofas.

She tried to distance herself from the power of his personality. She tried to avoid the searching glance of his dark eyes. It wasn't only that he was a handsome man, in the brooding, intense way she guessed Charlotte Brontë had envisaged Rochester to be or her sister Emily had dreamed up Heathcliff. He exuded some massive, inborn self-assurance that engulfed the other person. Except for the one time he had stood up to say good-bye, when she had felt hypnotized by his eyes, this was the closest she had ever been to him and she immediately wanted to be nearer, not in a sexual sense, but to receive the approbation of his touch, approval laid on by his hands as well as seen in his eyes.

"You are my star, my chosen star, you know that, Alexa, do you not?"

She slowly nodded, knowing his eyes were commanding hers to meet his.

"Barry has talked to your people, your agent. In a few months, your contract with them will be at an end. You will be one of the most important people in the Devi empire. You will be one of the most important businesswomen in the world. As an inspiration to women all over the world, you will embody all that Madame Devi's search for eternal youth can and has produced."

Alexa's head was swimming as she found she could not move her eyes away from his. "People are already waiting for you in Rio, in Buenos Aires, in Tokyo, and of course in Paris and London. You have never been to those cities."

It wasn't a question. He wasn't touching her, yet it was as if he held her firmly in his grasp.

"We are going to spread the Devi doctrine to the four corners of the earth, and you, my beautiful Alexa, are going to the four corners of the earth—and to the moon. Do you know what going to the moon is like, beautiful Face, Now and Forever?"

Again she shook her head, at that moment longing to go to the moon, to the four corners of the earth, anywhere with him.

His voice was so melodious, it was like the ocean breaking on the cliffs of Mendocino, like the breeze whispering through the palms of Santa Barbara. "You are a star, but you will need help to maintain your star quality, my flawless Alexa. You will begin to feel you want to be more like yourself than you already are—a superstar, a comet above the crowd. I will help you achieve this."

He stood up, turned away and the spell was broken. She felt she might have sighed with relief out loud, for as Forga started to walk toward a far door, instead of a master dominating her, taking her mind willingly to wonderful, unknown places, here was just a man still enormously powerful, but nevertheless just a man, not a god, not a master. All the same, her mind reeled. Rio, Buenos Aires, Tokyo . . . did he mean she was about to go there?

"Come here, Alexa." She followed him into an anteroom and gasped. There on a cinema-size screen was a film of Marc and herself, hand in hand, walking, talking in Greenwich Village. She remembered immediately they had been on their way to a Moroccan restaurant that Marc wanted to introduce her to.

Baxter Forga said gently, "He is a wonderful man, but you cannot go to Morocco with him now. There are too many important things to do."

She had had a speech ready, a strong line of argument to use, but every word of it had gone out of her head. Instead, she said only one word, "Why?"

"It is all part of our strategy, our multimillion-dollar empire strategy, my dear. On Thursday, when you were hoping to fly away, you have a very important appointment with an old friend."

They were back in the large, luxurious sitting room, and this time he touched her, stroked her hair in a way that made her feel again like the star she now accepted she had to be.

She waited patiently, hands clasped on her lap, for Mr. Forga to tell her who the old friend was.

"You are expected at the *View* office to discuss a sitting for the all-important September cover with the owner and executive editor and, perhaps more important, Penelope Waverly." Forga looked at her fondly. "Morocco will still be there next year and by then you will be able to buy a slice of it for yourself if you so desire."

He led her back to the precipice of a staircase. "After the photography session is completed we will celebrate—on Sunday. I will send Barry to collect you. We are going to celebrate in a special way. I am going to show you what it can be like to journey to the moon."

CHAPTER NINE

"WHY DID YOU DISAPPEAR SO SUDDENLY?"

If Jo had ever thought Alexa was right, that Barry Hunter could strike like a piranha, it was hard to believe today.

They were lunching at The Four Seasons—in the Bar Room, which Barry had already told her was the place to be seated, not the glamorous, showy Pool Room next door, where out-of-towners sat around a nonstop fountain looking for celebrities.

He had just ended his own celebrity-spotting session, telling her who was who on the banquettes around the room, not familiar faces of actors, models, TV personalities, but real power brokers, men and a few women who, it seemed, controlled the world or could if they put their minds to it. Barry told her with a note of reverence she found both appealing, yet also disquieting, that these power moguls lunched there nearly every day, so had their own reserved seats at the well-spaced-out tables "to preclude commercial espionage or eavesdropping with no infernal fountain splashing to interrupt their megabucks deals."

Barry squeezed her hand and Jo knew it was time to concentrate on being as clever as he was, if not cleverer. She felt cool.

Everything Mike had told her over the phone was clear in her mind; about Adele Petersohn's disfigurement at the Spring Skin Clinic, ". . . the evil witch, Magda Dupaul . . ." Magda, also a model, who had been her mother's friend, and about the all-important link between the Spring Skin Clinic and The Fountain, Denny Upton, lawyer for the first, owner of record of the second. Uppermost in her mind, though, was the name Dr. Lane, who, Mike had told her, the owner of the Magic Shop had implied ". . . was different from the rest of them . . ." Jo looked directly at Barry. Alexa had once told her. If you want a man to believe you think he's wonderful, look him directly in the eyes and don't look away. Apparently Alexa had read that in a book about the duchess of Windsor, whose huge blue eyes had so mesmerized the king of England he'd fallen off his throne.

But it wasn't easy to keep looking straight into Barry's eyes, which were also so blue; Jo immediately thought of the Mediterranean and fish and . . . piranhas. Oh, please God, help me to concentrate, concentrate. "I had to work things out, Barry . . . You know, I have this . . . this boyfriend back home. After that evening with you, he called me late that night. I felt all mixed up." Jo could hardly believe how easily her imagination threaded the lies together. "He called to tell me my dad was moving out of the house. We hadn't been getting on so well. We hadn't kept in touch. I didn't even know where Dad was moving to. I just felt I had to see him. My dad, I mean. To patch things up and . . ." she longed to look away but, as Barry's hand went to her knee, she forced herself to keep her eyes fixed on his. "I had to sort things out for myself. To see how I still felt about . . ." She hesitated; should she mention Mike's name? Of course, she told herself, there was no reason not to. ". . . About Mike, my boyfriend."

"And how do you feel?" Barry gently squeezed the soft part of her thigh before moving away to pick up his glass of Perrier.

There was no way she could lie about Mike. She didn't have to give the game away, but she couldn't, wouldn't ever be able to say she didn't care. "He's a wonderful man . . . Who knows what's going to happen?" she ended lamely.

"Is it serious?"

The waiter helped, arriving with their first course, a sorrel soup that Barry insisted she try. Jo attempted to. "Is anything called serious today?" It was a remark totally out of character, but then Barry couldn't know that.

For a second he put his arm around her shoulder. It increased her uneasiness because she didn't object to it at all. It was odd. This man's arm made her long for Mike . . . for sex with Mike . . . but when he took his arm away, she wanted it back, gripping her shoulder.

"One thing's serious." He smiled.

"Oh?"

"Mike's three thousand miles away—and I'm right here."

She was blushing, but that was all right, too. Mike loved her. He'd told her so. She felt it, knew it. Perhaps that needed boost to her self-confidence had made her more attractive to someone as sophisticated as Barry Hunter. Perhaps she'd become more interesting to someone like Barry because she'd become less attainable, had more or less told him she was "unavailable," or at least not uncommitted.

"What does this lucky guy Mike do?" The question was casual, but she, foolish girl, hadn't expected it.

"He's—um—he's a writer, a free-lance writer . . ."

"Successful?"

She felt disloyal now, but there was no way out. "Up and down. You know, like most free-lancers . . ."

To her relief, Barry changed the subject. "Well, there won't be any more downs in your life, Jo. There's a big reason for this lunch."

A nerve in her throat jumped. She quickly drank down some Perrier, determined not to be distracted by anything "unexpected." Svetlana, she told herself fiercely. Find out more about Svetlana Sorgiokov. Find out about the link between Lanning and *Lane!*

"We don't want you to go unrewarded. Your sister is doing the most remarkable job for Devi. We don't want you to think we don't know how much you are contributing to that."

She tried to continue the eye-to-eye confrontation, but it was too difficult. She looked down at the tablecloth. "How am I helping?"

"Well, we know you helped us keep Alexa from flying off

to Morocco." Before she could speak, the look of surprise on her face was enough for Barry to continue. "Kiko doesn't miss much." He paused, frowned, then hastily added, "Not that there was anything wrong about the trip. Obviously, we have the greatest regard for Dr. Lanning . . . We introduced him to Alexa after all. The timing was wrong. We know your influence keeps Alexa concentrating on her job. It's particularly crucial that she give Devi all her attention now."

We . . . we . . . we . . . had Barry always used the plural when talking about Devi? She couldn't remember.

"I don't understand. Why is it so crucial now?"

Barry looked stern. "You have a lot of insight—intelligence, Jo. I told you before that Madame Devi has been backed from the beginning by a man of considerable . . ."—he paused dramatically—". . . extraordinary wealth. Madame Devi's search for active principles . . . her research to find ways to stabilize, modernize the formula she discovered in India, her immunology labs, her team of biochemists—all this has taken hundreds of thousands of dollars . . ."

"Where are the labs? Where does all this take place?"

Barry waved a vague hand. "In Paris. I told you before . . . in many places in the world . . . on the West Coast . . . but everywhere, there is the best talent, the best equipment, all paid for, backed by this one man who is convinced Madame Devi has begun to find a way to tap the fountain of youth." Now Barry was staring at her. Jo clutched the seat of her chair, praying she still looked calm, that his last sentence ending with the chilling words "the fountain of youth" hadn't immediately revealed her suspicions, her terror.

Barry went on as earnestly as he had that night at Mortimer's . . . about the brilliance of Madame Devi, this time extolling the amazing facilities that had been provided for her. "She has a memory bank that is bigger than the one in Santa Monica." A lot of what he said went in and out of Jo's mind faster than the soup went down her throat. She was waiting for an opportunity to get back to Madame Devi the woman, Madame Devi who had been born Svetlana. It didn't come, and suddenly, there was reason to pay close attention to every word Barry was saying. "We want you to come on board the Devi ship. We're going to offer you a substantial salary . . ." His arm surrounded her shoulders again. "We want to make you official. How does a hundred thousand dollars a year sound?"

"What!" There was no way she could hide her stupefied reaction. "How on earth could I be worth that much to you?" She was so mortified by her lack of cool she could have stuffed the elegant Four Seasons napkin into her mouth, but apparently her innocent reaction couldn't have been better, for she realized Barry must have been tense himself. Now he seemed to relax suddenly, leaning back against the banquette, roaring with laughter.

"Jo, you are such a delight to deal with . . ." He took her hand and with a courtly gesture brushed his lips against it. "You are worth your weight in gold because you have such a commonsensical head on your shoulders. We want you to guard . . ." he corrected himself, ". . . guide Alexa. As you know, we're going to open Devi Now and Forever face clinics in selected markets across the country. We're going to take Devi overseas, everywhere. Alexa's participation—financial rewards in terms of equity and, when we go public, stock options—are being worked out now with the main financial team, but how do you feel, Ms. Shapwell, about being one of the top-salaried women in the country?"

Guard Alexa! What a Freudian slip. Jo smiled, she hoped her most angelic Alexa-like smile. "I am, well, obviously overwhelmed . . ."

And obviously no one at Devi dreamed she might turn the offer down. Her acceptance had been taken for granted. She repeated, "I'm just overwhelmed—but what does Madame Devi think about all this?" She giggled like a schoolgirl. "After all, she is the genius—we all know that—but isn't she . . . well, she is a woman, after all . . . although the way you speak about her she could be a goddess, but isn't she likely to become, well, jealous about all this attention being paid to Alexa? And now me? Does Madame Devi understand Alexa's role and importance in the Devi company's expansion plans?"

Barry squeezed her hand again. "That's a very intelligent observation and I'm not surprised you made it. The answer is I'm not sure. It's quite likely she doesn't know—and doesn't care to know. She has never wanted anything to do with the business side of the operation. You mention *goddess,* but perhaps it's more like a Wizard of Oz."

Witch . . . thought Jo, *witch.* She tried to lose the negative thought as Barry went on. "Madame Devi lives in her own world of research, development. Few of us have ever met her. I am one of the fortunate ones."

So much had happened, so much had changed. Jo looked down in surprise to see a coffee cup in front of her. She had eaten the main course, or probably not eaten it without realizing what had been placed in front of her. Her hand was trembling. She hadn't accomplished what she had set out to do. It was ten to two. She didn't know how much time Barry had allocated to the lunch. She had to steady herself somehow . . . had to go to the ladies' room, even if a few precious minutes would be lost.

"Barry, this offer—well—I don't know . . . it's made me so nervous. I just have to go to the ladies' room. You don't have to rush away, do you?"

"I'm all yours, baby. All afternoon if you like. How about coffee in my apartment—it's only a couple of blocks away."

She shook her head quickly. "No, no, I can't. I promised Alexa I'd go over to the studio—they're starting work on the *View* cover shot this afternoon, but I'll be back in a second." She didn't make the mistake of heading for the phone to call Mike this time. She really did need to go to the bathroom. Her stomach was playing tricks. She slapped cold water on her face. Probably the cloak-room attendant thought she had drunk too much. In a way, she wished she had had a drink, but Barry had never offered her one.

He was talking on the phone by the reception desk when she ran back up the stairs to the Bar Room. He gestured for her to go back to the table. When she did, she gasped. There was a huge bouquet of red roses beside her plate. "Welcome to the Devi family," said an attached note.

Oh, if only everything she had ever suspected could turn out to be just one horrible, amazing coincidence. If only, as Mike had tried to point out, Ann Pershing's death and all the other events surrounding it were circumstantial evidence, that in a court of law would be immediately dismissed.

Barry caught her sigh as he came back. He kissed her cheek. She thanked him shyly, then summoned up courage to say, "Should I thank Mr. Forga, too?"

There was no surprise on Barry's face that she knew his

name. "I think that would be a nice polite thing for a well-brought-up girl like you to do."

She rushed on as her nature always made her rush on. "Alexa said something to me on the phone about Madame Devi coming to New York to make an announcement about big changes—the expansion—will I meet her then?"

Again, there was no change in Barry's expression as he said easily, fondly, "Well, no, I don't think so. In fact, she's not coming to New York now. As I've told you before, she's a recluse—not interested in personal publicity. All she wants is to continue her work—to find the magic solution to solving old age. I suppose you could also say she's dedicated to proving Mr. Forga is right to have so much belief in her."

Barry's hand was on the soft part of her thigh again. "You know, the highest-paid executives in this country are paid about two million dollars . . ." He looked tenderly at her. "Rock stars, of course, earn a little more, shall we say someone like Kenny Rogers, about ten million a year." He brought his face closer to her as he whispered, "Mr. Forga controls an empire with assets estimated, some say conservatively, at two-point-five billion. One of his most lucrative enterprises provides him with about forty to fifty million dollars in annual income. Isn't that the kind of family business you want to be associated with?"

Jo's spirits soared. Her suspicions began to evaporate. One day she would find out the real identity of Svetlana Lane, but now she was beginning to think that perhaps she'd been crazy all along. No man with an empire of that size, of that importance, could be involved with anything as tacky as a face clinic that five years before had disfigured her mother. It was ludicrous. Before she could answer, now genuinely smiling at him with her eyes as well as her mouth, Barry asked, "Do you party?"

She hesitated, not sure what he meant. He went on fast, "If you don't, you're going to, my dear Jo. Mr. Forga is going to give a very exclusive party—just for the family, the Devi family, and that definitely includes you."

Jo could hardly wait to get back to the apartment to phone Mike. Now the phone, owned by Devi, like everything else in the apartment, the phone that she had regarded with such suspicion, was an instrument like any other. If Kiko was around, listening or not listening, he wanted only the best for Devi—that was what it was all about. They were right to employ her to guard, guide, do whatever was best for Alexa, who goodness-only-knew could be a self-destructive wildcat just when she had the most going for her.

Before calling Mike, Jo dialed the studio where a new assistant to Penelope Waverly told her brusqely, "Pen would prefer that you don't come over for an hour or so. She wants to be alone with Alexa." That suited her. To her relief and joy when she dialed the San Diego office number, Mike answered the phone himself.

"Mike, I feel so much better. I can't explain it. I'm sure it's you . . . you who made me calm down . . ." She related the events of the lunch with Barry Hunter. When she mentioned the hundred-thousand-dollar offer, Mike whistled through the phone.

"That's incredible, baby Jo . . . whoa!"

Mike went right along with her newfound longing to believe she'd perhaps been wrong . . . that incredible coincidences could happen in life. When she put the phone down after hearing over and over again how much he loved her, Jo couldn't remember feeling so happy in years, and soon Mike would be in New York. His real-estate probe was coming to a climax. He would arrive in New York perhaps in time for Mr. Forga's party. He would see for himself what she was at last beginning to believe—that Devi was not rooted in evil.

On the West Coast, after Jo's call, looking out toward the great span of the Del Coronado Bridge, Mike was grim. He had bolstered Jo's feelings of optimism, reinforced her decision to be less suspicious only for her sake.

As far as he was concerned, the hundred-thousand-dollar annual salary, the emphasis on the huge fortune behind Devi only made him more apprehensive that there was something sinister about the whole affair.

Umberto Ritaldi was proud he represented a unique kind of bellboy, who, as one of a specially trained corps, carried his business with him on an equipped beeper belt as effortlessly as, he supposed, members of the five families carried their weapons.

He'd been to training school to understand how the electronics of his beeper worked, how to repair it, so he could be on call twenty-four hours a day, ready to provide snow for plush sales meetings to impress out-of-town buyers or for private parties—as he told his best friend from his native Colombia—for those really in the fast lane.

Today, though, he was tired of working so hard. He wanted to catch the Yankees game but first he wanted to pick up a particular skirt he'd been lusting after since the night before on Eighth Avenue and 43rd.

When the personal code number of a very important Wall Street client came through loud and clear on his beeper at 5:50, Umberto was at first tempted to ignore it. He looked at the gold watch he'd been able to buy with his first week's commission, thought about the fullness of the black breasts he'd been shown when shopping the night before, the thick black bush he'd also seen as the woman had opened her thin raincoat to show him more of the naked merchandise beneath. He'd been interrupted by an urgent call then, too, but he'd made it clear he'd be back to sample plenty the next night . . . and now this!

He was about to shut off his beeper when the code came through again, insistent, not to be ignored. He knew there was really no way he could ignore it. Somewhere out there was someone who somehow would know he'd turned his back on an important order, and that would be very bad news for him. Bad news like ending up dead in a concrete mixer. Two signals meant "rush"—just like in the bad old days when he'd been a cycle messenger for the two-bit delivery service, carrying manila envelopes with URGENT and RUSH written all over them.

If he was lucky with the subway he might just be able to do his duty, deliver the gentleman's nose candy, drive his rod into that sweet black Eighth Avenue ass, and still hit the stadium, when he could legitimately switch off his beeper until 11 P.M., when business went back to prime time.

He looked at his watch again. There was a rule that if delivery couldn't be made within twenty minutes he had to call H.Q. It had been made clear at the outset the fewer calls the better. It had also been made clear it wouldn't necessarily mean just losing the job. Umberto looked at his watch again. Twenty minutes was a breeze. He could do it.

Whoever invented the touch-tone beeper had to have been a genius, he thought, as he struggled through the rush hour crowds. Anyone with a good memory could make a fortune. His memory was improving all the time. He had regular clients and could recite their personal codes in his sleep, just as he could also match code to order with no trouble at all. Some wanted pure "rock," others half "sand," half "rock." He was part of a major league. He could and did supply whatever was required. In his vest were six or seven white business envelopes, all carrying in heat-sealed plastic containers the sweet white powder that was first-class cocaine, seventy percent pure, no shitty street stuff busted up with lidocaine and speed or borax. No sirree. Mr. Umberto delivered the best "size eights" in the business and he didn't need to be reminded what this particular celebrated client wanted, although it was unlike him to punch his number twice. He knew this gentleman, a top Wall Street lawyer, would be taking his usual order of a beautiful size eight for the evening . . . an eighth of an ounce, about three and a half grams, for a cool six hundred dollars in cash.

As Umberto emerged into the Wall Street canyon and walked down the street to enter an impressive white stone building, there was his client, handsome, erect, buying a cigar at the cigar stand. He waited as he'd been told to wait in the past by the swinging door until his client looked up and saw him. He went back out into the street, and then, as he saw his client approach, he went back in, envelopes changed hands, and Umberto headed toward Eighth Avenue.

Two miles uptown, the Park Avenue drug dealer, Madeline Abbott, the third name she'd adopted in two years, looked like a successful young female executive in a snappy dark navy sheath and designer sunglasses as she sat in a matching dark navy Mercedes coupe in a spot marked RESERVED in an underground parking lot. Although Madeline could not be described as anything but "well dressed," the customer in the passenger seat was obviously in another class, from another world.

From the charcoal-and-pale-lilac cashmere shawl draped so casually, yet landing with precision in perfect curves around her body, to the gold-and-pearl Elsa Peretti pin securing it at exactly the right spot on the shoulder of her pale gray suede suit, from the small deeper charcoal beret that emphasized perfect lustrous sideswept dark gold bangs, this woman was an obvious nominee for the best-dressed list.

"Do you want me to drive you somewhere?" Madeline

asked. There was an obsequious tinge in her voice that she detested. It was often there when she dealt with this customer. She knew why she'd hesitated, too. She'd also felt she should have added, "ma'am".

The beautifully shaped head leaned back wearily against the car seat. "Yes," she spoke so quietly it was almost a whisper, almost a moan. "Drive me to the usual corner, but give it to me now." Madeline got out of the car as if to inspect the tires, looked around the almost empty garage, got back into the driver's seat, and handed Blair Benson the ration of snow already prepared for her, the ration she had been told by her boss to supply.

As usual there was tension between them and, as always, Madeline foolishly tried to dispel it, to get through somehow to this woman, always so stunningly dressed and about the most inscrutable human being she'd ever set eyes on. "Going somewhere special tonight? You look . . . well . . . just incredible, but then you always do."

She didn't expect an answer and she didn't get one. As she drove up Park Avenue and stopped at a red light before making the left turn toward Fifth, Blair Benson after a few inhalations stopped slumping, sat upright, her cheeks slightly flushed, a sense of regained authority about her.

"I've changed my mind," she said. Her voice was still low, but now distinctly haughty. "There's no need for me to go home. I'd like to get to the party early." She laughed humorlessly. ". . . Before the guest of honor arrives."

Madeline was amazed. She never knew where her customers went or were going when, their self-confidence regained or whatever it was that they needed the snort or the snow for, she dropped them where they told her to drop them. "Are you sure?"

"Of course, I'm sure." Blair Benson opened a burgundy alligator purse that Madeline had coveted ever since Blair got into the car. She took out a thick gold chain that also looked like a manacle and clipped it around her throat. She studied a business card. "Take me to East End Avenue. I'll tell you when to let me out."

It was the call from Forga that had made him call for an order and he was glad he had. Barry told himself the party was already something so outside Forga's normal pattern of behavior, it wasn't showing any lack of control on his part to get a quick snort before picking up Jo and Alexa. There were already enough guys on the fast track, he knew, who had the habit and it certainly hadn't slowed up any of their deals. He already felt better, faster, in fact pretty much invincible, and he looked good, too.

Who had Forga invited to this "family party"? He didn't have a clue, but, to ready himself for any eventuality, he'd given in to an impulse to get a little self-protection. He'd regretted it for about twenty seconds. Now he knew he'd been right.

As the car approached Central Park South, Barry did some swift calculations on the slim gold calculator he always carried with him. Until Forga's phone call, he'd never been totally sure whether the master plan for the huge Devi expansion was for real or for show. He'd also never been sure how much equity he was in for. For obvious reasons. Forga had never told him, although he'd implied in a way that only he could imply that he, Barry, was one of his very special boys, a chosen one.

Barry shook his head as if to shake away a cobweb. Being with Forga was like the first time he'd ever taken a snort. Although it was always good, nothing could ever repeat that first time, the intense pleasure had been so unexpected, the feeling of being so smart that you could run the world. Only Forga could still make him feel that he could really do anything—and for Forga he would do anything.

Barry leaned back, tension seeping out of him. His first serious love affair had led him to score his first dope. He'd liked it, but he'd been far too smart to get hooked. It had been recreational then. It was recreational now.

Forga liked him for his knowledge and control of the sweetest powder in the world.

In fact it was Forga who had once told him it was useful, because it could help him "reprioritize the brain's drive." He'd liked that. Forga had a way of putting things that were exactly right. Snow didn't just unlock libido or help a guy get more fun from sex. It just made everything about life more intense, more interesting; particularly business.

Were Jo and Alexa about to be introduced to the moon shot that would "reprioritize" their endeavors, their goals? Barry doubted it, but then you never knew with Forga, who from his earlier psychiatric work certainly knew how to get the most out of human beings.

Barry took out the calculator again. On his private line Forga had told him what he'd half been expecting to hear for the past three or four months. A giant pharmaceutical group had sent an emissary. There was interest. More than interest. For some reason, Forga, unaccountable to anyone except himself, had not turned the emissary away. He wanted new financial projections based on the offer in twenty-four hours. Barry was sure Forga had already projected them himself. For some reason, Forga's passion for finding the solution to "youth, now and forever" had either waned or had been replaced by something else. Either way, Barry smiled complacently as the car turned into the girls' driveway. He was going to be rich, not just rich but very, very rich—with or without Forga at the helm. Forga had made it clear that if he sold out to the drug company, Barry was part of the deal and there was no way he could lose.

Jo couldn't believe how adorable Barry was being—just like the first time he had escorted her to what in her mind she'd always called "Alexa's coming-out party."

She'd changed her dress three times, brushed out the tangled hairstyle she'd allowed herself to be talked into by one of *View*'s fancy hairdressers, who prided himself on never going near a salon, only to a studio to work on models' hair for sittings.

It was Alexa's fault that she was nervous. Only an hour before Barry was supposed to pick them up, Alexa had announced that although Marc Lanning hadn't been invited to Mr. Forga's party, he was still taking her there and ". . . afterward, to make up for not going to Morocco, he's borrowed a friend's yacht to sail us around another exotic place—Manhattan Island."

Okay, okay, so she should be pleased that Alexa was acting like a human being—acting as if she were in love or something . . . Still her own personal gremlin haunted her, whispering that Marc Lanning could be Marc Lane, son of Svetlana, son of the peeler.

But it wasn't only that. Jo knew how much this party meant to Mr. Forga. She knew how much he was counting on her, Jo Shapwell, to produce an Alexa who was a shining example of belief in what she was doing, who was not going to go off on some moonshine trip with a lover, even if he happened to be the son of the remarkable woman who had made Devi possible.

As she changed into the third and last dress she would wear that night, Jo tried to think more positively—at least it was preferable that Marc Lanning was the son of Madame Devi. What if Alexa's chosen beau had been someone else—a movie producer, a timberman from Mendocino, a dropout from Santa Barbara. Jo sighed. She would do her best to do her job, to guide, and if necessary guard Alexa, but Alexa would always make it difficult, trying and mostly succeeding to do exactly what she damn well pleased.

And now Barry was being so adorable, not even frowning, when, on arrival, he'd had to be told that Alexa had already left with an uninvited Marc Lanning, en route to the East End Avenue address where the party was being held.

Barry's only complaint had been he had not been able to get through to her on the phone. Jo had blushed. It wasn't surprising. Kiko had had the nerve to hover in the door and try to get her off the phone. She hadn't even realized that she'd been talking to Mike for fifty-two minutes—at least that's how long Barry told her he'd been trying to get through.

Barry was terrific. There was no other word for it. There was something that radiated out of him tonight, something so catching she felt she radiated, too.

He collected her in one of those long stretch limos that Alexa had told her about. "See out, can't see in." Alexa was right. They were wonderful cars. She had never felt more cosseted, private, privileged.

"You look very pretty."

"It's my third try."

She wasn't trying to be coquettish. Barry made her feel pretty in a way Mike somehow never could, however madly in love with Mike she was. Was it possible to be in love with two men at once? No, it was just the magic, the excitement of what was happening to her life. She was sparkling from the adrenaline Barry had created, adrenaline that meant her fragile bud of self-confidence was starting to bloom. She hoped it would stay that way.

"I'm scared."

Barry took her hand. "Don't be. I'm not saying Mr. Forga isn't an extraordinary man. He is, but you just stay yourself, your sweet natural self; he'll know why you're worth so much money to the company."

"That's not the reason. I don't care about money, the position . . ." Before she knew what was happening, Barry stopped her speaking with his mouth. He was kissing her, not thoroughly, not probing, but all the same a kiss that was a real kiss, nothing brotherly, nothing dispassionate about it.

"Oh, please don't do that. Please don't . . ."

"Jo, that was called a 'relax kiss.' Don't give it another thought. You don't need to call the West Coast to confess . . ."

By the time the stretch limo pulled up outside an imposing house, they were both laughing and although Jo's knees were trembling, with Barry's arm around her waist she was able to enter the house without stumbling.

It was like no other house she had ever seen. If she'd thought the Devi apartment on Central Park South was grand, she now knew immediately it wasn't in the same class. There was an aura of opulence from the moment the door was opened by someone who was not Kiko, but who looked exactly like him . . . except it was a her! The beautiful Thai girl bowed low. There was wonderful music. "Schumann," Barry murmured, more to himself than to her.

The flight of stairs ahead looked like black ice, black and shining as if they were at the north pole at night. At the top of the stairs were—who else but Alexa, laughing, confident, looking like the moonbeam Barry had once described, and Marcus Lanning, who seemed amused by the whole affair. Beside them stood a man, tall, dark, and formidable was the word that came instantly to Jo's mind. It wasn't because Mr. Forga had a beard or huge eyes or features that stood out in some extraordinary way but, well, she supposed, his commanding presence was something a huge fortune automatically brought into being.

Jo thought they were in a receiving line, but no sooner had Alexa hugged her and Marc shaken her hand than Mr. Forga, with a smiling nod, led her into the most enormous sitting room she had ever seen.

It was enormous, yet in one way it was like a maze, created by different seating areas, screens, a huge media wall with lights flashing on and off, a grand piano in one corner, in another a low table that had to be at least twenty feet long, surrounded by gold, bronze, and black cushions. Everywhere there was an intoxicating, heady smell.

Sipping Champagne with Barry beside her, she strolled more and more confidently around the room in the dress that was a cloudy pink haze of tulle found at Lord & Taylor without a recognizable label.

For only one second did she find herself alone, and in that instant Alexa was beside her. "If anyone asks you 'if you party,' say 'no' . . ." she hissed.

"Party?" Jo repeated.

"It's dope—coke—nose candy . . . here, I've seen it." Before Jo could answer Barry was back and asking her to come to sit down with Mr. Forga, the master genius of the whole apparatus.

Nose candy. Dope. Jo felt like laughing. As if she would ever try anything so ridiculous. As usual, Alexa was exaggerating. There was no way anyone in such an exalted circle, making so much money, living in such luxury, could descend to that depth. For what reason? Why? There was no need.

It couldn't be the Champagne. It couldn't be anything she'd inhaled, but as Barry brought her over to the sofa where Mr. Forga was sitting, she felt as if she were on another planet. There were familiar faces around the room. Could it be Frank Sinatra? It couldn't be and yet . . . was it John Travolta? Goldie Hawn? Jo didn't want to appear naïve. They were probably all there, all the stars, but she'd gone past the autograph-collecting phase. She was an executive of Devi, one of the highest-salaried women in the country. She gulped down more Champagne before Mr. Forga turned to put his full gaze on her.

She was drowning in a sargasso sea of sexuality, feelings that were erotic, exotic, yet fearful as his dark eyes looked deeply into hers. He didn't say much. He didn't need to. "Thank you," he said, briefly touching her hand. "Thank you for helping your sister so much."

Jo was aware of a disturbing element, of someone standing above them, an element Mr. Forga didn't want and wasn't used to having to put up with. It was only when he turned his eyes away from hers that she found herself able to look up. It was a shock. There was Blair Benson, the immaculate conception of fashion herself, looking down at Mr. Forga and herself with an expression nobody could misinterpret. Loathing. It was pure and simple loathing.

Whatever Mr. Forga had been about to say to her was not going to be said. He stood up. He seemed ten feet tall to Jo. "How kind of you to come, Ms. Benson. Have you greeted your own discovery?" Jo knew something strange was going on. There was a current of emotion between them, moving so swiftly Jo had the impression if they didn't move away, something dreadful would happen. But they did move . . . not toward Alexa, who was standing happily beside the grand piano with Marc, but toward another area of the room shielded by an ornate Japanese screen.

Jo was having a wonderful time. She had the best big brother that anyone could have, she decided, in Barry Hunter. He was her protector while her lover was away, Mike, the man she loved more than she thought she could ever love anyone.

As Barry spooned caviar into her mouth, occasionally stroked her hair, and introduced her to scores of chic people she would normally have run a mile from, she could feel again an attraction growing between them. She tried to force it down. It wasn't love, she told herself. It was the brand-new sexuality Mike had aroused in her . . . mixed up with a strange kind of maternal sense, and above all pure, simple gratitude.

They sat together by a glass wall that gave a tremendous scenic view of the East River, eating more caviar by the tablespoonful, sipping a mixture of ice-cold vodka and less cold Champagne. Jo felt she wanted to stay there forever. Over to the right she could see Alexa and Marc looking at their watches and beginning to make a surreptitious exit. It didn't worry her anymore. She had overreacted about that as she had overreacted about so much.

Barry, his face as innocent as a choirboy's, the same obstinate flick of sandy hair not staying in place, said to her, as if he needed to say it, "Don't move. There's an old buddy of mine just arrived that I haven't seen in ages. I'll bring him over."

He returned with an older-looking version of himself, the same sharp blue eyes, the funny irresponsible hair. Despite the euphoria brought on by the ease with which she had adapted to such a ritzy occasion, months later Jo could still remember the way her skin had grown cold as Barry said, "Here's a pal from your part of the world, Jo. Denny Upton, another member of the Devi family."

She knew she held out her hand. She knew she mumbled a few words, but just as if an earthquake or a hurricane had hit the East End Avenue house, she was a different girl sitting there. Some miraculous combustion of chemicals coursing through her veins diluted the alcohol as if she had never sipped a sip. All sense of being "someone" . . . high-salaried, high-powered meant nothing. Upton. Devi. Svetlana. She had been right from the beginning.

It had come out of nowhere, like a rifle shot or an arrow in her side, but now she knew how to react. There would be no frantic rush to the phone to Mike. Later but not now. She was cool, although she saw no more sign of Alexa—or Mr. Forga for that matter. As Barry and Denny Upton talked animatedly, happily together, she watched them carefully. A couple of times Barry turned to her and apologized for talking so much to him. "Haven't seen him in a couple of years, although we talk on and off over the phone." She smiled serenely, said, "I'm perfectly happy," and continued to observe them—for how long she didn't know. Her mind was clear. If Denny Upton knew, as he had to know, of Madame Devi's origins, she was as sure as her love for Mike that Barry did not know, and if he didn't know, neither did Mr. Forga. Could it be possible? Anything was possible. Change of name, change of place, change of face—particularly change of face. She shuddered.

Barry saw her looking at her watch. He was about to speak when, from across the room, Jo saw Mr. Forga appear from behind the Japanese screen and beckon to him. Barry came back looking like a crestfallen child, but his remarks were addressed only to Upton. "Mr. Forga asked if you will come back tomorrow. I'm sorry, Denny . . ." Barry looked embarrassed. "It seems you've come twenty-four hours too soon—at the wrong time."

Upton bit his nail. "For once Forga's wrong. Something's happened that needs his attention now . . ." Before Barry could stop him, Upton went toward the screen. Barry pulled her to her feet. "Let's get out of here."

Jo nodded gratefully, but before they could leave, Forga appeared again and angrily beckoned to Barry once more. What was going on? Jo was about to go over to them, seeing how agitated Barry looked, when their conversation came to an end and Barry came toward her with a forced smile on his face. "Let's hit the road. Mr. Forga says the celebration is at an end."

As they went toward the colonnaded entrance hall, Mr. Forga was waiting for them there with two glasses in his hand. "To Alexa." He handed Jo a glass and sipped the other himself. "To Alexa," she dutifully repeated, swallowing down a drink she had never tasted before . . . almonds, oranges, something piquant, something strange.

Barry helped her into the car outside and although she was sure the car was moving, she didn't feel she was moving with it. The dark panel between driver and passengers closed. Barry was laying her down on the long back seat, slipping the tulle sleeves of her dress off her shoulders, burying his face in her breasts, cupping them, licking them, pulling her nipples, until, she wasn't sure, but she thought she was crying out, "Mike . . . Mike . . ." as well as "Don't . . . don't." The car was traveling so slowly she felt she was in a movie as Barry's hands slowly but deliberately began to take the tulle down to her waist, stroking the sides of her body like a massage, murmuring in her ear. She was becoming dizzy, desperately, horribly dizzy.

She could see herself as if there were a mirror in front of her and when Barry said, "Is anything worrying you?" the words came out as if she were addressing herself in a mirror, as if she were attached to a truth machine. The horrible dizziness didn't go away.

"Oh, yes, Barry. Oh yes . . . you have to warn . . . have to warn Mr. Forga . . ."

He was unzipping the tulle dress from the waist down. She wanted to resist but with every movement came more dizziness, and worse, nausea. She struggled but it was no use. The tulle dress fell in a cloudy puddle to the floor and Barry ran his fingers down beneath her pantyhose, reaching the crease of her behind until he probed with full force into her vagina. She moaned. She could feel her wetness pouring out as the car moved slowly on and on and on. "Warn Mr. Forga about what, darling Jo?" he murmured.

She was naked with her pantyhose around her knees, his lips nuzzling her breasts. As he made her wetter and hotter, again he asked, "Warn Forga about what?" And she found herself talking and talking as if she could never stop . . . as if talking would stop her betraying Mike because although she didn't want to, her body was responding, urging another man to mount her, but Barry never moved to do so. Only his fingers played with her as she talked. Did it take minutes or hours to pour out her fears . . . that part of her reason for coming to New York had been to find out who was behind the face clinic that had disfigured her mother . . . a disfigurement that had led to her mother's suicide . . . the unsolved murder of Ann Pershing and, tonight, the horror of meeting Denny Upton, who she knew for sure had been the owner of record of the bogus clinic that had ruined her mother's life and led to her death.

Barry was redressing her. The tulle sleeves were back on her shoulders as they'd been designed to be. He half led, half carried her into the Central Park apartment. She knew she was sobbing and laughing and talking all at the same time, but she couldn't stop herself and the dizziness grew as if some demon had entered her body.

"The nurse . . . Ann Pershing . . ." How she remembered the name she would never know. "She must have thought she was sitting on a gold mine. She probably came to New York to blackmail . . ." It was the last word she remembered saying. Blackness descended. She passed out, not even sure if Barry's arms were out to catch her.

It wasn't quite light when she opened her eyes again. The room swam upside down for a moment and then settled down. There was the sofa, the rug, the pictures on the wall, and Barry—Barry Hunter her friend and nearly lover oh, she prayed, it was 'nearly' lover—sitting apparently sleeping in the armchair by the window. She must have made a noise because in seconds he was beside her on the bed. "What happened?" she cried. "Was I drunk?" Everything that happened the night before was a blur.

"I don't know." Barry looked stern. "Kiko," he said without looking away from her. "Bring Miss Shapwell some coffee."

"Barry," she cried, "It isn't even morning, or is it?"

"It's six o'clock but we've got to talk. You said some pretty crazy things last night." In seconds the coffee was on a tray beside her bed. Her memory was coming back and along with it her sense of self-preservation. Oh, God, what had she said?

Barry knelt by her bedside. "Jo, something very strange went on last night. You made some incredible accusations. Do you remember anything at all?"

With two cups of coffee her mind was clear. She couldn't remember everything, but she knew she had said some of the things to Barry that had been on her mind for so long. As she leaned back against the pillows, the horror hit her. Upton. Denny Upton. At last there was the link she had hoped, prayed would never be found.

She searched Barry's face, found it as anxious and as concerned as she now believed him to be. He didn't know and if he didn't know, probably neither did Forga. It wasn't impossible. People who headed huge organizations didn't always know every detail about those they discovered, employed. Since coming to New York, Jo had learned that every day, just by reading the papers. Neither did presidents of countries.

She sat up, the dizziness and nausea of the previous evening still haunting her. "Barry, I must have sounded crazy. I don't know what happened, but after that last drink with Mr. Forga, I don't know, I just lost my head . . . I told you things about myself, my life, about my family, but they're all true."

Barry sat impassive, as Jo, this time calmly and quietly, told him the story of her mother's death. *Suicide*—she repeated the word twice. She told how, with Mike's help, she had learned of her mother's attempt to peel herself back to youth at The Fountain, a face clinic where she had been disfigured . . . of the name Svetlana on the back of the checks, of the owner of record, Denny Upton, who had been the lawyer involved in the closure of another clinic in Las Vegas after another disastrous face peel.

Barry closed his eyes. He couldn't believe what he was hearing. It was like a Freudian nightmare, a cocaine withdrawal, a horror story, and all this on the verge of either a mammoth expansion or a takeover that would make him a millionaire plus. It was crazy, yet here was this naïve little girl, sure that there was a connection between Devi and a tacky face clinic place on the West Coast. He got up and paced up and down as Jo looked at him as if he were her savior. There was only one thing to do, he decided. Only one thing that would bring the necessary time to prove everything false that Jo believed. Again he knelt at Jo's bedside. "Jo, God, what can I say.

I had no idea of what you've been going through. It's all . . . all . . . what can I say—it's insane. There's no way that a man like Baxter Forga could be involved with anything like this, but I swear to you I'm going to find out. There's obviously something sinister here." Again, he paced around the room. "Jo, will you trust me?" Before she answered he went on, ". . . at least for a few days?"

She nodded.

"Whatever the truth, I know Baxter Forga can know nothing about this. I swear to you he would be the first person to want to bring whoever was responsible for your mother's . . . for your mother's disfigurement to justice."

Jo held out her arms to him like a little girl. "Oh, thank you, Barry. I'm sure—I know you're right. Mike always said I was jumping to conclusions. Now I know I wasn't and yet I'm sure Mr. Forga knows nothing about this. What will you do?"

Barry clasped her hands tightly in his. "Promise me you'll say nothing until I've told Forga about all this. He always knows what to do. Promise—at least not for twenty-four hours."

Under the sheet Jo crossed her fingers. She would say nothing to anyone—except Mike. Somehow she would leave the apartment to call him. Her worst fears had now been confirmed, but at least she had an ally in the enemy camp—and would have a still greater one in Forga. He always knew what to do—Barry had said so . . . and, she was absolutely sure he was right.

CHAPTER TEN

MUST BE FIVE-FOOT-TEN, WITH WONDERFUL LONG ARMS, LONG legs, laser slim, a bushel of gleaming hair and a face like a blank, pristine canvas you can paint anything onto . . ."

Alexa threw her head back and laughed till tears ran down her cheeks. As he meant to, Marc sounded exactly like Blair Benson clipping out sentences like bullets from a machine gun; standing with the kind of awkward, yet commanding stance Blair sometimes adopted before her minions.

"I can't . . ." She couldn't get the words out. She was choking with laughter and happiness. "I can't believe you asked her that with a straight face and that's how she replied . . ."

"Yep." Marc bent down to refill her glass as, crossing the wake of a fast-moving police boat, some Champagne slopped onto the table. "I asked her to give me the necessary credentials for a *View* model and that's what she said—except for the adjective 'blank' I'd say you were born for the role." He bent down again to smooth back her hair blowing in the breeze.

Stop. Stop now. Don't fall in love, Alexa told herself. You said you would never allow yourself. Stop . . . stop . . . but even as she said it to herself, she was stretching out her arms toward him. He went into them, his body cupping hers on the huge navy-blue-velvet cushioned sofa—she couldn't call it a "bunk"—which in a perfect half circle was set at the stern of the yacht they were on. "Here's *Night Star,* it's a seventy-foot power yacht, owned by Ben, an old navy pal of mine," Marc had told her casually as they'd boarded the gleaming white vessel moored in the Hudson, high up on the West Side.

Ben. Why did his old navy pal have to have been named Ben? She even loathed the name and certainly everything it stood for. She had never been more convincing than when Jo had called with the startling news that their father was moving out of East Mission without a word to them—not even telling them where he'd stored the possessions that they'd left behind . . . it was incredible to believe that he hadn't even left a forwarding address. She'd been able to hide the fierce hatred Jo's news had provoked—for Jo's sake, only for Jo's sake. Even the sound of the name Ben, her father's name, had for a brief moment stolen some of the joy of sailing away into the night with Marc.

But it had really only been one moment from the past encroaching on a present that was perfection—on a dream yacht with a crew so silent and skillful, by the time they moved away from the dock Alexa had forgotten they existed. As the yacht headed south, she was conscious only of Marc, of a new and attractive assertiveness about him, a sense of taking charge, of total reliability that made her want to reach out to him all the more.

"Would you like to sail around the world?" he whispered into her hair. The world. Only a few days had passed and here was another man, one so different from Forga, offering her the world—but there was no hypnotism here, no strange mesmerizing or feeling of being drugged into submission. In Marc's arms she felt tranquil, safe.

"Yes," she said dreamily. "Oh yes. Let's sail with great white sails . . ."

"We will, Lex, we will, one day when you've grown tired of your life in the spotlight."

As the yacht began to move away from the might of the

Manhattan skyline, Alexa felt she was escaping from the glittering skyscrapers which like luring sirens tried to beckon her back to the world of artificiality she despised, to the world where only money and power seemed to count, where values were measured in gossip columns. She never wanted to go back. She could already smell the ocean . . . the same heady, sweet smell of freedom she'd absorbed in Mendocino. "Are we heading out into the ocean?"

"We're in the Lower Bay, but there . . ." Marc took his arm from her waist and pointed into the darkness, "the Atlantic . . . three thousand miles of Atlantic and, then, Europe. Shall we set sail?"

It was a story, of course, a fairy story that they whispered to each other as the wind whipped up and knocked their Champagne glasses over and they knelt on the deep-blue-velvet-cushioned banquet looking out into the dark as the ocean crashed against the stern.

It was odd. They were so close to each other, and for the first time it was she who longed to get close, to intensify the mood. She, who had always run away from the sexual, the sensual. It was Marc who kept turning them back into children, out on a skylark trip, as the yacht sailed around Manhattan's harbor, pointing out Staten Island off in the southwest corner as if they were just discovering it, talking like Robinson Crusoe as he told her stories of coves in Rockaway, egrets on Coney Island, crab hunting on Far Rockaway, and wildlife in Jamaica Bay.

"You're a poet," she said shyly. She didn't know him and she wanted to—desperately. She knew that now. And if Marc was a poet, surely his mother, Madame Devi, had to have had something to do with it. It came as a surprise to realize it was the first time she had ever credited Madame Devi with anything.

Marc pulled her to her feet as *Night Star* changed direction, first east, then north. He led her into the main stateroom lined with row upon row of beautifully bound dark leather books. "Here's a poet . . ." he took a book from the shelf. He didn't seem to need to read the title. Like a woman knows her makeup case, her kitchen, Alexa thought, Marc knows these bookshelves well. He opened a page. "There is now your insular city of the Manhattoes, belted round by wharves as Indian isles by coral reefs. Commerce surrounds it with her surf. Right and left, the streets take you waterward. Its extreme downtown is the Battery, where that noble mole is washed by waves; and cooled by breezes which a few hours previous were out of sight of land. Look at the crowds of water gazers there . . ." He smacked the book shut and returned it to its place as she looked up at him wide-eyed. "Herman Melville's hundred-year-old vision of Battery Park . . ."

He helped her down into a tiny dining salon, lit by silver lamps. "Why did the poor poet of Tennessee, upon suddenly receiving two handfuls of silver, deliberate whether to buy him a coat, which he badly needed, or invest his money in a pedestrian trip to Rockaway Beach?" He pushed her shoulders down so she sat at a white damask-covered table set for two.

A slim sailor who looked more like a boy than a man served them. "Tim, this is Alexa Shapwell." Alexa could see by Tim's awed expression he already knew who she was. "Tim can walk on his hands as well as his feet, can't you, Tim?" The boy sailor nodded and scuttled away. "He's the fastest putter-up of sails I've ever known," Marc told her. Tim served them fast, too . . . turtle soup that was like nectar, lobster with a sauce that, Marc winked, "is Ben's secret weapon," and a wonderful melting brie en croûte with celery that tasted as if it had just been picked. They talked and talked . . . she about Mendocino, her love of the ocean there, he about poets, old and new, sunsets and sunrises and favorite sails with Ben "from Cape May to Montauk . . . from New York to Bermuda . . . and in Sydney, Australia, where everyone's born half in and half out of the water . . ."

She tried to get him to talk about his work, but it was obvious he didn't want to. "With very few exceptions, I'm only interested in people from the neck up." He tried to sound as if he were joking, but he didn't look it. He leaned across the table to tilt her chin toward the light. "You are one of the few exceptions."

"I'm glad."

He went on as if she hadn't spoken. "I'm an otolaryngologist." He said the word phonetically, as if to a child. And she acted like the child she felt he wanted her to be at that moment, touching with exaggerated movements her ears, her nose, her throat.

"That's right," he said gravely. "Head and neck, ear, nose, and throat . . ." He paused and added laughingly, "You could say, lovely Lex, we're in the same business. As a member of the American Academy of Facial Plastic Surgeons, I deal with women who believe in your line of work, in the 'now and forever' youth bit . . ."

Did he hear her gasp? If he did, he paid no attention, but tension made her body stiffen as he told her he occasionally carried out facelifts, eyelifts, SMAS jobs . . . could he see the fear in her? Fear of suspicion rising again . . . fear that she would be unable to trust him after all? Either because of some dreadful irony or for a worse, more treasonable link, that he, the son of Madame Devi, was also a 'youth doctor'?

As Tim served a sinful chocolate cake, Marc went on talking, occasionally picking up her spoon to make her taste the cake, which was tasteless to her now.

"SMAS—it sounds like something out of James Bond, doesn't it? Jack Owsley, a great plastic surgeon up in San Francisco was one of the first to use it . . . superficial muscolo aponeurotic system—working with muscle, not skin. It's changed the art of facelifting forever. . . ." Marc was silent for a moment and then spoke as if to himself, "for those well qualified to do it." He moved his face nearer to hers. "You'll never need it. Stay out of the sun—you're naturally golden, aren't you? There's some Creole in you somewhere, I bet. . . ." As they laughed together, most of the tension went away.

Oh, God, he's so wonderful, Alexa thought. Please let him be really wonderful. Don't let this dream turn into a nightmare, too.

As they sipped a golden Château d'Yquem, Marc leaned forward, his expression serious, no more stories, no more fantasies. "Why aren't we in Morocco tonight? What did Forga say to make you change your mind so easily?"

Alexa, who never blushed, could feel herself blushing. Off guard, uneasy, she stuttered, "But I told you, the *View* cover—its importance to Devi—to your mother's company—my new role, my share in Devi . . ."

"Forget it." Marc stood up, his back to her. He was angry, she could see from the set of his shoulders. It was such an abrupt change of mood, such a brutal return to the present, the future, tears burned her eyes. He gestured for her to precede him back to the book-lined stateroom, out again to the cushioned stern. There in the distance was the city of dreams, the pinnacles of power that she was climbing so easily, yet with such uneasiness inside.

The water was rougher now. They were against the wind. As the yacht turned north toward the East River and the magnetic skyline, Alexa stumbled over a footstool to sprawl on the floor. Marc made no motion to help her up. She grabbed his leg. She put her arms around his body. She buried her face in him, for the first time in her life knowing what it meant to long to be taken, to lose yourself in someone else's body. He still didn't move, until, her mouth open, she breathed her hot breath against his hardening crotch.

In a second he had lifted her high above him, his mouth on her neck, her chin. As the yacht plunged through a sudden turmoil of waves, they fell together onto the dark velvet cushions. With one hand he pulled her long gold hair up high away from her face like a golden rope, looking at her in such a searching, longing way she wanted to cry out, "I'm yours, Marc. I'm yours. Don't worry. From now on I'll do as you say . . ." but she didn't. She couldn't. There was still a nagging doubt, a lack of trust, but it was no longer strong enough to stop her from wanting him. It was she who put his hand inside the diving neckline of her gold lace dress. She who moved nearer as he lifted her skirt, to feel her, finger by finger, stroking, probing, searching, opening, learning, she was sure, with a doctor's knowledge that—amazingly—she was still a virgin, an old-fashioned, stupid virgin. She who had been whipped and imprisoned by a sex fiend, who had had endless fondles but who had never been penetrated—never, because she had resisted and fought against it—until now. And now, oh, how she wanted it.

There was a fierce look on his face, his mouth was tightly smiling as he built her desire for him, sucking her nipples, pulling them delicately until they ached and grew hard, taking her hand to his penis, kissing her until she was panting, "Oh, please, please . . ." The gold lace dress was on the deck. He threw her tiny bikini out into the sky where the wind caught it, a flash of silk, before whipping it away into the waves. Again he pushed her down by the shoulders, but this time into the deepness of the couch, burying his face in her wetness, his tongue deep, deeply sucking. "Oh, oh . . ." she had never dreamed it could be like this. "Oh, more, more . . ."

"Yes, my girl, you shall have more . . . and more . . . until you beg me to take you to Morocco . . . you beg me and beg me . . ."

She didn't hear, didn't listen. The whistling of the wind and the roar of the sea was part of the sensation of his ramming her again and again, her other mouth clinging, opening, gulping, fever mounting until they were both gasping as they reached a climax together and she had to cry out, "Oh, God . . ."

Did she sleep? She didn't know, but her eyes had been closed and when they opened for a second she didn't know where she was. She was alone, a soft wool blanket covering her, the yacht still moving, but so slowly and smoothly it was as if she were in a movie, not on a real yacht, but a set yacht with Manhattan again the backdrop. Her dress was still at her feet. She sat up slowly, gingerly as if she was setting out to walk, to live normally again after some kind of operation. She had her dress up to her waist when Marc came toward her, looking as shy, as awkward as she was sure she looked.

"What beautiful breasts. Let me hold them again." The desire to be taken again came back with the force of the appetite she'd had to battle with all her life. She was about to slip out of her dress again, but he stopped her. "No, not now. We're too near land. Remember, Cinderella, you told me you had a curfew."

As he spoke he knelt at her feet, cupping her breasts as gently as if they were baby sparrows. Had she told him she had a curfew when she'd agreed to play hooky from her Devi role and leave Forga's party early? It had been another girl, another day.

As he caressed her, she saw the time on his watch. One fifteen. It was another day. She didn't know the date, but she knew she faced another day in the studio in eight or nine hours' time . . . plenty of time to stay in his arms, and then go to the studio, go anywhere for the first time in her life with a new look on her face, a radiant look because she had given herself to a man she loved.

Loved? She tried to throw the word out of her mind. He had taken his hands away from her naked breasts, was lifting the lace dress up onto her shoulders and saying in the voice she was used to hearing, the slightly mocking but also sweet voice, "Zip yourself up, my lovely." He stood up and pointed toward the shore. "That's where I used to crew when I was at Columbia. Soon, my love, we'll be in the beautiful Bronx . . . and Spuyten Dyvil and then the Cloisters and back to the Hudson River, always hurrying to the open sea. You'll step on land to be The Face, Now and Forever . . ." It was the same half-mocking, half-sweet voice, but she didn't want to hear that tone anymore.

She stood up, shrugging the lace from her shoulders, knowing that without the zip, she could shrug the dress again to the floor. "Don't they have any bedrooms on this yacht? Does Ben always sleep in the open air?"

He pulled her to him so tightly the buttons on his shirt pressed into her skin. "Don't you want to obey your curfew?"

She shook her head slowly from side to side to side.

"Follow me below . . . to the master cabin. There are never any bedrooms on water."

It was a totally white cabin. Alexa shuddered, remembering the whiteness of the room at the Fairmont Hotel so long ago. Why did bad memories have to invade such a glorious present? Marc left her there with, "I'll be back. I have to give new instructions to the captain." Captain? Of course, there had to be one, but he had never appeared, had simply guided *Night Star* through her night of dreams.

She lay on the huge white piqué-covered bed. There may not be bedrooms, but this was certainly a bed, and through the porthole, Alexa saw the lights of the city, but now they were on her right, not her left. *Night Star* had turned again. For a moment she felt alarmed. Would Marc think she now need not go back for days? Was he taking her to Cape May or Bermuda or . . .

He was back in the cabin, taking it over, taking her over. She saw the black curly hair on his chest, around his rod for the first time. Man. He was all man, desirable, enormous, demanding. Her throbbing began as he stood looking down at her.

He sat in a swivel chair that was latched into the floor. He opened his arms wide and whispered, "Come here." It was so natural to lower herself onto him, to wrap her long legs around the chair so she crossed her ankles tightly together at the back, to move with him as the yacht crossed the waves, up, down, up, down, both moaning, moaning, she stifling screams of pleasure as wave upon wave of orgasm broke in her, until again they were on the bed, he on top, she on top, biting, sucking, he exploring until she felt his imprint all over her.

As she finally fell asleep, she knew she would never be the same person again. She was at once liberated and totally captured. *Doomed* was the last word she heard in her mind.

At 7 A.M., wearing a pair of Tim's trousers and a *Night Star* T-shirt, both enormous on her, she faced her unshaven, stern-faced lover, at a breakfast she found for once she couldn't eat. She had another appetite now.

"How much do you know about your company, the company you tell me you will now hold equity in? How much do you know about Devi?" There was nothing mocking in his voice now. It was tender, quiet, but he wanted answers.

"You must know more about it than I do." She was trying to be candid, but he cut in impatiently.

"That isn't an answer."

"All right, all right. As you know, Mr. Forga put up the money for Devi, because . . ." she hesitated, not understanding why he was scowling, "because of the formulations, the formula, whatever you call it, that your mother created." When he didn't respond, she went on defensively. "Women love it. I know you've teased me about the 'young-now-and-forever bit,' but it isn't as if they buy one pot and never come back. They can never seem to get enough of it. It must have some worth. In any case, women have been trying to buy back youth since Cleopatra's time. I should know."

She hadn't meant the bitterness to show in her voice, but it was impossible to hide it. Part of her would always be bitter over Mom's death.

"What do you mean 'I should know'?" Marc had a piece of delicious ham on his fork, which he pushed toward her. She didn't want it, but she ate it all the same. It gave her time, time to be suspicious again, time enough not to tell him anything about Mom's death and all the confused circumstances surrounding it, always too "circumstantial" for comfort.

She tried to sound lighthearted but it didn't work. "Well, all the women who clamor to talk to me around the country say, 'There's no hope for me, is there?' hoping damn well that there is still hope, that Devi will turn back the clock and make them ravishing—even if they weren't ravishing in the first place."

"Don't give me all that crap. That's not what you meant."

She pushed her plate away and rubbed the greasiness from her mouth. "Why don't you tell me about your mother? You don't call her Madame Devi, do you? You never want to talk about her? Why?"

His expression didn't change. "We were never very close." Now he sounded sarcastic again. "Like you, I suppose you could say she was always a career girl—her products came before me . . ." He paused and added, "and my father."

"Tell me about your father. Was he a doctor like you?"

Marc shook his head and looked at his watch as if to indicate it wasn't the right time to start talking about his life, her life, but she persisted. "Marc, why are you so . . . so secretive about . . . well, I suppose, everything?"

He laughed, but it had a bitter sound. "I'm not secretive. I just want to leave the past alone—to cut myself away from it." He saw how troubled she looked. "My father was a decent, straightforward man, no genius. He was—well, I suppose you could say a bit of an entrepreneur, without the talent for it. He had car dealerships, was in import, export . . ."

"Where?"

Marc looked at her strangely. "Is this going to get me anywhere? Am I applying for something?" Again he looked at his watch. "It's getting on toward eight A.M. What about that curfew you were so adamant about last night?"

"I don't care," she said mutinously. He came over to kiss her lengthily, both starting to breathe heavily, to want, but he was the one who broke away.

"I was born in Paris, but as my father was American, I became an American right away. What was Dad doing then? I was too young to remember, but it was almost certainly a scheme to make us rich."

"And what was your mother doing then? Was she already a chemist? Not a Madame Devi but a Miss What? When your father met her . . ." Alexa persisted. "Was she a chemist, Miss . . ."

"I can hardly pronounce it. Miss Svetlana Sorgiokov . . . yes . . ." Marc looked strange again. There was a wistfulness there she couldn't begin to comprehend, but just at the sound of the word *Svetlana* she realized how Jo must have felt at Mortimer's, learning from Barry Madame Devi's original name.

They were pulling alongside a dock that Alexa recognized. The Water Café. There was physical pain at the thought of leaving *Night Star,* of leaving Marc. She sat staring at him, sure he was going to say more. "She was a student when my father met her. Yes, a young Russian emigré student of chemistry in Paris—young, ambitious, and I suppose beautiful, too . . ."

It was as if he were talking about a stranger. "Isn't she still beautiful? She must be." Alexa wasn't teasing him now. If she kept talking, perhaps doors in his mind would open and mysteries would be solved. If only their time together were beginning and not ending. She was sure she was on the edge of learning so much.

He pulled her to her feet and put his arms tightly around her. "There's no more time now, lovely Lex . . . and perhaps time's running out on us altogether."

"No!" she cried. "Don't say that. Why do you say that? I'm sorry about Morocco, really sorry, but . . . Morocco will still be there next week, next month, next year." As she spoke, she realized she was parrotting Forga. Damn Forga, but the words were out before she could stop them ". . . I'll be able to buy a piece of Morocco next year."

Marc pushed her away from him as if she'd turned into a vampire, but when he spoke there was no anger in his voice, only a dead dull sound. "I've heard it all before, Lex. I've heard it all before. There's only one thing I feel I want to say to you. You have to make up your own mind but . . ." he hesitated. She could see he wasn't sure whether to say anything.

The yacht wasn't moving. They were moored. It was time to go, yet she couldn't move, felt paralyzed, longing for him to say . . . what? She didn't know . . . that he loved her? That wouldn't change things. Seven-forty A.M. In an hour, she was supposed to be at the studio. Thank God, it was the studio and not a public appearance. It never mattered how a model appeared at a studio—like a bag lady wrapped in rags or straight from an all-night party with lipstick smudged, bags under the eyes. Models were canvases to be painted on, dressed or undressed. Today, when she appeared in an oversize sailor suit with her three-thousand-dollar dress in a plastic bag, no one would care or probably even notice . . . except, surely, her face and body must somehow announce to the world she had been made love to all night . . . that she was in love.

"Tell me, Marc . . . tell me . . . what is it you want to tell me?" Alexa timidly put her hand on his shoulder. He covered it with his own but didn't look at her.

"Be careful," he said slowly. "Be careful with Forga. He's a ruthless manipulator." He hesitated again and said slowly, "He may give you the moon, the stars, the equity—whatever he's promised you, whatever his lawyers appear to be drawing up for you to sign. That's perfectly true, but then again, he may . . . may . . ." He looked at her searchingly, eyes to eyes. "He may change his mind and leave you on a garbage dump without a backward glance."

"I can take care of myself," Alexa replied defiantly. It was an automatic response, one she had been making ever since she could remember.

"Can you, Alexa? I hope you're right. Others have thought so—and found out too late they were wrong."

She wanted to grab hold of his coat, ask him to hold her again, promise he would rescue her if she was left on a dump, but suddenly he was all business, removed, talking quickly to a sailor she had never seen before, turning to tell her "You know where you are? I thought this would be the best location for you to get to the studio. Isn't that where you're headed? Outside the café, on the right, there'll be a sedan—it's from London Towncars. Just give the driver the address. You've got plenty of time unless you want to go back to Central Park South first." He'd thought of everything, yet Alexa felt like a piece of nothing. She fought back the question she knew so many women ruined their chances with . . . "When will I see you again?"

Time's running out, he'd said. She would have to prove to him somehow that she knew she had a choice now—or at least she hoped she still had.

He'd had a hell of a time getting through to Forga. After the third number he'd been told to try, Barry had had this terrible thought that had almost made him throw up, that maybe Forga had already left the country, was perhaps en route on one of his jets, as he so often was, to some far-flung destination halfway across the world. But no, the third number reached him and at last, at 7:40 A.M., drenched through with nervous sweat with no black coffee or a snort of anything to calm him down, he was about to face the great man in his East 62nd Street office.

It was where they had first met. On the way across town he tried to think of a way to start, how to begin telling Forga about the preposterous string of accusations Jo had spewed out, at first incoherently, obviously drunk out of her skull the night before in the car, but then, again when she'd been able to open her eyes and had talked and talked concisely and coherently.

An hour later, Barry cursed himself for having so little trust. He needn't have suffered that hideous early agonizing hour, wondering how to approach Forga about Jo's crazy outpourings. As soon as he sat down, facing Forga across his huge marbletop desk, Forga relaxed him. As usual he was in command, immaculate, unassailable, immune it seemed to whatever might be affecting anyone or anything else outside in the world.

Before Barry said a word, Forga pointed to a side door. "Why don't you freshen up? Don't worry. I know what's troubling you."

Barry did as he was told, not only slapping cold water on his face but putting his head under the forceful jet of water until his mind started to clear. Although he'd only hastily shaved at the Central Park apartment, using Kiko's resourceful bathroom supplies, he felt he now looked calm and could act with more resolve.

There was Turkish coffee on a small side table next to his chair when he emerged. He loathed Turkish coffee but he drank it down in one gulp, its burning bitter taste further sharpening his mind.

Forga leaned back in his brass-studded leather chair. He closed his eyes for a second, then opened them to stare at Barry so penetratingly he felt he was under an X-ray. He started to speak, "Bax . . . Mr. Forga . . ." Still staring at him, Forga put up his hand to stop him.

"What did she tell you? What is worrying the little girl—the sister of our star?"

Barry twisted uncomfortably in his chair. "How'd you know . . . it's incredible . . . I don't know how or where to begin."

"Relax. I thought by now you would have some understanding of the depth of my perception of human beings. As soon as our West Coast colleague made his untimely, unfortunate visit here last evening, I sensed immediately something was disturbing the newest member of our Devi family. I thought it was important we learn what it was before any time was lost."

Barry leaned forward, anxiety wrinkling his forehead. He began fidgeting with his tie, clutching it as if it were a lifeline. Again, Forga said serenely, "Please relax, Barry. There is nothing whatever for you to worry about. I gave you some help last night to help myself—and to help unlock or should I say unburden Alexa's sister. You will remember the last drink we had together? I added a little powdered ketamine, an anesthetic. I discovered its usefulness some time ago." He smiled at Barry as if he were discussing a new and innovative balance sheet. "It is usually used by veterinarians to tranquilize potentially dangerous animals. Possession of the drug is, of course, totally legal."

Barry's tension began to seep out as his admiration for the extraordinary man across the desk escalated and he listened more and more intently. "It has remarkable effects on human beings, providing you give exactly the right amount—not too much, not too little. The only uncomfortable side effects can be possible nausea, a little dizziness, but under ketamine's influence, I believe I am right, am I not, the young woman . . ." Forga paused, smiling again as if it gave him particular satisfaction to say the name, "Jo Shapwell remained totally conscious but could not control her actions or hide her thoughts, her secrets? Am I right?"

Barry nodded. He was in charge of himself again. Thank God, he hadn't made a complete fool of himself and shown Forga how much Jo's crazy charges had unhinged him. "You're right. Well, up to a point." He allowed himself a quick man-to-man smile but quickly went on when he saw that Forga was no longer interested in any niceties of conversation. "In the limo going back to the apartment last night I thought Jo just wasn't used to dealing with alcohol. As I told you earlier I knew neither Alexa or Jo partied . . ." Barry corrected himself hurriedly. "Maybe a little kid stuff, marijuana, but maybe not even that. Jo started to tell me a long messy story about her mother . . . their mother . . . committing suicide, driving her car over a cliff or something because she'd gone to a California face clinic for a youth peel or some such treatment and been disfigured." Barry paused to see Forga's reaction but he sat expressionless, leaning back in the chair with his arms crossed.

Barry went on hastily. "The reason I said you were right up to a point is that perhaps because Jo has a low tolerance of drugs, the ketamine knocked her out when we got to the apartment, but first she told me the real reason she came to New York was to find out who was really behind the face clinic . . ."

Forga interrupted him. "What condition was she in when she came round this morning? About six, you say?"

"That's what bothered me most, sir . . . Bax. I expected her to tell me she'd gone crazy or something—that the whole thing was some hallucination, but when she woke up after a couple of cups of coffee she was as levelheaded as I've always known her to be. She repeated the whole story coherently, clearly, explaining the reason she felt Svetlana . . ." Barry couldn't keep his face from twitching with nerves as he said the name that had been almost sacrosanct to him ". . . was now in New York, because of the head nurse's sudden visit here and subsequent murder. Apparently Jo has a boyfriend on the West Coast who over the past few years has been trying to discover what really happened to her mother. He was the one who found out . . ." The words stuck in Barry's throat. Now, instead of the fear he had had over facing Forga with the story, the reality of what he had to say was making his palms moist with sweat. "He found out Denny Upton was the owner of record of the clinic. Goddamn it, that was what Jo kept saying this morning . . ." Barry punched one hand into the other.

"What exactly did she say?" Forga's voice was as calm as ever, but his expression was brooding, his hypnotic glance again drilling Barry's psyche.

"She said—she said meeting Denny—Denny Upton at your party was the link she had been looking for—to Svetlana—the link that until last night she had begun to hope and pray she would never find." Barry looked pleadingly at his boss. "She said over and over again I had to warn you—tell you that Svetlana—Madame Devi . . ." Again Barry almost choked on the words, ". . . had been involved with this . . . this face-peeling operation that killed her mother and . . . with at least one other similar setup in Las Vegas, where Upton was the defending lawyer in a multimillion-dollar suit brought by . . . by . . . well, another dissatisfied patient."

When Forga still did not respond, Barry agitatedly leaned across the desk. "Does this make any sense to you? Can any of it be true? There must be some crazy mix-up somehow. Where is Upton? Can't we get this mess straightened out right away? God, with Pershall about to make their offer . . . any murmur of malpractice, disfigurement . . ." Barry shuddered. "And even murder . . . murder of this nurse . . ."

Forga put up his hand again. "I told you to relax, Barry, and that is what I want you to do. Take the day off. I'll arrange for Umberto to give you something to improve your self-image, to renew your trust in yourself. I can assure you your belief in Devi—in Madame Devi—in Svetlana is not misplaced. She is a genius. The product she brought to me, as we all know, is miraculous and the public—women—know it, buy it, are buying it, and will continue to buy it, millions and millions of jars . . ."

He stood up. Barry was always surprised by Forga's height, his dominance, his presence reinforced whenever he stood up behind his giant desk.

Forga walked to the window and talked to Barry although he didn't turn to look at him. "We have not made a mistake with Madame Devi, that I can assure you. It appears, however, I have made one mistake—and I rarely make mistakes. I do not like to admit it. I find it painful. Listening to you, it appears I have made a mistake regarding Alexa's sister. She sounds like an unbalanced young woman—hysterical, creating a mystery out of something that was unfortunate, but was not a mystery—the suicide of her mother. Regrettable. Understandably distressing to a daughter, but imagine the audacity of this immature creature . . ." Although Forga's back was to him, Barry winced at the ice in his voice. "This hysterical dangerous creature daring to present Madame Devi, a woman of character and dedication as a . . . what do you call it in America . . . a medicine man, a quack, a phony, a cheap facialist. What can an ignorant little piece of trash know about the years and years of research, of setbacks, of inexorably working on, only wanting to find the truth, the right formulations, the years of persecution, of anxiety, of the final redemption of finding the formula . . ."

Barry's heart began to pound. Oh God, where's Umberto? I need it now, NOW, he told himself, but all thought of instant help, instant renewed self-respect went as Forga came to stand over him. He was smiling again, tenderly, like a brother, a father. "There are millions of dollars at stake, Barry. This hysterical little girl has to be made to leave New York but, of course, leave with her fears lulled. There is nothing she can do, but—shall we say—she is an unnecessary irritation, a blip on the perfect screen that must disappear. We need time—a couple of days—to conclude our negotiations. Not much time, but enough time. She will, of course, tell her sister everything—if she has not done so already." Forga frowned and looked at his watch. "Probably not. As you know, Alexa embarked on *Night Star* with Marc Lanning, the very respectable Dr. Lanning . . ." Forga laughed. It was not an attractive sound. "It was probably her first experience with sex."

Barry shook his head in disbelief. He couldn't keep himself from laughing nervously. The man was a phenomenon. There was nothing he didn't know, couldn't control. Forga continued, "She will be at the studio now with Penelope Waverly as a watchdog. I am sure not even her sister will be able to get through to her for several hours. I will give instructions to that effect."

Forga returned to sit at his desk, drumming his fingers, not impatiently but slowly, serenely, as if marking time to some inner composition. "I am afraid you will not be able to take the day off today after all, Barry. There is work to do. The most important work of your life, for your future. You must reassure Miss Shapwell, make her understand how appreciative we are, you are, I am . . ." He emphasized the "I" in a way Barry hoped he would be able to convey to Jo ". . . for her warnings, her openness in telling us her most unhappy family story."

Again Forga stood up. This time Barry sensed menace in his posture. "It is your responsibility now, Barry, to reassure her that I am looking into this very serious situation at once." He paused, then laughed sardonically. "Indeed I am. I have a meeting with Mr. Upton in precisely thirty minutes. Tonight you will take Miss Shapwell to dinner with Mr. Upton, who will be able to explain to her how such an unfortunate coincidence of name should have resulted in her very understandable, but totally misguided conclusion. He will invite her to return with him to California where he will show her relevant papers, which will put her mind at rest—at least until we can divest ourselves of the operation to everyone's satisfaction. With your considerable charm you will make sure she accepts Upton's invitation. Take her home with you tonight. If she is in love, which I am afraid she probably is, with this interfering young man on the West Coast, at least make sure she is not back at Central Park South until midnight . . ."

"But then—Alexa—however much I reassure her, she'll tell her sister. Alexa is much smarter . . ."

Forga broke in and smiled his coldest smile. "Yes, Alexa is much smarter, tougher, much more interested in becoming rich—as rich as you will be—if you are able to do the job I have just told you to do." He turned to the credenza behind him and took out a vial. "Slip a little of this into her glass tonight to encourage her faith in you and Upton."

"Is it . . . is it . . . ketamine?" Barry asked.

Forga shook his head reprovingly, as a father would to a foolish child. "Of course not. It is a mixture from Umberto—for special clients. For special flights of happiness to the unknown. By the time Miss Shapwell returns home her sister will be away on an assignment, but this . . ." Forga tapped the vial. "This will give her sweet dreams . . ." Again he looked piercingly into Barry's eyes. "You will not fail, Barry." Barry shivered at Forga's tone. He shook his head slowly as Forga repeated the words. "You will not fail. You cannot afford to fail."

"So you hit the big time, the real *big* time . . . but I can't do anything with your face, baby, if those pieces of salt are going to keep running down those high-class bones of yours."

She'd had her eyes closed, hadn't even been aware that anyone had come into the dressing room after Penelope had gone whizzing out in search of another bra. It was "Imagine" that had turned on her tap, John Lennon's "Imagine," which she'd listened to at least four hundred times without really ever hearing one word. It was on the radio and she'd listened to the lyrics with her new mind in her new loved-and-touched body and the words were more than she could stand. When was Marc going to call? When was she going to see him again? She couldn't believe the change in herself; she who had *never* been able to understand until this second how another human being could mean so much; it was almost impossible for a person to function on her own.

Alexa opened her eyes. It took a minute or two to remember who he was, the extra-tall black man looking down at her. Then she remembered. It was the makeup artist who never smiled, until you squeezed one out of him. It was the makeup artist who had once long ago tried to proposition her on behalf of a "collector of 'boo-ti-ful' women."

"Mims."

She could see he was pleased she remembered his name. There was a glint of white as he peered down to examine her face as he had done the first time around in Cal Robinson's studio. It seemed a lifetime ago. It was a lifetime ago.

"I'm not going to ask why you're cryin', though I know from *Models' Showcase* you're the hottest thing around."

"Why not?" Alexa didn't care about the answer. It was a question to give her time to pull herself together, to make her think about the job and not about Marc, but Mims's answer jarred her.

"I know why. You're the Devi girl, The Now and Forever girl. That's enough to make anyone cry." As he spoke, Mims swiftly marked her face with big white strokes, beneath her eyes, along the bridge of her nose, down both sides of her cheeks. "White lights, dark recedes"—she'd said it herself to women all over the country, explaining how makeup could transform a face "once the canvas is right. Devi skin care first, color next."

Penelope came whistling through the door. "Oh, good, Mims, you've started. Isn't it great, gal, he's come to New York just for us and for an enor-mous amount of money." Penelope looked as arch as she knew how to look. "You'd better be worth that fortune today, Mims, my friend. This is the most important cover shoot of the year—even if we're not paying for it."

"What do you mean by that, Pen?" Alexa asked irritably. She knew what Pen meant. It was a veiled reference to her Devi position, and she wanted to get the link out of Pen's mind and mouth. "You used to want me for *View* once."

"I still do, m'dear, but it's very strange. Let's say I think we're giving your company a wonderful free advertisement—but you're certainly looking more like the 'Now and Forever' story than you did forty minutes ago." Penelope held a necklace of ruby beads interspersed with diamonds close to Alexa's neck. "Nope—too red, too bloody red and real." She pressed her face against Alexa's, receiving a white smear on her own cheek in the process. "Do you know, gal, we spent forty-eight hours brainstorming what to put around your precious little neck and I was right. I knew I was right. Nothing against you, but real ruby is too red. I'm going to buzz my idiot child back at the office to bring over some . . ." She was out of the door before anyone could hear the end of her sentence. Alexa sighed. She was back in the old crazy world.

Mims sighed, too, but then as he worked, he talked about why he'd left the West Coast for the East Coast and why he'd probably soon be going back. Alexa couldn't have cared less, but at least his voice stopped the radio from getting through to her. She was so deep into her own thoughts, it took a while to realize Mims had stopped work, had stopped talking, was staring at her reflection in the unsettling way he'd stared before. Was he just waiting for her to pay some attention?

"What's up, Mims? The salt still showing?"

"Do you know the real reason I came east for a while honey? It was because of you . . ."

Alexa thought he must be kidding. She stifled a yawn. "That's great. Thanks a lot."

"I know your Devi boss, gal." Mims cackled as he said the last word to make sure she realized he was imitating Penelope. "I know your boss and he owes me. He owes me plenty." The big white teeth were on view, but not in a smile.

"My Devi boss . . . ?" She was being slow, but the adrenaline started to flow. "You mean . . . Mr. For-"

He finished the word for her. "Forga, who used to be Mr. Baxter, Mr. Boris Baxter. He's the one to make you cry like he knows how to make 'gals' cry, but he doesn't make boys cry, not big boys like me, oh, no . . ."

He picked up a blusher stick and deftly made her cheekbones jump out in the mirror. She tried to turn to look at him directly, but with one big hand he forced her back. "You don't need to look me in the eyes, sweetheart. This could be your lucky day and maybe mine, too. If he made you cry, would you like someone like me to call on some friends with knuckles? My hands are insured for a million bucks. They're my living, but I've got friends who use their fists for . . ."

"Wait a minute. Wait a minute, Mims. You're going too fast for me . . ."

"Gotta go fast. Madame Room with a View will be back in a minute busybodying herself. We've got to take it as we can get it. Does he still have the club on West Eleventh?"

"Yes," she lied, not having a clue what Mims was talking about. Perhaps yes, perhaps no. Perhaps it was a case of mistaken identity, but there was no mistaking Mims's fury. It was the kind she understood only too well—fury that builds up like a volcano until it has to burst out. If Mims thought she was crying over Forga and it helped find something out, anything out about him, it was worth going along with Mims's wrong ideas.

"He's a beast," she whispered.

"He sure is, my lovely."

"What's your problem? What did he do to you?"

Mims bared his teeth again. It wasn't pretty. "You could say I used to work for him, too . . . in a sort of way. Models. He likes models. I know models. I help models. I introduce them to the big time . . . to photographers, magazines, TV commercials . . ." He paused, then, "To Mr. Bigtimers with money—like Mr. Boris Baxter." He frowned as if trying to remember something, then said accusingly, "Why, Devi girl, I believe I was going to introduce you to him when we first met . . ."

"Why?" Alexa knew why, but she asked all the same.

"He paid well, honey. He paid me for the recommendations, for the easy way I got the 'gals' to go to him . . . the better the 'gal,' the more I charged." As he talked, he continued to work, with color, with powder, with cream. "Why shouldn't a black bastard like me have money, too? Not the crappy by-the-hour, by-the-day makeup-man shit. Why shouldn't I have a custom-made Mercedes, a fur-lined Bijan coat for the cold. The models he really liked got a trip to big-time New York, to the club on West Eleventh. But he screwed me. He screwed me big." This was a new Mims, as menacing as black ice.

Alexa no longer looked at him. It was too frightening. She looked at her reflection without seeing anything. "Okay. Okay. So he screwed you. How?"

The black man clenched and unclenched his million-dollar hands. "A girl I know killed herself because of the fucker. It scared off the others. He never paid up and he blamed me for no more supply . . . he owed me fifty g's to begin with. He had this 'Now and Forever' youth idea years ago . . . years and years ago. He set up this empire, gal . . ." Again there was heavy sarcasm behind the way he used Penelope's favorite way of addressing her. "You weren't the first inspiration by far. He set up youth shops all across the state, then in other states, small-time operators . . ."

Alexa felt the blood rush to her face; in the mirror she could see the sudden redness changing, her makeup appearing fudgy, strange.

Suddenly, Mims knelt down and with his big hands forced Alexa to look at him directly. He was whispering, far more chilling than if he'd yelled at her. "He had my kid brother killed, gal . . . a little kid, not even twelve, do you understand? Mowed down on the sidewalk eating his ice cream. Hit and run . . . he didn't stand a chance . . . no witnesses . . ." The whisper was getting hoarse; the black eyes dilated.

"Why are you telling me this?"

Mims stood up. "I've been looking for the fucker ever since. He disappeared, dropped out of sight, and then the fun started. I started to get all these hard-luck calls from kids he'd been playing around with—some for sex, some for what he called 'formula experiments.' They were in plenty of trouble. I've been looking for the son of a bitch for two years. I got lucky. I was in Paris working the shows. I saw a picture of a man in *Ola,* half hidden behind some bosomy duchess. I was sure it was him, even half a face—it's the kind of face you don't forget—even if it has a new name. 'Said to be the brains and the money behind the great new Devi Company,' *Ola* said. Then, what next do I read in *Models' Showcase,* but the big news about Cal Robinson's little Alexa being chosen as The Face, Now and Forever." There was poison in his voice. "It seemed as if Jehovah had decided it was time I got a break. Time at last to collect and get my revenge . . ."

"Why didn't you just go find him at the club on West Eleventh?"

"I did. I have. I do. There's a neat little plate on the door. Doctor's office it says. That's all. Bars on the window; some bloody dog showing its fangs at the window, but never anyone there. No more showtime. My friends have been checking it out. Waiting for him, for someone to arrive. It's the only clue, the only address I had. The only way to reach him until I learned about your connection." Again Mims bared his teeth. "That's where I had to cable him whenever there was a new broad I thought he'd like; that's where the best lookers went for being 'specially good.' " Again the heavy sarcasm. "But as I tell you, that was years ago. I want to be sure. Don't want to B and E for nothing . . ."

"B and E?" Alexa asked.

"Break and enter . . ."

Alexa looked startled, but Penelope didn't notice as she bustled in singing in a high falsetto voice, "Buy me, buy me, buy a bottle of Devi, too, and stay young now and forever . . ." She was carrying what looked like a coil of red electrical wire. Neither Mims nor Alexa made any comment as she started to wind it around Alexa's neck. Whatever Pen decided to use for a necklace Alexa didn't care—providing she didn't pull it too tight.

Her pain over Marc was receding. She winked at Mims through the mirror. He didn't know it, but, she thought, perhaps Jehovah had decided it was time she got a break, too. As usual it took an interminable time before Penelope decided she was ready to face the camera of the photographer usually referred to as God. It took so long, Mr. God himself came into the dressing room, shut the door quietly, perched beside Alexa on the dressing-table stool, and spoke in a low voice to her reflection. "Do you think we can take some pictures before you turn twenty-five?" He got up just as quietly, opened the door, and started to walk slowly, head down, toward the studio. Penelope darted after him. "Oh, Dick, dahling, let me just tell you I think . . ."

Mims quickly shut the door. It was the first time they'd been alone for about an hour. "Well . . . ?"

"I'll do anything to help, but what can I do?"

Mims spoke urgently. "Where is he now? This Mr. Baxter Forga? Now, today, tonight. There's never any time to lose with him. He can disappear in a minute . . ."

Alexa answered him just as urgently. "I never know where he's going to be. He changes our meeting place all the time. He's got offices, property, homes for all I know, all over the city. Last night I was at his party . . ." Mims twisted his mouth in an ugly expression, as if he wanted to spit, but she went on hurriedly, "I usually never see him socially. If he gives parties, this is the first one I've been to—at an enormous place on East End Avenue."

"Number?" They could hear Penelope approaching, whistling again.

"I don't remember. A car took me. Number twenty I think—but why don't you—what did you call it—B and E West Eleventh? Make sure Baxter is Forga? Perhaps find out more locations?"

"I need help. Will you help?"

"Yes."

Alexa sat, as she remembered she'd first sat for Penelope in Cal Robinson's studio, isolated on the set, surrounded by high white boards and many standing, glaring lights. It was ironic the mood Penelope told her she wanted to produce. She didn't have to simulate it now. "Abandon yourself. Abandon . . . wild abandon . . ." Penelope mouthed behind God the photographer. But despite her new knowledge of what it was like to abandon herself to another, at first the mood didn't come. Alexa had to keep her mind from "showing," from working like a computer, trying to put into order the astonishing things Mims had told her.

After a short session before lunch and two hours after of fifteen-minute segments, trying to relive for the camera the real face of abandon she'd shown so often the night before, Alexa passed her tongue over red glossed lips longing for a long cool drink.

"That's it. That's it. Again . . . again, Lex . . . tongue. Tongue. Think tongue . . ." ordered Penelope.

Another hour passed. One bare shoulder forward, then the other. Twist . . . writhe . . . head back, head down. Right side, left side. Long white-nailed finger on pale gold cheek . . . right arm across the strapless vivid red bugle beaded top . . . arms behind her back . . . barely covered pale-gold breasts thrust forward. The red wire coil had been on and off half a dozen times, replaced by the rubies, and then by a necklace that looked as if it had been made from red bottle caps.

When it was time to change film rolls, Alexa called out, "Can I get out of here for a minute?" Although there was no consent, she knew there would be no objection because Penelope and God were arguing about the size of her lips. It would probably go on for a while. Mims had just given her a paper cup of iced water from the water cooler when one of the studio minions sidled in and said she was wanted on the telephone.

Mims looked at her expectantly. He knew as she knew that on very important shoots, models rarely took calls unless it was an emergency. It was a black mark against them; evidence that, however successful they were, they might be developing an "attitude" that could interfere with performance. A "good attitude," which meant strict adherence to instructions, along with all the obvious vital statistics—could keep a girl in work in the most fickle profession on earth.

"I wouldn't even know if anyone called me, unless it was Blair . . ." Alexa muttered, "but then she'd ask for Pen, not me. Unless it's an emergency call from Jo, it has to be . . ."

"Him?"

"Him."

Alexa's stomach cramped at the sound of Forga's voice, singularly sweet today, which made it even more unnerving after her runaway act from his party the night before.

"There are some important people I want you to meet." There was no change in his tone as he made his message clear. "That you must meet—for the sake of the company. It is inconvenient for me and perhaps for you, too, but we have to meet them in London."

"When?"

"Tomorrow for lunch, an all-important lunch. A car will collect you from the apartment at nine-thirty tonight. Kiko has packed your bag. You won't be away long—two or three days."

"But . . ." she realized there was no *but*. She either escaped and it was all over or she went on with her Devi role. Forga provided more details. "We will leave from Teterboro about ten-fifteen. There is a comfortable bedroom on the plane. You will arrive refreshed—in time to make a sensation, my dear. I have already informed *View* that no matter what happens you must leave the studio no later than eight-thirty. After so much of your very valuable time I am sure they must now have the cover they—we—want." *Click.* She held the phone off the hook for a second, seeing a trace of the red gloss on the mouthpiece. It looked like blood.

As she returned to the dressing room, she could hear

Penelope's voice in the studio, placating, soothing, persuasive, still discussing the merit of a big or little mouth. She rushed inside to tell Mims Forga's latest command.

He was lying on a chaise longue, eyes closed. Once again Alexa thought back to seeing him the first time that way in Cal Robinson's studio. She felt guilty. She hadn't thought of Cal in months and months, let alone called him.

"I don't like it. It smells. It could be the most important trip of my life—I just don't know. It's part of my contract with Devi. I go where I'm told to go. This is the first time overseas." Her voice was defensive. She felt foolish.

Mims didn't move as he spoke with his eyes still closed. "It's nearly four o'clock. Around five you will look tired. I will convey that message to Pen, even if she doesn't see it herself." Mims opened his large black eyes and winked at her. "You will do a bolt. There's a back exit. You won't be seen. You'll wear this, baby . . ." He pointed to a drab-looking raincoat hung over a chair. "A car will be waiting downstairs. It's the right time of day, rush hour, and we're lucky. It's pissing with rain. People anxious to get where they're goin'. You're goin' to West Eleventh with my guys. Get me that guarantee that your Mr. Forga is my Mr. Baxter, baby, and we'll take care of the rest. We'll follow you home and make sure you don't have to cross the ocean . . ."

Alexa shuddered. "What about the dog?"

"Poisoned meat."

Mims didn't need to explain further and the thought of poisoned meat stayed with her for the next hour. If they didn't already have the cover in the can, then the red bugle-beaded top and the violet chiffon she was now wearing weren't going to do it for them. She cared and she didn't care.

If any other model had been around, for once in her life she would have asked for a lude, something, anything to calm her nerves. What a twenty-four hours she'd been through—and now she was going to take part in a dangerous break-in-and-enter job. Was she going out of her mind?

After a whispered consultation with the photographer, Penelope, looking agitated, ran out of the studio calling, "Mims . . . Mims . . . where are you?"

He came in and carefully surveyed Alexa. "Yeah," he drawled. "I see what you mean. There's something negative 'bout the eyes with the chiffon. Let me try something. I've got an idea . . ."

Penelope jumped up and down like a little girl. "Oh, goody, good for you, Mims, my dear friend. I knew you'd see our point."

Incredibly, it was exactly five. Penelope had collaborated with Mims's plan without either of them having to do a thing.

Why was she doing it? Why was she taking such a risk? If she'd had more time to think, perhaps she wouldn't be going to West 11th Street, but she knew why Mims's urgency was propelling her fast forward . . . why she was looking for proof on Mims's behalf that he had the right man. It was because she was desperate to prove that Mims was wrong, Jo was wrong. She had to find out once and for all that Forga had nothing to do with the West Coast chain of face factories, because she had to make sure Madame—Svetlana—Devi, the mother of the man she'd fallen in love with, had nothing whatever to do with the tragedy in her past, the death of her mother.

It wasn't until, wearing the raincoat over the diaphanous violet chiffon, her hair stuffed into an overlarge tan beret, she was on her way down the gloomy back stairs that Alexa realized Mims wasn't coming with her. As she stopped, obviously wavering, Mims looked down at her and said firmly, "If I come too, it will be too suspicious. I'll tell them you told me you had to make a phone call. I tried to stop you but you wouldn't listen . . . don't worry." Even in the dim light she could see him roll his eyes. ". . . I'm a good actor, baby. I'll dish you dirty. Tell 'em I've been coping with your tears all day. Then, you damn well come back here and tell me I've found my man, baby."

She was as scared as she'd ever been in her life, sick-to-her-stomach scared, but there was the car just like Mims had said and the back door opened as she appeared in the street. She'd expected black men like Mims, huge black men with visible, frightening fists, but the three inside looked more like Puerto Ricans. They grunted, looked embarrassed, and looked away, as if her beautifully made up, naturally gorgeous face was a light bulb lighting up the dark interiors of their lives.

The only thing said to her on the way downtown was, "Don't move," as the car neared West 11th Street. It was pissing rain all right. The man in the front passenger seat muttered, "It's enough to wash the rat out of the cow." She wondered what he meant until she saw the driver hand him what looked like a butcher's package. The poisoned meat. Oh, God. It was too late to back out now. Her teeth chattered. She was shivering all over.

Two of the men jumped out and the car circled the block. As they turned the corner onto West 11th again, the car slowed to admit the front-seat passenger. He smirked to show a mouth with many missing front teeth. "I don't know what your black guy was worried about. It was a breeze, man. Take out the lousy dog and bury it and no one will ever know they've had any visitors."

They turned to look at her. No mistaking the look. It was her turn now to do whatever the black guy wanted her to do.

There were three steps down to the front door that looked closed, but which opened as she approached it. With the rainy, gloomy day, it was already nearly dark inside. She turned to look for a light switch. "No," said an angry voice. "I don't know what *you're* looking for. I'm looking for the snow that Mims says is stashed here, the snow and the dough . . ." He cackled without a trace of humor. "Someone's been livin' here, but there's sure nothin' worth stealin' . . ." He handed her a flashlight irritably. "Keep it low."

She passed a paneled room that looked like a doctor's waiting room with magazines on low tables, standing lamps, a sliding glass window set into the back wall. "I have an appointment with Dr. . . ." Dr. who? It was all so bizarre, but there was a smell about the place she recognized instantly. It was the faint but unmistakable, intoxicating odor of the dark blue Rigaud candles that Forga always had lit in every place she had ever visited him. Her palms grew moist.

She was with a glove-wearing pro. It was obvious. He told her to follow him and she did, into every room where with a low-angled flashlight and practiced eye he took in every door to open, every cupboard, every picture that might conceal something behind it.

There was nothing. Nothing except books, hundreds and hundreds of books on medicine, law, psychiatry. No letters. No diaries. No documents.

She followed the pro upstairs into a boring beige-colored anteroom that also resembled a waiting room—waiting for what?

There was a shoji screen and Alexa gasped as her guide silently slid it back. The bedroom beyond was magnificent. The bed was covered with a mink blanket, the walls mirrored to reflect dark red Eastern poles that supported a rich gold silk canopy.

Despite the professionalism of the guide, it was she who inadvertently found what Mims was looking for—and what she had dreaded to find.

She tripped as she went down one step into a silver-walled vault of a bathroom and grabbed hold of a large ring set in a wall. The "wall" opened to reveal a huge walk-in closet where, in neat precise rows, hung whips, straps, canes, chains. In the corner of the closet was what she imagined an electric chair looked like, not because it was connected to any electricity, but because at every level from the ground up were restraining straps, clamps, chains. The house of a torturer, but that still didn't mean it was owned or occupied by Baxter Forga, or for that matter, the Boris Baxter that Mims had once "pimped" for.

And then she saw it—at the same time as her gloved companion saw it—a safe, paneled as the cupboard was paneled and locked with an intricate-looking lock. Her companion knelt down, opened his jacket, and revealed a variety of small tools hanging from his belt. Alexa held the flashlight, amazed that her hands had stopped trembling, as he tried first one, then another instrument to open the lock.

It wasn't easy. She wasn't wearing a watch and sweat poured down her face from anxiety over the time it was taking and from the heat in the oppressive closet. She estimated at least thirty minutes had passed before at last he broke the lock open.

"I've paid my dues now to that black punk," he whispered. "Now, goddamn it, someone will know we've been here. Okay, lady, get to work. I'll look around, but if what you or he wants is in this house, I bet you'll find it here."

There were dozens of books of traveler's checks, with no name on them, issued by the European New York Bank of Commerce. There was an envelope stuffed with photographs of beautiful girls, pornographic pictures that only made Alexa think of poisoned meat again, but no pictures of Baxter Forga. There was a slim black leather book with MEMBERS monogrammed in gold. Alexa flicked through the pages. There were dozens of names, some with symbols and initials beside them, meaningless to her, but not to those who had set out to entertain the members. She had a hunch . . . yes, there he was under *G* . . . Paul Gruen with three telephone numbers and LTW and CONT in the margin. "Likes to whip"—she bit her lip as the words came to her mind. What the other initials stood for, that had once ensured Mr. Gruen's membership, she didn't know or care. The club seemed defunct, thank God. This was getting her nowhere.

Then suddenly she came across letters, three or four letters that she knew without reading them would tell her what she most feared to know that Baxter Forga, the man Mims had recognized from the photograph in *Ola* as Boris Baxter, the mastermind behind a huge experimental face-clinic operation, was one and the same man who had been behind The Fountain. A one-name logo on top of pale mauve writing paper was all she needed to see. MAGDA it read, in the bold darker mauve logo Jo had told her about . . . letters from Magda to Svetlana and to "Bax"—Boris Baxter.

It was all there, everything Mims wanted to be true. Everything she didn't want to be true. She read so quickly the words attacked her like deadly germs. "He's no good. Break with him . . . not worth it . . . don't trust him . . . he's ruining your life, encouraging these experiments. I can't be a part of it anymore. Where is he going to lead us? It's getting more and more dangerous . . ." Alexa, who a few minutes before had felt so hot, now grew icy cold as she read on: "Bax, this is the end. I'm leaving the country and taking my sister Svetlana with me . . ." Sister! Svetlana and Magda were sisters! Alexa leaned back against the door. It was incredible and yet so obvious . . . one sister helping another, one sister providing patients for another. She began to feel ill but she read on. "Your big ideas have just about ruined Svetlana's life, other lives, but at last she's decided to listen to me after what happened to Teri . . ." Alexa moaned. The Puerto Rican came quickly, angrily to the doorway. "What's up, chick? You've found what you came for?" She shook her head, gasped, "I'm not sure. Give me a minute or two . . ."

He looked at his watch. It was a gaudy gold affair. "Bring the stuff wid you, kid. It's gettin' late."

"Just a minute." She had to recover, had to read on, and prove without any doubt that Boris Baxter and Baxter Forga were one and the same.

> My sister Svetlana and I are going back to Europe. I warn you if you try to contact her again, I'm going to the police. I know even if she won't believe me that you've made thousands out of her work. We can prove you've driven us to do what we did. You're the one who's caused all the trouble. We were doing well before you came along and turned Svetlana's head with all your crazy ideas about eternal youth. You should rot in hell. You're a monster . . .

The Puerto Rican came in and roughly pulled her to her feet. "We're going. Take the letters. Leave 'em. I don't care. But we're on our way. There's no snow, no cash. It's a setup. I can feel it. I want out . . ."

The safe was still open. With a sense of authority she didn't feel Alexa turned on the man. "There's something more than dope, than cash that Mims needs. He wants proof of identity. He won't like it if I don't find it conclusively . . ."

She didn't know why she'd said it . . . she was working in the dark . . . there had to be more clues, clues as to where Magda had gone. Magda was the key to everything. Where on earth was she? But there were no more letters, nothing more about Magda or Svetlana. With the Puerto Rican now glaring at her dangerously, Alexa leaned inside the safe and pulled out what looked like a slim manuscript from the bottom. It was a photocopy of a chapter of a book by someone called Dr. Eugene Kennedy, Ph.D., Professor of Psychiatry at Loyola University.

Alexa gasped as she read the first line. *"There is an everyday loneliness that has never been identified. The loneliness that fills the hours when we can do nothing but wait . . ."* She knew the words by heart. She could see the cover of the small volume she kept in the drawer by her bed with the prominent byline, *By Baxter Forga, Ph.D.*—truly a forger, a liar, a plagiarist. Here was the proof that despite everything she had still stubbornly hoped never to find, . . that Boris Baxter and Baxter Forga were one and the same and Magda had not been successful in convincing her sister Svetlana to leave the country. Svetlana had obviously not believed that "Bax" was a monster. She had believed he would provide the support for her to continue her crusade to find the youth portion . . . and he had . . . Devi, Now and Forever.

Alexa couldn't stop shuddering. What was she going to do? How could she successfully hide her feelings for the next few hours, let alone days in London?

Mims could hide her, but what good would that do? If she went to the *New York Times* or a television producer with the story, what would a couple of letters written on tasteless mauve writing paper prove? How long would it take to put the evidence together with all the pieces to show what a sham Madame Devi was, as was all that she stood for? She had no real proof even now that Madame Devi and Svetlana Sorgiokov were the same person. Marc. Tears again rolled down her cheeks. He was the last person she could tell, confide in, ask for advice. He had to know, if not about the true nature of the face clinics, then certainly something about the relationship between Forga and his mother. He had tried to warn her about Forga without telling her anything specific.

"We're off now." There was no "maybe" in the man's tone. There was in any case no more reason to stay. Alexa stuffed the Kennedy manuscript and two of the letters, one to Svetlana from Magda, one to Boris Baxter, deep into the raincoat pocket, and she put the others back where she'd found them. She watched as the Puerto Rican attempted to close the safe and lock it. "Fuck, this one's a real bitch." He wasn't satisfied, but it looked locked to her. He looked at his fancy watch again. "I could do it better, but Mims said you've got to be back in an hour—and we've spent nearly two . . ."

"What time is it?"

"Seven-twenty. You've gotta catch a train or something?" He didn't expect an answer but train rhymed with plane. The plane from Teterboro. She didn't even like to think about the pandemonium at the studio caused by her absence. On the ride back it was as if she were two people. One terrified, shuddering at the thought of what was ahead, of having to pretend to be the immaculate, perfect Face, Now and Forever; the other as cold as a calculating machine wondering if on her trip to London she could find out in some way where Magda was . . . Magda . . . the name rang in her head like a familiar dirge of death. Magda, the one who had once hated Forga enough to warn him she would go to the police; Magda, the witness to Forga's involvement with the face-clinic ring, the cash-register ring of misery.

The driver broke into her thoughts. "Tell Mims to give us a call. We're ready when he is—thirty minutes—call in thirty minutes."

Mims. Alexa stiffened. Did she want Mims to know Forga was his man? Did she want Mims's guys with knuckles to get rid of Forga now? Or give him a lesson, slice him up so he disappeared again—to reemerge later, probably as rich and powerful as ever?

Wouldn't it be a sweeter revenge to see him publicly disgraced, he along with his Madame Devi? But how could she remain unscathed by that? Inevitably, her career, her reputation would be besmirched, too.

She didn't know what to think, didn't know what to tell Mims. As the car stopped and started in heavy traffic in the pouring rain she began to feel drowsy, her practically sleepless night, followed by this incredible day, catching up with her. She was dozing when the slim guy next to her prodded her in the ribs and whispered, "Looks like you've got a welcoming committee ahead . . ."

For a minute she didn't know where she was. She'd been dreaming she was back, trapped, at the Fairmont. Ahead she could see a long gray stretch limousine outside the main entrance to the studio. Something told her that Forga was inside. "What time is it?" she asked again.

"Ten of eight . . ."

She didn't hesitate. "It will be bad for Mims if I go in now. I am sure the guy he's after is in that stretch. I don't want him to see me now. Take me home."

The driver looked around suspiciously. "Why?"

She almost screamed at him. "Can't you see—something's happened. They're waiting for me. I'll call Mims immediately when I get back to the apartment."

The driver spoke. He seemed to be the boss. "She's right, Sid. Where do you want to go, lady?"

Mercifully, the traffic eased up as they crossed over to the West Side. Before the car dropped her a block away from her building, the driver turned around. "What do we tell Mims?"

She hesitated. Before she could answer, the one who had

been with her in the house said accusingly, "Let's see what you took, lady. Maybe Mims will want it."

"He won't—it doesn't prove anything to him." All the same, she took the copy of the manuscript and the two letters out of the raincoat pocket. He passed them over to the driver.

"Doesn't look like much to me—but I think we'll give the letters to Mims . . ." He tossed the manuscript copy back over his shoulder as she cried, "Oh, please, at least let me have the letter to Bax . . ."

"Nope," he said coldly. "If Mims thinks you should have 'em, you'll get 'em. Tell him we've got something for him when you call him like you said you were going to do and make it quick. These two letters prove he's the guy Mims is looking for, right?"

"Right," she said. "He's the guy Mims has been looking for."

As she ran into her apartment building, her heart pounding, the doorman indicated someone was waiting for her, sitting on the corner sofa. She tried to smile, but her mouth trembled too much as Forga stood up to tower over her. He put one finger under her chin as he said, "Oh, the foolishness of love. I hope you enjoyed your tryst, my dear, but I am afraid you are going to find it was very expensive. You will find out why on our way to London."

CHAPTER ELEVEN

THE PHONE CALL FROM BROWN SCHNEIDER COULD NOT HAVE COME at a better time. Jo was stunned that Brown would call her, although she had always had the feeling, for some reason, that Brown liked her. Even so, to be invited to lunch at Brown's apartment was . . . well . . . so flattering. She was also relieved out of all proportion to the invitation to have somewhere to go that would keep her mind—momentarily—away from the horrors of the night before.

She had no exact recollection of what she'd rambled on about to Barry—under the influence of alcohol to an extent she had never been before in her life. She could remember word for word what and why she'd told Barry when she'd awakened at dawn to find him dozing in the big easy chair in her bedroom.

Had she been right to trust him? Since his flustered departure she'd been tossing and turning, dozing as if she was recovering from an anesthetic, until the midmorning call came from Brown.

Her invitation to lunch that day had made the world more

like a normal place again. "If you've nothing better to do . . . it's time we really got to know each other . . . just a picnic . . . yes?" Jo's immediate yes had been followed by "Good . . . about one then . . ."

When she showered and dressed, still feeling like a sleepwalker, Kiko was acting strangely. What was it? He was agitated, that was the only word for it . . . Kiko, who was never anything but impassive, phlegmatic. When she asked him if anything was wrong, she received only a stilted "nothing at all, miss" with a slight bow. She was still wobbly, walking from room to room. She vowed she would never, never drink more than one or two glasses of anything in the future and certainly would never mix her drinks . . . Champagne and vodka and then the last mysterious drink with Forga! Wow! No wonder her head had almost fallen off.

As noon approached she began to feel shy, apprehensive at the thought of time spent alone with Brown in her apartment. Number One Lexington Avenue—she'd already heard that Brown's apartment overlooking Gramercy Park was stunning.

When Mike wasn't at home or the office at 9 A.M. San Diego time, Jo left a long message on his answering machine at home. Not knowing where he was worried her, but then everything seemed to worry her today. For a moment she thought of trying to phone Alexa. It was the last day of shooting . . . trying to get through to her would be like trying to get through to her in purdah. In any case, she couldn't talk about the horrible revelation of the night before on the phone. It would have to wait until early evening. By then she prayed she would have been able to get some advice from Mike.

It was pouring rain, but Kiko's strange and obvious jitters, hovering about as if he couldn't wait for her to leave the apartment, made her decide to leave for the lunch early.

As she waited for the elevator with Kiko standing in the front door, showing—for him—almost a relieved expression, she heard the phone ring in the apartment. For a second she was tempted to go back in case it was Mike, but the elevator doors opened and she couldn't bear the thought of Kiko listening to what she had to say. She would try to reach Mike again from outside.

As soon as she reached the lobby, Joe the doorman asked

her to go back up because a Mr. Hunter was anxiously trying to reach her. Some instinct told her not to go and, as if to prove her instinct was right, at that second with the rain heavier than ever, a taxi arrived to drop someone off. "I'm late, Joe," she said over her shoulder as she jumped in the cab. "Tell Kiko I'll call Mr. Hunter at his office after lunch."

They sat in a book-lined room, not just floor to ceiling, but wall to wall, tumbling and neatly piled books, books over the door mantel and on the marble top of the mantelpiece, books of every description, paperbacks next to leather-bound tomes, some huge and horizontal, others no more than six inches high, grouped together between improvised bookends—an empty Coke bottle with a silver Ganesh, a small bowl of goldfish with an onyx vase stuffed with dry flowers.

It was a room full of contradictions, half tidy, half messy, with a huge desk dominating the floor space, a desk Jo immediately coveted.

"It's a partner's desk, late eighteenth century," Brown told her as she admired the mellow glow of the wood, the huge but elegant rectangle shape with drawers with bamboo handles on both sides. "I had to have it; saw it in one of those dimly lit, broken-down bric-a-brac shops London specializes in. I never want a partner but I had to have my partner's desk."

To Jo's surprise, they lunched there, manuscripts, files, magazines, newspapers pushed left and right, placemats made of shells pulled out from one of the drawers, knives and forks from another.

Jo looked carefully around as Brown went into the kitchen. It was an intriguing apartment, probably not too large, but giving the impression of size with two book-lined corridors seen through half-open doors leading somewhere. It was her kind of place, much more than the mini palace she lived in on Central Park South or the museum showplace on East End Avenue. For a second Jo felt faint, but the moment passed as Brown returned with a big earthenware bowl of salad Niçoise in one hand and a carafe of red wine in the other.

"In a second our repast will be complete." Brown looked as if she were enjoying herself, grinning broadly as she strolled languidly back to the kitchen and returned with a basket of hot bread and a stone jar. "Stilton," she said. Jo winced as she banged it down on the polished desk top. "It's especially good with this bread from a great Italian baker around the corner . . ."

Denny Upton, Forga, even Barry Hunter and all they stood for seemed a million miles away, but Jo wasn't relaxed. How could she be with so much on her mind? Nevertheless, the warmth of Brown's welcome, the clumsy coziness of the much lived-in apartment was like a temporary balm to an open wound as the rain poured down outside.

She hardly touched the glass of wine Brown poured for her. After Brown had had a couple of glasses, she leaned across the desk, her owlish glasses slipping down her shiny nose. "I'm concerned about you. While your sister blooms like the Rose of Tralee, you, the dedicated serving maid, are wilting."

Before Jo could answer, Brown's tone changed, became more abrupt. "I meant what I said about getting to know you. I'm fascinated by sisters, especially those as close in age as you two are—especially those who appear to have such different values—as you two have. I loathe procrastination. I have to get to the main point of this lunch."

Jo stiffened. Was there another surprise, shock in store?

"You don't have to answer me, but I'm curious . . ." Brown looked at Jo for so long without speaking that Jo gulped down some wine to cover her embarrassment. Immediately the dizziness, even a remnant of nausea returned. It passed, but Jo quickly pushed the glass of wine away. No more, not even a sip for her. Brown didn't notice. Her voice sounded deeper, solemn, as if she were about to make a confession. She was.

"I have a simple question to ask, but I'm going to explain why first." Querulously she added, "Nothing to do with *View*. Nothing I'm writing for *View*. I'm going to trust you—because I know, I observed you don't gab. Now, I'm going to trust you to keep that private little mouth of yours even more tightly shut. Fact is, I'll be leaving *View* soon . . ."

"Oh, that's too bad." It popped out, but Jo meant it. Today, for the first time, she realized at the back of her mind she had always in some way counted on Brown as an ally in a hostile environment.

"Yes, it's too bad, but Blair knew I was a pinch hitter. It started out as a game for me, a solution for her after a disastrous series of beauty editors who couldn't even hit the ball."

Jo loved Brown's baseball references—they totally fitted her unexpected, irreverent personality—but where was this leading?

Brown got up, went over to an old-fashioned drinks trolley and came back with a bottle of port. She poured a drop or two into the Stilton and then dug out a generous portion and put it on Jo's plate. "Funny thing, I've known Blair's family all my life. Loaded, m'dear. Loaded with bucks. I admired Blair for branching out on her own—the Benson family has always been in the paper business, you know that—Georgia, Florida . . . mostly paper, but Blair's brother Clem moved the company into the twentieth century with diversifications. Clem was killed in a plane crash a few years ago . . . he and Blair were so close—she went into a tailspin, but then with true Benson grit seemed to get over it . . ."

Jo nodded, said "oh" and "um" when it seemed appropriate while Brown talked, ate, and drank without pause. "Anyway, funny thing, I woke up this morning, realized I was getting stale. I've been slogging away for too long and, worse, I've been getting too close, too fond of some of the beauty types I have to deal with."

"What's wrong with that?"

"Everything, my dear. Halfway through my *View* stint, I was approached by a publisher—doesn't matter who—who asked me to write an objective book about women and how far they are prepared to go for this abstract, ill-defined prize of beauty."

Jo wanted Brown to shut up right there. She fidgeted, scared of what Brown was going to trust her with, scared of what she was going to ask her.

Jo tried to eat the Stilton, the bread. They were excellent, but she had no appetite for anything. Already she was watching the time, urging it to move faster, so she could try once again to get Mike and get the call to Barry Hunter out of the way. In the back of her mind was an idea to go over to the studio and wait outside until Alexa emerged.

"The book is nearly finished—got a neat subtitle—Hype and Hypocrisy in the Ugly World of Beauty."

Jo shuddered. She wasn't timid anymore. Too much had happened to her.

"Why are you telling me this? I don't understand."

Brown pushed her chair away from the table, her sharply angled unmade-up face full of purpose. She went over to the bookcase and picked up the small silver Ganesh. The books it supported leaned over but didn't fall.

"D'you know what this is?"

"I think so. Someone had one at school once—it's a lucky elephant charm, isn't it?"

Brown snorted derisively. "Don't say that to my Indian friends. There's nothing charming about it. This, my dear, is an Indian god—the god of good fortune. I'll explain why it has the elephant head some other time, but that brings me to my question. When your beautiful sister became The Devi Face, Now and Forever—Devi, an Indian Goddess of beauty—I assumed, in common with other members of the staff including the obsessive, possessive Ms. Waverly, that she would no longer grace the covers of *View.*" Brown beckoned to Jo to sit beside her on the chintz-covered chesterfield. "Perhaps you are not aware that it is a continual problem for all fashion and beauty books . . . that the magnificent unknowns they discover and work with so assiduously and introduce to the big world are, alas, often in a very short time snapped up for enormous sums of money by big advertisers, the major fashion and beauty houses."

Brown crossed her long trouser-clad legs and lit a cigarette. "It's a peculiar irony, since this usually jeopardizes the model's future appearance in magazine editorials and especially on covers. Obviously because it would be worth hundreds of thousands of dollars of free advertising for the company she represents."

As what Brown was getting at began to sink in, Jo knew the question before she asked it.

"It's happened to so many. Lauren Hutton, Karen Graham, Isabella Rosellini—all regular cover girls until they signed respectively with the likes of Revlon, Lauder, Lancôme . . ."

"And now Alexa is thoroughly established as the Devi girl, you're wondering why *View* is still using her for a cover?"

"Yes, my talented friend. And not only for the cover shot going on now. Pen Waverly, I hear, is a joy to watch and hear as she struggles with conflicting emotions—pleasure that her discovery Alexa has been booked for two out of the three spring covers . . . uneasiness that Alexa is now firmly fixed in the reader's mind as Devi's Face, Now and Forever. Why is this happening?"

"I don't know." Jo hated to sound dumb, but with everything else going on, the conflict of interest had never occurred to her.

Brown blew a perfect smoke ring into the air. "Something fishy, my dear . . ." She poured coffee into two dark-blue mugs. "Watching you both, from near and far over the past year, I decided there was a serious omission in my book. I had to devote a chapter to those born with great beauty; the maintenance, the reality of it, living with it. Beauty corrupts, absolute beauty corrupts absolutely . . ."

"Alexa isn't corrupt!" Jo was so angry, Brown put a placating hand on her shoulder. Jo shrugged it away.

"I really hate your saying that, Brown. Alexa is . . . is . . . well, incorruptible."

Brown took her hand away. "Have you met Forga?"

Jo's astonishment that Brown knew Forga's name showed. "How do you know about Forga?"

It was Brown's turn to be angry. "You seem to forget, it's my business, my job, to know the real decision makers, to get behind the PR crap and see what's really going on. For the first time in my professional life, I'm frustrated, Jo. I can never get to Forga. I can never get to Madame Devi. 'Madame Devi never gives interviews,' " she mimicked. " 'Madame Devi is not available. She is traveling, she is in India . . . in Paris . . . about to leave California.' "

"Why don't you write about the mystery? Isn't that a story?"

Brown laughed heartily, her coffee almost spilling onto the Portuguese rug. "Exactly on target, Jo. I did write a splendid story, an incredible story based on all the broken appointments, the excuses, the astonishing life of a man who, because of his giant wealth and power, can seem to disappear almost off the planet . . ."

"When did it run? I have to read it." Jo's expression was so grim, Brown stopped laughing.

"Something's troubling you, Jo. I want to know what it is . . . I think it's related, tied up somehow to the mystery. Blair killed the story. Even when I threatened to leave when it didn't run, she didn't budge . . . and I stayed. Do you know why?"

When Jo didn't answer, she got up to lean against the mantelpiece, staring down at her to be sure of her full attention. "Because, my dear, my curiosity is whetted. I intend to find out what's behind this strange conspiracy . . . which won't take much longer."

"Oh, really, what have you found out?" Jo asked excitedly.

Brown looked at her slyly. "A turf dispute is bringing speedier answers."

"Turf?"

"You've met Mr. Arthur Reddish, otherwise known as the unique 'Radish,' who never repeats himself."

Jo nodded. What on earth was Brown talking about now?

"I discovered through my astute assistant, who has befriended most of the assistants on the staff, that Radish has been invading my turf—my area of coverage."

"So?" Jo no longer cared if her ignorance showed. Too much was at stake. Her mind was in turmoil. No one could miss seeing the large clock on the mantelpiece—two-forty—how had she let so much time pass . . . but now she couldn't leave before Brown told her everything she knew.

"I confronted him two days ago with the undeniable fact that he had had the audacity to invade my territory. He has been working on an 'I-reveal' piece about Madame Devi. As usual, he blustered belligerently, but when—also as usual—the wind went out of his bluster, he told me my hypothesis was correct . . . that Blair had not given him the okay to go ahead. On the contrary. She expressly told him to lay off . . ."

"And is he?"

"We are pros." Brown was at her haughtiest. "I stimulated his journalistic instinct. I rather think he will try to outdo me, thinking that with a fait accompli interview with Forga or the mysterious Madame, Blair will capitulate and print—but she won't . . ."

"Why not?"

Brown drew heavily on her cigarette. "Forga has some kind of hold over Blair." She hesitated. "I used to think I knew her. Since her brother's death I'm not sure, but I know for sure, if not now, at some time in the recent past Blair and Mr. Forga have had, shall we say, some kind of personal relationship. She is preserving the anonymity he wishes or perhaps commands. Your sister's return as a—shall we say—'Devi' cover girl is another example of Forga's influence. What is more, Radish, perish his tart tongue, told me he had reached the same conclusion."

It was too much. Suddenly the dam burst. Jo was crying, couldn't stop, despite the embarrassment, despite Brown's startled expression. Her pent-up fears, emotions, flooded out in tears as steadily as the rain fell outside.

With another cup of coffee and some uncharacteristic pats and "there, there" from Brown, Jo regained some calm, but she still shivered, not sure what to do or say.

"Tell me about it, Jo?"

She bit her lip, shook her head. She'd already blurted out everything to Barry Hunter. Was she now going to go around telling her story to anyone who asked, who listened, who showed her sympathy?

"I have to go."

"Why? It's pouring down. You're upset—relax with your feet up. Talk if you want to, stay silent if you don't . . ."

The thought of going out into the rain, to find a phone booth on the street, to call Mike, and, then, depending on what he said, to return Barry Hunter's call, was anathema.

"Can I use your phone?"

"Yes, in the bedroom, back there, second door on the right . . ."

"I'll call collect. It's . . . it's . . . to California."

"Call the moon. Do what you have to do." Poor woebegotten little child, Brown thought. She was sure Alexa's extraordinary looks had to have given her disfigured values, while Jo carried Alexa's career responsibilities on her shoulders. Something was fishy. Brown Schneider was sure of it, as sure as she was about her judgment of character.

The bedroom was book lined, too. Jo almost expected to find Brown slept on books. There were also photographs everywhere, so many it was hard to locate the phone, not conveniently by the bed, but connected to an answering machine on a table in the corner. Jo could just imagine how many times Brown let her answering machine pick up while she stayed in bed devouring page after printed page.

It was three-fifteen, twelve-fifteen in San Diego. "Please, God, don't let Mike be at lunch."

He wasn't. At last he was there and, as she poured out all

that had happened, his concern blanketed her with care, so positive it was almost a tangible rope to cling to.

"Just a minute . . ." Jo heard him call an assistant. "Is there a plane to Los Angeles from New York or Newark tonight?" He came back on. "Catch the six-thirty American to the Coast—you can't stay in New York now. I don't know whether Hunter or Forga know everything or not, but it's not important. I want you out of that Devi apartment now. I'll book your ticket with my Amex card. You'll arrive in time to get a connection to San Diego or I'll drive up to L.A. to meet you. Where are you calling from?"

She told him and all that Brown had just told her, hearing his sigh of relief. "Thank God. Well, don't waste another minute. What's the number there?"

She told him, then said urgently, "Mike, I can't leave without telling Alexa. She's locked up in the studio. I can't get through to her, unless I go there . . . and then how can I tell her with some of the *View* crowd around?"

She understood the irritation in his voice. It was another indication of his love for her. She knew he wanted to say, "screw Alexa," but he didn't.

"Look, Jo, I'll look into flights. I'll call you in fifteen, twenty minutes. Don't do anything until you hear from me. Stay with that good lady . . ."

"Shall I tell her about Mom . . . about everything?"

"Hold it till I call you back. Let me digest all this."

"Shall I call Barry Hunter back?"

There was a pause at the other end, then reluctantly Mike said, "Well, yes. Find out what he wants, but don't let him talk you into any meeting with Forga—or him, for that matter. You haven't put any ink on that one-hundred-thousand-dollar contract. Something tells me it's not going to happen. You're a free agent. Stay away from them."

With fingers that hardly knew how to function, Jo dialed Barry's number. There was no boyish charm, no sense of caring, or an arm tucked protectively under her elbow now. He almost snarled into the phone, "Where the hell have you been?"

She was so startled by the venom in his voice, so angered by it, it took all her willpower not to yell back at him. His attitude helped her control.

"Out to lunch. Am I supposed to check with headquarters to get permission?"

He got her message. Swiftly, he tried to make up. "Jo, I'm sorry I sounded so rough, but I've been crazy with worry. God, you nearly passed out last night—I thought you'd had an accident. I've left so many messages at the apartment, Kiko must think I'm sick."

"I'm okay." She tried to sound friendlier.

"Look, Jo, I understand how you feel. You have every right to feel that way. I talked to Mr. Forga this morning . . ." Every so often Jo could hear Barry catch his breath as if he were running as he spoke. "He is very concerned, very concerned, but he thinks the best thing is for you to meet Denny Upton. I want you to have dinner with us tonight, the two of us. I want to hear what he has to say with you sitting right there. He says he can explain everything . . ."

It was the last thing in the world she expected. It was a startling suggestion—but how could she believe a word either of them said? In any case, Mike had told her explicitly not to see any of them until he called back. She would play for time.

"I still don't feel well, Barry. I'm not sure . . ."

"Are you home?"

"No." She knew he would go to the apartment immediately if she had lied and said she was at home. If she was going to go to the Coast, however, she had to pick up a few things after she'd somehow got through to Alexa.

"Where are you?" He was angry again.

"At a friend's house."

"Where?" He was shouting. "What on earth's the matter with you? Don't you realize the seriousness of the allegations you've made. How damaging . . . you've got to meet Denny—got to give Devi—Madame Devi—a chance to clear her name."

"I'll call you later." She couldn't listen anymore. It probably wasn't wise, but she put the phone down before he could bully her into some kind of submission.

She sat staring into space, then at the photographs on Brown's table. There was one that looked like a young Blair, as elegant as today, but rounder, with no strain on her face, sitting on a garden swing with an older woman—perhaps her mother—and a laughing-eyed man—perhaps Clem, the brother she'd lost.

The phone rang, almost to the second, fifteen minutes later. Mike sounded frantic. "Can't get you on a plane, puss. I gather the weather's foul in New York, right? Everything's delayed, and everything's overbooked. Oh, God, can you stay there with Brown—what's her name, Schneider? I'm worried sick about you."

When she didn't answer, he said, "Puss, I wasn't going to tell you, but I'm going to see your father tomorrow. I've found out where he is. We're going to have a man-to-man talk about a few things."

"Oh, Mike . . ." For a second when he'd told her about the plane situation she'd felt hurt, bitterly hurt that he hadn't said he was on his way to her instead, but there he was working away for her all the time. She told him about her conversation with Barry.

"Are you up to it? Can you pretend you believe them? I think it's risky. Really risky . . ."

She interrupted him. "I think I've got to for Alexa's sake as well as mine." She could see herself in a small mirror beside the table. She looked calm. She was calm. The facts weren't all in. She would give Madame Devi the chance Barry had asked for.

"Where will Alexa be tonight?" Mike asked anxiously.

"God knows, probably at the apartment. She's usually exhausted after a major shoot."

"Good. Give her a call at the studio—tell her you have to see her, meet her at the Plaza, anywhere, before you meet Upton. She has to share the responsibility with you." He paused. "Damn it, she should be there—at the dinner. You shouldn't have to face this alone. Then stay together. Don't, whatever you do, stay in that apartment alone. Fly to the Coast tomorrow. I've booked you on the ten A.M. direct to San Diego. I need you, Jo. Go to my apartment like before. I'll be home after I've seen your father. Things are moving at last, puss."

She felt embarrassed, using Brown's phone again, but there was nothing else for it. She called the studio. Just as she expected, she was told Alexa was on the set and couldn't be disturbed for anything. "Call back about five-thirty—she'll probably be taking a break then."

"This is her sister Jo. Before she goes home, it's vital I meet with her. Tell her that, *please.* I can't tell you how important it is." She paused. "Who am I talking to?"

"Mims—I'm doing her makeup. I'll be sure to give her your message."

Jo paced up and down the room, nervous again, trying to

cool down before she made the second call to Barry Hunter. She wanted to sound trusting and as eager as he and Upton were to discover the truth. She thought she had psyched herself into sounding exactly right when she dialed his number. It didn't matter. "He's left for the day," his secretary told her emphatically and, no, he hadn't left any message for her.

Jo didn't think about how much she was using Brown's phone now. She had to call Mike again. Every minute counted. Every action had to be the right one.

This time there was no hesitation in his instruction. "We've got nothing to lose. Brown took you into her confidence. Bring her completely up to date, darling. See if you can stay with her if you can't make contact with your sister." He sounded as if he could hardly bear to say Alexa's name.

Almost an hour had passed. She felt like a different person going back to the sitting room where Brown was stretched out on the sofa, reading *The Economist*. "What's up?"

Brown was an excellent listener just as she was a superb speaker. She didn't interrupt once, although Jo occasionally stuttered and stumbled as she went through the whole saga. At the end, Brown's expression remained the same—resolute, reliable. She was a friend.

"Mike doesn't want me to go back to the apartment, but I must get some things before I leave tomorrow morning. I ought to go back anyway—in case Barry Hunter calls. I ought to meet Upton, don't you think? Hear him out?"

It was four-thirty. In an hour, she would either call or go to the studio to make sure Alexa didn't elude her. It still gave her enough time to go back to Central Park South to grab a bag. She appealed to Brown. "Do you think I should move out of the apartment tonight, which shows them I don't intend to believe a word they say—or should I try to brave it out? Could it all possibly be a coincidence?"

Brown sat up and lit another cigarette. "I'm as sure as anyone can be that all these links are not coincidental. I am certain Forga knows everything that he wants to know about the Devi woman." She shook her head irritably. "You told me yourself how angry Forga appeared when he saw Upton arrive unexpectedly last night . . . and from the description of your condition last night, your inability to stop talking, telling Hunter all you have now told me. I am sure Forga put something into that last drink of yours." Brown stood up, a powerful woman, sure of who she was and what she was going to do. "Mike's right. You shouldn't stay in the apartment. Let's go over there now—get your things, then collect Alexa. You can both sleep here . . . one on the chesterfield, the other in what is laughingly referred to as my maid's room."

"You mean, you'll come with me to the apartment now . . . ?"

"Of course. I am an important editor, my dear. Devi is unlikely to want to make a bad impression on me. I'll get my wheels out of the garage. We'll never get a cab in this weather."

As they drove up Central Park South, it reminded Jo of the day she'd arrived at the house on East Mission Drive, not sure whether her key would fit anymore, feeling paralyzed by fears she couldn't explain.

Brown parked in the Central Park South apartment garage. Jo was relieved they didn't have to go through the lobby. It was exactly five past five. She would throw some things in a bag, then alert Alexa to wait their arrival at the studio.

The key fit. "Kiko, Kiko, are you there?" No reply. Her bedroom door was shut. It was Brown who opened it. They both stood momentarily stunned. There was chaos inside. Her room had been ransacked, drawers left open, contents on the floor, her bed, sofa, moved to one side. Someone had been looking for what she didn't have—evidence that the The Fountain and the Spring Skin Clinics' Svetlana—Dr. Svetlana Lane—was the same person as Madame Svetlana Devi, savior of women, purveyor of youth. Someone had also wanted to leave her a message . . . that it was known she no longer believed what she had been told; that she was an adversary, a dangerous adversary and nobody cared that she now knew it was acknowledged.

"Call Alexa now," Brown hissed. "Then grab your toothbrush and let's get out of here. We've got a lot of work to do." Brown's cool, terse orders were just what she needed. Five-twenty. Jo dialed the studio ten minutes before break time. No matter what anyone said, she was determined to hold on until Alexa could come to the phone. Mims answered again. He sounded upset.

"Ma'am, I gave your sister your message, but we don't know what happened. She came off the set a few minutes ago and she's vamoosed . . . walked out on us . . . bolted . . .

they're yelling bloody murder over here . . . Do you have any idea where she may have gone? I bet there's a guy involved. She's been salting up all day. If you know where she is, you better tell me . . . and if you don't, when she gets home you better tell her to call Pen Waverly right away before she has a heart attack."

There was a sense of unreality about everything. Alexa was aware of every movement she made; every word she spoke. They weren't idle sentences. They were lines that she had to be sure were the right lines, not giving anything away. It was the only way she could live through the hours, maybe days ahead. The deep burning anger in her mind was a crutch, not an obstacle to dealing with the fiend who now sat facing her in the Central Park South living room, as Kiko served them coffee and baclava and, then, with just the modicum of noise to show he wanted her attention, carried her overnight case into the front hall.

"There's a slight delay. The weather. I'm afraid Americans have a lot to learn from their Japanese competitors. The control-tower equipment is hopelessly inferior . . ."

Was he going to talk about the trade deficit, too? Alexa had a line that had to be said, that would take Forga's mind away from control towers. "I must tell my sister I'm leaving—or does she know?"

Forga smiled paternally. "Of course, she knows. She is a member of our team, is she not? You have just missed her. She is dining with Barry and our lawyer from the West Coast. Mr. Upton." Why was Forga studying her so intently? Was there a message he was trying to convey? If so, she was missing it—but perhaps that was all to the good, because he relaxed his posture and waved a casual hand, continuing, "She tried to reach you at the studio to wish you bon voyage. She was concerned that you had acted so unprofessionally." He leaned forward to tap her knee as if to reprimand a naughty child, then smiled again. "Why don't you leave her a note? Here is our telephone number in London."

She accepted the piece of paper without looking at it. She knew no note she wanted Jo to receive would ever reach her. "When do we have to leave?"

The phone rang before he answered and he waited as Kiko picked it up to ask who was calling.

Her body chilled as Kiko looked at Forga for permission to

pass on the information. There was an imperceptible nod. "Ms. Wells, Dr. Lanning would like to speak with you . . ."

"Tell him I can't."

Forga interrupted with another paternal smile. "Speak to him, my dear. Put his fears at rest. My, my . . . he can't even let an hour pass before he hears your voice again. Why don't you take the call in your bedroom—in privacy."

She didn't want to speak to Marc, didn't want to see him ever again, but there were lines to be said tonight in this play for her life . . . lines that would give no suspicion to the enemy, that all her dreams and hopes had been crushed forever in a house on West 11th Street.

Was it really possible that only twelve hours ago Marc and she had had breakfast together after a night she would remember all her life? It had been a night that had introduced her to the ecstasy of sex and an understanding of what love could mean.

Marc was saying all the things she'd ached, longed for him to say that morning so many memories before. Tears came to her eyes, remembering the pain of listening to John Lennon sing "Imagine" in the studio, wondering when—if—she would hear from him again.

"Alexa, thank God, you're there. I haven't been able to work today. I made the mistake of my life this morning . . . I have a lot to say to you . . ."

"Oh, Doctor, don't say that. Doctors never make mistakes." It was a perfectly delivered line, light, yet sweet, uninvolved. She circled her ankle, concentrating on the circle exercise, instinctively knowing that outside everything was being listened to and probably recorded.

But Marc wasn't listening, wasn't getting the message that she had moved forward, had made a discovery that meant she could never allow herself to care for him, could never trust the son of a woman whose whole life was a lie. No, he wasn't listening. He was saying incredible things. "I love you . . . I want you. I can't believe it, but I think . . ." He laughed the carefree laugh he had laughed at sea. ". . . If you promise to meet me in thirty minutes, I might even propose."

"Save your breath." It wasn't a perfect line. It had come from the place in her brain she had wanted to bury, the place where the pain was so bad, any words said would be meant to hurt someone else.

There was silence at the other end. She laughed again. It wasn't a bad attempt at a laugh. "It's a very tempting thought, Marc, but who knows how you'll feel in thirty minutes . . ." she paused. What better way to kill two birds with one stone . . . with Kiko and/or Forga listening. With the right sentence, she could perhaps avoid the questions and even the "expensive" toll Forga had mentioned he would extract for her strange disappearance from the studio that afternoon. "I loved playing hooky, Marc darling, but my boss wasn't very happy about it. He's here now . . ." Her stomach twisted as she heard Marc gasp. She went on resolutely. "He's mad at me. I have to make amends. We're leaving for London tonight, an important business meeting. I'll call you when I get back . . . maybe . . ."

"Save your breath." *Click.* He'd hung up on her. Alexa looked bleakly across the park. No lights, no park, just darkness, rain, and clouds. She heard the click of the receiver in her head like the click of a revolver ending something. She had ended it before it began, before it was too late.

She was still wearing the diaphanous chiffon. Crazy. Forga had said the plane was delayed. There seemed to be no sense of urgency about leaving. She took a hot shower, trying to drown her growing sense of loss and aloneness. What should she wear to arrive in London for such an important meeting, something that would help her camouflage and support the greatest act of her life? She went to her wardrobe. The Geoffrey Beene tweed, like no tweed the English would ever have seen—and the suede sombrero to cast a shadow over her face, to hide real shadows on The Face, Now and Forever.

There was a knock at the door.

"Yes?"

"Time to go, Ms. Wells."

When she reappeared, Forga gave her the most dazzling smile she could remember receiving from him. Again there was that frightening sense of time standing still as his dark eyes probed hers, so she could only look at him until he looked away and like a matador, swirled a cloak in front of her, a fur cloak, a sable.

"A present for the trip. You are about to meet some of our new investors."

As Kiko picked up her bag and accompanied them to the door, he bowed politely. "Did miss leave note for Miss Jo?"

Alexa shook her head as contritely as she could.

Loathesome parasite, she thought. What hope would there ever be that Jo would receive anything, let alone what she really had to write . . . but there was still the act to play for two, three days and then it would be face-the-music time for them all. Marc included? She would face that when she had to face it.

Forga patted her fondly. "We will telephone Jo from London." He turned to Kiko. "When Ms. Shapwell returns tonight, be sure to give her this number. Tell her that I personally asked her to call her sister. Take care of her, Kiko."

As they went down in the elevator, Alexa made a silent prayer that Mims wouldn't suddenly appear to ruin her own plan of revenge. There was nobody in sight. She had to gamble that for the duration of the trip. Forga wouldn't learn about the raid at West 11th. Wouldn't guess that she now knew the truth that Magda and Svetlana were sisters in crime and he the mastermind behind it all.

The gray stretch was at the curb. See out, can't see in. Alexa prayed that for the next forty-eight hours or whatever time the trip took, she would be just as impenetrable—outwardly the perfect example of The Face, Now and Forever; inwardly, the one who intended to destroy Devi once and for all.

CHAPTER TWELVE

It was amazing the way things turned out sometimes. Mike had gone with a camera crew to the Westgate to cover a Mastermind Negotiating Seminar, run by an outfit that was the talk of the Coast, so successful, the owner, Max Masters, Mr. Mastermind, had been talking about going public.

Over the phone, Mike had been astonished by some of the big corporations on Mastermind's client list, all apparently willing to spend thousands of dollars "to turn potential into power" and intrigued by the Dale Carnegie fervor of Masters himself.

It hadn't been a wasted day. No sirree. Not only had the footage been turned into a neat five-minute spot, it had led him directly, of all incredible pieces of luck, to Mr. Ben Shapwell, one of Max Masters's many success stories, printed for all to see in an impressive four-color selling brochure of "real-life turnarounds." There was a captioned, straight-into-the-camera smiling picture of the now supersuccessful Ben Shapwell, who wrote candidly how his whole professional life had been upgraded by ". . . the most significant career training ever."

"I'd like to do a follow-up story sometime, meet this guy Shapwell, for example," Mike had told Masters, who'd flown into San Diego from his Santa Monica headquarters to run the seminar personally for the station.

Masters had fallen over himself with joy. Once a member of Mastermind, always a member, he'd enthused. Not only had Ben Shapwell been an enthusiastic subscriber for a couple of years to any new cassettes or audio tapes for "review and reinforcement," but he'd learned so much, he'd occasionally been used as a "stand-in" lecturer for seminars in and around the Bay Area.

It had been a piece of cake.

"Is Ben Shapwell there?"

A bubbly light voice answered. "Who's calling, please?"

"Well, he won't know me, Michael Stewart . . ." Mike felt no guilt. He'd never used a false name before, but this was a necessity. "I'm interested in this Mastermind Negotiating course. Someone gave me his number. Is this . . . this Mrs. Shapwell?"

Whoever it was giggled and didn't answer the question. "Just a second. Ben's coming right now. Yep, this is the right number."

Confidence oozed over the wire. The review and reinforcement disks had obviously been studied well. "Glad to hear from you. I tell you, this is probably the most valuable phone call you ever made in your professional life . . . Michael . . . Mike . . . is that right?"

Mike played it cool. "Yep. Mike Stewart. I've heard, read about a lot of these courses. I've never been sold before, but perhaps this is . . ."

Shapwell interrupted him. "Why don't we get together? It's easier to answer questions face to face. I could come to your place or we could meet somewhere . . ."

"Okay, where do you suggest?"

There was a pause, then Mr. Supersalesman got into his stride. "What about brunch on Saturday, Mike? The Cellar Café, Serramonte Center, eleven-thirty? I guess you know it's one of the most profitable malls in the world, over seventy-two acres . . ." Before he could be asked why he wanted to meet a prospective client in such a mammoth place, Ben was quick to explain. "If you haven't seen this place, it's a must. I had a lot to do with putting some of the deals there together and . . ." He laughed in a way to show he was such a big guy, he didn't mind admitting now, "I was a loser until I hit on Mastermind. When you see Serramonte, you'll know the world's the limit."

"I'm not sure exactly where it is?"

"Take Interstate 280 in Daly City . . ."

As Mike finished taking the directions and put the phone down he said aloud, "What a schmuck!" Shapwell hadn't even asked where he was calling from or for his phone number. Would he have smelled something if he'd learned this "prospective client" was calling from a couple of hundred miles away? Did he cruise the seventy-two acres of Serramonte Center looking for Mastermind clients? Who cared? It was more than time he had things out with Jo's father.

Mike flew up to San Francisco, hired an Avis, and despite Ben's expert directions, found it difficult even finding his way into the mall from the acres of parking lots. God, the place needed radar. As Mike headed toward a gigantic concourse called Food Court, so huge its floor seemed to bend with the curvature of the earth, he dismissed any belief that Shapwell had had anything to do with putting even a crumb of the Serramonte pie in place. He'd never seen anything like it anywhere. The Cellar Café was just where Ben had said it would be. Mike felt he had already carried out a morning marathon when, after crossing a kitchenware department, he saw the sign.

He supposed Ben thought it was a chic kind of place and it wasn't bad, rustic with lots of baskets, pitchforks, and wheat sheaves around to summon up an earthy atmosphere. A good-looking hunk of a guy came toward him. In the dimly lit café he looked about thirty-five. When they found a trestle table and Mike saw him across two feet of space, he saw ten to fifteen more years etched over the deep tan. There was a swagger about Ben that would have made Mike uneasy, even if he didn't know all he knew and detested.

"How'd you hear about us? Through *Forbes?* They're hot for us, always give us a good plug . . ."

Over a bloody mary and quiche lorraine, Mike let Ben give him the Mastermind spiel. Target setting . . . telephone advantages . . . the Japanese patience technique. Ben was good at it. Perhaps Ben had found his niche at last.

Mike listened attentively, asking all the right questions. "I read it really changed your life?" Mike waved a hand around him, looking impressed. "Did you really have something to do with making Serramonte happen? I've never seen anything like it in my life."

Ben leaned back, his crisp collar extra white against the dark tan of his neck. "Yep, a few deals . . . got the fitness guys interested. I'll take you over to the gyms, the aerobic centers, later, if you have time."

"Well, you sure look fit. Do you work out?" It was like taking candy from a baby.

Ben literally flexed his muscles as the boasts poured out. "Gotta keep in shape. Gotta stay young. Mastermind tells you "fit mind, fit body.' I've always believed that."

"Your wife sounded real young on the phone."

Ben smirked. "Who said she's my wife? I play the field, buddy . . . but well, yep, Sally's a favorite member of the team, you could say. You married?"

Mike shook his head. "Not yet. Do you work for Mastermind full time?"

"Hell, no. I do the occasional seminar for fun . . . keeps my hand in. I'm a developer, put together the right folks, been doing it all my life, but Mastermind really showed up my weaknesses, built my strengths . . ."

Mike waited for the question he knew would come if Ben really was as good a salesman as Max Masters had indicated. He would give him ten minutes more before he changed the subject. Ben ordered another round of bloody marys. Good, it would soften him up still more. Mike pushed the remainder of his first drink to one side. Ben leaned forward earnestly. Mike could see the faint flecks of gray that Jo had mentioned, the gray that looked so good in Ben's dark, almost black curly hair. He remembered Jo talking about the injustice of a pretty man looking better as he grew older, while a pretty woman just looked old.

"The fee is damn good. It covers tuition, ten-hour audio cassettes, workbooks, success lunches . . . but you probably qualify for a discount. Let's see, I bet you're a candidate for vice president for a big-time company—Polaroid—American Standard—U.S. Steel . . . a bright guy, surrounded by dozens of other bright guys, all out to cut your throat, right? If you work for any of those and dozens of others, you get a discount . . ."

Mike cleared his throat. It was time to get to the point. With a note of reverence, flattery in his voice he asked, "Don't you have a famous daughter? What's her name, Alexa? The Devi Face? Did you teach her some of your tricks to get to the top?"

Ben opened and closed his mouth. Mike looked at him innocently, still apparently impressed by the older, successful man.

To Mike's relief, Ben swallowed down a good portion of the second drink. "I sure do have a famous daughter. How d'you know that?"

"Doesn't everybody?"

Ben snorted derisively. "Hell, no. That's another lesson to learn, sonny. Never trust a woman, not even one of your own flesh and blood. That famous daughter of mine might just as well not exist for all she thinks or cares about her dad."

"But doesn't she make millions from that Devi job? She's just about the most famous model in the country, isn't she?"

Ben drank down the rest of his bloody mary. Mike gestured for the waiter to bring another. "No, no more . . ." Ben demurred, but the drink came and he immediately took a gulp. There was a trace of perspiration on the tanned forehead.

"Yep, my famous daughter makes millions. So what? I never see a cent, hear a word. As far as I'm concerned, she might as well be dead." He stared at Mike as if seeing him for the first time. "Let's get back to the discount situation. Which company are you with?"

"Station KCST . . ." It didn't sink in. Ben stared at him stupidly. Mike grasped Ben's wrist across the table. It seemed to paralyze him. More perspiration broke out on his head. "What the hell do you think you're doing? What the hell is Station KCST?"

"I'm from San Diego. The NBC affiliate. Your other daughter, Jo, used to work for me. She's been a very unhappy girl." Ben tried to wrest his arm away but something had happened. The shock had knocked the strength out of him. His jaw went slack. He looked like a man about to have a seizure.

"My God, you slimy, lying louse . . . you phony . . ."

"Wait a minute, Mr. Shapwell, that's not entirely true. I

did meet Max Masters. I did do a program about the seminars, as a matter of fact. He showed me the brochure, talked about you, was impressed with you, wanted me to follow up—all that's true. It seemed too good to be true to me. A perfect opportunity to sit down with you and bring you up to date on a few things . . ."

"Up to date on what?" Once Ben heard Max Masters's name, some of his color came back, some of the bluster, too. "What did you say your name was? Mike . . . I can't remember . . . I know Jo worked on and off for some Mike, but that wasn't the name I remember . . ."

"I apologize for that. I didn't give Sally my real name. I was eager to see you. I thought you might remember me—Mike Tanner—and then we wouldn't get anywhere. I'm not here to trick you into anything, to revive sad memories. You never followed up on the check to The Fountain to find out what it was all about, did you? Or bothered to find out who Magda was?" Mike took his hand away as Ben's face turned a brilliant red. It showed up the booze in the man, years of booze that months of aerobics hadn't been able to eradicate. Now, he was belligerent.

"I don't know what business it is of yours."

Mike interrupted him. "I want to marry Jo." He hadn't expected to say it, but he knew it now and it made him feel especially good to say it to the man who ought to hear it. "Why have you neglected her? Why didn't you tell the girls you were going to move or send them your new address?"

"I called Alexa, wrote to her. The little bitch never answered . . . then . . ." There was a crafty look about him. "I got the word I'd be better off staying out of their lives. Alexa's in the big time. Jo, too. Seems it was wiser for me to stay away . . . wrong image, you know, not big time enough for them."

"Who gave you the word? You mean someone told you to stay away from them? Who?"

Ben shifted uneasily in his seat. "That's not what I said."

Mike looked at him with ill-concealed contempt. "I talked to the Mexican police, you know. They were evasive. Did you deal with a Captain Gonzalez the night you drove to the . . . the wreck? A Captain Gonzalez?"

Now, Ben looked furtive and scared. He looked around for a waiter, called out, "Bring me the bill."

Mike persisted. "Did you deal with Captain Gonzalez?"

"I can't remember, buddy. What does it matter? God, it's four, five years ago. How long do I have to carry the cross? Okay, okay, yes, it was Gonzalez. If you met with him, I'm sure you did all your homework, like a smartass reporter, didn't you? Saw the car record . . . Teri's signature . . . read the police report? What else can I tell you?"

"No, I'll tell *you*, Mr. Shapwell. Your daughter Jo with my help found out your wife Teri Shephard spent over two thousand dollars at The Fountain for a youth-peel face treatment that disfigured her . . ."

Ben put his hands over his face. "No, no . . ." he moaned.

Mike ignored his act of misery. "We learned this from the head nurse at The Fountain, Ann Pershing, who was murdered in New York City. It's pretty certain Teri went to The Fountain on the recommendation of a model friend of hers, Magda Dupaul. Teri probably didn't know Magda also had a vested interest in the place . . . and . . ." Mike hissed out the next part; "A year or so before Magda had been involved with another so-called rejuvenation clinic, which closed down after disfiguring another poor woman. It gets worse, Ben. You won't tell me who told you to stay away from your girls. You probably didn't need anyone to tell you, but I'll take a guess it was someone involved with Devi, the company that pays your younger daughter millions of dollars, Madame Devi, otherwise known as Svetlana Lanning—the same Svetlana who signed the back of the check you took away from Jo."

"That wasn't the name . . ." There was no conviction in Ben's voice.

"Oh yes, it was. You see, Ben, Jo found another check and this time she didn't make the mistake of entrusting it to you. One step followed another, and it won't be long now before the whole bloody mess becomes unraveled. Your wife committed suicide because of what was done to her by a woman who since then has been backed by a multimillionaire to produce a product that's supposed to maintain youth . . ."

"I don't know. I don't understand . . ." Ben was breaking down fast. There were tears on cheeks that now looked weather-beaten, old. "What's it got to do with me? What good does telling me this do?"

Mike looked at him with disgust. "Don't you want to help?

Isn't there anything you can tell us—anything you know that will prove all I've told you? Did you know that Gonzalez left the police not long after the accident, that he took early retirement on policeman's pay that couldn't buy shit in Shinola? That he moved to a ritzy apartment somewhere near Manzanilla? How could he afford that? Why was he paid off? There's still something missing."

Ben got up and stumbled toward the door, brushing past the waiter who tried to give him the check. Mike watched him go, paid the check, and sat back to finish his bloody mary. He had a hunch that telling Ben how much they knew would produce some kind of action. He would call again on Mr. Shapwell and he was pretty sure, like Nurse Pershing, he would find that Ben had been called away on urgent business . . .

Blair was alone when the pale-gray phone rang. No wonder. It was eight o'clock at night. Only the cleaners would still be on the floor. The air conditioning went off at six. It was about eighty degrees and until the phone rang, she had begun to feel damp all over, as if she were outside, where it was still pouring rain as it had been all week. The phone ringing chilled her, as his voice, his exorbitant demands, his hypnotic gaze always chilled her.

"I'm in London."

"Yes . . ." she breathed the word as if he had just paid her an extravagant compliment. "Two members of your staff have continued to express interest in meeting me, interviewing Madame Devi . . ." His voice was cutting.

She was about to apologize abjectly when he continued, "I believe a meeting with Madame Devi would be useful now. Timing is important. You can tell Brown Schneider you have changed your mind about an article on the Madame Devi subject . . ."

Blair was so surprised that she asked a question, something she knew he disliked. "Why?"

As he answered, she knew he was smiling sardonically, the smile she knew so well was in his voice. "Perhaps I am being influenced by my companion. I brought Alexa to London with me to meet some new investors and to teach her obedience. She will be ready to do as I say tomorrow . . ."

Jealousy broke in waves through her body, bringing nausea with it. She almost vomited into the receiver as he continued to talk calmly, coolly. "Tell Brown Schneider you have been told Madame Devi has just arrived in California. If she calls Barry Hunter he will arrange an interview." Blair was too sick to reply. Perhaps he knew it . . . of course he knew it, because his voice softened, not too much, but enough to make a difference. It was as if it were his eyes that were now speaking to her, not his mouth.

"It is a new day here in London. I am alone in my bed. I will stay alone. When you reach home you will find I have sent you a reward . . . a trip to the moon. Smoke naked, my dear, and then you may masturbate with my boot, the black patent boot I gave you . . . masturbate every night until I return."

It was the only time Jo hadn't heard the phone ring since moving to Brown's place two nights before. She hadn't gone to San Diego on the ten o'clock plane. How could she leave New York until she knew what had happened to Alexa? Only Brown's common sense had stopped her from going to the police when she'd learned from Kiko on the phone that Alexa had had to go to London unexpectedly with Forga for an important business meeting.

Without her asking for it, Kiko had given her the London number. Then she had told him she wouldn't be returning to the Central Park South apartment for a few days. So far the London number had never answered.

"Cool it." Brown must have said that a dozen times during the past thirty-six hours. Mike said it, too, on his way to meet her father, who, it appeared, was now living outside San Francisco, working for a career-management outfit, giving seminars. It didn't ring true.

As Jo came out of the shower there was a sharp rap on the door. "Jo, can you hear me?" There was excitement in Brown's voice.

"Yes, what is it? I'll be out in a second. Have you found Alexa?"

"Much better than that, m'dear," was Brown's dry response. "For a reason we shall no doubt shortly discover, I have just received a communiqué from my leader . . ." Jo didn't bother to dry herself, but wrapped herself in a towel and opened the door.

"Yes . . . yes . . . oh, what is it?"

"I not only have the seal of approval, I have just received a *View* command to proceed with my story on Madame Devi."

"What!"

Brown nodded, her mouth twitching with amusement. "Things are moving fast. The great lady has apparently landed on this planet—in Northern California to be precise. I am to call Mr. Barry Hunter, who will then arrange a meeting forthwith." Brown winked. "I am sure he will know I am taking an interested party with me . . . an associate, shall we say, with astute questions of her own to ask." Brown looked at her watch in an exaggerated way. "Is it too early to call Mr. Hunter? Eight forty-five A.M.? I don't think so. From what you have told me he sounds like a dawn breaker, a workaholic. He is probably waiting for my call."

For the first time since the terrible night two nights before when Jo had discovered that Alexa had flown away with Forga, she did not feel the paralysis that had made every movement and every thought a monumental effort.

In fact, after Brown told her they were leaving on the lunchtime plane for San Francisco and would be met and taken to Madame Devi's laboratory in Northern California, she could hardly sit still.

"Mr. Hunter, was, alas, not at his desk," Brown drawled, "but a very competent assistant knew all about my request. It's astonishing, isn't it, how suddenly doors that have always been firmly closed are now miraculously open, and the person giving you the information finds it hard to understand why one should be at all surprised. Hype and Hypocrisy in the Ugly World of Beauty personified . . . perhaps I'll make it my title. It's too good for a subtitle."

Jo tried to pay attention, to make it clear how much she appreciated Brown's interest, but for Brown it was a journalistic challenge, a grand finale to her work at *View* magazine before she moved back to her cloistered existence of more postgraduate study, more books to read and, after the beauty book, other books to write.

They were at the front door, leaving for the airport, when the phone rang again. Even as Brown was drawling, "Let the answering machine pick it up," some instinct drove Jo to the phone in the hall. There was a lot of static, before, with a euphoric relief, Jo heard Alexa's voice. There was no preamble.

"Jo, this has to be quick. I'm in London. I'm okay. My Face, Now and Forever, is working wonders . . . but . . ." it was difficult to hear. Jo realized there had to be a reason for Alexa to talk softly, "Magda and Svetlana are sisters. Forga's a phony. You were right all along."

Jo gulped. Sisters! It was a startling piece of news. "Oh, Lex, I'm so worried about you. Thank God you called. You'll never guess. Madame Devi has agreed to Brown Schneider interviewing her, obviously with Forga's permission. I'm leaving for the West Coast with Brown now. When will you be back?"

There was a different note in Alexa's voice. Someone must have come into the room. "I'm coming. I'm ready . . ." Jo heard her say with a light laugh. "In a couple of days . . . bye."

Brown showed how considerate she could be after Alexa's call. She knew when silence could be a blessing and on the long flight across the country, apart from patting Jo's cheek and admonishing her not to drink alcohol, "Bad for you at this altitude . . ." she left Jo mostly with her own thoughts.

Why had Blair Benson given her approval for Brown to probe the mystery surrounding Madame Devi? Brown had immediately concluded it was Forga who had asked Blair to proceed and obviously ordered Madame Devi to speak. Why? How could this woman possibly exonerate herself from a past that would ruin all prospects of a future for her company? Was it possible there could be an explanation that was eluding her?

After two sleepless nights worrying about Alexa, frustrated she was doing nothing positive with what she now knew, Jo suddenly fell asleep, then woke with a start as a stewardess instructed her to put her seat-back up and fasten her seatbelt. They were landing.

As Brown had told her to expect, a uniformed chauffeur, holding aloft a card marked SCHNEIDER, met them as they went into the baggage claim area. They only had hand baggage. "Quick in, quick out," was Brown's usual method of carrying out a *View* assignment anywhere in the world.

"We made a reservation for you to fly up to Eureka this afternoon. I was told only to get one ticket but there shouldn't be a problem. I will show you the way to the terminal." The chauffeur bristled with efficiency. On his lapel Jo noticed a small gold *D*.

"A local car service will meet you at Eureka airport and take you to a hotel. Madame Devi apologizes, she has only just arrived. It is not convenient at this time for you to stay with her at her estate. Your appointment is at eleven o'clock tomorrow morning." The chauffeur directed all his remarks to Brown as if Jo didn't exist. "Madame Devi would be honored if you would stay for lunch. You will then be driven back to Eureka airport for a connecting flight to San Francisco."

Brown acknowledged the arrangements with a curt "Thank you." Jo tried to remain calm but her heart pounded until she had the ticket to Eureka in her hand.

The small plane flew along the coast over dark green forests, barren hills, streaks of silver river like glittering threads. Jo stared at the coastal road circling coves, lost in shadow and forest, emerging from tunnels, moving on and on. It had to be the famous Highway 1 that Alexa had told her about, the road she had taken with Barb so long ago, the road she had felt would lead her to fame and fortune. It had . . . to Cal Robinson, the San Francisco photographer and the *View* editor, and to Forga and Devi. Coincidence? Life stranger than fiction? Brown had said it was feasible, possible. Soon, she would know.

Although she'd hardly eaten, Jo couldn't look at food. "I can't face dinner, Brown. I'm going to take a pill and try to sleep. Do you mind?" They had been taken to a motel midway between Eureka and Arcata. It was a motel trying to be something else, with expensive-looking red carpet and atrocious toffee-colored furniture in the foyer, a bar still decorated for a Fourth of July celebration and slot machines in the bedrooms to buy thirty minutes of vibrating mattress.

"I'm going to do the same myself. Something tells me this is going to be an ordeal. Jo, I think it's best if I do most of the talking."

Jo nodded. It was best—unless she felt Brown was getting nowhere.

They were up and waiting at nine-thirty for the small gray sedan that had picked them up at Eureka airport. Stan, the driver, had already told them he had never heard of the place they were going to, but that he had been sent a map and it shouldn't be difficult.

It was bizarre. A chauffeur with a *D* for Devi to show them the way to a terminal everyone could find in San Francisco; a local driver to take them to the Devi headquarters in a place even he had never heard of. However, after the hour Stan said it would take, they turned left off the main road to Oregon onto an unmarked drive lined with cypress and poplar trees. They drove for about five or ten minutes up and up, round and round, until on a high ridge a long, low, and undistinguished gray stone building came into view. Brown muttered, "It looks like a sanitorium. See those outbuildings in back with the smoke belching out. Maybe that's where the alchemist brews her brews and carries out her experiments."

Jo was icy cold, body and mind. At last she was going to meet Svetlana.

The door opened as the car pulled up in a large cobble-stoned courtyard. A motherly looking gray-haired woman in a nurse's uniform shook their hands and ushered them into what looked like the waiting room of a high-class doctor's office. There were roses tumbling from large and small vases, the latest copies of *Architectural Digest, House & Garden, Vogue, View, Newsweek,* and *Time* on low round tables. "Madame Devi will be ready to receive you shortly. Would you like some coffee after your long journey?"

It was all so normal. Taped music, Chopin, played softly in the background and as if to emphasize normality and friendliness, sun rays came and went through the long casement windows. Brown was restless. She checked her tape recorder, went to the window, commented on a pretty brook coming down the hills, sat, stood, picked up the copy of *Time,* put it down again.

The door opened. It was she at last, Svetlana, Madame Devi. It had to be: a tall, maybe five-foot-nine or -ten, woman with magnificent white hair, swept up and coiled in a large chignon, white hair that was a sign of time passing in dramatic contrast to the unlined beauty of her alabaster skin . . . and she was beautiful.

Jo remembered the note of reverence in Barry Hunter's voice when he'd talked about Madame Devi, remembered as if she were thinking about another girl, her irrational jealousy that night at Mortimer's.

There was an austere quality, a remoteness that made Svetlana's sharply etched features, the high slanting cheek-bones, the straight perfect nose, all the more compelling. Had her features always been perfect? Or had she been "remade" to hide a past life?

"I am delighted you are here." The words were welcoming, the voice was not. Perhaps Madame Devi was trying to appear relaxed, but a taut, tense atmosphere had entered the room with her. "Please come to my private sitting room." The nurse who had let them in followed with a silver tray of coffee and cookies.

"As you know, I do not give interviews. This meeting . . ." Madame Devi brought a hand to rest for a second on her chin. It was an affected gesture, but one that emphasized the whiteness of skin on skin, of shining perfection. "I was asked by someone I can never refuse. You want to talk about my work, of course . . ."

Brown didn't waste time. "You have achieved a great deal, Madame Devi. Your product is acclaimed. Whether it can achieve the remarkable results you predict will only be proved with time."

"That is so. But my research has taken many years."

"Of trial and error?"

"Yes, working with active principles, with unknown forces in the skin, one affecting another. There were many things I discovered over the years. For example that the time of application could be of utmost importance . . . that certain ingredients, when mixed in a certain order, could be less effective than when mixed in another order. All research is, of course, based upon trial and error." She turned majestically toward the far window, where the view was endlessly green. "I learned long before other researchers, other students of the skin, that at night during sleep the body's energy is directed totally to skin-cell regeneration, so skin metabolism functions at an optimum level. I constantly reexamine my formulas. I work constantly to see where improvements can be made . . . introducing rare botanical elements, recognizing that just as some plants grow better in proximity to others, some botanical extracts work more synergistically than others. Palm kernel, palm oil, ginseng . . ." She allowed herself a slight smile. "For example, black-currant extract helps bind water in skin cells for extra hydration. If you would like to see them, I have some interesting slides and statistics—the result of real-life testing on stewardesses on the longest flights in the world. Young women carried out tests for me, applying my formula to only one side of their face for comparison studies. The herb, alpine lichen, has a natural antibiotic healing effect . . . saponaria brings brightness to the skin, as well as to the hair, but it is in the synergy of these things that I have found the key to the maintenance of a youthful skin. Others, of course, have experimented and learned much about these ingredients . . . however, it is in the synergy that my secret lies."

Her voice was hypnotic, but Jo waited—as each sentence was meted out—for Brown to start to get to the truth.

It was only when Madame Devi had been speaking for about twenty minutes that Jo realized Brown's strategy was to lull any suspicions Madame Devi might have by getting her to talk about the subject that obviously obsessed her—her work.

Then it came, like lightning, cutting through everything. "Madame Devi, we know you have worked long and hard. We also know you used some of your original youth-seeking formulas in peel treatments at clinics in Nevada and California, at The Fountain, for instance, in the San Fernando valley."

Madame Devi didn't miss a beat. It was only as she answered in a firm, resonant voice that Jo heard for the first time the faint inflection of a foreign accent. "Yes, I did once practice at The Fountain. It was a clinic much praised for its remedial, rejuvenative work."

Jo gasped. Had she made a sound? She didn't know. It didn't matter. Madame Devi was continuing without the slightest indication of shock, displeasure, or even surprise. "Unfortunately, a zoning change in the area forced the clinic to close. Now I look back at what then appeared to be a disaster for me and realize it was the turning point in my success."

The gray-haired nurse was back. "Lunch is ready, Madame Devi."

They followed her into a circular room overlooking a deep gully, where a waterfall cascaded over rocks into a pool far below. If lunch had been timed at that precise moment as a diversion, it didn't work.

Even as she held a succulent shrimp on her fork, Brown looked directly at the impassive face of Madame Devi and continued her interrogation. "You say the closing of The Fountain was a blessing. In what way do you mean?"

There was a golden, almost auburn liquid in the glasses in

front of them. Before Madame Devi answered Brown's question, she smiled serenely at Jo. "This is an interesting experiment of ours. The black-currant extract I mentioned, blended with ginseng, becomes a delicious and excellent tonic to drink for the digestion and helps rid the skin of toxins."

She turned to Brown and said in measured tones, "It brought my work to the attention of an enlightened man, whose faith in me and investment in my work allowed me over the years to expand my research. As you both know, today, thank God, thousands upon thousands of women instead of a mere handful are able to benefit from my formulas. I believe Divine Intervention brought into being the Devi products . . ."

Brown had had enough. "I think I should tell you, Madame Devi, if you do not know already, that my associate here, Jo Shapwell, was the person who told me about your association with The Fountain. Her mother went to your clinic for your youth-peel treatment."

"Shapwell?" There was no recognition of the name.

Jo intervened. "She used her professional name, Teri Shephard. She was a model. She entered the clinic about the end of May 1977. She was killed . . ." Jo cleared her throat to speak more clearly, "she was killed in a car crash when she left the clinic. Her car went over a cliff in the Sierra Madres in Mexico."

There was silence in the room. A tense silence of at least two minutes before Madame Devi spoke again, still with the same resonant voice, but now tinged with appropriate sadness. "My dear, I am so sorry. So much has happened, for a moment I could not remember your mother . . . but yes, of course, now I do remember. Such a delightful young woman. I was very grieved when I heard about the accident. She was so happy after the treatment. She was looking forward to the rebirth of her career—as a woman with new confidence and the skin of an angel."

Madame Devi looked at her searchingly as Jo obviously struggled to keep her composure. "But, then, you, of course, are the sister of our star, Alexa . . ." She stretched out the long beautiful hand, this time to touch Jo's wrist. "I was overjoyed to have the opportunity to give my sanction to the choice of your sister to illustrate my work . . . as The Face—Now and Forever. It was so fitting after the tragedy of your mother's death, a reward that, who knows, may well have gone to your mother had she lived."

Shock waves were making Jo dizzy. Madame Devi, Svetlana, had known all along that Alexa Wells was Teri Shephard's daughter? The full purport of it was too much for Jo to take in, but not for Brown. She seemed intent on rupturing the perfect exterior of this extraordinary woman, who had sailed across the sordid facts of The Fountain's existence and closure without the slightest hesitation.

Dessert was brought in, crêpes so thin the sheen of the porcelain plates could be seen below. "It is gratifying to hear what you have to say about the results of Teri Shephard's treatment, but I am afraid Jo was told an entirely different story by the chief nurse, Ann Pershing, who was present at the operation. She told Jo that her mother was disfigured, seriously disfigured by the peel. Ann Pershing, I am sure you will also remember, was mysteriously murdered in New York a week after making that statement."

Jo and Brown waited for a crack to appear in the veneer, for even a flicker of dismay, a change of expression, anything, but Madame Devi didn't waver. If anything, instead of withdrawing, her demeanor softened slightly, became a shade more intimate. She sighed. "Poor Ann. I discovered too late Ann was a deranged woman, another tragedy. She had undesirable friends, lived in a twilight world of drugs. I discovered this all too late . . . however much I tried and, oh, we tried . . ." Madame Devi paused to sip her black-currant elixir. "She would not listen. Instead, she turned on me, on her colleagues, her friends. She never understood the seriousness of our, my work, never comprehended that what we were working toward—in such a humble way at that time—was to bring happiness and beauty to women everywhere. Alas, we had to dismiss her."

Madame Devi made it all sound so plausible, and no matter how much Brown tried, her voice sharp, almost impertinent, asking question after question to dent Madame Devi's composure, she remained serene and had convincing answers for everything.

"I am a very busy woman, you know. I have only just returned from a fact-finding trip to Asia. I would be most happy, however, to arrange for one of my senior staff to show you our laboratories here, our computer link with laboratories around the world . . ."

Jo didn't answer, her mind still reeling with what she had

been told, more confused than ever. There was only one other person who knew the truth—if Ann Pershing had, in fact, told a vindictive lie. Magda—and Alexa had just dropped the bombshell piece of news that Magda was Svetlana's sister . . . Magda, who had obviously encouraged their mother to go to The Fountain in the first place. There had been no time to learn how and where Alexa had stumbled on this amazing fact, but Jo knew from the tone of Alexa's voice, that she had been absolutely sure of what she was saying.

As they walked back toward the waiting room, Jo cried out, "Where can I find your sister, Magda, Magda Dupaul? She was the one who influenced my mother to go to The Fountain . . . and she worked at the other clinic . . ." Jo faltered. There was no proof that Svetlana had had anything to do with the Spring Skin Clinic, no evidence that she was the Doctor Lane the Magic Shop's Adele Petersohn had mentioned.

She had hit a nerve. Svetlana *hadn't* known that they knew the relationship. Jo was certain of it as she watched blood rush into Madame Devi's face. Her breath was labored. For the first time she showed anger, her mouth hardening as she spat out, "There is nothing Magda can tell you about your mother. She hardly knew her. Your mother's death had nothing whatsoever to do with her."

She hadn't denied Magda was her sister. Jo's resolution returned. "There must be a way you can help me find Magda," she persisted. "Please, where is she? She had arranged to meet my mother after the treatment. I'll go anywhere . . ."

Jo's persistence enraged Madame Devi even more. "Enough! I tell you, Magda can tell you nothing. There is nothing more to say, nothing to tell . . . Your mother's death was a tragic accident . . . the peel a total success." She whirled around to face Jo, towering above her, her face still contorted with rage. "How dare you mention my sister? She has had nothing to do with my work, my research . . ."

"But . . ." As Jo protested, the gray-haired nurse came out from a side room, no longer sweet faced, but looking stern, like a guard.

"Good afternoon," Madame Devi said curtly. She turned swiftly around to go back the way they had come. The front door was open. There was nothing to do but leave.

As they walked into the courtyard, they heard Madame

Devi's voice calling to them. They looked up to see her standing glowering from an open window. "Please do not come here again. Do not send any of your colleagues either. I am a serious, dedicated scientist. I cannot have my concentration disturbed. I have answered your questions to the best of my ability. I have nothing more to add."

Jo tried to choke back tears as she got into the car. Stan, the driver seemed to sense something was wrong and drove very slowly away from the house. It was fortunate for all of them, because as the car reached the first bend, he had to swerve violently off the road to avoid a car speeding around the corner. Jo screamed, not with fear, but because, as the other car screeched to a stop, she saw clearly that her father was at the wheel. Their eyes met, and Jo turned to open the door, but before she could get out, her father had stepped on the gas and driven right past them.

"It's, it's my father . . ." Jo gasped.

"Turn around. Follow that car." Brown commanded. By the time Stan reversed and drove back up the driveway, there was no sign of the other car. They reached the forecourt of the long low building once again. It was empty. They drove around the back. There was no trace of a car anywhere. He had known how to give them the slip.

Marc. He came into her mind against her will all the time. She was in love with him, but she would fight it as she had been able to fight so much . . . but the pain of missing him was acute, pain mixed with fear that he was as guilty, as involved as the others. Her mind was a seesaw. How could he be? There was such openness, honesty about him, such a sense of dedication to his work . . . yet how could he not be involved, the son of Svetlana the peeler, despite his obvious distaste for the moneymaking machine, Forga. Thank God she'd been able to catch Jo before she left for the Coast. It was ironic. There was a complete role reversal. Gone forever, it seemed, was the carefree Alexa of Mendocino. Now, she was the one worried sick over Jo, her older sister, who had been fighting for so long to discover the truth. Well, soon it would all be over. It had to be . . .

Alexa looked at herself with loathing. She looked perfect, the merest trace of blusher and pale coral lipstick emphasized the gold of her skin; a tan shadow emphasized the strange color of her eyes. Her hair had been styled that morning by Michael of Michaeljohn, hairstylist to the young "royals," a deceptively simple-looking plaited chignon working perfectly with her stunning bone structure.

Forga had chosen what she should wear for the all-important lunch meeting—an expertly cut pale gray Yves St. Laurent coat dress. It hung in its silk container on the door. A matching pale gray suede purse and shoes, still in the Raynes' box with the Royal Warrant on the lid, were on the dressing table.

Forga had been watching her since their arrival, but he'd received a phone call the night before that had transformed the phlegmatism to which she was accustomed. He told her abruptly, "I have a business appointment at ten tomorrow morning. Please be ready by noon, when I will be back to collect you."

She had locked her bedroom door in the Curzon Place house where they were staying, a house sumptuous and comfortable with huge English chintz sofas and deep armchairs, Constable paintings, boiserie in the library and dining room, a profusion of flowers in porcelain câchepots everywhere and Wedgwood plates in the flower-tiled kitchen. It was the kind of house she had never expected Forga to own. It was too cozy, too cheerful. He said he did own it, but perhaps he didn't . . . in any case she was sure they were staying there to allay her fears, to emphasize normality. There was nothing in any way reminiscent of the other places where she had met Forga. All was light and bright and for the last twenty-four hours she had concentrated on appearing light and bright, too. She thought she had succeeded very well.

The all-important meeting had been postponed because of their late arrival. Now, it was only a couple of hours away.

At ten-fifteen she went downstairs in jeans and a sweater, ostensibly for some coffee, but really to check that Forga had left the house. There was a rosy-cheeked Betty in the kitchen, humming along with Radio One, a bustling, bonnie, normal girl. If Betty only knew . . . but then perhaps she did. Perhaps she knew how to turn into a jailer when necessary.

"Has Mr. Forga left?"

"Yes, mum. He said to remind you to be ready by twelve sharp."

"Okay . . ." She said a laconic "See you" to Betty before returning to the bedroom. She had calls to make, arrangements to confirm. The phone was dead. She couldn't believe it. She jiggled it up and down, thinking there was an English trick to it. It had worked the afternoon before when she had just managed to catch Jo when she had heard Forga talking to somebody downstairs in the study. It was dead now. She felt a second of panic. Was she a prisoner? Would the front door be locked like the Fairmont Hotel suite had been? She ran back to the kitchen. "There's something wrong with my bedroom phone."

"Is there, mum?" Betty looked genuinely puzzled. She picked up the kitchen phone. A dial tone came through immediately. She held out the phone to Alexa, who shook her head.

"It isn't working upstairs. Perhaps I did something wrong." She ran upstairs quickly, but no, her extension didn't work and neither did the one in the study.

She summoned up her courage to say, "I'm going out for some air, Betty."

Betty grinned. "Good idea, mum . . ." So there was to be no opposition. Alexa could hardly believe it. She appeared to be free to do what she had to do.

There was an exhilaration about the London streets. If only she were walking hand in hand with Marc, along Park Lane, into Hyde Park, to see all the places she had only read about . . . If only . . . if only life was normal, but it wouldn't be until she took action.

She asked her way to the nearest airline office. Pan Am? TWA? British Airways . . . After two or three false leads she was directed to British Airways. Thank God for her Gold American Express card, too. She would never leave home without it. She booked a ticket on the 6 P.M. plane back to New York the following night. "Have you any change for the phone?" She asked a cheeky-looking girl behind the desk.

The girl grinned at the twenty-pound note Alexa held out. "What sort of change?"

"Well, how much is it to call a London hotel, the Dorchester or someplace like that?"

The girl laughed. "Ten p. I can't change twenty pounds for that . . ."

Alexa looked desperate. "Well, can you give me ten p. and keep the change."

The girl grinned again. "I can do better than that. You can

use the phone over there in the corner. You're a first-class passenger. I think we can let you make a free phone call."

God, the English were great. The girl even looked up the numbers for her—the Dorchester, the Savoy, and when Alexa had an even better idea, a hotel called Skyways at London Airport. That was the best bet. She had to take every precaution she could.

"Can I make the reservation for you?"

Alexa shook her head. It was hard enough to lie on the phone. She couldn't think fast enough to explain why she wanted a hotel reservation in another name.

"I'd like to make a reservation for this evening . . ." She paused, looking at a Rome travel poster on the wall. "A single room, Theresa Rome—she spelled the name carefully. "Yes, I understand. I'll arrive about four. Okay, you'll hold the reservation until six-thirty, but I'll be there before."

She ran back to the house, terrified Forga had returned early, but everything was as she had left it, the radio playing, the sound of a vacuum down the hall. She had to keep pushing down her fear of what she was about to do.

It was still only eleven. She started to write the letter to Marc, the letter she'd thought about as she'd waited in the British Airways office. It had come to her suddenly that whatever the truth was about him, he had to know the truth about her. "I do care for you, more than I've ever cared for anyone, but . . ." It was hard to put in words the whole terrible saga. She wrote it out once. It sounded so melodramatic she tore up the letter and flushed it down the toilet. Eleven-thirty. The letter would have to wait. It was best written afterward, anyway, to explain why she had done what she was about to do.

As she finished dressing, her mind was cool. She left her bedroom door open so she could hear Forga arrive. She thought about taking a lude but she didn't dare. She had to be totally in control.

With the airline ticket zipped in the inner compartment of the pale gray purse, Alexa went gaily down the winding staircase to show Mr. Forga how perfectly ready she was for the all-important Devi meeting.

It was held in a private room at the Connaught Hotel.

Forga introduced her with Old World ceremony to three men, all directors, he explained, of the giant Pershall Pharmaceutical Company, two British, one tall and almost totally bald whom Alexa guessed to be either German or Dutch. They were noticeably impressed with her and, in the beginning, ill at ease as to how to treat her. There were covert glances, stilted compliments, and then desultory conversation. She worked hard at showing them she had a brain. They began to relax and at her request gave her their business cards as they downed a couple of sherries while Forga and she stayed with Perrier.

As the first course, smoked sturgeon, was consumed with a fine Montrachet, the three resumed what Alexa imagined was their usual tough business, let's-get-down-to-it manner. They asked for an update on Devi, for figures, for a clarification of Forga's expansion plan for Europe, the Far East, and South America.

They were enjoying themselves, all of them, including Forga, although he rarely smiled and his answers were brief but always to the point. She hadn't been asked to say much. She answered questions professionally and succinctly about her nationwide tours, and the almost universal acclaim that had come from The Face, Now and Forever campaign.

Forga leaned back, occasionally speaking in German to the tall, bald-headed member of the trio. It didn't take Alexa long to understand they were meeting to finalize the deal; the major part of the work had been done. The about-to-be-new investors already had an enormous amount of information. They had probably expressed a desire to meet her, to satisfy their curiosity, to see if they agreed she provided the necessary magnetism Forga had probably boasted of. She realized for the first time that she herself, the Devi Face, Now and Forever, had become as valuable as the product.

It was two-fifteen. The moment had come to show them all another side of her magnetism. "Gentlemen." Her tone demanded attention. As she stood, she smiled the radiant smile she had given as she first entered the room. Even Forga seemed to remain relaxed, regarding her with a benevolent look, despite what was, in fact, an interruption in the so-far smooth forward momentum of the meeting.

Alexa was proud of herself. He had obviously not learned about the break-in on West 11th Street and she had managed to deceive him for over thirty-six hours. She had rehearsed what she had to say in her head all night, but the words sounded shocking when she heard herself in the suddenly quiet room.

"Madame Devi is not only a phony, she is a dangerous woman. Her product is a good product, but her past is disastrously bad. It is a past about to catch up with her. To my knowledge, she owned two disreputable face clinics that were closed by the American government and may have owned more. She disfigured people. She disfigured my mother, who committed suicide. I have stayed silent, working for the company until I had the proof. Now I have the proof." There was no movement. The three men all wore expressions that were almost theatrical in their degree of stupor and shock. She didn't dare look at Forga as she waved their business cards in front of them. "I will see that you receive a report and the proof. As you can imagine, after today I doubt my Devi contract will be renewed. I'm not sure there will be a Devi company to renew it."

She walked out of the room quickly, out of the hotel, praying she would have time to cross the street before Forga came chasing after her. She ran across Carlos Place, not knowing where she was going, entering a small garden. There was a small colonnaded walkway . . . it led into a church. She had to hide, had to wait somewhere a long time before she made her way to the airport hotel.

It was a Catholic church, old, very old, with magnificent leaded windows. Alexa waited there nearly an hour, hunched down in a back pew.

Slowly her courage returned. It was difficult. She had to force herself to look around the church, to the left, to the right, behind her. When she saw it was three-thirty, she stood up with an effort. Fear was paralyzing. She forced herself to overcome it. Before she left the church she had decided when she reached the Skyways Hotel, she would cancel her reservation for the next day and take another plane, whichever one was available. It was safer. Although British Airways had assured her passenger names were never given out in advance, with Forga's influence, there was no way she could be sure he wouldn't know, wouldn't end up sitting in a seat beside her.

She would spend the time at Skyways writing the long letter to Marc, writing to explain why she had done her best to ruin his mother's company; but why, because of her feelings for him, she had decided she would do no more to seek vengeance by linking his mother and certainly Forga to Ann Pershing's death. She would mail the letter as soon as she got back to New York. If anything happened to her, Marc would then at least know why and who was to blame.

It was easy to make the plan, much more difficult to carry it out. By the time Alexa checked into the hotel and finished the letter to Marc, she was a wreck, incapable of moving, of even thinking of catching a plane to New York the next day.

Jo . . . she had to reach Jo somehow, somewhere, and tell her what she had done. She had never felt so alone, so friendless. Her planning had left out the basic necessities. She went down to the lobby. "Where can I buy a toothbrush?"

"Everything's closed. Tomorrow morning. Eight A.M. over there . . ." Stifling a yawn, the desk clerk pointed to a kiosk on their right.

A pretty stewardess was checking in. She must have seen something disproportionately tragic in Alexa's expression on hearing she couldn't buy a toothbrush.

"I've got a spare Pan Am kit if you'd like . . ." the stewardess said.

Alexa started to demur, then thanked her profusely. She went back to her sterile room, clutching the kit like a talisman. Who would know where Jo might be . . . where Madame Devi was giving this long sought audience? Mike Tanner, of course. The English phone system was hell. She couldn't get through to San Diego information. In the end, she got through to NBC in New York to get the San Diego affiliate number. Mike was away "on assignment" and no one seemed to know where or at least they were not prepared to tell her.

Alexa sat staring at the floor, trying to think what to do. There was only one person she could turn to for help now, one person she could think of who she could trust, who might still consider offering the shoulder she now realized she needed. Cal Robinson. Would he be willing to help her find Jo? She'd never returned his generous call, never thanked him as she should have thanked him for all his help. She had to risk it. There was no one else.

Tears came when she heard Twinny's voice answer, as he answered every day Cal was at home base. He sounded overjoyed to hear her, so happy he didn't wait to be asked if Cal could be interrupted. Minutes passed, dragging her deeper into depression, but then there was Cal on the line, laconic but not cold, casual but not uncaring. "Is this the star calling herself? I can't believe it. To what do I owe this honor?"

"Cal, I'm . . . I'm in London."

"Give my regards to the queen. It's a pity, I was coming to New York in a week or two." He paused, then added cattily, "With a new face, someone I guess, you've heard about . . . Patsy Brook?"

"No, no, I haven't heard . . . I'm glad." Alexa went straight on. "I'm in trouble, Cal. I need help. I know I don't deserve it, but . . . but . . . there's no one else . . ."

"So what have you got yourself into now, baby?" Now he sounded as if he couldn't care less. Why should he care? "Surely nothing that money can't get you out of? You're rich, baby, rich and famous. *Time* magazine told me so."

He was quiet as she tried to break through his cynicism. If what she was trying to tell him didn't do it, her fear spoke for itself. "Can you try to find out where my sister Jo might be? I've burned my bridges with Devi. I didn't act on impulse . . . I can't explain everything, anything now . . ." Alexa hesitated. Whether Cal thought she was behaving hysterically or not, there was no other way to say it. "Cal, my life could be in danger—so could my sister Jo's. Everything's about to fall apart. I thought I'd go to New York, but since Jo's in Northern California, obviously I ought to be with her . . ." She tried to sound confident. "Two's better than one."

There was a long low "whew" and then silence before Cal asked, "Where did you say you are now?"

"The Skyway Hotel at London Airport."

"Can you bear to stay there?" He paused, then laughed. "Hell, why should you suffer that, you little delinquent? There's a great place I know, not too far from the airport—it's called The Bell at a place called Hurley. I know the owner. It's peaceful . . . sounds like you need some R & R before you get back in the jet stream. If you have to hole up somewhere, that's the place to do it. I'll call them, then give me twenty-four hours to find out what I can about your sister. Don't ask me why I'm bothering, but maybe I've still got you under my skin or on my conscience or something. After all, I guess I put you on the fast track in the first place . . ."

When Alexa hung up, she felt she'd been hugged. At

6 A.M. she gave up trying to sleep. She put the coat dress back on and went out to mail the letter to Marc. It would help to know it was on its way. In the elevator was the pretty stewardess again. She looked inquiringly at Alexa. "Anything else you need?"

Alexa asked, "Are you on your way back to New York?"

The stewardess nodded. "Yes, it's a tough week for me. I've got some hours to make up . . ." She paused, then asked shyly, "Aren't you the Devi Face? I have a bet on it with a member of the crew . . ."

Alexa gulped, then said, "Yes—but please don't say anything. I don't want anyone to know I'm here." As they walked into the lobby the girl said cheerfully, "Okay, but can I have your autograph? I'll collect on my bet later on."

Alexa took a Devi business card out of her purse and scribbled her name across the back.

"Oh, gee, thanks. You sure I can't do anything for you in New York?"

Of course, there was something the Pan Am girl could do. Who knew how long the mail would take from England. Alexa opened her purse again and took out the letter to Marc. "Could you mail this for me as soon as you arrive in New York? It's very, very important."

"Sure." The girl took the letter as if it were a precious jewel. "I'll be happy to. Can I call you sometime, about that . . . that youth product? I'd love to try it."

"Give me your address. I'll send you a year's supply . . ."

CHAPTER THIRTEEN

IT WAS EERIE ARRIVING BACK AT THE CENTRAL PARK SOUTH APARTment. Without Cal at her side, Alexa couldn't have done it, but Cal was beside her, paying off the taxi, taking charge as he had from the moment she'd come through customs, shaking, expecting an assassin's bullet in her back.

It had been the worst journey of her life, despite the promise Cal had made to take time off from his New York sittings to be at Kennedy to meet her. She'd looked and acted like an eccentric, wearing no makeup, her hair squashed into an English cap and wearing the overlarge dark overcoat she'd bought during her stay at the English inn, despite a seventy-five-degree welcoming temperature in New York.

The doorman was not his usual cheery self. Far from it. For the first time Alexa could remember, Joe was red faced, belligerent, as he said, "I'm afraid I have instructions not to let you in—or anyone inside the apartment, Ms. Wells. I've been expecting you for over a week. There's been a call here for you every day . . ." He handed her several pieces of paper from a message pad. They all said the same thing. "Call Blair Benson's office at *View* magazine immediately on your return. Urgent."

"Where's Kiko?" Alexa asked coldly.

"I don't know." Joe began to sound a little more apologetic. "Sorry, I almost forgot. He—Kiko—packed your things in these suitcases. There was mail here for you, too, but Mr. Hunter, who represents the owner of the apartment, arranged for it to be sent up to *View* for you to collect there."

Cal was already in the street, signaling another cab. As they climbed in, Alexa asked, "Where shall I go?" For a minute she looked like the girl he remembered in Mendocino, a mixture of defiance and insecurity, but even as she asked the question, she had the answer. "I know. I'll go to the actors' hotel, the Wyndham—they have maximum security there. They won't let anyone up without checking first . . ."

The maddening thing was she still hadn't been able to make direct contact with Jo. Cal had spoken to Mike Tanner, had asked him to call Alexa in Hurley, but for some reason the independent bastard hadn't called. Cal told her Mike had been cagey, not totally trusting him, because all he'd divulged was that the Madame Devi interview had taken place, but Brown and Jo were still moving about in Northern California, that the facts were slowly coming together.

Lack of real knowledge hadn't made her days at The Bell easy to bear. In the end, Alexa hadn't been able to stand it. She had had to come back. Anything was better than living with daily uncertainty.

When Alexa got into the hotel suite, she immediately tried to get through to Mike Tanner. He wasn't in, but was "expected." She left the Wyndham number and asked him to call her as soon as possible. "It's an emergency."

"See if you can find out where Brown is from her office. I couldn't," Cal said apologetically. Brown's secretary took a long time to answer. When she heard Alexa was calling, she breathlessly asked her to hold on. Another five minutes passed. Alexa was about to hang up when the despicable Rab came on the line to say "One minute please." In seconds, Blair, at her iciest, asked, "Where have you been? You have to be the most incredible ingrate it has ever been my misfortune to meet. How dare you run away in the middle of a sitting . . ."

Alexa didn't even realize what Blair was talking about.

Then she remembered. It all seemed as if it had happened years ago . . . it all seemed so unimportant, but, yes, she did owe Blair an explanation, not then, not tomorrow, but soon, when she had recovered some of her strength.

"I have to see you, Alexa. Can you come over now? I have something serious to tell you."

"I'm just back from . . . from Europe. I don't feel too well. Can't it wait?"

"No. Where are you?"

Alexa hesitated as Blair repeated, "Where are you? No, this can't wait."

Alexa looked at Cal. He winked at her reassuringly and gave her a thumbs-up sign. For some reason it gave her confidence. She sighed.

"Okay, okay, Blair. I'll be over at . . ." She started to look at her watch but, as always, Blair was the one who gave the orders.

"Be here by five-thirty. Thank you."

Cal persuaded her to rev herself up, to open one of the suitcases and pick out a "knock 'em dead outfit." Kiko had packed her things the same way he always did—with layer upon layer of tissue paper, so skirts, tops, suits fell miraculously into shape with no creases. Perhaps Kiko didn't know how to do it any other way.

She washed and blow dried her hair, put on a dark-green linen jumpsuit. "I can't face makeup," she said defensively.

"You don't need it." Cal meant it. "Let Madame *View* off lightly—don't blind her with your natural brilliance, baby."

Although she tried to protest, she was relieved when Cal said he'd come right up to Blair's floor with her and would wait outside until Blair delivered her urgent news. "Then I'll give you that Chinese raincheck you asked for three years ago." Cal grinned.

Until she walked into Blair's office, despite Rab's posturing and his unsuccessful attempt to make Cal move downstairs to the editorial reception area, Alexa felt sure of herself again, certain if she showed enough remorse and intimated she would be able to explain everything to Blair one day, somehow she could make amends.

She was wrong. Blair was obviously receiving an enormous amount of pleasure delivering her speech but, God, Alexa thought, she looked a wreck.

There was no preamble. She didn't ask Alexa to sit down. "In case, through your hugely inflated opinion of yourself, you believe you will ever work for *View* again, I have to inform you your career in New York—in America—is finished. I have taken steps to ensure from now on you are virtually unemployable as a model."

Alexa sat down anyway in the chair facing Blair's desk. She knew Blair wasn't finished and remained silent as Blair opened her desk drawer and handed her an envelope with the Devi logo.

Alexa's head began to throb, but she remained silent, intuition telling her to wait, that something was happening to Blair. She was losing her cool as an inner rage began to surface.

"This letter will confirm what you may already know. Your Devi contract is not going to be renewed. You're finished—out in the street . . ." Blair stood up. Alexa could see the veins on her neck. She was skeletal. As Alexa got up without opening the letter and walked toward the door, Blair started to screech, "You're both meddling busybodies, stupid, interfering no-accounts. If you don't blame yourself, you unprofessional ingrate, you can blame your sister for ruining your career."

Two hours had passed since she had followed his instructions and personally delivered the death blow to Alexa Wells's career.

He had promised to send her a reward. It had arrived thirty minutes ago in a package she had so far resisted opening. He had also promised to telephone to tell her if they could spend the night together. It was that expectation that gave her the strength to push the package out of sight. It was also at times like this Blair knew she was beginning to lose control.

If she took the cocaine now, without him, she knew the high would be followed by an emotional payback so black that she might not be able to cater to his wishes or even begin to deliver or experience any sexual pleasure.

She bathed, opening her legs to the force of the Jacuzzi jet, contracting her vagina, drawing water in and out as he had taught her, punishing her when she had not performed to his satisfaction. She dressed herself in the thin gold chains, one pulled tight from the waist down, across her belly, up high between her legs against her vulva, through the crease in her behind to the small of her back. She was ready . . . but would he come? She looked longingly at the cupboard containing the package. What could she do to take her mind off its contents?

Blair went to her desk. The cold gold chain chafed her, even as it increased her desire . . . but she also felt empty, disoriented, disappointed that Alexa had not broken down, had hardly reacted.

Blair opened her briefcase. Inside was a bundle of mail for Alexa, forwarded from the Devi apartment on Central Park South to *View* for her safekeeping. Forga had asked her to keep them for his return. Why? Why was he interested in reading mail to someone he had ordered her to destroy professionally? Why did he care about someone he had told her he intended to leave on a garbage dump?

She flipped through the bundle . . . bills, invitations, mail order catalogues until she came across a thick envelope with initials on the back, F.O.T.M.D.P.S.M.M.

There was something about the strong handwriting, the initials, that made her sure this was what Forga was looking for. Suspicion, jealousy, anger went into the way she ripped open the envelope.

It was a love letter from Marc Lanning to Alexa, a love letter she could hardly bear to read, the opening lines were so tender and caring. She hunted ferociously for the name she expected to find.

> I now know how much influence Forga has over you. I know only too well he has the ability to make the sanest people behave like lunatics, let alone anyone like you, an impressionable, beautiful girl who thinks she is in love with him . . .

Blair screamed out in pain. "Bitch . . . bitch . . ."

She crumpled the letter, then with trembling hand straightened it again, reading more outpouring of Marc's devotion. Angry tears ran onto the ink. She turned to the second page.

> I have a lot of explaining to do. My father married a simple young Russian chemistry student, Svetlana Sorgiokov, when I was six. My mother had died two years before. I think it was a happy enough marriage in the beginning, but looking back I realize everything changed when they

met Forga. I never liked or trusted him. He turned their heads with talk of a worldwide beauty empire. My father went bankrupt investing in this pipe dream and died soon after of a heart attack. I was sixteen. I hardly saw Svetlana after that. I wanted to stay away when Forga was around, and he was more and more around. It was only when I came out of the navy and took my plastic surgery boards that Svetlana began to take more interest in me. I made a big mistake. I went along with the charade she asked of me—one I thought was innocent—not bothering to correct the impression that I was her son, not stepson. I stayed away from everything to do with the business, but I knew my medical background added to the Devi credentials. I am to blame for not taking it seriously enough. I went along for my father's sake. After receiving your letter, I am determined to find out the truth, no matter if I've already lost you to Forga. I must do it for my own peace of mind. I must get to the bottom . . ."

I've lost you to Forga . . . to Forga.

Blair crumpled up the letter again, stood up to pace the room, the chains cutting into her. She wrenched them off, scratching, tearing her skin. Forga and Alexa! She ran to the cupboard and opened the package to get the drug. It was all becoming obvious. Forga must have found out about Marc and Alexa . . . that was the reason he wanted to destroy her, to cancel her Devi contract. He wanted to teach her a lesson the way he knew how to teach everyone a lesson, choosing the way that would hurt the most . . . in the bitch Alexa's case, her career, to make sure her cocksure, egotistical face never saw the light of fame again.

Blair had just begun the ritual when the phone rang. The chains were gone from her body. The initial rush of pleasure that the first inhalation gave her made her feel the chains had gone from her mind. She could and would triumph over him at last. When Forga told her that he couldn't get away, she was able to soar above her disappointment. He must have sensed it. There was a pause. Then he said, "I will send for you tomorrow morning . . . early, very early . . . to bring you to the 62nd Street house to fit you with something that I will insist that you wear to work . . ." She knew he wanted her to know he was planning a particular punishment, but when she hung up and deeply inhaled, it was as if she had never smoked before. Her brain was fired with resolve. She wouldn't wait for the morning. She would confront him tonight with all she knew.

The phone was ringing as Alexa walked wearily into the Wyndham suite. She was so tired, she shook her head, hoping it would stop. No one knew she was there—except Mike Tanner, and he had never bothered to call her before.

Cal picked up the phone and, smiling that sweet slow smile of his, said, "Just a moment, Jo."

"Oh, Sis . . ." Alexa just saved herself from a nosedive as she fell over a suitcase to pick up the receiver.

"I've been calling the Central Park South number for days. When did you get back? What happened?"

As Alexa told Jo about her performance in London, to her amazement—and anger—she heard Jo sigh.

"It was wonderful of you, brave and wonderful, Alexa, but . . . I wish in a way you'd waited . . ."

"Why?" Alexa felt betrayed, distraught.

"Alexa, Dad's involved . . ." Jo quickly recounted what had happened at the Madame Devi interview, how Madame Devi had had explanations for everything, remaining majestic and apparently totally convinced of her contribution to mankind. "The only change came when I tried to find out where Magda is. She almost fell apart, showed us the door fast . . . and then, as we were leaving, Dad was arriving. He saw me—but he didn't stop. He gave us the slip. Brown, Mike, and I have been trying to find him ever since. He isn't home. He's disappeared. What can it all mean? The incredible thing is that Madame Devi knew all along that you were Teri's—Mom's daughter. How did you find out that Svetlana and Magda are sisters?"

Alexa's heart was thumping, her palms wet with sweat. "Forga apparently ran a club in New York, had talent scouts, an organization all over the country . . ." Alexa laughed harshly. "Pimps, procurers would be a more accurate description. I found letters from Magda to Svetlana, to Forga . . . letters that explained so much . . ."

When they finally said goodnight, Alexa leaned back wearily on the couch and told Cal about her father's appearance at the Devi headquarters. He kissed her on the forehead. "I'm going to leave you now. You're zonked out. Everything seems larger than life. Let's talk in the morning when things will seem clearer. There are always explanations for everything."

It was only eight-thirty when Cal left, but she couldn't wait to climb into bed. She was so tired she didn't even undress. Cal had been good to her as he had always been . . . kind, considerate, but Alexa had a feeling he was humoring her, that he had no real understanding of Forga's power. He hadn't been surprised that *View* had canceled her out. She had run out on a sitting, had disappeared to London without telling anyone, so what else could she expect?

Cal hadn't been surprised that her Devi contract had been canceled so quickly either or that she had been locked out of the Devi apartment. After what she'd told him she had said at the Connaught meeting, how could she expect anything else? He thought she'd acted impulsively.

She went over what Jo had told her . . . that Ann Pershing, according to Madame Devi, had been on drugs, involved with dangerous people. The phone rang, cutting through the maelstrom of her thoughts. It was the desk clerk. "Mr. Robinson is here to see you."

"Mr. Robinson?" She was slightly irritated that Cal had returned, although she knew it was because of his concern for her.

"Okay, it's okay. He can come up."

Alexa brushed her teeth and combed her hair, glad that she hadn't taken off her jumpsuit. Perhaps it was good that Cal had come back. Perhaps she should talk it all out with him right from the beginning.

When the doorbell rang she was smiling as she went to answer it . . . but it wasn't Cal. It was Barry Hunter, not the boy-next-door version, but Barry Hunter the piranha, who before she could fight to close the door, jabbed her arm through the green linen sleeve of the jumpsuit.

Down below on West 58th Street, three men sat in a small sedan, parked in front of a long gray stretch. The same small car had followed Alexa and Cal from the Central Park South apartment to the Wyndham and from the Wyndham to and from the meeting at *View* magazine. The men had watched the rangy Californian leave and continued to wait, as they had been told to wait by their black leader, for Alexa to emerge and lead them straight to the man they still hadn't been able to find.

Pen Waverly's assistant had kept her promise to Mims and phoned immediately once she knew through the office grapevine that Alexa was coming in to be properly admonished and probably demolished by their owner and leader, Blair Benson. When girls got too big for their boots and believed they could get away with anything, no matter who got hurt, it was always gratifying to see them cut down to size . . . particularly when they were gorgeous cover girls.

It came as no surprise to Mims to see Alexa come out thirty or forty minutes after Cal Robinson left, leaning so heavily on another guy's arm that he almost had to lift her into the stretch limousine. Fetch and carry. Dolls like Alexa liked that kind of treatment, probably liked to be fed, top and bottom. It was a Forga trick to spoon honey into a cunt to suck, securing legs and arms wide apart with gold chains. Mims knew it all, had seen it all. He should have guessed that, despite Alexa's obvious fear and loathing for Forga, she was just like the rest of them, obsessed by him, hypnotized by his money and power . . . but he hadn't expected her to give him the slip and go straight to London with the bastard.

Mims prided himself on his patience. He knew Alexa would come back . . . and she had . . . later than the two or three days she'd said, but at just the right time as far as he was concerned.

They didn't have to go far. As the gray stretch pulled out, they followed it to a house on East 62nd Street with dark shuttered windows and—a sign of special wealth in this city of the superrich—its own garage. As the car approached, a big black door cantilevered up and the stretch smoothly moved inside to be swallowed up in the gloom.

Mims and his best pair of knuckles got out of the car. The place was obviously wired but probably not when visitors were expected.

As they approached an impressive front door with its giant brass knocker, Mims thanked his blessed grandmother in heaven, for it opened just as if they were expected, too, and the sandy-haired guy who had brought Forga's booty over came out.

He never knew what hit him; Knuckles was so quick and

quiet with the giant knuckle-duster he'd brought from a pal in the Chinese Mafia. Mims easily caught Barry Hunter's weight as he lurched forward and, Knuckles having wedged something in the door to keep it open, they moved him like a drunk back to their small car.

They were about to return when the driver pointed out that someone else was on the scene. It was obviously going to be a Forga orgy night.

It was impossible to miss this one. You could see right through the pale green dress she was wearing. She looked naked beneath. It figures, thought Mims. It was going to be a fun night, all right, letting Forga's selected dames see him get a very special "facial" of his own.

The woman walked imperiously up to the door as if she expected to find it open. Silent like giant cats, Mims and Knuckles followed seconds behind her, step by step, up the stairs, into a corridor, stopping on the threshold of a drawing room.

They were intent on carrying out their business, extracting the revenge that Mims had waited to extract for more than two years, but first they watched an interesting pantomime. The new arrival stood as if she had been turned into a block of ice, not moving her body as she watched Forga, with his back toward them, carrying a struggling, crying Alexa into another room. The man was sick. He was crooning, "Don't look in the mirror tomorrow, my darling."

"Baxter Forga . . ." Blair's voice reverberated across the highly polished floor. "You have betrayed me for the last time."

In shock, Forga released his hold on Alexa. She crumpled to the floor, then half crawled, half scrambled to where Mims and Knuckles were standing in shadow.

"Git," Mims hissed. There was a vacant look in her eyes, but he had no time to spare for her. As Forga, his face blazing with hatred, sprang at Blair's throat, the two huge men moved.

"You . . . so it was you . . . thief." It was the last word Forga would utter for weeks, as Knuckles, steel-encased, purposeful fingers crashed into his mouth. There was a sound of teeth breaking and a higher, thin scream as Knuckles used his hands as a punching bag to demolish Forga's eyes, nose, and chin.

As he lay unconscious against the wall, blood running in a

wide stream down his body to the pale carpet, Mims moved. Slowly, methodically, as if he were cracking lobster tails, Mims broke each one of Forga's fingers. As he snapped, a faraway look on his face, Mims recited: "This one for Mary. This one for Sue. This one for Agatha . . ." Ten fingers, ten names. The enormous man stood up and looked at the wreck on the floor. "I think I have to finish him off for my kid brother's sake," he whispered.

"Don't do it," said Knuckles. "He ain't worth going inside for."

Mims thought for a minute, then lifted his huge boot and with all of his strength kicked Forga violently in the crotch. "You're right, Knuckles. That sure finished his sweet dreams. It's better he has to live like that . . . a living death, yeah, that's good."

Blair was calm now. She had been through the eye of a neurochemical hurricane, the worst descent into hell she had ever experienced. She looked for a long time at the photograph of herself with her brother Clem; the photograph of a young woman she could remember. As a new outbreak of cold sweats began, she reached for the phone: 800-COCAINE. It was a number they had printed more than once in stories that often ended in hope . . . a number that was apparently a lifeline to so many, a medical crutch that promised anonymity. Now, terror stricken, Blair knew she hadn't much time left. She dialed the number. When she learned where she had to go, she dialed the police to tell them where they could find one of the biggest drug dealers in the country, if not the world, a Mr. Forga was lying in a bloody pool in an elegant East 62nd Street brownstone.

Jo clutched Mike's hand too tightly as he parked the car on Shady Drive. She knew it without seeing him wince, but she couldn't help herself. Dad had come back to his hot tub, his new girl, his audio/video wall. She could feel a lump in her throat, a lump of love for Mike, who had kept up a remorseless phone crusade to find her father. He'd known that Ben would finally give up, creep back home, and he'd been right.

He opened the door before they rang the bell. If Jo felt sick, her father looked it. There were circles beneath his eyes, deep dark circles that made him look as if he'd been in a fight. He walked like an old man, hunched over, ambling from side to side. God, Mike thought, Ben Shapwell has aged twenty years in two weeks. Ben turned, still without speaking, and held his arms out to Jo, trembling arms. She wanted to respond but she couldn't. She reached up and pulled his hands down to his sides. "Dad, we've got to talk. You can't hide anything anymore . . ."

He started to sob. There was no sign of his girlfriend, Sally, only her presence in gewgaws, baskets of potpourri, and, outside in the yard, Jo could see the hot tub bubbling, the steam rising up.

"Mr. Shapwell, look, there's no need for this. We're not here to trap you, blackmail you, we just want the truth." Without being asked, Mike went over to a well-stocked bar and poured Ben a brandy.

"Dad, tell me what happened to Mom . . ." It was all she needed to say for the dam to burst, and for the facts to start pouring out.

"Jo, Jo, I've wanted to tell you and your sister for so long . . . but it just got harder and harder . . . with Lex's success and all . . ." Ben bit his lip, wrung his hands, started to pace. "I got this call. It was about one, or maybe just past midnight. I don't remember. There was this crazy foreign voice screaming at me that I had to come at once, that your mom . . ." He retched as if he were going to be sick. He collapsed back into a wicker chair, his hands over his eyes. ". . . That your mom had been in this accident, this car crash. She said Teri was injured bad, real bad . . ."

"Who was 'she'?" Mike asked sternly.

Ben didn't answer, moaned to himself. Jo patted him awkwardly, silently pleading with Mike not to say anything. Her father kissed her hand, looked down at the floor. "She . . . she was Svetlana Lane . . . Dr. Lane, although I didn't know it then. That night she screamed I had to come . . . that her sister, her sister . . . the car had gone up in flames before her sister Magda could get out . . . that it was all Teri's fault, that Teri had been driving. She kept screaming your Mom had killed her sister Magda."

For Jo the room swung around. Mike drew her to him protectively as Ben now seemed as if he would never stop. "I drove over the border like a maniac. I don't know how I did it now. It took me about two hours or so up in the Madres to where she said they were." Ben buried his face in his hands. Sometimes it was hard to hear him, but Jo was too stunned to move, to do anything but just sit there. Now Ben started to weep again, as if his eyes were diseased, his body fluids pouring out as he pounded the chair. "Your Mom didn't know me. She was like this . . . this terrible ugly version of Teri. She'd lost her memory, her speech, but . . ." The words were said bitterly, that wasn't all. She'd lost her face. It was all white patches, blotches. She was unrecognizable. It wasn't until later, much later, that I realized her face had had nothing to do with the crash. I thought she'd been burned in the car crash, too. When I found out—after you found the check from The Fountain and the note from Magda, it was all too late." He shuddered. "I'll never forget the car lights coming up over the hill, the bloody car lights that lit up what was left of your mother's face."

Mike snapped out, "Was Forga in the car?"

Ben wasn't listening or couldn't hear. He went on in the same bitter tone. "It was Boris Baxter coming to collect them. They told me, Svetlana and he, that your mom was driving. That she'd killed Magda. Svetlana said it was a miracle that she had been able to escape. Over and over again they said it was all your mom's fault."

"Svetlana . . . Dr. Lane . . . of course you also mean Madame Devi?" Mike asked quietly.

Ben gulped, nodded. "He said they'd sue, I'd be ruined."

"Who said this?"

Ben sat up and looked at Mike for the first time. There was hatred in his eyes. "Baxter. Boris Baxter Forga. I'll never forget the way he made me look at Teri. She was . . . was . . . just hideous. I'll never forget him saying, 'Do you want to wake up in the morning to see this face on the pillow for the rest of your life.' It was a nightmare. It's still a nightmare."

If Mike's arms hadn't been around her, restraining her, Jo would have hit him. Her hands were aching to wring the tanned neck. She screeched, "What are you saying? What are you telling us? What do you mean?"

Ben gulped the brandy down. "Baxter—Forga—whatever name he was using, said it could all be hushed up, that the car had been hired in Teri's name, that he could fix it as if Teri had died . . ." Ben looked pleadingly at Jo. "He said Svetlana was a chemist, that perhaps she could mend Teri's face, but that it would take years and years and thousands of dollars." His sobs grew quieter. "Teri didn't know me, as I told you, her memory had gone. I didn't have that kind of money. At the time I didn't think right. I was half crazy . . ."

Mike interrupted coldly. "In the end, Forga paid *you* for your silence instead, didn't he?"

For a few seconds all that could be heard was the bubble of the hot tub outside. Then Ben whispered, "Yes."

Jo broke free, pummeling his shoulder, shouting, screaming, "You mean my mother is still alive? You monster. Where is she? *Where is she?* Or did you agree to her murder, too?"

Ben looked up dazed, shocked. "How can you say that, Jo? Svetlana always said in time she'd be able to get Teri's face back to normal . . . that she was a skin doctor. It took months, years before I understood and put two and two together. I didn't even go into why she was with Teri that night. I thought it had something to do with the Mexican location your mother had told us about—don't you remember?"

Jo violently pushed him back in the chair. "I never want to see you again after tonight. But where is my mother *now?*"

The image he had carried in his mind for as long as he could remember was so strong that when Svetlana first came into the room, Marc didn't recognize her. His first reaction was, This is an impostor . . . the second, Svetlana is up to her usual tricks; followed by a familiar rush of anger and, "Does she still think she can fool me? Does she still think I'm the awkward, anxious-to-please stepson she can send to her native Siberia or wherever she chooses with one glance?

As she came nearer, walking slowly, precariously, like someone newly released from a wheelchair, Marc saw it was no impostor and there were no tricks. This was a shell of the woman who had married his father. Just as he had never been able to make up his mind about her in the past, trusting her, longing for her approval one minute, detesting her the next for her superiority, her indifference to him and, often, he was sure, to his father, so it was now.

The complex mixture of feelings that had been accumulating since he'd received Alexa's tormented, pathetic letter didn't pour out of him in bitter denunciations as he'd expected. Svetlana's appearance stripped him of all emotion, except shock.

He had been burning with anger on the long drive north from San Francisco airport, so angry he'd been oblivious to the trees Alexa had talked about with childlike awe on one of their early dates. It had been an awe so out of keeping with what, until that evening, he had cynically labeled her to be, an empty, dressed-up doll, especially since she was the most beautiful doll he had ever seen. She had talked about the soaring, glorious redwoods the way he felt about the soaring, glorious ocean. It had been a glimpse into the hidden real Alexa, the girl—woman he'd tried so hard not to fall in love with, the Alexa who had forced him to face the hypocrisy of his relationship with his stepmother Svetlana and with her company Devi. By doing, saying nothing, he realized now, he'd appeared to endorse the "Now and Forever" concept, coming to terms with his conscience by dismissing it as "commercial trivia that can't do any harm." He despised himself because with Forga's involvement he should have been suspicious from day one.

"Marc, this is . . . this is such a surprise. What are you doing here?" To his continuing astonishment, Marc could see Svetlana was actually struggling to regain her usual regal demeanor of total control, command, but something had happened. She couldn't do it. The lights had gone out in her world. When she went on, "You have always refused to visit me—to see and evaluate my work . . ." the words came out in a pathetic bleat.

The gray-haired nurse who had finally answered his angry ringing of the front doorbell appeared nervously in the doorway. "Madame, as I told you, this gentleman said he is Dr. Lanning, your stepson. I told him you were sick. Do you want him to leave?"

Svetlana could still stop nervous chatter with an imperious hand and wave the chatterer away out of sight.

As the nurse retreated, Marc's sense of purpose returned. "I know everything," he said sternly. "Alexa has told me everything."

Svetlana began to cry. It was like seeing a monument crumble. Although she made no sound, the tears creeping from her eyes onto her face and her suddenly bowed shoulders stirred something strange in him. He didn't want to deal with this broken-down Svetlana. He wanted to touch her shoulder, remind her who she was; who he was. As if she sensed his turmoil, Svetlana visibly recoiled as if he had touched her, turned to look out of the long casement windows where the sun was painting a high range of coniferous trees with giant gold strokes.

"Don't judge me, Marc," she said in a low voice. Again she repeated—this time piteously—"Don't judge me, Marc, please."

He slumped down into one of the deep buttoned armchairs, a flair of memory from the past reminding him of another day, a different confrontation—a young boy by a window, trying to accuse an imperious woman of something the boy didn't really understand . . . of not caring enough for his father . . . of causing his death through neglect . . . of being influenced by another sinister man, Baxter Forga . . . an imperious woman in an armchair in Paris, listening, waiting without caring for the outburst to be finished. Now it was his turn to wait, and he would wait forever until she talked.

The tears were still there when she turned to face him. "I don't know what you mean when you say 'everything'? Does 'everything' mean my years of torture? Does 'everything' mean you know how I've lived like a recluse with the knowledge for years that I was wrong?"

Svetlana sank in the chair beside him, reaching out with her beautiful white hand, a hand he could not take. "It was an accident . . . a terrible accident. I was too sure. I thought at last we'd found the perfect formula, the perfect youth peel."

"We?" His voice held no promise of belief, let alone forgiveness.

"Magda and I—we were working together—she made mistakes. I had never made a mistake. Forga knew that. He hated her, but he believed in me. Magda believed in me, too . . . she always said I was the real genius in the family. Your father—he thought so, too. He believed in my experiments, don't you remember?" The tension in the room was palpable.

He remembered all right. Because of his father's unseeing eyes and blind devotion he'd left home, hadn't he? If "home" could describe the tiny room under the stairs where a cot had been reluctantly put up during his school vacations. He'd left "home" as soon as he'd left school to join the navy.

Marc shut his eyes to blink back his own tears as he heard

pain in Svetlana's voice, pain he realized he had been waiting to hear for years—pain over his father's death. But the pain was still for somebody else—for Magda, Magda her sister. The sentences weren't smooth; the pain made them jagged, gasped out.

"She saw—Magda saw Teri Shephard's face after the accident! It was terrible! Magda had personally selected Teri as the perfect candidate for my new treatment, the one who was going to bring us both vindication from our past battles with the government. She was perfect. Teri was perfect material . . ." Svetlana's voice broke. "But it was still too early. Despite Baxter Forga's investment, his funding for all the things we needed . . . it didn't work. It was the worst—the worst accident of all."

Marc stared woodenly at his stepmother . . . Mrs. Lanning . . . Svetlana . . . Madame Devi, the Dr. Lane of The Fountain Rejuvenation Clinic. Her words burst in his consciousness. The perfect candidate had been Teri Shephard, Alexa's *mother!* He looked with loathing at the woman silently sobbing before him, sobbing because her beloved sister had seen her "perfect experiment" fail.

Svetlana leaned back against the armchair, the silver of her hair like a halo against the deep-blue silk cushion. She closed her eyes, but there was no doubt that as she spoke she was reliving a personal agony. "Every night—still—Magda returns to me. Sometimes she is angry, but usually she is forgiving. I see her standing in my surgery again, wringing her hands after seeing Teri's terrible scarring, knowing Teri had lost her memory, might lose her life."

Her voice grew lower and lower until it was little more than a whisper, almost a hiss. "As usual, Forga had the solution. He knew it was only a matter of time before I had the right formula. After Teri, there were to be no more major experiments."

Marc clenched his fists. He was full of self-hatred, looking back at his smug condescension toward Devi. Svetlana remained sightless, eyes closed, still talking. "We were to take Teri to a clinic he had over the border in Mexico. There we would have time to address what could be done. We had to get her out of the States after what had happened in Las Vegas. We did what Boris told us to do—we always did what he said. He is a Svengali."

Svetlana opened her dark deep eyes, leaned forward to grasp Marc's knee. "You know that, don't you, Marc? You never liked him. Your father, Victor, always told me you hated Forga."

He didn't answer, didn't need to answer, and as if that movement had been too much effort, Svetlana collapsed back against the chair, a ray of sunlight eerily hitting her face like an interrogator's spotlight. "He—Boris—Forga—told us to hire a car in Teri's name. He knew Magda had told her to lie to her family to explain her time away at The Fountain—to say she was going to Mexico on location. It was easy. Magda used Teri's license from her purse. Magda drove the car . . ." Svetlana's voice suddenly clogged up like a drain. It was difficult for her to get the words out, but each one sent shock waves through Marc's brain. "I was nursing Teri in the back. Magda was driving. It was terrible, terrible . . . the mist, the rain, the misery of it all—driving to Boris's clinic, which wasn't a clinic at all. It was another one of his clearing houses for drugs, but we never got there. The car went over the cliff. My Magda—Magda . . . !" Svetlana suddenly screamed one sharp, shrill scream. "She couldn't escape. Trapped. Burned to death. My Magda died thinking I was a failure."

Marc grabbed Svetlana's bony knee. "I know 'everything' " he had said. Now, he knew that he—and Alexa from her letter—had known nothing, but Svetlana didn't realize that.

"And Teri escaped." It wasn't a question, it was a statement.

Svetlana sighed a long, low, despairing sigh. "Teri escaped and I became a prisoner . . . Forga's prisoner. He has been blackmailing me ever since." Svetlana's eyes were suddenly empty of tears, sharp, brilliant. "Teri has made great progress. Her skin is showing signs of cellular renewal . . ."

Marc barked out, "Her memory?"

Another sigh. "Of course the doctors caring for her do not know her true story. They say her past is locked up following the shock of the car crash."

Marc looked at Svetlana with contempt. Even now she seemed to have no understanding that she was responsible for the whole terrible mess. She went on, not looking at him. "They say if someone appeared who she loved very much in the past it would help . . ." Svetlana was begging for his approval now. "But of course I have never let Ben, her worthless husband, near her. I asked the doctors to show her the *View* covers. I persuaded Forga to try Alexa out for the Devi job—I hoped to find salvation that way—to gain Magda's forgiveness in Heaven. Teri wrote fan letters to Alexa without, of course, knowing who she was . . . It gave Teri happiness, I know it did."

"Happiness? How dare you talk of happiness after all that you've done." Marc stopped abruptly. There was nothing to be gained in letting his fury out. What he had to do now was get involved in Teri's treatment as soon as possible—Teri, Alexa's mother. There was a glow in his mind even thinking of Alexa. He would soon be able to call her with the incredible news that her mother was still alive, but first he had to see what he could do, if anything, to improve Teri's condition. Then he would ask Alexa once more to marry him.

A cloud came across the sun, bringing darkness to the unhappy room.

Marc stood up abruptly. There was no time to lose. "I want to examine Teri Shephard myself—as soon as possible. Where is she?"

Svetlana seemed unable to move. She sank farther into the deep buttoned chair. "Only thirty minutes from here—in a small, secret, experimental center—just thirty minutes away in Oregon." She laughed bitterly. "Very small, thank God. Teri is my only dermatological patient. Otherwise there are a few lost souls—alcoholics, drug addicts."

"Oregon?" Marc repeated.

"Thirty minutes away from here, in Oregon," Madame Devi said emphatically. "Are you ready to see Teri Shephard now?"

The handsome doctor who had come into her life—was it days or weeks ago, well, it didn't matter—told her he had a wonderful surprise for her. She hoped it would really be wonderful—not another exhausting session with Dr. Lane, who despite being very clever never had satisfactory answers to her questions . . . not even as to why there were no mirrors on the walls.

It had taken Teri a long time to remember what the word was. Mirror, mirror on the wall . . . she still got things mixed up. She sometimes called a cup by the wrong word, then the next day the right word would come. All the same she'd come "a long, long way, baby . . ." She giggled, feeling modern as she heard the phrase in her head. Piece by piece her brain was coming back. It had helped, no mistake about that, encouraging her to dictate those notes to the model on the *View* covers, who, Dr. Lane said, looked so much like her.

She believed it. There was something about the girl that brought back all kinds of thoughts and memories. Teri sighed. She hadn't seen Svetlana, Dr. Lane, since she had brought the handsome new doctor along, so she hadn't seen any pictures of the girl either.

Was Dr. Lane getting old or something? She *looked* old, well, older, sagging, not her usual self, which in the beginning had intimidated her, but that was all such a long time ago.

If Dr. Marc Lanning were to take Dr. Lane's place full time, Teri decided she didn't really care. In fact, she might even prefer it. She touched her face. The last operation, the one she'd cried about, did seem to have made her skin smoother, and this nice young man had told her he was optimistic there was soon going to be a major improvement in her looks. It was about time. Although there were no mirrors around, she knew she'd be too frightened to look in one anyway.

She'd gone through a rough patch before the new doctor arrived, waking up one morning to remember, one, two, three, just like that, that Magda, her lovely friend Magda, had died in the car crash. Magda had been driving the car, while Dr. Lane nursed her in the back, on the way to a recuperation clinic in Mexico. At least that's what Dr. Lane had told her, because she had never been able to remember where they were going . . . and why they were going there. It was just one big blur. She couldn't even remember leaving Mexico and being taken to this place in Oregon where she'd been living for so long.

Dr. Lanning had told her the day they met that his first name was Marc, which she liked because it sounded French. He'd given her a small black silk purse, which she must have touched maybe fifty times since his last visit. There was something about it that was sweetly familiar; it smelled of lily-of-the-valley. She loved lily-of-the-valley. Soon, he said, he would take her shopping, and maybe find some perfume that smelled like lily-of-the-valley, but first there was going to be this wonderful surprise. Apparently it was one she was now ready for—whatever that meant.

The calendar said Wednesday the First in bright red letters, as red as the magnificent sun rising over the Oregon hills, where she had lived such a strange life of small happinesses, then unexpected snatches of unhappiness about things she could never quite understand. Mostly though, she loved her little cottage in the landscaped grounds of the clinic, where there were always more nurses than patients.

Wednesday the First. Teri smiled happily as she opened and shut the black silk purse. She was sure it was the day of the surprise and there were roses on her breakfast tray, too.

She had a wardrobe to choose from, now that she could move about more easily. Teri frowned. Once she'd hardly been able to move at all, and she was still scared when far away in the distance she sometimes heard the sound of something she knew was dangerous, a car, the sound of a car far, far away, but thank God, never coming near where she lived.

Teri walked through the garden, the air sweet with the scent of roses, to the terrace overlooking the valley.

There were voices inside the room with the glass doors, soft, sad voices. There was the handsome doctor—Teri could hardly believe it—with the pretty *View* cover girl, who reminded her so much of herself. There was another young man there behind him—Teri put her hands out without knowing why—there was another lovely face, a familiar, loving, cheeky face with tears in her eyes. She knew her. In fact, one, two, three, suddenly she knew that she knew both girls very, very well. It was scary, but because Dr. Lanning—Marc—was there, it was all right . . . it was going to be all right.

As she moved toward them slowly, he took her arm and said sweetly, "Teri, this is Alexa, someone very important to me, and to you, someone I want you to meet . . ."